PRAISE FOR *TH*

'Intricately plotted with a rich cast of characters,
The Circus Train is a compelling story of
magic and survival against the odds'
The Sunday Times

'An enchanting story of love, loss and
survival in a world wrecked by war'
Mail on Sunday

'Impeccably researched ... an uplifting read and
a welcome escape from our turbulent times'
Guardian

'A magical, vibrant parade of a novel about extraordinary people
finding light in history's darkest decades. Spellbinding stuff'
Erin Kelly, author of *The Skeleton Key*

'One of my favourite books of the year'
Stacey Thomas, author of *The Revels*

Parikh's storytelling skills evoke the world of duplicity
and desperation lying behind the scenes of circus
dazzle. A compelling story of love, loss and betrayal'
Daily Mail

'Lucinda Riley fans will love this heartwarming
novel ... a story full of hope and bravery'
Prima

'A gorgeous debut, full of wonder, hope and heartbreak'
Woman's Weekly

Amita Parikh received an honours BSc from the University of Toronto before moving to London, England, where she completed the Curtis Brown creative writing course and the Royal Court Theatre's writers' programme. *The Circus Train*, her first novel, was an instant bestseller in Canada and has been published in thirteen countries around the world.

the

CIRCUS
TRAIN

AMITA
PARIKH

SPHERE

SPHERE

First published in the United States in 2022 by HarperCollins Publishers Ltd
This edition published in Great Britain in 2023 by Sphere

1 3 5 7 9 10 8 6 4 2

A CIP catalogue record for this book
is available from the British Library.

ISBN 978-0-3499-9412-3

Typeset in Caslon by M Rules
Printed and bound in Great Britain by
Clays Ltd, Elcograf S.p.A.

MIX
Supporting
responsible forestry
FSC FSC® C104740

Papers used by Sphere are from well-managed forests
and other responsible sources.

Sphere
An imprint of
Little, Brown Book Group
Carmelite House
50 Victoria Embankment
London EC4Y 0DZ

An Hachette UK Company
www.hachette.co.uk

www.littlebrown.co.uk

For Rishi, the first believer

This novel touches on the experiences of living with polio in the 1930s to 1950s. Anyone wishing to learn more about the reality of individuals affected by polio and/or disabilities in this era should refer to the Author's Note at the end of this book.

The first appearance deceives many.

—PHAEDRUS

PROLOGUE

May 1929 – Thessaloniki, Greece

'Twenty-four, maybe forty-eight hours.' Dr. Komninos delivered his diagnosis as though he was reciting a weather report or the answer to a maths problem. He tucked his stethoscope in his black leather medical bag and snapped it shut, the shiny front buckle casting a shard of light across the room.

'Is there anything I can do?' Theo asked, grief cloaking his face.

Dr. Komninos hesitated. He knew Theo lived in a world of hope, of make-believe, of what could be. But there was no denying the truth about his wife.

'I'm afraid it's too late for Gia. A cold towel will make the pain more bearable. Your daughter, however,' Dr. Komninos trailed off. Over the years he'd learned that the most difficult aspect of being a doctor was giving people false expectations. It was always better to err on the side of caution.

'Yes?' Theo asked.

'Once the fever subsides, I'll have a better idea of what her limitations will be. To be honest, I wouldn't have expected her to survive,' Dr. Komninos admitted, stacking rolls of gauze on the bedside table. 'Saint Demetrios himself must be watching over her.'

'So she'll live?'

Dr. Komninos sighed, thinking about the pile of paperwork

1

waiting for him back at his office. 'If her fever breaks tonight, as I expect it will, then yes, I see no reason why she won't live. As for what kind of *life* she'll have . . .,' he picked up his medical bag, forcing himself to look Theo in the eye. 'It's too early to say. But take it from me. In these types of situations, expectation usually leads to disappointment.' Dr. Komninos pushed open the bedroom door. 'I'll be by first thing tomorrow to check in,' he said, descending the white stuccoed staircase.

Theo stood at his window, watching the doctor walk east on *Kassandrou*.

From the crib in the corner, he heard the muffled sounds of the baby, barely twenty-four hours old. Fear rose inside him as he rushed to check on her. But when he looked in, he saw that she was fast asleep, her tiny fingers curled up in two tight, little fists. Relieved, he sat down on the edge of his bed, where his wife, Gia, lay sleeping. Her face was pale despite the deep glow of the glaring late spring sun. Though the hottest season in Thessaloniki was yet to come, the room was smothered in an invisible layer of heat and Theo noted that her breathing was laboured, but rhythmic.

Around six o'clock in the evening, as Theo pressed a cool flannel against her forehead, Gia's eyes fluttered open. Theo's heart leapt.

'Gia! Can you hear me?'

'Where is she? Is she ok?' Her words came out in a whisper, her voice scratchy and dry.

Theo picked up the little girl, holding his breath as he lowered her slowly into her mother's arms. Her eyes were still glued shut, but her mouth opened wide, forming a perfect 'O' as she nestled her warm head into the crook of her mother's collarbone.

'Helena,' she whispered, beaming. 'We will call her Helena. Lena for short.'

Theo leaned over and kissed her forehead. 'You might recover. Dr. Komninos—'

'I know what Dr. Komninos said.' Gia smiled. She appreciated

2

that Theo always tried to look on the bright side, but this time, it wouldn't be enough.

Helena stirred in her arms and Gia used what little strength she had left to lean forward and kiss her lightly on her forehead, her nose, her cheeks. Suddenly, all the things she wouldn't be able to see, all the moments in her daughter's life she would never live to witness flooded her mind. Was this the price she and Theo were to pay for their respective pasts? Something good had finally come of all their lies and now, she wouldn't be around to see Lena blossom.

She gazed up at Theo. 'I kept your secret for you. Now, you must promise to keep mine for me.'

Theo cradled mother and child in his arms as a response. He didn't want to let go.

Eight hours later it was apparent that the end was near. Resisting the urge to climb into bed next to Gia, Theo remembered the promise he made. He sat down at his desk and took out a clean sheet of stationery. He picked up his pen to write, but paused. Eventually, he began what would become a lengthy explanation, covering two, then three pieces of paper. Towards the end, he stopped, crumpled up the pages, tossing them in the rubbish bin.

He looked at little Lena, the new light of his life. In less than five hours, Dr. Komninos would return to confirm Gia's death. His visit would be followed by the arrival of a wet nurse, who would show Theo how to test the milk temperature on the inside of his wrist, tell him what to do if Lena required a nappy change, show him how to massage her legs with a special kind of apricot oil, and demonstrate how to use chilled compresses to soothe a heat rash.

But first, Theo had to close the door on the past. He took out another piece of paper and began writing. This time, he got straight to the point.

I cannot be with you. I must think of the girl. Please. Do not contact me again.

PART I

My object is to mystify and entertain. I wouldn't deceive you for the world.

—Howard Thurston

CHAPTER ONE

September 1938 – London, England

'How many do you think there are?'

'D'you think any of them are handsome?'

'Trust you, Suze, to ask that!'

Lena Papadopoulos stared at the two girls standing a few feet in front of her. They were gathered at the end of the hallway, trying their best to gauge what was happening behind the closed doors of Horace, the circus director's, study.

Laura, an acrobat from Brighton, pulled her long blonde hair into a ponytail and crouched down on the plush blue carpet. She was what Horace called a circus chameleon, possessing the rare ability to slip into any number of acts – aerial silks, trapeze, contortion – on a moment's notice.

'Maybe I can spot something from this angle.' She splayed herself flat on her stomach and rested her chin in the tiny gap where the carpet met the cool marbled tile that made up the study's foyer. Lena thought she looked like an elegant, upside down starfish.

'Oh, do get up! This is pointless,' Suze moaned, a spray of springy red curls bouncing madly around her face. Suze had joined the circus from Dublin a year ago and was training to be a water ballerina. She jutted her hip out, brushing lint from her leotard, and glanced at Laura. 'I dare you to go up there.'

'No thanks.'

'Go on.'

'No.' Laura stretched her slender arms overhead and arched her ribcage forward.

Suze pouted and began kicking at the hallway baseboards, her bright green eyes roving around impishly before settling on Lena.

'Why hello, Lena. Didn't notice you there.'

Lena blushed. 'Hi,' she squeaked, tentatively inching herself forward. A wide smile spread across Suze's face.

'How'd you like to play a game?' She pointed towards Horace's study. 'If you go up there and see if there are any handsome boys, I'll give you a shilling.'

'Suze,' Laura warned.

'I'd like to play,' Lena answered, grateful for the chance to be included.

A satisfied smile settled on Suze's face and she nodded towards the study. 'Whenever you're ready.'

Lena took a deep breath and began rolling herself forwards. As she crossed over from the carpet onto the smooth marble, she felt her stomach turn somersaults and told herself firmly not to mess up. She had a chance to be a part of Suze's friend group. Everyone loved Suze. She was like a bright, red firefly with a magnetic temperament that attracted the attention of boys and girls alike. As she drew closer to the double oakwood doors Lena imagined what it would be like to sit next to her at meals and have those same children clamouring to speak with her.

Horace's study was housed in its own carriage, styled in a way that one could only expect from the wealthy entertainment impresario. A giant spotlight shone from either side of the doors, ensuring that whenever Horace entered or exited, he was always the centre of attention. A tiny row of hand-painted blue and gold tiles ran around the perimeter of the foyer. In the centre, a stunning Ming vase, crafted from the finest porcelain, sat on a stone pedestal. The marbled floor had been imported from a quarry in Italy and the space just outside the doors was inlaid with a custom mosaic emblem of Horace's initials.

Lena came to a halt outside the entrance, positioning herself so that she could peer directly into the keyhole that was level with her line of sight.

'Well?' Suze whispered loudly.

Lena squinted, pushing one of the blue velvet tassels that hung from the brass door knockers above out of the way. She could make out two young girls, a boy who looked to be a bit older than her, a set of older boys who were probably teenagers, a few adults, some children, and a mother jiggling her baby in her arms.

'I think I see him. Tall, black hair? Holding juggling balls?'

'That's him!' Suze nodded vigorously. 'What's he saying?'

Lena placed her ear against the keyhole and tried to listen. While she waited, she thought about the initiation dinner that evening, the marquee event that kicked off the World of Wonders tour. Every year, Horace threw a lavish feast in the grand dining hall before the tour commenced. To be accepted into the World of Wonders was a prestigious thing and Horace saw to it that no expense was spared. Last year's dinner had an *Alice in Wonderland* theme and featured dishes like mock turtle soup, glorious icebox cakes in every shape and size, and glasses of champagne with little tags that read 'Drink Me'. After the meal, everyone had spilled outside, engaging in games of croquet with wooden mallets designed to look like flamingos and running through the maze that had been decorated with bushes of white roses splattered with brilliant splashes of red. This year's theme was based on the classic Russian fairytale *The Firebird*, and Lena could hardly wait, remembering the fat stacks of fluffy *blinis* she'd seen Mario preparing earlier in the kitchen.

'Suppose I do like one of them. What of it?'

Lena re-focused on the task at hand, straining to catch onto a word. But the new recruits had moved around in the study and she wasn't having any luck hearing, so she looked through the keyhole again and tried to lip read.

'Remember that Jamie fellow? A fine mess you got yourself into!' Laura scolded. 'All I'm saying is you don't want a repeat—'

Suddenly Lena drew back sharply. 'Quick! They're coming!'

Suze and Laura took off like lightning, sprinting away from Lena towards a set of heavy blue velvet drapes hanging further down the hall. It was only after they'd reached the safety of the curtains that Laura looked back, realising what they'd done. Her face fell as she watched Lena, furiously trying to manoeuvre her chair away from the door.

'Lena! The vase!' Laura jerked her head towards the pedestal.

Lena twisted her head, her eyes falling on the vase. It wouldn't hide her completely, but she didn't have any other options.

'Laura!' Suze whispered loudly from behind the lush folds. 'Leave her!'

From her position in the foyer, exposed beyond belief, Lena caught Laura's eye, noting the pity on her face.

I'm sorry, Laura mouthed, before diving behind the drapes with a speed and grace that Lena would never have.

Lena shook her head and tried to move, intent on reaching the vase. But her right wheel appeared to be stuck.

'Come *on*,' she muttered, bending over, trying to see what was wrong. 'Why won't you move?' Then she noticed that there was a small groove between the tiles where her wheel had become stuck.

'Lena!' Laura's voice echoed down the hallway and Lena looked up to see the golden knob of Horace's door twisting. Out of ideas and time, she sat up and pushed extra hard, *Good!* She said to herself. *If I can just get away from the doors*, she thought. *That's it. Almost there.* She stole a quick glance forward. Horace had opened the door but was exiting with his back towards her. She just needed a few more seconds.

'As I said, dinner will begin—'

Crash.

Horace came to an abrupt halt and the frightened shouts of the new cast members filled the foyer. From her place a few feet away, Lena squeezed her eyes shut. But when she finally dared to look, her heart sank. Tiny bits of blue and white porcelain lay scattered all over the tiles.

'Lena!' Horace boomed. 'What have you done!'

Out of the corner of her eyes, Lena saw the tips of Suze's red hair disappear behind the curtains. 'It was an accident,' she said, forcing herself to look at Horace.

Horace was down on his knees, picking at the hundreds of pieces in front of him. 'Have you any idea how expensive this was?'

'I'm sorry,' Lena whispered, wishing she could sink into the floor. She knew this wasn't the first impression he wanted to give to the new performers. Indeed, the dozen or so people who'd been in Horace's study were now staring at her uneasily.

'What's wrong with her?' A young girl pointed at Lena.

From the floor, Horace stood up with much difficulty, brushing bits of porcelain dust from his bespoke midnight blue suit jacket. 'Everyone, I'd like you to meet Lena, daughter of our renowned illusionist, Theo Papadopoulos.'

Lena cringed, wishing Horace would let her go. She knew what was coming next and, sure enough, the question landed right on target.

'How'd she get that way? Not on account of your circus, was it?' A young man who Lena surmised was a knife thrower from the set of blades that gleamed in a bag slung over his shoulder eyed her suspiciously.

'Of course not,' Horace replied hastily. 'We uphold the highest standards of safety at the Beddington and Sterling World of Wonders. In nearly a decade of operation, we have yet to lose a performer to a long-term injury. Sprains and the occasional break are to be expected in this business. But Lena,' he continued, pointing to her like she was an exhibit at a museum, 'tragically, was born this way.'

'Oh my,' one of the women whispered.

'Still. We count ourselves lucky to have her on board,' Horace said, his voice full of false care. Lena swallowed. She wasn't afraid of Horace, but she'd always had the feeling that he viewed her as a never-ending bill he had to pay in order to keep her father happy. 'Everyone, I apologise for the disruption. You'll find your carriage assignments on your key tags. I invite all of you to start getting settled. As for you,' he turned to Lena, his eyes gleaming with contempt. 'I trust you can keep yourself out of harm's way until the evening's festivities have concluded?'

Lena nodded and rolled her chair away, not bothering to glance back at the band of performers staring after her.

'What time do you think it will end?' Lena asked. It was a few hours later and her governess, Clara Smith, had just finished braiding her hair and was now tying a length of midnight blue ribbon to the ends.

'Why d'you ask?'

Lena pointed to the book on her nightstand. 'I'm at the part where Alice meets the Cheshire Cat!'

Clara chuckled. 'Might I suggest you forget about reading for tonight and try to make a friend or two? There's bound to be a few new children on board.'

Lena frowned. 'They won't like me.'

'They don't *know* you. If you talked to them, you might be pleasantly surprised.'

Lena shook her head, wondering at what point adults forgot what it was like to be young. 'I won't. They'll only pretend to be nice, in front of all the grown-ups. Then they'll go back to ignoring me,' she explained, reaching back to feel the silky ribbon in her hair.

'That's not true.'

'It is!' Lena insisted. 'And grown-ups do the same. I know because Johannes pretends to like everybody, but as soon as they're gone, he starts making faces.'

Clara burst out laughing and Lena smiled at her governess in the mirror. Clara wasn't anything like the stuffy, uptight governesses Lena read about in her books. She'd grown up in a place in London called Fulham and had come into Lena's life three years ago. Fed up with the sub-par choice of suitors who kept calling at her family home and not wishing to waste years of education, Clara did what most women her age would never do: she joined the circus.

Lena loved Clara. She liked the smart tweedy skirt suits she wore and the smell of the *Amami* shampoo she washed her hair with every Friday. She liked the way she wrote her capital letters neatly inside the crossword puzzles she completed at breakfast at the weekends. She liked that Clara had a proper job, not a circus job, and the way she sometimes paired men's trousers with bright red lipstick, her brown hair falling in soft ringlets around her face. She liked that she was young enough to chum around with Lena, often playing checkers and Snap with her in the evenings, but old enough to be firm when required.

'Lena?'

Lena's smile vanished. She turned around to see that her father, Theo Papadopoulos, had returned from his trip into town. Lena noticed how pink his cheeks and nose were from the cool autumn air as he tugged off a pair of grey gloves.

'Papa. You're back.'

'I am indeed,' he said, hanging up his coat and draping his scarf over the door hook. 'Clara, would you mind if I spoke with my daughter alone?'

Clara stood up. 'Not at all, sir. I'll use the time to press my dress.'

Theo smiled at the governess as she left, then took a seat in front of his daughter. 'So? How was your afternoon?'

'Fine. I've almost finished the book.'

'Already? Goodness, I wouldn't be surprised if you were the fastest reader this side of the ocean. Anything else happen?'

Lena bit her lip, wondering if she could get away with lying about the vase. But her father knew everything. It seemed to be a special kind of magic power all parents possessed, the ability to know about every little mistake their children made without having to ask. 'I didn't mean for the vase to fall!' She threw her hands up in the air. 'It was an accident!'

'But what were you doing outside Horace's study in the first place? Did I not leave you with enough activities?' Theo gestured to the table by her bedside, where a stack of books, colouring pages and a compass set sat, untouched.

'I wanted to play with the other girls,' Lena whispered, twisting her hands in her lap. 'I'm sorry I broke it. Was it a lot of money?'

Theo leaned forward, his eyes crinkling affectionately. 'It's not the money. I know you like being around those girls. But they are a few years older than you and always getting into trouble.'

'They're my friends.'

'Would your real friends let you take the blame for something that wasn't your fault?' Theo raised an eyebrow and Lena blushed. 'Next time, please, listen to me and stay here.'

Lena glanced sadly at the shelves around her, which housed the books and trinkets her father had purchased. From a hand-painted doll house they'd found in Utrecht, to a set of brilliant watercolours from Bern, to the latest Beatrix Potter books, Lena had everything a child could have ever hoped for. So why did she feel so empty?

But, not wishing to start an argument with her father – especially ahead of the dinner – she braced herself and smiled. 'I promise.'

Theo beamed and plucked a silver bag with strands of sparkly ribbon tumbling out of it from behind him. 'Good. Now, every girl deserves something special before the initiation dinner.'

Lena perked up on seeing the bag and grabbed at it, tugging off the ribbon and removing the gift.

'Oh, Papa.' It was a deep red velvet headband, laced with an intricate pattern woven from thin golden thread, with three fake rubies shimmering at the centre. She placed it on her head and twisted back and forth, admiring herself in the mirror. 'It's beautiful.'

'You look just like a Russian *tsarina*,' he said, bending down and planting a kiss on her forehead. 'Now. You must help me decide what to wear.'

The grand dining hall was the most magnificent carriage at the World of Wonders. Gargantuan chandeliers crafted from the finest Austrian crystal hung from the ceilings, their shards of light giving the appearance of diamonds raining down on the tables. Blue paper flecked with gold leaf lined the walls and the doors that faced the inner courtyard had been unlocked so that guests could go outside. From her table, Lena watched, enthralled, as cast members entered clad in traditional Russian dress; the men in white *rubhakas* embroidered with red, blue and green thread and the women in colourful *sarafans* and glittering *kokoshniks* perched atop their heads. The tables had been rearranged in a rectangle around the perimeter of the hall, leaving the centre open for performances and speeches.

After the main courses had been served, it was tradition for Horace to give a speech. Tonight he was dressed in a midnight blue tuxedo with tails and suede stripes, and wore a matching suede top hat. As he waddled to the podium, Lena heard snickering. She turned and saw Suze trying to stifle a laugh two tables over. Laura caught Lena watching them and gave her a sympathetic wave and smile. Lena smiled back sadly then refocused her attention on Horace. Her father was right, she thought. As much as she hated to admit it, she would never be like any of the children here. It was best to not get involved with them.

'If I could have everyone's attention please?' Horace boomed. 'As is customary, this dinner marks the beginning of a journey that will take us across Europe. I have been running this show for ten years and each time I think it can't get any better, it inevitably does.' The audience whistled and howled and Lena joined in with the clapping. 'I shan't bore you with the intricacies of every act, costume and musical piece that I've planned, but I would like to give the newcomers a brief glimpse of what to expect.'

Theo had left Lena's side at the start of Horace's speech and was now standing in the centre of the room, flanked by two fire jugglers. On his cue, the jugglers lit the ends of their sticks and tossed them high into the air. Behind them, the orchestra began to build, the strains of a traditional Russian folk song filling the carriage.

Theo held up a handful of feathers, coloured red, yellow and orange, for all to see. They were the kind easily found in a children's crafting shop for pennies a pound. But in Theo's hands, the mundane became magical. He scrunched them up into a tight ball in his fist. Then, with the flick of a wrist he tossed them into the air at the exact same time the fire jugglers threw their sticks up. The audience gasped as the flames touched the feathers, setting them alight. A loud *crack* reverberated through the hall, a blast of orange illuminated the room, and out of the centre, a magnificent firebird emerged.

The onlookers pointed as the firebird gathered speed, floating majestically through the air. Its wings were a rich ombre, starting from the deepest crimson at its breast and feathering out to canary yellow at the tips. A halo of orange encircled its head and a hint of gold glinted off the feathers whenever they caught the light.

Suddenly, the firebird swooped down and stopped in front of Theo, who was moving his right arm like a musical conductor. The bird looked to the ceiling, hovering, as though trapped in a trance. Then it spread its wings and soared upwards, weaving in and out of the chandeliers.

On the ground, Theo motioned to the fire jugglers to toss their sticks one last time. On the count of three, they threw them as high as they could, just as the orchestra reached the apex of its piece. Smoky ash filled the air and the bird looked like it was about to burst through the roof when Theo made one final sharp hand movement. There was a loud *bang* as a brilliant ball of red washed over the entirety of the carriage. And then the whole room went dark.

'The lights!' Horace yelled over the murmuring cast members, who were all trying to figure out what, exactly, had just transpired before their eyes. 'Chadwick, the lights!' He scolded his assistant, who scurried to the back wall and flipped a switch, flooding the room with beams of white. Lena rubbed her eyes, adjusting to the brightness, then took in the scene unfolding in front of her. All around her, people were on their feet, cheering. Children had abandoned their dessert and were clamouring around Theo, demanding to know how he had done it. Young women batted their eyelashes coquettishly in her father's direction, showering him with praise. Shouts of *Was it real? Where did it go?* echoed through the room. Beside Theo, Horace clambered back to his position at the podium, revelling in the spotlight.

'Bravo,' he yelled, clapping his stubby hands together, motioning to the orchestra, the jugglers and Theo. 'Quiet. Quiet please, everyone please be quiet,' he ordered. A silence settled over the crowd. 'Thank you, gentlemen, for that spectacular performance. Remember, this is but a small taste of the magic and luxury you can expect to unfold over the course of the year. Now, I invite all of you to raise a glass.' Horace held up a flute of champagne, the golden liquid sloshing out onto his expensive suit.

As the performers seated around her followed his lead, Lena

grabbed the steel cup that was sitting upside down at her place setting. When she picked it up off the table, she gasped. Staring back at her was a single feather, shaded red, orange and yellow, the tips doused in a sparkly golden sheen. She plucked it off the white linen cloth and glanced at her father, who was looking directly at her. He smiled and winked.

'Welcome,' Horace said, his lips turning up into his signature charismatic smile as the crowd held up their glasses, 'to the World of Wonders.'

CHAPTER TWO

To understand what made the Beddington and Sterling World of Wonders so unique, one has to begin in Boston, 1913, where a seven-year-old boy named Horace Beddington the Third lived. As the heir to the Beddington fortune, Horace didn't need to work. But his father beat him and his mother cried and Horace decided early on that he couldn't be a part of this family. People envied their wealth, but Horace remembered yearning to be poor if it meant having parents who cared.

Every morning during his summer breaks, Horace woke early, walking up and down the streets of the sleepy suburb of Somerville, delivering *The Globe* newspaper. Following this, he accompanied his father to his office on Atlantic Avenue, setting himself up outside Quincy Market with a box of shoe polish, an assortment of cloths, and the will to make something of himself. His father had already decided that Horace would follow in his banking footsteps, but when an eight-year-old Horace heard the voices of the men whose shoes he shined, talking about mergers and oil prices, he knew he couldn't do it.

Horace was an only child and the constant bickering between his parents meant he never wanted to invite any of his classmates over. He grew up somewhat isolated, dreaming of the day when he'd finally be able to leave home. Horace's grandmother Esther noticed his reticence and began buying him toys and books.

Among these gifts was a magic set. Horace quickly took a shine to it, thrilled that it required no extra people to use it, unlike the board games his parents bought him every Christmas. Horace holed himself up inside most nights, practising. On weekends, he retreated to his grandmother's house in Lexington, where he would perform for her, pulling scarves out of hats and sending cards soaring through the air. Esther would watch patiently, clapping politely at the end of each trick. She didn't have the heart to tell her only grandchild that he was mediocre at best. And she liked his company, liked the fact that finally, someone could see her as something more than a widow, a burden to be taken care of, or an endless source of easy income.

When the family went up to their plot on Long Island on long summer weekends, Esther would often take Horace down to Manhattan. She'd buy tickets for whichever vaudeville or magic show happened to be playing and then sit, observing Horace lose himself in the performances of Thurston and Cardini. Afterwards, she'd take him to Martinka, the magic shop on Sixth Avenue, giving him extra spending money to buy whatever he wanted. They'd frequent the back parlours of Hell's Kitchen and Chelsea, where soothsayers sat behind beaded fringed curtains, holding crystal balls and spouting fortunes to anyone willing to pay.

On a particularly memorable trip, a clairvoyant proclaimed Horace's future as 'Full of promise. You will do great things.' Horace beamed and Esther smiled knowingly. She knew her grandson was capable of greatness. He simply needed to hear it from someone else.

A trip to Harry Houdini's residency at the Hippodrome would prove to be a turning point. In the lobby of the theatre, Horace saw a mermaid. Later, he would come to realise that she was just a woman dressed in a gold bustier with a greenish-gold tail to match, her long blonde hair splaying out in the water each time she dove back down. But to Horace, she was an ethereal, celestial being. As she floated around a tank filled with water, smiling coyly at the onlookers, Horace pushed his way to the front and placed his hand on the glass. The glass was thick and he could see his reflection looking back at him. A lonely teenager, he was extremely uncomfortable around girls. But the mermaid propelled herself forward and placed her hand against his, their palms separated only by a few inches, and smiled. At that moment his fate was sealed. Only in a world like this, he thought, could a creature so beautiful connect with someone like him. He wanted to bring this feeling of euphoria to everyone.

After that day, Horace dedicated himself to practising magic. He made repeat trips to Martinka and spent hours in front of his mirror trying to make something out of nothing. But quick hands and a deft touch were not among Horace's strong points and he began to lose hope.

During the summer break before his final year of school, Horace overheard a conversation between two men behind him in the line at Lyndell's Bakery.

'Audrey wouldn't shut up about it.'

'How long's it in town for?'

'They come through every year. Stick around a few days, then pack up and it's as if they never existed.' The man traced a circle with the toe of his shoe in a layer of flour dust. 'But one thing I do know is that showman's makin' a lotta dough!' Horace twisted his head and saw the man rubbing his thumb and forefinger together.

'Hey kid! You orderin'?'

Horace blinked three times before realising they were referring to him.

Outside Lyndell's, with a loaf of bread for his mother and a cinnamon bun to nibble on for himself, Horace made a decision that would change his life. He would never be the leading man, the lothario, the Casanova. But what he could do was see possibility where no one else did. He could be the architect, the visionary that pulled together a show so mesmerising that it would blow everything else out of the water. What he lacked in looks and skill, he made up for in taste. Plus, he had the backing of a grandmother who hated seeing him bullied by her own son.

Following a heated argument with his father and a lot of crying and begging from his mother, Horace Beddington the Third, aged seventeen, boarded a Red Star Line ship to England with an early inheritance from Esther.

As the ship sailed eastward, the smells of rotting fish, sweat, and salt tickling his nose, Horace watched a deckhand pull at a piece of thickly twined rope, winding it around the barrel. When the deckhand paused to wipe his brow with the back of his page boy cap, he noticed Horace looking at him.

'Where you headin', sir?' he called out in that signature Bostonian accent.

Horace smiled. No one had ever called him 'sir' before. Things were different already.

'To London. I hear the streets are paved with gold.'

In London, Horace quickly settled himself in a house on Fitzroy Park, conveniently located but a stone's throw from the Witanhurst mansion. Thanks to Esther's social circle and connections, Horace was welcomed into the upper crust of British society. Still, it was up to him to put his plan into motion. He took a job as an usher at St. George's Theatre, determined to learn everything from the ground up. He worked there for years, taking notes, thinking about how he would do things differently and wondering how he could improve upon the acts if they were his. Even after he'd seen every performance, and could recite what each magician would say, word for word, he continued to watch, perched in the corner, his flashlight turned off.

'Why do you keep watching the same acts over and over?' his boss asked one day. 'Are you daft?'

'I'm not watching the act. I watch the audience. I want to see what leaves them breathless.'

In the evenings, he nursed pint after pint at the Flask, flagging down the bartender by clanking his shillings on the wooden tables. In his growing collection of leather notebooks, he drafted the details of what would become his masterpiece. He would call his show The Beddington and Sterling World of Wonders. In doing so, he would be paying homage to both himself and his grandmother, Sterling being her maiden name. The colours would be blue and gold. And this wouldn't be like a typical circus or vaudeville act. This would be different to the shows in cheap dime museums, different to the shows in shady back parlours that stank of stale cigar smoke. It would be different to watching the groups of poor street performers that lined the cobblestones of Covent Garden, different to the solo magician act in the Alhambra. Gone was the red and yellow striped tent, the hum-drum lions and elephants, the stale popcorn, candied apples, and sticky children's fingers. No, the Beddington and Sterling would elevate the circus into a luxurious sphere, bring together the best parts of all these travelling shows and then some. It would be, quite simply, the finest circus that had ever existed.

With his money and unprepossessing looks, Horace charmed his way into many a pocketbook. Men didn't see him as a threat – no self-respecting woman wanted to date Horace – and women looked upon him as a friend, a confidant to whom they could entrust their dreams and fears. When it came time to raise funds for his show, the family at Witanhurst mansion were only too happy to host a cocktail party in the ballroom of their estate. But this wasn't just any cocktail party. It was a Beddington and Sterling party. Horace had spent six months cultivating talent he'd met over his years in London and convinced all of them to band together to perform a new set of tricks, for one night only. By the time the rapt crowd had watched contortionists squeeze

23

their limber frames through gilded cages, a card magician turn the ace of hearts into smoke, and acrobats made up like mermaids execute a synchronised swimming routine in a giant rectangular tank filled with lilac-hued water, they were reaching for their chequebooks.

While the party-goers watched, Horace did the rounds, clad in a blue and gold tuxedo from Huntsman and Sons. As bankers, lawyers and landowners signed over their savings, Horace swelled with pride. No matter what people said they wanted (Real estate! Stocks! Bonds!), their actions always spoke louder. People wanted an escape. They wanted entertainment, a place where they could revel in wonder and forget about the drudgery of everyday life. And that night, Horace proved that he could provide it in spades.

Flush with investor cash, Horace traipsed the globe building the vision he'd first drafted in a smoke-filled tavern of North London. In Romania, he scoured the playgrounds of the poorest schools, hand-selecting girls who turned cartwheels at a dizzying pace and boys who used tree branches as playthings, swinging and twisting like it was second nature.

At an orphanage in Persia, he spotted a young girl curled up in a corner, staring at him with eyes of deepest, startling aquamarine.

'How much for her?'

The orphanage director proceeded to spin a tale about how the girl, named Pari, was royalty, a direct descendant of Nader Shah, but that no one in her family wanted her because of her Russian mother. Horace sighed. This tale, no doubt, would hike up the price, but as Horace left the orphanage, Pari's little hand clutching his, he somehow knew the girl would be a good return on his investment.

In the Atlas Mountains, he found strongmen who could lift 200-pound barbells with ease. In a Nigerian church, an uncommonly tall ten-year-old girl named Nneka took his breath away. Her skin was a dark brown, save for a perfectly symmetrical patch of cream cascading down the middle. Her hair splayed out in all directions like it had a mind of its own and refused to be tamed. When she noticed Horace staring at her, she immediately cast her gaze downwards. For a moment, Horace's heart ached. He knew what it was to be an outsider. When he inquired about her face, the church director shrugged.

'Some kind of skin condition she was born with. She's been sleeping on the corn sacks in the back. Her Mama's dead. Her Daddy don't want her. She just sleeps there, sweeps the floors and sings. All day long.' The church director shook his head. 'It's a shame.' And then Horace heard it. Her voice, so melodious, so powerful for someone so young. When Nneka sang, it was like she transformed into another being.

'Name your price,' he said. The church director shook his head.

'God has bestowed upon this child a rare gift. Something so holy cannot be bought.' But after a few more rounds of haggling, the church director decided that Nneka and her voice were indeed worth something and, armed with a string of rosary beads and a bible, she joined Horace on his tour.

Across the ocean in Bahia, a troupe of capoeira dancers and drummers were only too willing to join Horace, as their form of entertainment was being suppressed by the authorities. In Germany and the Soviet Union, he found swimmers who'd been cut from Olympic teams and still had something to prove.

And so it went. For nearly a year Horace travelled, adding to his collection of performers. He never went for the best, most popular ones. Instead, he was careful to choose the ones who had either been consumed by the grief of losing someone (a parent, a child) or who were consistently finishing third or fourth in their respective sport or art form. These, he reasoned, were people right on the edge of glory, the people who would fight for acceptance, who would continually strive to be the best.

His cache of acts almost complete, Horace returned to London, installing his recruits in a home next to his own under the supervision of his assistant Chadwick. The only thing Horace was missing now was an illusionist. One act that would culminate each performance and leave people's jaws hanging. He got his wish in Thessaloniki, where he spotted Theo Papadopoulos.

To many, Theo Papadopoulos was the greatest illusionist of all time. When he performed by the Amsterdam port, sailors from as far as the Caspian Sea would halt expeditions, anchoring their boats, so they could see him walk on water. Children gasped as he turned the tepid beige of the stray goats dotting the Italian hillside into all the colours of the rainbow. In Vienna's famed *Burgtheater*, women swooned as he transformed simple pebbles into glittering diamonds with the squeeze of his hand. Grown men regularly forgot they were men, and unleashed childlike squeals of disbelief when he emerged, intact, from a wooden box which had been pierced all over with Japanese knives. Everywhere he went – London, Prague, Berlin – people came to marvel. There was nothing Theo couldn't do, no miracle he couldn't perform.

As Horace watched him spellbound, he felt his skin tingle with the sensation that what he'd been working towards was finally complete. Theo had the showmanship of Houdini, the skill of Devant and the intelligence of Kellar.

When the performance finished, Horace waddled through the dispersing crowd like a penguin, sweating in the searing Greek sun. It was important to maintain an air of professionalism, he told himself, glancing down at his long coat-tailed suit. He didn't care what he had to promise the illusionist, he thought, as he mopped his forehead with a cotton hankie. He was determined to sign what he knew would be the crown jewel in his World of Wonders.

But Horace's smile faded when he saw the dapper illusionist's wife, Gia, turn around. She was a classic beauty, her face that of a goddess. She looked like she had been carved from marble. Her long dark hair was swept to one side and fastened with a clip. But her stomach, although not as big as Horace's, was certainly larger than normal. Still, he forged ahead, introduced himself, and invited them both to dinner.

Later that night they dined on Cypriot food at the top of a hotel overlooking the Thermaikos Gulf. Theo told Horace how he got his start in the business. He'd fallen in love with magic after visiting a circus that had come through the city when he was five. After his father had cast him out of the house for choosing an unconventional career, Theo worked as a carpenter to pay his bills and honed his magician skills at children's birthday parties. It took many years, but he eventually worked his way up to being one of Europe's most in demand illusionists. By the time Theo was finished, Horace had decided he was perfect. Tall and commanding, but unthreatening. Relatable to adults and children alike. And women loved him, Horace observed, catching more than one lady sneaking a glance at the handsome performer while he spoke. Horace outlined his plan for the Beddington and Sterling World of Wonders and, not wishing to waste any more time, made them a verbal offer. Theo glanced at his wife.

'You must understand, I can't travel at the moment.'

Horace nodded. 'We can wait till after the baby's born. Our carriages are outfitted like first-class train cabins and I'll see to it that a nursery is built. The child will want for nothing.' Gia cleared her throat. Horace continued. 'And for you, madame. We have a state-of-the-art games room. Billiards, darts, mahjongg, cards. Access to the finest European society gatherings. Quite often, it is the rich who are clamouring to associate with us. Martha, my head costumier, and her team were hired away from Lanvin. They can make anything you want. Velvet gowns, silk flapper dresses, diamante skull caps. Anything.'

Gia sipped at her San Pellegrino and glanced at Theo. 'What do you think?'

Her husband placed a protective hand on her stomach. 'We'll wait, of course. But afterwards . . .'

Gia nodded thoughtfully but didn't look entirely convinced. Horace played his trump card.

'My staff physician, Dr. James Wilson, ran the best clinic on Harley Street before joining us. He was educated at St. Bart's and graduated first in his class.' He smiled, satisfied at the look on Gia's face.

'We'll join, but on one condition,' Gia said. 'I want my child to have an education. The best tutors. The finest books. Access to the top universities. All at your cost.'

Horace couldn't believe his luck. If all the most talented illusionist in the world and his wife wanted was a few good school-teachers, he had hit the jackpot. He wiped the corner of his mouth with his cloth napkin and extended a hand.

'You have a deal.'

The next morning, Theo signed his contract and Horace promised to return in three months.

Producers are used to being ready for the worst-case scenario: performers suffer injuries, things go wrong, contracts don't work out. But Horace wasn't expecting a widower. When Theo opened the door on a hot July morning, one arm holding a bottle, the other clutching a baby wrapped in a white blanket, a shock of dark brown hair peeking through the folds, he looked worse for wear.

'Forgive me, Horace, but I don't see how I can honour our agreement,' Theo said, after explaining what had happened to Gia and his daughter. The baby stirred and Theo rocked his arm back and forth. Horace was flummoxed. He'd been prepared for any situation but this one. He briefly considered trying to find another illusionist, but he knew that no one could hold a candle to Theo. Besides, he thought, he was Horace Beddington the Third. He was used to hard work, used to things not going right the first few times.

So Horace called Chadwick and told him there'd been an unexpected obstacle and that he'd be back in a few weeks. He took up residence in a two-bedroom flat on Tsimiski Avenue. Horace rose with the morning market peddlers, bringing fresh leek and spinach *plastos* to Theo's doorstep. He hired a team of the best medical doctors, instructing them to do everything they could to make the girl's life as bearable as possible. He found round-the-clock wet nurses and had a cook prepare fresh meals using ingredients he picked up at Modiano market each morning. Though the forty-day mourning period had passed, Horace insisted on paying for a new tombstone to mark Gia's grave, and he watched from a distance as Theo paid his respects every Sunday following the weekly service at the Agia Sophia. Horace ploughed all his remaining energy and money into Theo and his daughter's well-being. He had to have him onboard the World of Wonders, and if that meant giving this man more than he'd bargained for, Horace was willing to do it.

His persistence paid off. One morning in September, Theo showed up outside Horace's flat, the baby swaddled in a pink linen blanket. If the show would pay for Lena's medical expenses and a governess, plus allow him two months off to return to Thessaloniki each year, they'd have a deal.

A month later, Theo Papadopoulos arrived at Victoria Station with two trunks, his daughter, and a desire to leave his old life and the secrets he'd kept hidden for so long behind him. The Beddington and Sterling World of Wonders would open at the London Palladium and from there, begin traversing the continent. It was 1929. Trotsky had been exiled, Hoover was now president, and the stock market had just crashed. No matter what happened, Horace insisted on moving forward. The show must go on, he said.

Yes. When Horace Beddington the Third wanted something, nothing stood in his way.

CHAPTER THREE

Lena Papadopoulos didn't believe in magic. At least, not the kind that thrilled people who came out in droves to watch the World of Wonders, night after night. Although she'd grown up around the pomp and circumstance of the circus – a universe where literally anything was possible – Lena's world was rooted firmly in reality. Having used a wheelchair since she was old enough to remember, her condition acted as a great divider, separating her from the other children and adults she lived with. Though they ate the same food, slept in the same carriages, and enjoyed the same music, Lena's disability had taught her a harsh truth: she was different, and people didn't like different.

It hadn't always been so bad. As a very young child, Lena's physical condition had the opposite effect, drawing children to her like bees to honey. Four-year-olds had yet to form strong opinions on what was right or wrong, good or bad, and they flocked to her in droves, daily. She recalled one occasion when a group waited outside the infirmary for hours. When she finally emerged, they threw themselves at her, begging to be taken on a ride. They'd crowd around her during meals, running their hands enviously over the metal and wooden framework of her chair, peppering her with questions and looks of envy.

'I don't *want* to walk!' one had pouted, crossing her arms.

'Don't be silly,' the child's mother had said. 'The poor girl had polio as a baby. Would you like polio?'

'Yes!' the girl had screamed back. 'I want to ride around everywhere like her!'

But as the years sped by, curiosity gave way to rejection, the limitations of what Lena could and couldn't do dawning on the others. She quickly turned from attraction to liability. At first, the children made valiant attempts to include her. But it eventually became clear that it was easier to not ask her to participate in their activities in the first place. No matter how hard they tried, it was impossible to play hide-and-seek or netball with Lena without having to make drastic adjustments to the rules.

Slowly, the gap widened, made worse by Lena's frequent coughs and colds, a result of a chronically poor immune system. Stuck inside the infirmary carriage for long stretches of time with nothing to do, Lena took to observing Dr. Wilson. She sat in her bed, listening as he diagnosed all manner of ailments that plagued the performers who came through to see him. Measles, tuberculosis, influenza and typhoid. Ankle sprains, bruised quadriceps and torn ligaments. High blood pressure and hairline fractures and, for one poor fellow, a case of early-onset diabetes.

Lena watched curiously as Dr. Wilson talked each patient through their condition and prescribed a course of treatment: medications, rest, cold or hot compresses, lymphatic massage and more. While other children her age practised card shuffling and tightrope walking, Lena slowly but surely learned the names of all the muscles, arteries and veins that snaked through the human body. She memorised home remedies, writing down recipes for tonics in a little leather notebook she kept by her bedside. She observed how pills were measured and dispensed. When she was old enough, Dr. Wilson let her conduct an inventory of his plethora of tinctures and vitamins, and Lena would sit for hours, copying the names and dosages carefully into the ledger. When

Dr. Wilson wasn't around, she paged through his collection of textbooks and medical journals lining the back wall of the infirmary carriage, learning about calculus, astronomy, physics and organic chemistry.

As her knowledge grew by leaps and bounds, Lena soon realised that the magic that surrounded her at the circus was just a matter of careful scientific and mathematical calculations. The effortless trajectory with which Johannes Larsen, the trapeze artist, soared across the stage was nothing more than hundreds of hours of practice coupled with the physics of good balance and the mathematics of impeccable timing. The 70-degree angle at which Anna Maria Bianchi, the multi-talented water ballerina, acrobat and contortionist, arched backwards, appearing to defy gravity as she rode bareback on a show pony, could be explained using Newton's Third Law. The flash of blue fire that burst forth from Jussi Forsberg's flame juggling sticks was but a simple chemical reaction: a rag affixed to the end was generously soaked in copper chloride. When lit, it blazed a brilliant bright blue.

Even her father's tricks were the result of hours of cutting, sawing, building, calculating, practising and precision. What other people didn't understand, Lena thought, was that it wasn't magic. It was science. There was a science to everything that her father, and everyone else in the circus did, be it sleight of hand, misdirection, or a perfectly timed escape. And it was science where Lena found her passion, science that thrilled her. Science, Lena thought, was where the real magic lay.

'Do you know,' Lena said, during a stop in Stuttgart not long after her seventh birthday, 'that the first description of rubella was made in 1740, by a man named Friedrich Hoffmann?'

'I am aware of Mr. Hoffmann and his contributions to German measles, thank you, Lena.' Dr. Wilson drew a drop of liquid into a pipette and squeezed it into a beaker, turning the liquid inside a pale green colour.

'How did you learn about all these potions and things?'

'Medical school.' Dr. Wilson busied himself sterilising his equipment. 'We did coursework in chemistry, genetics, physiology, anatomy.'

'Is medicine a sort of magic?'

'I suppose some might say that.'

Lena glanced down at her legs, lying limply underneath a thin cotton blanket. 'Maybe one day some medicine magic will happen to my legs. Then I can be your assistant,' she announced proudly.

Dr. Wilson put down the tool he'd been holding. 'You're a perfectly fine assistant now. No need to change anything.' He felt for the little girl, who approached learning with a gravitas he had yet to witness in any of the other children on board. But there was no sugar-coating her medical history. 'Besides, you must understand. Infantile paralysis is nothing to scoff at. You were so sick as a baby.'

'But it would be an interesting experiment, wouldn't it – to try? I'm much better than when I was little, aren't I? And you said medicine is always improving!'

Dr. Wilson hesitated. The girl had been lucky to survive polio and the host of other ailments she'd had as a baby and toddler at all. To think that she would one day improve to the point that she would walk normally was next to impossible. Not wishing to let her down, he hastily changed the subject, relieved when she didn't bring it up again.

But when Theo came by that evening to check on her long after she'd fallen asleep, Dr. Wilson pulled him into the hallway.

'What's the matter?' Theo whispered anxiously.

Dr. Wilson cleared his throat. 'It appears Lena has reached an age where she's aware of how different she is. She can see her limitations, but she no longer wants to accept them. The doctor who delivered her told you as much: it would have been difficult for her to walk in the best of cases.' Dr. Wilson paused. 'On the upside, her mind is sharp and she loves to learn. But the girl is lonely.'

Theo's eyes crinkled and he burst out laughing. 'Don't be absurd. She's with you or Clara all day, and I spend hours with her at night, reading, drawing—'

'She doesn't *want* us – she wants to be with children her own age. D'you know, she's asked me twice if she can go to a school outside of here?' Dr. Wilson shook his head. 'She doesn't feel she fits in.'

Theo rubbed his eyes. He wasn't blind and had observed with crushing disappointment the way the other children ignored his daughter. But he'd naively hoped that she'd be too busy with her toys and books to notice. 'Tell me, James,' he said, wistfully. 'Is there a prescription for loneliness in that medical bag of yours?' He smiled sadly, lapsing into quiet thought for a moment. 'James,' he began cautiously. 'Might I take her out? Her lungs do seem stronger, she hasn't actually had polio for years, and there's much to see outside these circus walls.' Theo felt a buzz of excitement, thinking about a world of possibility that might be open to his daughter. 'Mondays would work, apart from when we're travelling. Would it be too risky?'

'On the contrary, I think it would do her a world of good. Such a curious, bright mind deserves to be nurtured,' Dr Wilson replied.

So the next day, Theo visited Lena in the infirmary, draping a blanket and woollen scarf on her bed.

'Come,' he announced. 'We're going out.'

Lena dropped the book she was reading. 'We are?'

'I've got permission from Dr. Wilson to take you on a little trip. There are a few conditions, of course. One, you have to keep warm,' he said, gesturing to the blanket and scarf. 'And two, if you start feeling ill, we come straight back here. Understood?'

'Oh Papa, thank you!' Lena clapped her hands, colour flooding her face. She threw off her sheet and hoisted herself into her wheelchair. 'Where are we going?'

'It's a surprise,' he said, winking at her, as he walked beside her down the hallway.

The *Musée Fragonard*, part of the *École Nationale Vétérinaire de Maisons-Alfort*, was not open for public viewing but Theo managed to schedule a private appointment just the same.

At the museum's entrance, they were met by the chief scientist and curator, who led them to the current exhibition. The room was musty and a few students of the veterinary school of medicine looked suspiciously at the man and the girl in a wheelchair peering into each of the glass box displays.

When her father told her about Honoré Fragonard during their journey, Lena was mesmerised. A surgeon who obtained his brevet in 1759, he was dismissed from his post as an anatomical professor because of his outlandish ideas. As she travelled between the rooms, stopping every few minutes to trail an index finger across the glass enclosures, she thought that perhaps he had been misunderstood, that his thoughts were ahead of his time. The *Musée Fragonard* was famed for its teratology collection, a fantastic amalgamation of genetics gone wrong. Lena looked, fascinated at a three-headed calf, a cyclops monkey, a Janus calf, a ten-legged sheep and Siamese twin lambs. Each one looked like they would have made good additions to the World of Wonders had they still been alive.

When they reached the final room, Theo pulled out a notebook and pencil and gave them to Lena, who sat silently in her chair and sketched what she saw. Honoré Fragonard was best known for his écorchés, skinned real-life cadavers preserved in death as they had been in life. The most famous of these was one based on Albrecht Dürer's print, *The Four Horsemen, from the Apocalypse*. It consisted of a man sitting on a horse, the horse's rope leading through the gilet. Lena stared at it, transfixed. It was as though someone had cast a spell that froze man and beast in time, then peeled away the outer layer of their respective skins, allowing her to see the insides. Such things were too grotesque for many to look at, but where others were repulsed, Lena saw beauty: numerous arteries and veins, a network of axons and capillaries all working harmoniously to breathe life into every living being. She sat perfectly still and sketched out an amateurish replica of the exhibit.

As Theo stared at his daughter's face, his heart leapt. It was this face he yearned for, the one that he failed to see when she watched the death-defying acts at the circus. But in the musty space filled with ancient relics preserved behind glass, Lena's face shone, and Theo beamed with pride.

'Papa,' Lena said. She was next to him now, clutching at his hand.

'Yes?'

'Why are you crying?'

Without realising it, tears had welled up in Theo's eyes. He brushed them away, bending down to pinch Lena's cheeks and bundling her in a hug.

'Because you are perfect.'

And so it began. Whenever they had a spare day, Theo and Lena would leave the circus grounds, in search of enrichment. They visited the *Palazzo Castellani* in Florence, the *Josephinum* in Vienna and the *Anatomisches Museum* in Basel, which housed the oldest human skeleton in the world. At the end of each stop, Lena would add to her growing souvenir collection, either by sketching what she saw or purchasing one of the trinkets they found in shops along the way. A thermometer, a vintage brass hourglass, a heavy metal compass. In a scientific shop in Hamburg, Theo found a petri dish that now served to hold Lena's earrings and bracelets on her dressing table.

On one occasion, Horace, who had been observing the jaunts with amusement, let his inquisitiveness get the better of him and asked Lena what she was carrying when she returned home. Lena opened her bag and presented an object to Horace. It was a circular bronze device, etched with numerical markings. Horace turned it over in his hands, a baffled look on his face.

'It's an astrolabe,' Lena explained, reaching up to take it. 'It was used to measure time relative to the stars and planets.' She spun the object around.

Horace watched, waiting for it to land on a specific set of numbers.

'That's it?' he said expectantly. 'What a useless piece of metal.'

Lena watched as Horace walked away, shaking his head. She was disappointed but not surprised. The astrolabe, after all, was not the kind of magic Horace appreciated. It was pure fact, based on truth, created from a linear process of deduction and hypothesising.

So while the other cast members rehearsed, Lena sat patiently, pouring over her box of assorted objects and drawings, dreaming up ways to manipulate time, thinking of what it would be like to traverse the constellations on foot, imagining the feeling of weightlessness as she dove to the depths of the Pacific Ocean. Science, and the realm of possibilities it represented, became her world. True to her father's prediction, the mementoes she'd collected served to inspire her over the years and unleashed a love for studying things she could see, touch and feel. Things that were real. Stuck in a universe where the sole aim was to distort the truth, the evidence-based nature of science brought Lena a kind of comfort she didn't know she craved.

Chapter Four

October 1938 – Europe

Following the inaugural dinner, the string of blue and gold carriages sped south. As they journeyed towards Luxembourg, Lena rolled herself down the hallway towards the library. Of all the carriages on the World of Wonders, the library was her favourite. For one thing, she seldom ran into other children. And the walls and walls of books provided an escape from reality, a myriad of characters and worlds she could lose herself in for hours on end.

Once inside, Lena surveyed the scene with dismay. Before the start of each tour, the costume and makeup carriages underwent a deep cleaning. During this time, the library became a makeshift storage centre. The heavy oak reading tables and lavish armchairs had been replaced with movable racks of gorgeous dresses, silk and cashmere leotards, elegant bespoke suits, sequinned jackets and more. There were piles of gilded trunks done up in midnight blue leather and lined with gold silk stacked neatly in one corner, holding a bric-a-brac of performer accoutrements. Towards the back, a line of chairs and dressing tables had been set up. The end table held stackable clear containers, filled with jewellery – Art Deco earrings and chokers, delicate studs, gigantic sapphires and opals fit for a Rajput prince, rose gold, silver, and copper rings – all organised and catalogued by colour and type. To the mere outsider, this room was a glimpse of the secrets the World of Wonders held, a tiny sliver of what was the most magical place on earth for anyone lucky enough to attend a show.

Yet for Lena, it was the opposite, a stark reminder of all the things she couldn't do. She sighed, moving her chair along one of the walls, and selected a book from the bottom shelf. While *Rock Formations Native to Australia* didn't sound particularly interesting, it was one of the only books she could reach. The temporary reorganisation meant all the books she liked had been placed on shelves higher up.

Lena thumbed through the pages, barely concentrating on the words. Every year she got her hopes up that this would be the season things changed. This would be the year she'd meet someone who accepted her for who she was, or the year Dr. Wilson finally came up with a medical cure for her ailments. But it was always the same. The new children would be polite to her face, but she'd never really be a part of their group. They'd say *Good Morning!* and *Good Night!* and might ask her to sit with them at breakfast from time to time. But she'd never be trusted to share their secrets or inside jokes.

Still, she told herself, trying to remain optimistic, she couldn't be that upset. She loved losing herself for hours in books, was an exceptional student and enjoyed helping Dr. Wilson. When she really stopped to think about it, it wasn't as though she was missing anything. She'd never used her legs, never known what it was to stand firmly in an upright position, to walk from one room to the next, to sprint on the sand of the beaches in the Mediterranean. Life in a seated position was the only life she knew.

Lena sighed, trying to focus on her book. *Australia boasts a fascinating geological history,* she read. *It is a continent that includes virtually all known rock types spanning 3.8 billion years.*

The main sections are Archaean cratonic, Proterozoic fold belts and sedimentary basins.

Suddenly she heard a noise.

'Hello?' a voice called out.

Johannes, Lena thought, placing the book back on the shelf. She inched her chair in behind a rack of beaded flapper-style leotards, removing one from its hanger and draping it over her feet, to make it look like she was nothing but a mass of jumbled fabric.

'Is someone there?'

Lena didn't answer. She didn't want to get into a discussion with Johannes. The Norwegian trapeze artist could be so tiresome. But it was too late. She could hear his footsteps coming towards her. A few seconds later, he pulled apart the rack of clothes, the beads making a swishing sound, and frowned.

'You know I can see your shoes and legs, right?' Johannes rolled his eyes as Lena wheeled herself out from behind the rack, pushing her long, chocolate brown curls away from her face. Johannes had spiked his hair up in tiny points that looked like miniature icicles. He was wearing a golden silk robe, Chinese printed blue and white silk pyjamas and had finished the whole look off with a pair of blue velvet smoking slippers that sported the Beddington and Sterling crest embroidered in gold thread on the tops. 'Shouldn't you be with Clara?'

Lena wheeled herself behind Johannes to the makeup area, eventually coming to a halt in her chair next to him. An assortment of palettes and brushes lay open on the table. He picked up a black pencil with a whisper-thin tip and began tracing the outline of his top eyelid.

'I finished all my schoolwork.' She undid the brake on her chair and began rolling it gently forward and then tried to push herself backwards when she reached the table using the soles of her shoes.

'So you decided to come here to annoy me?' Johannes blinked animatedly before starting on his other eye.

41

'I didn't know you'd be here,' Lena retorted. She pushed and pushed but nothing changed. Sighing, she rolled herself back and tried again.

'What about your father?'

Lena shrugged. 'He'd just tell me to stay inside the room.' She furrowed her brow as she strained herself, willing her feet to work.

'I don't know how you do it,' Johannes continued, letting out a loud sigh. 'Must be awful to be stuck inside all day, unable to move the way you want.'

Lena pressed her lips together. Johannes suited the circus perfectly, so dramatic was his temperament.

'It's not actually bad.'

Johannes dipped a brush into a pot of gold flakes and gingerly began patting it on his cheeks. 'I guess. But don't you ever wish things were different? That you could change? That you could finally have some friends who weren't an old British doctor and a spinster of a governess?'

'Clara's not a spinster!' Although there was more than a thread of truth to what he'd said, she would never admit it to him. Johannes gossiped like it was his job and she didn't want anyone – especially not her father – ever thinking she wasn't happy or grateful for what she had.

She placed her arms on the table and leaned over, then pushed back with all the force she could muster. But she over calculated the power in her upper body and shot back into the dresser on the other side, sending a palette of eyeshadows crashing to the ground.

'Lena!' Johannes shrieked, leaping up from his seat. He picked up the palette, cradling it like a beloved animal. 'Why can't you just sit quietly?'

Lena was about to shoot back that Johannes was by far the loudest person she had ever heard, but she held her tongue. 'I didn't know it would work.'

Johannes tutted as he settled himself back in his chair. He used a furry brush to remove the tiny particles of eyeshadow that had mixed in with each other. 'Sometimes I just feel so sad for you.'

'Why do you wear makeup?' Lena asked, after a moment's pause. Johannes stared at her like she was an insect.

'*Everyone* wears makeup. It's a circus.'

'Only girls and ladies, at least outside of shows.' Lena watched as Johannes dragged a stick of gold across his cheekbones, then patted it into his skin, giving it a bright sheen. 'JoJo,' she said impatiently. 'Tell me why!'

'Goodness, Lena! I wear it because I feel like it!' Johannes answered, exasperated. 'Because I can. Because I *want* to,' he said, pausing to look in the mirror. Satisfied with his reflection, he stood up. 'You know, just because someone says you have to be a certain way, or only do certain things, it doesn't mean you have to listen.' He whipped the ends of his robe across his body, the golden lengths of the ties flying in the air, and sashayed towards the door.

'And what came after the fall of the empire?'

A month later, Lena sat, staring outside the library window at the dreary Amsterdam sky. It was early December and they'd arrived in the capital the night before. Despite a good night's sleep, Lena was having trouble concentrating, mostly because she knew everyone else was out. It was their day off, and she'd watched with envy as the other children took off that morning, running out of their carriages to join the other performers for a tour of the city. She knew her father would have done his best to take her along, but he was tied up in meetings with Horace all day, so Lena had no choice but to stay behind.

'Did you hear me?' Clara arched an eyebrow.

Lena twirled her pencil around until it dropped on the ground. She bundled herself over in her chair, straining to reach it. 'Yes.' She loved Clara, but there were days when she yearned to be away from the circus. She wished, at times, that she could simply attend a normal school, with regular classmates who weren't off studying the art of contortion or training in acrobatics. She'd thought about asking her father many times but always stopped just short of getting the words out. *He would never,* she thought as she retrieved the pencil and straightened up, *let her go.*

Clara glanced at the clock. 10:45 a.m. It might do the girl some good to have some free time, an opportunity to explore the carriages without fear of running into children who might poke fun at her. She cleared her throat and began rubbing the sides of her temples.

'Do you know, I'm suddenly not feeling well. Why don't we take the rest of the day off?'

'Really?' Lena brightened, then quickly did her best to hide her excitement.

'Really,' Clara smiled. 'We'll pick up tomorrow.'

Lena stacked her books and pencil case on one of the lower bookshelves and set off for the kitchen. Mario, the resident chef, always had something scrumptious for her to eat. Lena moved leisurely through the halls, stopping to admire the paintings and furnishings in a way she would never do in the presence of other people. The World of Wonders was a series of luxurious train carriages, instantly recognisable by their blue and gold colouring, an upscale alternative to the other circuses, which Horace deemed 'pedestrian.' At each stop, a palatial octagonal tent was erected out of thick, midnight blue panels flecked with gold that made it look like it glittered from afar. Inside, a foyer with heated lanterns allowed patrons to mingle before proceeding to the grand stage and seating area where the performances took place.

The carriages were linked together by blue metallic planks. Residents could move easily between them by pulling the levers on the blackened glass doors that enclosed each one. Unlike most carriages, the World of Wonders circus train had a path that ran down the middle of its carriages, like a hallway, with rooms on either side. The carriages could also be disconnected from each other easily and rearranged to create an interconnected labyrinth if Horace so desired for a particular performance. Theo had gone to great lengths to ensure that the entire operation was easily navigable for Lena, insisting that every lever and doorknob be placed at a height that was low enough for her to reach, that the hallways were wide enough to safely accommodate her wheelchair and that the connector planks had tiny rubber markings to stop her from skidding.

Lena had nearly reached the kitchen when she saw the door to the food supply carriage slightly ajar. Mario always kept it securely locked to prevent people from stealing the food stuffs he stockpiled from the Marks and Spencer in Marble Arch before leaving London.

'Mario?' When no one answered, Lena pulled back the door, her hand flying to her mouth. A body was lying on the ground. Without thinking, she wheeled herself towards it to get a closer look. It was a boy, who looked to be a few years older than her.

'Hello,' she said tentatively, placing her hand on his arm. His skin was ice cold. Ignoring her father's rules, she shrugged off her extra blanket and draped it over him. Already she began to shiver. The inner doors of the food supply carriage could be pulled back to allow for easier transport of items to the kitchen and Lena saw that it was wide open. That morning she'd woken up to see a sprinkling of snow covering the Dutch capital, and she could feel the cool air wafting in freely, clinging to her cheeks.

'Excuse me,' she tried, a little louder. When the boy still didn't move, she quickly rolled herself out of the hallway and into the kitchen, hoping to catch Mario. But there was no one there. And then Lena remembered Mario had said he was taking his kitchen staff to a cheese factory in Zaanse and wouldn't be back till the evening.

Unsure what to do, she pushed herself back inside the food

supply carriage, right next to the boy. *Ok*, she thought. She needed to remain calm. That was the first thing Dr. Wilson always did when presented with a new patient. Taking a deep breath, she closed her eyes. Yes, she was far from being a doctor. But at nine years of age, she knew how to quiet a colicky baby, create a sling for a broken arm out of a man's shirt and name all 206 bones in the adult human body. She knew that blood deprived of oxygen travelled through the veins to the heart and then to the lungs, where it was re-oxygenated and subsequently dispersed via a system of arteries back to every area of the body. She was neither repulsed nor afraid of broken bones, bloody gashes or the assortment of bodily fluids that humans managed to produce. It was just one boy. She could do this.

Lena stretched her fingers, trying to touch the boy's neck. But she couldn't quite reach, so she tipped herself forward a bit and subsequently tumbled out of her chair.

'Ow!' She yelped, her hand flying to her leg. Her chair had fallen down with her, landing firmly on her lower right leg. She hauled herself up into a sitting position and pushed the chair back upright, then grimaced as she pulled up her skirt. As expected, a gash had opened up and fresh blood was now pooling around her shin. But it was her ankle she was worried about. She'd twisted it as she fell and she could see it starting to swell in her stocking.

Ignoring the pain, Lena dragged herself closer to the stranger. She took in his filthy, ripped clothing and torn shoes and wrinkled her nose, the stench of unwashed fabric making her retch. But she needed to do her best to make sure he was alright. Holding her breath, she placed two fingers on the left side of his neck and waited.

Please, she said to herself. *Please be ok.*

She felt a faint but steady heartbeat thrumming against her fingers. Lena breathed a sigh of relief. He was alive. She began touching the boy's pockets, trying to find some kind of identification, and landed on a rounded lump in his coat. She reached in and pulled out a packet of half-eaten chocolate digestives. Placing it on the side, she continued patting his clothes, eventually feeling the outline of a thin book. Carefully, she took it out of his trouser pocket. It was a German passport, with a weathered cover.

Pushing herself up on her elbows, she began thumbing through it. The boy was well-travelled, the pages full of stamps from across the continent. Perhaps he'd arrived for an audition and got lost on his way to Horace's study?

Outside, the wind was picking up and bringing with it an even greater chill into the carriage.

'Oh dear,' Lena said, touching the boy, whose cheeks were ruddy with cold.

Leaving the passport on the floor, she dragged herself back to her chair and hauled herself up, taking a moment to catch her breath. Then she took one last glance at the boy.

'Don't worry. I'm coming right back,' she said, before exiting the supply carriage.

'In here,' Lena said to Anna Maria, not ten minutes later. She'd run into the water ballerina on the way to Horace's study and immediately told her what happened. Anna Maria had tasked one of the other performers she was with to alert the others, while she accompanied Lena back to the food supply carriage.

Anna Maria knelt beside the boy as Lena pulled up next to her. While the water ballerina tried to wake the boy up, Lena frowned at her own leg and pressed the fabric of her skirt against the cut.

Around them, a crowd of performers began to swell in the tiny space, their harried queries ringing through Lena's ears.

'Is he dead?'

'Where did he come from?'

'Should we check the other carriages for stowaways?'

'Where's Dr. Wilson?' Anna Maria asked.

'Gone on a boat trip down the Herengracht,' one of the clowns answered.

'Don't touch him! You might get some kind of disease!' Johannes shrieked, as Jussi, a Swedish flame thrower, knelt by the boy and pulled a half-eaten currant bun out of one of his pockets. 'Thief!' Johannes continued, accusingly. 'Someone call the police—'

'That's enough!' Jussi scolded. 'The poor boy was probably starving.' Johannes sniffed but didn't attempt a rebuttal.

Lena glowered at Johannes as a flurry of murmurs rose up.

'The pogrom,' Jussi whispered.

Lena saw him pointing to the passport she'd found earlier. It was only then that she noticed the letter 'J' stamped in bold, red ink.

'Get out, come on, out of my way!' Horace steamrolled in, his humongous belly parting the crowd. He stopped abruptly upon seeing Jussi holding a passport over the boy.

'What's this then?'

'I found him lying here.' Lena pointed to the boy. Horace's gaze flitted from the boy to the passport, his eyes narrowing as he did so. He snatched it out of Jussi's hand and began thumbing through it briskly.

'Where is she? Where's my daughter?' Theo anxiously pushed his way to the front. 'Lena! Are you alright?'

Lena nodded. 'I came looking for some cake. But I found this boy lying here, all alone. I wanted to help,' she added, lest Johannes try to accuse her of being a thief as well. 'But I fell,' she said, pointing to her leg. 'I think it's twisted.'

'We must get you to the infirmary.' Theo wrapped his coat around her shoulders.

'Wait,' Lena said, watching Horace page through the passport, his face growing redder by the second. 'What about the boy?'

'Jussi?' Theo said. 'Bring him to the infirmary carriage. Dr. Wilson will—'

'They will do no such thing,' Horace fumed. 'We do not associate with such people.' He flung the passport onto the floor. 'Dispose of him. Immediately.' Then he clambered out of the carriage from the inside door, his breath creating miniature white clouds in the chilly air.

The cast members glanced at each other. No one wanted to say what they were all thinking. Lena's face crumpled as she stared at the boy.

'Why can't we help him?' she whispered, her lower lip trembling.

Theo stared after the circus director. He gripped Lena's shoulder reassuringly.

'Don't worry. I'll take care of it. Jussi?' He nodded at Jussi, who picked the boy up and carried him out.

A few hours later, Lena awoke in the infirmary. She yawned, then suddenly remembered the boy. Sitting up quickly, she pulled back the curtain separating her from the bed on her left.

'Ah. You're awake.' Dr. Wilson had returned and was buttoning up his white coat. The boy she'd found earlier was still asleep, his clothes still on.

'Is he alright?'

'I was just about to check his vitals. How are you feeling?'

Lena pulled off the sheet covering her body and observed her leg. Dr. Wilson had cleaned up and bandaged the cut, and her ankle, she noticed, was wrapped in layers of thick fabric.

'You got a slight sprain when you fell. Nothing a few weeks of rest and elevation won't fix.'

'Will he be ok?' Lena asked, more concerned about the boy's condition than her own.

'We'll soon find out.' Dr. Wilson pulled the curtain closed while he gave the boy a sponge bath and administered antiseptic. When Lena was finally allowed to see him again, she was pleased to see that the boy was wide awake, his blue eyes looking startled. But as she saw him looking around in wonder, she quickly drew the curtain closed, peeking out from the tiny sliver she'd left open on one side. She didn't want him to notice her until she'd had a chance to observe him first.

Three weeks earlier they'd received word of an attack that had happened in multiple cities on the continent.

'Storefronts, synagogues, schools and Jewish-owned businesses were ransacked, their windows smashed,' Theo stroked Lena's hair as she lay in bed. 'The newspapers are calling it *Kristallnacht*.'

'What does it mean?'

'The night of crystal.'

Lena imagined for a moment bits of shattered glass tinted ocean blue, brilliant white, bottle green and amber yellow, falling on the sidewalks of Austria, Germany, and Czechoslovakia. At the time, she thought it sounded beautiful. How amazing to have the sky raining with gems. But as she studied the boy in the bed next to her, taking in the scrapes on his arms, the bruises lining his exposed shins, and the dark circles framing his eyes, she felt guilty.

Theo knocked on the door, smiling with relief when he saw his daughter was awake. He joined Lena at her bedside and after she'd assured him she was feeling much better, she clutched at his hand as they waited for Dr. Wilson to finish his physical assessment of the stowaway. Apart from his stunning blue eyes, the boy sported a mop of hair that matched the colour of the hay bales that dotted the French countryside the circus trundled through each summer. When he leaned his head forward, his hair flopped all over the place, like it was incapable of holding a curl. His face was devoid of colour, and his cheeks were hollow, as if he hadn't had a proper meal in weeks.

'Hypothermia, severe bronchitis, a broken rib. Possible frostbite.' Lena's face dropped as Dr. Wilson listed off a string of ailments. 'But he'll be ok. As long as we can keep him here to heal.'

Theo nodded. 'I'll see to it that he stays.'

Dr. Wilson stepped to one side and Lena watched as her father attempted to sit on the edge of the boy's bed. But the boy shrank away, eyes wide. Theo held up his hands in surrender.

'I'm not going to hurt you.' He waited before proceeding with caution. 'Do you speak English?'

The boy gave a quick nod, his eyes roving from Lena to Theo, to Dr. Wilson and back to Lena.

'My name is Theo. This is Dr. Wilson – he's going to take care of you. And this,' he pointed 'is my daughter, Lena.'

The boy looked briefly at Dr. Wilson before settling his gaze on Lena with interest. Lena glanced at her father, who nodded.

'What's your name?'

'Alexandre,' the boy answered in a clear voice tinged with a French accent. Lena blinked in surprise. She'd been expecting German.

'I'm Lena.'

'Alexandre, do you know where your parents are?' Theo asked.

Alexandre lowered his eyes and began toying with the edge of the blanket. 'They're gone,' he whispered.

A melancholy silence hovered in the air. Lena couldn't tell if by 'gone' Alexandre meant that his parents were dead or if it meant that he was lost, but she was too embarrassed to ask. She poked at the blanket on her bed, waiting for her father to say something.

'Well, Alexandre,' Theo began, 'we'll take good care of you here until we've figured out a plan. In the meantime, there's no need to be afraid. On the contrary—' Theo reached up and grasped at one of the rolls of white bandages Dr. Wilson kept stacked on a shelf in his medical supply cabinet. He unfurled it, twisting it upside down and inside out. Lena watched Alexandre, who suddenly couldn't take his eyes off her father. 'We're here to have fun.' Theo snapped his fingers and a brilliant flash of white light appeared out of nowhere. When it was over, the bandage was nowhere to

51

be seen. In its place, perched happily on Theo's right hand, was a snow-white dove. Lena looked at it proudly, its eyes gleaming like tiny onyx beads, its wings fluttering gracefully. Then she looked at Alexandre, waiting for his reaction. But he seemed unimpressed.

'Don't you want to know how he did it?' she asked.

'I already know.'

Dr. Wilson let out a laugh. 'Preposterous! It's magic. Nobody knows how it's done.'

But Alexandre didn't laugh back. Looking at the stowaway with a renewed sense of interest, Theo took a seat on his bed.

'How do you think I did it?'

Alexandre shifted, wincing in pain before settling into a comfortable position. 'The bird. I saw it in your sleeve.'

Lena knew how the illusion worked. The appearing-bird act was one of the oldest and most basic tricks in the book. A dove was indeed hidden in the opening of a magician's sleeve. A diversion was then created and the bird released. Though simple, it was impressive to watch, and not easy to figure out if you'd only seen it once.

'Why were you watching my sleeve? Why wasn't your attention on the bandage?'

Alexandre didn't answer immediately. 'Because that's what you wanted me to do.' A cloudy look crossed his face. 'If I only did or watched what was expected of me, I wouldn't have survived.'

The smile on Lena's face vanished. Theo placed a hand on the blanket covering Alexandre's legs.

'Was someone trying to hurt you? Did they hurt your parents?'

Alexandre blinked but refused to offer any further information.

'The Gestapo?' Theo prodded.

Alexandre narrowed his eyes, so that only a sliver of blue was visible between the tiny slits. He didn't speak for the rest of the day.

CHAPTER FIVE

'Where do you think he came from?' Lena whispered to Clara. A few days had passed since she'd found Alexandre and she was sitting upright in bed, labelling the capital cities on a map of Europe. Her lessons had been moved to the infirmary carriage until her leg healed.

'Germany, I assume, from his passport,' Clara answered. Lena scowled. Lots of people could have passports to certain countries. It didn't mean that was where they lived. Besides, the boy's French accent clearly meant he'd spent a lot of time there.

'Do you think his parents are dead? How old do you think he is? Why doesn't Horace want him?' Lena put her coloured pencil down and pulled the curtain back to stare at Alexandre, who was fast asleep.

'Lena Papadopoulos! Let him rest,' Clara scolded. Grudgingly, Lena drew the curtain closed.

'Papa said he must be a magician, since he picked the lock on the food supply door *and* he knew how to do the bird trick!'

'If only you were as interested in correctly identifying the capitals of European countries as you are in the stowaway.' Clara pointed to the map.

Lena sighed as she picked up her coloured pencil and went back to her assignment.

After her lessons were over, Lena opened the *Complete Oxford*

Dictionary of English and began nibbling on the biscuits Mario had left earlier. One of the games she played to keep herself entertained was to open the dictionary to a random page, choose a word, and read all about its etymology. Then she'd try and challenge herself to use the word in an everyday interaction, which was actually quite tricky.

'*Metamorphosis*,' Lena said, 'from the Greek "metamorphoun", which means "transform or change shape"'. She picked up another biscuit, split it open and licked the chocolate cream filling inside.

'Are you going to eat those all by yourself?'

Lena dropped the other half of the biscuit. Alexandre had pulled back the curtain and was watching her with an amused expression.

'How long have you been awake?'

He pushed a lock of floppy hair out of his eyes. 'Long enough to hear you asking about me.' He pointed to the dictionary, a hint of a smile on his face. 'This is a fun game, *non*?'

Lena scowled. 'You shouldn't spy on people!'

'You were spying on me!'

'I wasn't spying!' Lena said, her face going red. 'I was simply making conversation.'

Alexandre slowly pivoted his body in her direction, grimacing slightly from the pain.

'Here are the answers in case you're still wondering: Your teacher was nearly right on the first one, I was born in Germany, but grew up mostly in France. Marseille, to be precise. Number 2: Yes. Number 3: I'm 12. Number 4: Because I'm a Jew.' He pointed to Lena's plate. 'I'm sick of the potato chowder the chef keeps serving. How do you feel about sharing?'

Lena grinned and passed him the plate of biscuits. She watched him take one, pull it apart and lick off the chocolate cream icing just as she'd done, smacking his lips happily. She closed the dictionary, trying to think of something to say. 'Where were you before you came?'

54

'Amsterdam,' he said, shovelling another biscuit into his mouth.

'Why?'

He paused. 'Family holiday,' he answered, before launching into a fit of coughing. Lena held out her half-empty cup of water and he took it, sipping it slowly. 'Thanks.'

'You're lucky you don't have pneumonia. That can kill you. So can pertussis. And diphtheria.' Lena ticked off the list of all the different tracheal infections she'd committed to memory.

Alexandre took another sip of water. 'You certainly know a lot about coughs.'

Lena shrugged. 'I read a lot. Not much else to do here.'

Alexandre's eyes widened and he opened his mouth to speak but instead launched into another round of coughing.

'Ah! Keeping our stowaway on his toes I see,' Dr. Wilson said to Lena, as he entered the infirmary. 'There, there.' He rubbed Alexandre's back then poured some medicine out of an amber-coloured bottle. 'Two spoons of this,' he said, holding out the teaspoon, 'and you'll soon be alright.' He glanced at Lena. 'I think it's best that Alexandre spend the afternoon resting. You can continue your conversation tomorrow.'

'Ok,' Lena said, reluctantly returning to her dictionary.

The next day, Alexandre pulled the curtain back as soon as Clara had left.

'I thought your lessons would never end.'

'Hello,' Lena said, delighted that he'd been waiting to speak with her. 'Are you well?'

'I'd be better if I could have some of those.' He pointed to the plate of macarons by Lena's bedside. 'What's your secret? Every day you get tray after tray of biscuits and I'm stuck with chowder.'

'Take as many as you like,' Lena gestured to the plate. Alexandre reached over and picked up a handful.

'What did you learn about today?' he asked.

'The Mesozoic era. Do you know it?'

He wrinkled his nose. 'I don't like school.'

'Why not?'

Alexandre shrugged. 'Say,' he said, picking up a deck of cards he'd noticed on Lena's bedside table, 'can we play? What games do you know?'

Lena felt her face growing hot and turned away. She knew everything from pinochle to rummy but didn't want to admit to Alexandre that she'd spent her life growing up playing both hands because no one wanted to play with her. When she was sure her face had returned to its original colour, she faced him, smiling.

'Let's go with ... rummy,' she said. As Alexandre dealt the cards, Lena studied him. 'Why is it bad? To be a Jew?'

'Who said it was bad?'

'You did. When I asked why Horace doesn't want you.'

Alexandre considered his cards, eventually playing an eight of spades. 'I guess it means you're different and people don't like that.'

'Why?'

Alexandre shrugged and bit into another macaron. 'Dunno. Maybe it's a disease inside.' He grinned, holding up his half-eaten biscuit. 'Careful who you share these with. Wouldn't want you to get even more sick.' He pointed to her ankle. 'How long till you can walk again?'

Lena looked up from her cards. 'Excuse me?'

'The sprain. Did the doctor say how long you'd be out?'

And then it dawned on Lena that Alexandre had never actually seen her in her chair. This whole time, he'd treated her like his equal. Her wheelchair was in her room, along with the extra blankets and a plethora of tinctures and muscle balms her father insisted she have on hand. But the bandages on her leg and ankle were the only indication that she might not be able to walk.

Lena glanced at Alexandre. If she told him now she might risk losing him.

'He didn't say,' she said, playing a Jack of Hearts.

Alexandre triumphantly threw down an Ace. 'I win,' he crowed. 'I'm sure you'll be back on your feet in no time,' he said, stacking the cards into a neat pile.

'Yes,' Lena nodded, burying the sadness in her voice. 'I'm sure I will.'

Lena and Alexandre's play sessions and conversations continued in the lead up to the Christmas holidays, the two children quickly falling into a comfortable routine. Alexandre would wait for Lena's lessons to finish upon which they'd spend hours playing games and chatting, until Dr. Wilson came round to tell them to rest or take Alexandre for another massage therapy session.

One afternoon, as Theo was coming to visit Lena, he paused outside the infirmary carriage, his heart swelling to hear his daughter's jubilant laughter.

'It's a miracle isn't it?' Clara whispered, watching the two children.

'I can't quite believe it myself,' Theo agreed. 'What with bronchitis and the internal bruising – it's a wonder he survived.'

'I meant Lena,' Clara said. 'I daresay I've never seen her this happy.'

'Absolutely not.' Horace didn't bother looking up from the stack of financial reports he was leafing through.

'He has no family.' Theo stood imposingly across from the circus director and raised an eyebrow. In the back corner, Chadwick sniffed. With his scraggy frame, poor posture and mousy presence, Chadwick was the antithesis to Horace's power-hungry, egotistical persona. Had they any stage performing abilities whatsoever, Theo imagined the duo would have made a brilliant comedic vaudeville act.

'Such things are not my concern.' Horace licked his index

finger and began scrutinising the page clenched between fingers that were as thick and stubby as the Cuban cigars he smoked after each performance.

'He's only twelve. What's he meant to do?'

Horace peered at his star performer over the tops of his gold-rimmed spectacles, tilting his head so much that they slid down the oily bridge of his shiny nose.

'When I was twelve, I was earning fifty cents per week through my paper route. I later set up a shoeshine business servicing the financiers of Atlantic Avenue. Each morning outside Quincy—'

'Market, Quincy Market yes, yes, I know, we all know about your rise from poverty to opulence.' Theo smirked.

Horace narrowed his eyes, regarding the prized illusionist with a mixture of admiration and contempt. In nearly a decade of knowing him, Theo had always been this way. Benevolent to a fault. It was a quality that so many admired, but that baffled Horace. Why do anything for anyone if not for some kind of benefit? He moved his brown leather chair back into an upright position and leaned so far forward that the edge of his desk jutted into his gigantic belly.

'Do you honestly think that, given a reversal of fortunes, the boy would do the same for you?'

'You've helped many orphans before. I recall that working out quite well.' Theo motioned to the balance sheets peppering Horace's desk. The smile faded from the entertainment impresario's face.

'Be that as it may, there is still the matter of his background. He's a Jew.' Horace leaned back, the chair groaning under his weight, as he refocused his attention on the January profit projections.

'Again. You were once young in a foreign land. If not for the kindness of strangers, would you be here? Have all this?' Theo made a sweeping motion with his arm, signalling not just the study, but the entire operation that was the Beddington and Sterling World of Wonders.

'And how do you propose we alter his genetic composition?'

Theo shrugged. 'We don't have to change anything. We simply don't tell anyone. I know how skilled you are at cooking the books.' To Theo's pleasure, Horace reddened. 'Oh yes. Don't think I didn't notice the reduction at the end of last season's pay packet. But as long as I keep my mouth shut, you will too.'

Horace thought about the proposal. The boy identified himself as Alexandre Robichaud, born to a French father and a German Jewish mother. It was a hygienic name, one that wouldn't cause offence or set alarm bells off. From what Horace observed during his visit to the infirmary carriage, the boy looked the part, too. Blond hair, white skin, sky blue eyes.

'He's as Aryan as they come,' Theo continued, hating himself for bringing it up. But he needed to do what he could to save the boy, for Lena's sake. 'Besides. It's not as though you aren't protecting others for your gain.'

Horace thought immediately of Johannes' penchant for lanolin cream and frequent requests for Max Factor mascara, and the two Romani twins he hired five years ago, who were so skilled at tumbling that he couldn't bear to give them up, no matter how dangerous it was.

Theo cleared his throat. 'Get him his papers. And in return, I shall produce an illusionist even greater than myself.'

'Don't be absurd. He's nothing but a young grifter.'

'He's different,' Theo insisted. 'He has a quick eye and raw talent.'

'And what if he turns out like Lena?' At first, Horace hadn't minded the girl. He'd been hopeful, in fact, eager to see if medical advances could change her prognosis and in turn, line his pockets. If she looked anything like her mother, she'd make a fine water ballerina down the road. Or perhaps, he thought, she'd inherit Theo's magical genes. A female illusionist. What a feat that would be. Horace waited as she turned four, then five, then six, for her to improve. But as the performers rehearsed, all the little girl did was sit quietly in the wings of the stage curtains during each show, her nose buried in a book. It wasn't as though Horace lacked empathy entirely. He knew her physical condition prevented her from participating in the majority of the typical circus activities. But she could learn to sew, or try her hand at makeup, or hairdressing.

'What does that mean?' Theo bristled.

'Simply that she does no work for the circus. Suppose the boy's medical condition doesn't improve? Having one mouth to feed that brings me nothing in return is one thing, but two . . ..' Horace instantly regretted his words. Without warning, the carefully organised stack of financial statements floated up off his desk. As he cried out in frustration, each sheet of paper began spinning around, slowly at first and then faster, before it was engulfed in a growing cobalt blue flame that materialised from thin air. Behind him, Chadwick shrieked, throwing his hands over his face in a protective manner.

'Confound it, Theo!' Horace slammed his oak desk with both hands. 'Alright! I'll give you until the end of the tour. If you can see to it that the boy is earning money for us, I'll re-evaluate his status. And he can only stay if he agrees to work in Mario's kitchen. The boy must earn his keep.'

Theo considered the offer. Eight months was not a lot of time, but it would have to do.

'Draw up his papers tomorrow.' Theo tossed the passport to Chadwick. 'Burn this.'

'Now. My papers,' Horace said irritably. Immediately the blue tornado disappeared and the bits of loose-leaf flying around settled themselves into a neat pile on his desk. Chadwick lowered his arms, whimpering at what he'd just witnessed. Horace grumbled, shaking his head as he picked up the top sheet. His face reddened as he bellowed. 'Theo! These are all out of order!' But when he looked up, the illusionist was gone.

CHAPTER SIX

The next morning, Lena was looking forward to a full day of playing checkers and eating cherry tarts with Alexandre. She checked the clock, noting that he'd be back with Dr. Wilson soon from his exercise session, and began dividing up the black and red pieces for their game.

'Hi!' Lena sang out, upon hearing the doorknob turn. 'You're just in time!'

'It's only me,' Theo chuckled, walking over to her bedside.

'Oh.'

'That happy to see your Papa, eh?' Theo laughed and bent down to kiss his daughter. 'Perhaps my news will change your mind.'

'What news?'

'I spoke with Horace and he's agreed to let Alexandre stay. But on one condition,' Theo said, his face serious as he saw Lena's eyes light up. 'We must protect his identity as a Jew. You mustn't tell anyone who he really is. It's too dangerous.'

Lena nodded. She still didn't understand why Horace didn't like Jewish people, but she wanted Alexandre to stay on board as long as he could. There was no chance of her saying anything to jeopardise that.

'The second bit of news is . . . well. I'll show you,' Theo said, leaving the room. Lena clenched her fists in anticipation. Perhaps her father had bought her a puppy. She imagined herself showing it off to Alexandre, thinking of what he would say. But instead of a new pet, her father re-entered with her wheelchair.

'What are you doing?' she asked, her face going pale.

'Dr. Wilson says your leg is fine,' Theo said cheerfully, bringing the chair to her bedside. 'We'll have you back to your routine just in time for the holidays.'

Lena recoiled from the chair, pulling the blanket up closer to her chin. 'No!' she said, miserably.

'No?' Theo gave her a confused look. 'Surely you don't want to spend Christmas in here?'

Lena rubbed her throat and coughed a few times. 'I'm . . .I'm actually not feeling well again.'

Theo placed his hand on her forehead, frowning. 'You haven't got a temperature. Still, we should wait for Dr. Wilson.'

'That's an excellent idea,' Lena said. 'Maybe take the chair back to my room until then?'

Theo chuckled. 'I didn't mean wait *here* for Dr. Wilson! Lena, you've been inside far too long. It will do you some good to get out. There's a lovely museum we can visit, they're open until five o'clock.'

Lena checked the time. Dr. Wilson and Alexandre would be back any minute, but even if she waited until they returned, Alexandre would see the chair. The jig would be up. Her best bet was to get out as quickly as she could.

'On second thought, I want to go now,' she insisted, throwing her blankets off and hoisting herself into her chair.

'I thought you weren't feeling well?'

'I'm better.' She pulled a blanket over her. 'Let's go!'

At that moment, Dr. Wilson walked into the room, Alexandre right on his tail. His eyes widened when he saw Theo and Lena. Lena tried to pull the curtain back but it was too late. He'd already seen her.

64

'Good morning!' Theo said, happily. 'Alexandre, I'm so pleased to hear you're feeling stronger. There's something I wish to discuss with you, but let me get Lena settled into her room first.'

Alexandre was too busy staring at Lena to reply. He took a few calculated steps forward, trying to process what he was seeing. Mortified, Lena gripped the sides of her chair, wishing the ground would swallow her whole.

'What's happened to her?'

Theo looked puzzled. 'Nothing. In fact, she's better now.'

'But . . . if her leg's ok, why does she need the chair?'

Theo burst out laughing. 'Such comedic timing!' he said, shaking his head.

Alexandre gripped his bedpost, baffled. 'I'm not joking. Why is she in that chair?'

Theo glanced at Lena, whose face had turned crimson. 'Surely she told you? Lena's been in a wheelchair for most of her life.'

Alexandre rubbed his eyes. 'Oh,' he replied after a minute. 'Yes. She did. I've been so tired lately, I must have forgotten.'

'Not to worry. But yes, we're lucky she's alive,' Theo said, bending down to pinch his daughter's cheeks. Lena tried to bat away his hand, embarrassed at being treated like a small child in front of Alexandre. She stole a quick glance at him, but his face was expressionless.

'Papa,' Lena whispered sadly. 'Please, I want to get out of here.'

'Of course. Alexandre, I'll be back later, but in the meantime, Mario will be sending your lunch over momentarily.' As Lena wheeled herself out, she could feel Alexandre's eyes on her, but couldn't bring herself to meet them.

Later that day Theo returned to the infirmary carriage with a few sheets of paper, an envelope and a pen. He found Alexandre sitting up in bed, stroking the dove, which was arching its back periodically, then flopping down in his lap.

'Dr. Wilson said you'd be out just after New Year's,' Theo said, settling himself on the edge of Alexandre's bed. 'It's wonderful news.' He paused and took a deep breath. 'Alexandre, I don't know if you've given any thought to where you'll go once you're better, but you're welcome to stay here. In fact, I'm hoping you will.' He handed a few sheets of paper to Alexandre. 'This is a contract Horace has drawn up. He's agreed to make you a new passport, so no one will know who you really are. We'll keep your identity a secret and train you in the art of illusion. In exchange, you'll receive full room and board. Horace did stipulate you'd have to work a few hours in the kitchen, but I'm sure I can get you out of that.'

Theo cleared his throat, fingering the remaining pages in his hands. 'The second part requires an omission of truth on your part. I don't like lying, but as you'll soon see, I don't think I have much of a choice.' Theo met Alexandre's curious gaze. 'My desire to have you join us is not entirely selfless. I've seen the way my daughter acts around you. You've managed to bring her out of her shell, making her laugh, play and show more zest for life than she ever has.' Theo passed him the remaining pages and an envelope. 'Lena hid her condition from you because she's ashamed. She tries to remain positive, but the truth is, she's terribly lonely. That's where you come in,' he said, pointing to the envelope and papers. 'You'll find an additional contract, one between you and I, and enough money to double your salary in there. If you agree to stay, you'll receive another payment for each year you choose to remain on tour. All I ask is that you be a friend to my daughter. A good friend, someone who doesn't only spend time with her when it's convenient for them.'

Alexandre stared at the contracts and stack of neatly folded bills silently. He'd never stayed in one place long enough to form ties with other children. His father had insisted his family were the only bonds worth keeping. But he was pleasantly surprised at how comfortable he felt around Lena, and it was a feeling he wanted to hold onto. 'Sir, I like Lena. I don't need a bribe.'

'You've pure, but naive intentions, Alexandre. My guess is you've never been privy to the boundaries that exist between children who are normal and those who are different. And Lena – my bright, bubbly, caring daughter – is different. She sticks out immediately and has no hope of hiding her condition long enough for people to look past her wheelchair. Children can be so cruel. I've had to stand by and witness her retreating further into her shell as the years go by. However, with you, I see a different side of her, a side I'd like to keep. I want her to be happy, here, where she's safe and I can keep an eye on her. But you must promise to keep the arrangement quiet. No one – not Horace, not Dr. Wilson, nor the other children and especially not Lena – can ever know.'

'But,' Alexandre said, wrestling with the newfound feeling of wanting to keep another person in his life. 'I'll do it for free. You don't have to pay me.'

'But I do,' Theo said, his normally smooth facade cracking slightly. 'A contract removes any ambiguity. If you choose to accept, I'd like you to begin right away.'

Alexandre frowned. That Theo cared about his daughter was obvious enough, but there was something about the way he was acting that made him wonder if there was a bigger reason he wanted him to stay – one that went beyond Lena's social life.

'So,' he began, going over the details in his head. 'I'd live here the whole time? In these carriages?' Theo nodded. 'Going from town to town?' Theo nodded again, a feeling of dread rising inside him at the thought of Alexandre turning him down. He needed the boy to stay put.

'We'll take excellent care of you and you'll have access to the best of everything. I will, of course, understand if you wish to follow in your father's footsteps. However, should you want to explore an alternate pathway, I see no better option than what I've presented you with.'

Alexandre was silent. While he felt sick about accepting it, it was a lot of money and would ensure he wouldn't need to worry about food or clothes or anything, really. His mind circled back to Marseille, Cartagena, and Forte dei Marmi. All the times he stood outside the music halls, revues, and amphitheatres that dotted the coastal towns of the Mediterranean. His mother would act as a decoy, telling anyone who'd listen that her son had gone missing. She'd plead with them in a distressed voice, begging for help. Alexandre used this opportunity to take whatever he could. Sometimes it was a few francs but other times he got lucky: a pair of ruby earrings, a Cartier Tank watch, a silver bracelet. At the end of each evening, his mother would wrap her arms around Alexandre's shoulders, stretching out the walk back to wherever they'd set up camp for the night. She'd point out the constellations lighting up the midnight-blue sky and promise that one day she'd take him from Orion to Cassiopeia and back again.

'If you ever feel lost or frightened, Alexandre. Look up. I am there, always, watching over you, just like a shining star,' she'd whisper in his ear, her breath hot on his lobe. Alexandre remembered feeling her grip tighten and her body tense as they drew closer to where his father was waiting for them, ready to snatch away whatever they'd taken, along with the tiny bit of happiness they had when it was just him and his mother.

Then the gruesome scene he'd run from flashed into his mind. The abandoned barn. The sirens blaring. The footsteps of the policemen. The golden necklace. And he remembered the last words his father would ever speak to him.

'You did this, Alexandre. Everything you love, dies,' he rasped. He reached a hand upwards, trying to claw at his son's clothing. But Alexandre was too fast for him, especially in his compromised state, and darted to one side. His father let out a bitter laugh. 'You want to be a coward? Then go. But remember this, my boy. Blood is thicker than water. You cannot outrun who you truly are.'

But he couldn't say any of this to the man who was looking at him with a mixture of hope and curiosity, so he simply nodded.

'Where do I sign?'

CHAPTER SEVEN

By the time the World of Wonders rolled into Copenhagen in mid-January, Dr. Wilson deemed Alexandre well enough to be up and about. Up to that point, Lena had successfully avoided seeing him. But that day he was being released and Lena had spent the entire morning fretting over how she was going to stay clear of him.

She sat across from Clara in the library, chipping away at a Renoir puzzle her father had purchased from the *Musée de l'Orangerie* the last time they were in Paris.

'This goes where that splotch of yellow is.' Lena stretched her hand out and tried to slot the piece in. She frowned. It had looked like a correct match initially, but was refusing to slide in perfectly.

'No matter. It's the right colour, so it's bound to be in this section,' Clara said. She glanced at Lena as she sorted through a pile of blue and green pieces. 'Alexandre asked about you yesterday,' she said casually.

'That's nice.'

'He's being released today and was hoping you'd show him around later.'

Lena focused her attention on trying to build out the bottom border of the puzzle, picking through the pile of pieces, setting aside the ones that were beige and white. Borders, she'd found, were trickier than they looked. 'Someone else can do it.'

'Lena,' Clara said softly. She noticed Lena's lip wobble. 'He didn't know, did he?'

Lena shook her head. 'But he knows now,' she sniffed. 'I can't hide it. He'll probably never want to speak to me again.'

'I just told you he's been asking for you!'

'Why would he want to be friends with me?'

'I can think of a number of reasons. You're kind. Smart. Curious. An excellent board game player.' Clara slotted in a piece of the border that Lena was working on, smoothing over the bit where the two pieces met. 'You know, each time mother writes me with news of a potential suitor, it makes my blood boil. None of them ever work out. Did I tell you about the one who, after I'd agreed to meet him, kept me waiting at the town fair for one and a half hours? It was only because his cousin – much nicer than him, mind you —dragged him away from whatever bottle he'd been downing that he bothered to show up at all. Awful people, I tell you.' Clara shuddered.

'That's rude,' Lena said, slotting in another piece of the base, pausing to admire her handiwork.

'It is. And I could let it stop me from ever trying again. It's so hard to keep experiencing that kind of disappointment.' Clara glanced at Lena. 'But, if I didn't try, I'd still be in the same position. By not trying, nothing changes. By trying, I *could* meet someone who leaves me waiting for hours. But I could also meet someone wonderful.'

Lena dissolved in tears and Clara moved her chair around the table, draping an arm over the young girl's shoulders.

'It hurts,' Lena hiccupped. 'All I want is one friend.'

'I know,' Clara said, squeezing her. 'However, sometimes a fresh perspective is all one needs. Take Alexandre. You're worried about what he'll think of you – but have you ever thought about what he's going through? Perhaps he's reaching out because he's lonely.'

'Why would he be lonely?'

'How could he not be? He doesn't know anyone here and just lost his parents. Did you ever think that maybe he needs you more than you need him?'

Lena had never thought about it that way. But then she remembered the sadness that stabbed at her each time she watched the other children playing hide-and-seek, not bothering to include her. How could she risk exposing herself again to that kind of pain?

'No. The chance is too low.'

'But there's *always* a chance.' Clara pushed two red pieces together, creating a small flower in the bouquet. 'So. What do you say? You give Alexandre a chance and I'll respond to mother about the latest potential, a chap from Hampstead named Maurice.' Clara frowned. 'I'm not sure I trust people named "Maurice".'

Lena arranged a line of yellow puzzle pieces, deep in thought. 'I don't feel like it,' she announced after a few moments. She expected her to argue back, to try and convince her again, but Clara just shrugged.

'Alright. I've said what I need to. But remember something, Lena. Try or don't try,' Clara said, snapping the final piece of the bouquet into place. 'The time will pass anyway.'

'Because it's mid-tour we had no rooms available,' Theo said, leading Alexandre out of the infirmary carriage later that afternoon, 'but Horace has agreed to let you stay in the help's quarters. Now, if you go down here . . .'

As Theo droned on, Alexandre zoned out. The circus was a labyrinthine network of carriages and rooms all connected by a series of hallways and passages that seemed to go on forever. Alexandre twisted his head from side to side, taking in the different scenes that caught his eye as he followed the illusionist. When they came to a bend in the hallway, Alexandre caught sight of two young children, giggling with delight at a juggler balanced on a unicycle who was tossing balls in the air. While ordinarily, this would not warrant a second glance, the balls turned into whatever animal the children asked for, while still airborne.

'Lion!' the older one yelled. The juggler clapped his hands as a yellow ball morphed into a stuffed baby lion and came to rest in front of the boy's feet.

To Alexandre's left, out in the open air, he glimpsed two contortionists twisting their bodies into unthinkable shapes around the ice white branches of a cluster of birch trees. They were wearing white and silver leotards, giving off the effect that they were one with nature. He had to blink twice before he was able to separate the humans from their surroundings.

'It's a bit overwhelming at first, but you'll soon get used to it,' Theo said.

After a few more minutes of walking, they reached the residential cluster of carriages. Each door was made out of heavy oakwood and stained dark blue. A gold room number in Roman numerals was displayed on each one. As he tried to keep pace with Theo, Alexandre noticed a series of portraits on one side of the hallway, framed in gold. They looked like performers who had since left the circus. He shuddered, feeling the eyes in the pictures following him, wondering who this new recruit was.

'The eyes?' Theo asked, chuckling.

Alexandre didn't want to appear afraid, but the portraits were scaring him. He nodded reluctantly.

'It's an optical illusion. You'll find that many things here are not what they seem,' Theo replied, and Alexandre took note of the twinkle in his eye.

They turned right and approached a dimly lit corridor, walking in silence to an unmarked door at the end.

'I'm afraid this was all we had available.' Theo twisted a golden key with a blue velvet ribbon in the lock and flicked on a light switch. Alexandre gasped. The room was bigger than any place he had ever stayed. On one side was a single bed with a plush blue cover and four plump pillows woven with silk gold thread. On the other side stood a dresser and a small closet. A side table nestled neatly in the space between the bed and dresser. Alexandre shook his head in disbelief. All his life, he'd never had a room of his own – and certainly not one that came close to having a door that locked, or a bed that wasn't fashioned out of scraps of old fabric stitched together, albeit lovingly, by his mother.

'I gave Martha your measurements before Christmas. If you check the drawers, I'm sure you'll find everything you need. Right,' Theo said, heading for the door. 'I'll leave you to get settled in. Dinner's at seven.'

'Wait,' Alexandre said.

'Yes?'

Alexandre's eyes darted around before coming to rest on the illusionist. 'There's no police here? No one will find me?'

Theo smiled. 'Alexandre, you have my word. No one will know who you are, or how to find you. You're safe.'

Alexandre held Theo's gaze for a moment. 'Thank you.'

'If you get lost on your way to dinner, just inhale. I'm sure your nose will guide you,' Theo said, winking as he left.

After he'd closed the door, Alexandre opened the dresser. Sure enough, stacks of coloured shirts and sweaters, fresh underclothes and at least ten pairs of matching socks in blue, black and grey stared back at him. On the floor beneath he saw two pairs of leather shoes, one black, one brown, lined up neatly next to each other. He slid his foot into one of the shoes and closed his eyes. He'd never owned a pair of shoes that wasn't lifted from a rubbish heap, and the feeling of the smooth, clean insole nearly brought tears to his eyes. He opened the drawers of his chest again, and ran his fingers over the soft cotton tops and warm woollen sweaters, nuzzling one up to his cheek.

But this hadn't been the plan, Alexandre thought, shutting the drawer and sitting on his new bed. He wasn't supposed to have been caught, contracted bronchitis, broken any bones, or been taken in by these people at all. It was supposed to have been a routine procedure. The easiest kind. Into the carriage and out. Take what you need and go. Leave no trace behind.

Alexandre winced thinking about what his father would have said about his current predicament.

A weak, useless boy. Can't even be trusted to pull off a simple job! Anja, I'm telling you, he wouldn't survive a day in the wild alone!

He clamped his hands over his ears. It wasn't his fault. Everything had happened so fast. He stood up, trying to shake off the memory of the worst day of his life and tried to focus on the present. He liked the affable illusionist and his daughter, but he didn't know them well enough yet to trust them. Alexandre weighed his options. The money Theo had given him was enough to get started on his own, following in his father's footsteps. On the other hand, he had no idea where to go and no family to turn to for help. Plus, he was still getting weekly check-ups from Dr. Wilson. If he left now, he'd be on the run indefinitely, living hand to mouth, always looking behind him. If he stayed, he would at least be protected from the authorities and receive the medical care he needed.

Alexandre reached out and ran his hand over the gilded blue velvet lining the carriage walls. The circus owner had money, that much was obvious. If he didn't like it here, he'd stay until he'd built up a healthy sum and was feeling well again, then take what he wanted and go.

He took out the items he'd managed to squirrel away whilst holed up in the infirmary carriage. A stethoscope, a few rolls of white bandages, two beautiful blue apothecary bottles and a set of stainless steel German medical instruments that looked expensive. Then he took out his mother's necklace, a thin, delicate chain with a tiny golden star pendant with a diamond gleaming at its centre. A bolt of sadness shot through him. He hadn't stopped to grieve or think about how much he missed her. But there was no time for that now. He crouched down on the floor near his closet. Using the edge of his room key, he pried at one of the floorboards until it came undone, then tucked the items into the cavity below, replacing the floorboard. His father had taught him that you could never get too comfortable. *Trust no one, Alexandre.* He needed to be ready to run.

Lena wheeled herself slowly down the hallway towards Alexandre's room, coming to a halt outside. She looked down at the deck of cards, sleeve of Jaffa cakes and two bottles of ginger beer in her lap. Was she really going to do this? Risk everything just to be friends with someone who would probably desert her in a few weeks? Then she thought about what Clara had said earlier.

Try or don't try. The time will pass anyway.

She swallowed and knocked on the door. Alexandre opened it and almost immediately her nerves turned to concern.

'Are you alright?' she asked, taking in his red eyes.

'Yes. It's just the dust,' Alexandre replied, rubbing at his eyelids. He looked hollow, like someone had sucked the life out of him. 'Hello, by the way,' he said, brightening and standing up straight, his old self starting to come back. 'Where've you been?'

Lena watched him carefully. If she'd known him better she would have asked why he'd been crying. But she didn't know him, not really, and that brief moment of vulnerability on his part was gone now. So she shrugged it off and held up the deck of cards.

'Rummy?'

Alexandre grinned and moved out of the way to let her in.

CHAPTER EIGHT

Later that week, Lena gave Alexandre a grand tour of the carriages. She pointed out the secret hiding spot where Mario kept the tins of Cadbury biscuits, proudly detailed the history of every single costume in the wardrobe carriage and beat him handily at darts in the games room.

She saved the Mirage Maze for last because it was her maze, the special place her father had created for her. On the previous season's tour, Lena had accompanied Theo to a castle in Tiszadob. She remembered her father shaking her awake after the hour-long drive from Debrecen and marvelling at the fifty-two room castle which belonged to the powerful Andrássy family during their reign.

'One for each week of the year. Imagine if you lived here. You could stay in a different room every single week.' Theo chuckled.

But it was the maze in the garden that truly astounded her. Her father explained that it was like a puzzle she had to solve.

'You keep going until you come out the other side.'

'What's on the other side?'

'You have to get there to find it.'

So Lena pushed herself through, turning her wheels slowly, eventually ending up back at the beginning. At one point, she stopped to study a caterpillar dangling from a twig before realising her father was no longer with her.

'Papa?' She turned, trying to orient herself, but each time she was met with brambles and twigs. 'Papa?' she yelled more urgently, her voice shaking, the hedges suddenly large and overwhelming.

'Lena?' Theo's voice floated through the thicket. 'You can get out. Just put your hand on the hedge and keep following it. Don't stop until you've reached me.'

Lena noted the sinking sun overhead and wiped her tears. 'Why can't you come find me?'

'You can do this. Don't be afraid. Follow the hedge with your hand.'

Lena hiccupped but clutched her wheels, determined to keep trying. She pushed herself forward, keeping her right hand softly on the hedge. She kept going, even though it felt like she was going back the way she'd come. When she finally spotted the opening and saw her father waiting, she burst into tears.

'Papa! I thought I lost you forever,' she sobbed.

Theo laughed. 'My dear! This maze is only a few feet long!' He patted her head. 'In Greek we have a saying. *Epiméno*. It means "to persist". If you think about it, life is like one long maze. Sometimes it's easy. Sometimes we get stuck. But if you persist, if you can find it within you to endure the hardships, you will reach your goal.'

Lena buried herself deeper into her father's arms.

'I have an idea,' Theo said. 'We shall make you a maze. And it will be a magical maze, with a secret hiding spot. You will be the Queen of this maze. We'll build it together and start from nothing, so that you'll know every twist and turn, inside out. You'll see there's nothing to be afraid of.' Lena stopped crying and looked up, the promise of something built solely for her having piqued her interest.

Back at the circus grounds, Theo had barely got the idea out of his mouth before Horace agreed to it. And so the Mirage Maze was built, constructed out of 250 curved mirrored panels of equal length and width. The width of the pedestrian path was made extra wide and Theo and his team of engineers worked to make the corners curved, to allow easy maneuverability for Lena. Lena arrived each morning as soon as work began, intent on overseeing the entire operation. What none of the builders knew was that Theo was working behind the scenes to create the secret passage accessible only to his daughter.

When the builders had a day off, Theo got his chance. He led Lena straight to the maze's centre, where a miniature clock tower spiralled up from the middle.

'Is there anything here?' Theo asked.

Lena frowned, twisting her body around. The mirrors disoriented her and she began to feel her heart racing, like she was trapped again. Theo placed his hand on one of the panels and pushed gently. The panel collapsed inward to reveal a hidden space. Lena gasped.

'It's modelled after a Proteus cabinet. Go on. It's yours.'

Lena wheeled herself into the cool space directly under the clock tower. If her father hadn't shown her, she never would have known it existed. When the doors were hinged together, Theo explained, they reflected the other side of the mirror, giving off the illusion that there was nothing there. Only Lena and Theo knew about it.

'If you're ever afraid, you can come here. No one will ever find you.'

The Mirage Maze was built up at each stop the circus visited. Horace had initially envisioned it as a cheap distraction to keep children preoccupied while they waited for their parents to finish their cocktails. But it ended up being a highlight of the tour. On any given night, hordes of tourists ran through, banging the sides of the mirrors obnoxiously, pulling faces at their reflections and creating an extra source of income, to Horace's delight.

Lena explained all of this to Alexandre but took great care to leave out the secret cabinet. They continued to make their way through, Lena watching as Alexandre glided his fingers along the mirrored corners, stopping every few minutes to re-orient himself. As they edged closer and closer to the centre, Lena bit her lip. Should she tell him? The Proteus cabinet was one of two secrets she had, the other being about Alexandre's true identity. But what good was a secret if you couldn't share it with anyone else?

'If I show you something,' she began.

Alexandre's fingers came to a halt. They'd reached the centre of the maze and Lena watched as his eyes flickered up to gaze briefly at the clock tower.

'Show me what?'

'If I show you something,' she continued, 'do you promise never to tell anyone about it?'

'Of course. I promise.'

Lena pushed at the middle of the mirrored panel, enjoying the look on Alexandre's face. She demonstrated how the Proteus cabinet worked and let him try the door. As he unlatched and latched the secret panel, mesmerised, Lena imagined the two of them hiding there during shows.

'It's amazing,' Alexandre said, gliding his hand across a panel. Lena beamed. She was thrilled that Alexandre approved, that something of hers impressed him. 'But something about this place frightens you,' he continued.

Lena's smile faltered. 'What do you mean?'

Alexandre frowned. He'd known she was afraid as soon as they'd entered the maze. Her fear was written in the quick, darting glances she kept throwing from side to side, anticipating a monster that never materialised.

To truly know a person, Alexandre, do not ask him who he is. Rather, observe what he does. His father had trained him well. People always told you who they were, if only you knew what to look for. But he didn't want Lena to know this.

82

'Nothing. Forget it,' he said, walking ahead nonchalantly. Lena quickly rolled after him and grabbed at his sleeve.

'Promise you won't tell anyone about the cabinet,' she pleaded. 'Remember. I know a secret about you,' she said, fully aware that anyone finding out about Alexandre being a Jew was far riskier than her childhood hiding spot being exposed. But it was the only thing she truly felt was hers and hers alone. 'Please. I kept your secret,' she said, unknowingly echoing the same words her mother spoke nearly a decade earlier. 'You have to promise to keep mine.'

CHAPTER NINE

As the circus moved through the Soviet Union, Alexandre and Lena became fast friends. In Minsk, they shared malted milk topped with whipped cream that they sucked through thick straws. In Tallinn, Jussi taught them to play poker and they wagered using Cadbury's buttons as chips, the winner generously dividing up their haul equally amongst players. In Kiev, they traded roubles for fat stacks of *syrnyky* dusted with powdered sugar and topped with apricot jam. And through it all, Theo watched carefully.

It was during this time that Theo decided to formally commence Alexandre's magic lessons. His initial instincts about the stowaway were proven right during a simple demonstration using misdirection. Theo lined up a set of three steel cups, placed a red ball under one and then manoeuvred the cups around quickly before asking Alexandre to choose which one had the ball. Alexandre pointed to Theo's suit jacket pocket.

'In there.'

Theo smiled, torn between praising Alexandre for having a level of perception that very few possessed and saying nothing for fear that he would let it get to his head.

Next, Theo demonstrated the basics of juggling, then handed the balls over to Alexandre. While he fiddled around, Theo used the silence as an opportunity to try to get to know him.

'Lena tells me your father was an art dealer?'

Alexandre's face went beet red and Theo wondered if it was too soon to ask about his parents. Such a huge loss was obviously still raw.

'Yes,' Alexandre responded eventually. 'He bought and sold paintings, all over Europe.'

'That explains the constant moving.'

Alexandre dropped the balls. 'How did you know that?'

'The stamps in your passport?'

'Ah yes,' Alexandre said. He stooped to pick up the balls, placing them on a nearby table. 'Could we perhaps go back to the shuffling? I want to master that backward palm one.'

'Certainly,' Theo said, pulling out a deck of cards from his suit jacket and handing it to Alexandre.

'The thing with art,' Alexandre continued, 'is it's always more valuable outside of its country of origin. Each time my father wanted to sell a piece, we'd go to a new town. Then, once it was sold, we'd move on to the next.'

'Is that so?' Theo asked, impressed. 'I never would have guessed. It must have made it hard to make friends with all the moving.'

Alexandre shrugged. He finished the backward palm shuffle then placed the cards in a neat pile, ready to go again.

'And your mother? Was she a homemaker?' Theo asked.

Without warning, Alexandre dropped the entire deck, clubs, hearts, diamonds, and spades scattering across the ground haphazardly. When Theo knelt to assist him, Alexandre sprang back, covering his face with his fists.

'I didn't mean to drop them.'

'I know,' Theo answered slowly, watching Alexandre pick up the cards, carefully placing them in a pile on the table.

Alexandre hesitated, wondering if the illusionist had caught on. But when Theo didn't say anything, he figured it was best to move on. 'Yes, she was a homemaker. Look, I better go. Mario's waiting.'

The lessons continued like this, Theo explaining how a myriad of tricks were done while Alexandre picked everything up faster than any student he'd ever taught. Theo waited to see a relapse of the scared, vulnerable boy he'd witnessed during that first lesson, but Alexandre was almost as masterful as his teacher. He was quick to hide his feelings, good at disguising his thoughts. It was clear the boy had an uncanny knack for reading people, manipulating objects, and subterfuge. At times, Theo wondered if Alexandre's skills were purely God-given, a magical feat of intuition, or if there was something deeper and darker behind them. But how he had acquired his talent didn't really matter, Theo thought at the end of a particularly excellent session. Alexandre was here now and it was up to him to make the most of it.

On a warm April day in Milan, Theo announced they were going out. The snow may have turned the cities they visited during the winter months into picture perfect fairytales, but it made it nearly impossible to navigate the cobblestoned, uneven pavement with a wheelchair. When spring broke, Theo made it a point to take Lena out as much as he could.

'What do you think?' He watched over Lena's shoulder as she looked through a list of places he'd compiled. 'The aquarium is meant to be amazing,' he suggested.

Alexandre, who'd been practising his magic in a corner of the library wandered over and looked at the list with interest.

'Are you going out?'

'Yes. The snow's melted,' Lena held up the list. 'Where would you go?'

Alexandre studied it and pointed to one. 'What's this?'

'The planetarium? It's amazing – you can see the whole universe in one room.'

Alexandre balked. 'Like a whole map of the stars in one room?'

'Have you never visited a planetarium?' Lena asked. Alexandre shook his head. Lena grinned and looked at her father. 'We have our destination.'

The *Planetario di Milano*, Theo said, as Lena eagerly moved from one display case to another once they'd paid their admission, was the largest of its kind in Italy. 'It also has an octagonal base,' he said, reading from a pamphlet. Lena craned her neck.

'Where's Alexandre?'

Before Theo could scan the crowd of noisy children and parents, Alexandre bounded up to them, breathless.

'This place is amazing! D'you know there's an entire ceiling of stars in there?' He gestured excitedly to the showroom.

'That's where we're headed,' Theo said, as the trio entered through the doors. An assistant informed them that the show would begin momentarily and Lena and Alexandre lapsed into anticipatory silence. But five, ten, then fifteen minutes passed and there was no sign of it beginning.

'Papa,' Lena said, tugging at her father's sweater. 'What's taking so long?'

'I don't know,' Theo glanced around and frowned when his eyes fell on the assistant. A member of the *carabinieri* had entered and they were talking in hushed tones. 'You two wait here, I'll go see what's happening.'

'But you'll miss the show,' Lena said, as the lights began to dim.

'You can tell me all about it afterwards.'

Lena was about to urge him to stay but the voice of the announcer interrupted them, explaining how the stars came to be. The two children gasped as a blanket of darkness fell over them.

'Look! Orion!' Alexandre pointed up excitedly.

'That's an easy one,' Lena teased. 'Find ... Delphinus!'

'You underestimate me,' Alexandre replied, outlining the

five-point constellation above them. And so they went, back and forth, Alexandre challenging Lena, Lena challenging Alexandre, as the map of constellations danced overhead.

'You know a lot about stars for someone who didn't go to a proper school.' Lena twisted her body, trying to catch a glimpse of Alexandre's face, but couldn't make him out in the dark.

'I could say the same about you.'

Lena was silent for a moment. 'It's my escape.' When he didn't say anything, she continued, running her hands over the armrests of her chair, glad the lights weren't on. 'I can't go out and see everything on my own. So all my books, my telescope, the photographs on my wall – it makes it feel like the whole universe is in my room.'

Alexandre opened his mouth to reply but just then light flooded the room. The show was finished and people were now emptying the space, a line-up of eager tourists ready to come in.

Lena frowned. Her father was nowhere to be seen.

'Come on,' Alexandre said, gesturing to the throngs of people leaving the room.

'We can't leave. Papa said to stay.'

'We can't.'

Lena bit her lower lip as she watched the room emptying.

'It's fine, we'll wait by the entrance. Your father has to come out that way.' Alexandre walked ahead of her and Lena reluctantly followed him towards the double glass doors. 'There,' he announced a moment later, having reached the entrance. The gardens where the planetarium was situated, were just beginning to show signs of a spring bloom, early tulips and tiny rosebuds peeking out from the dirt in the flower beds.

Lena unhooked the carrier bag slung across the back of her wheelchair while Alexandre took a seat on the stone ivy-covered bench across from her. She held up the bag. 'Hungry?'

Alexandre relaxed, a grin spreading across his face. 'Starving.'

Mario had packed boxes of pasta and the two children ate quickly, washing everything down with bottles of San Pellegrino.

'The reason I know so much about the night sky is because of my mother.' Alexandre crunched down on a potato crisp, dusting his hands together, trying to get the salt off them. 'My father was always working.'

'Making art deals would take up a lot of time,' Lena agreed.

'He was always out late, dining with clients. My mother and I spent a lot of time alone. Her father – my grandfather – was an astronomer from Germany.'

'He was?'

Alexandre nodded, pleased that Lena thought so highly of someone in his family. 'He taught my mother everything she knew. And she knew a lot. Every night she'd take me on a walk and teach me something about the solar system. For example, did you know that the Earth is 129 million kilometres away from Mercury at its closest point?'

'What do you mean closest?'

'The planets are always moving,' he explained. 'But even when they're the closest they could ever be, it's still millions of kilometres away.'

Lena nodded in agreement. 'You'd need a rocket to get there.'

Alexandre grinned. 'And did you know the stars are a map? Anywhere you want to go on earth, you can get there by looking at the stars. But only if you know how to read them. And I know how,' he said, finishing off his pasta. He reached into the bag and pulled out two slices of almond cake, placing one on a napkin and handing it to Lena.

Lena's eyes danced around as she stared up at the sky. 'I wonder what it would be like to be able to walk to the ends of the Earth.'

'I can teach you. Not now, but in summer?'

Lena's smile faltered. Summer was so far away. By then, he might have tired of her.

Noticing her change in mood, Alexandre backtracked. 'Unless you don't want—'

'No,' Lena interjected. 'I do! But . . .'

'What?'

'You might be bored of me by then,' Lena said softly, picking at the slice of cake in her lap.

Alexandre let out a laugh that echoed off the stone statues lining the garden. 'Hardly. You're my only real friend here,' he said, as the envelope he kept hidden in his floorboard, thick with cash flashed into his mind.

'Yes, but you're bound to make new friends. And then you'll want to be with them, to run up and down, play new games. Trust me,' Lena said, 'You'll get bored. Everyone always does.'

'I vow that I could never be bored of you,' Alexandre announced solemnly, putting a hand over his heart. Lena started to giggle. 'Besides, I can't do this with the other kids.' He plucked the piece of cake off her lap and took off down the path.

'Alexandre! Bring it back at once!' Lena yelled, pushing her chair after him, her giggle ringing over the hedges. When she finally caught up to him, he knelt in front of her, holding out the piece of cake as though it were a valuable object.

'Your highness. I hereby crown you the Queen of Marzipan. A country so steeped in almonds that everyone is . . . nuts.' Alexandre said, bowing his head.

Lena burst out laughing and grabbed the cake, stuffing half of it in her mouth before he could take any for himself. He stood up and grinned, plonking himself next to her on a bench.

'It's settled them. I'll teach—'

'Lena and Alexandre! What do you think you're doing?!' Theo's concerned voice cut through the garden. The smile on Lena's face vanished.

'Papa, I— '

'I told you both to stay inside!' Theo said.

'The show ended and we were just playing ...' Lena looked down at her cake, not hungry anymore. She didn't know what to say. She'd never lost track of time, never defied her father's rules.

Theo knelt down in front of her and she could see the fear in his eyes. 'Are you hurt?'

'I'm fine. Everything's fine, why do you keep treating me like I'm sick? I'm not a baby anymore.' Lena crossed her arms. She'd been having so much fun with Alexandre, why did her father have to ruin it? Then she glanced at Theo and noticed the hurt in his eyes. She sighed. Even if he was overly cautious, she knew it came from a place of love.

'It's my fault,' Alexandre piped up. 'They told us to leave and I thought you'd be able to see us from the garden entrance.'

'This isn't the garden entrance,' Theo said, pointing to the actual entrance a couple of metres away, before glancing down at his daughter. 'You should know better. Come, let's go. They're shutting the planetarium.'

Lena looked at the crowd of *carabinieri* congregating outside the doors, barking orders. 'What happened?' she asked, as she pushed her chair over a slight bump that separated the gardens and the pavement.

'One of the items on display went missing,' Theo explained.

'Goodness,' Lena said, 'I hope they find it.'

Beside her, Alexandre shoved his hands into his pockets. He looked briefly over his shoulder, as the mass of police officers began to swell at the main doors.

'Yes,' he said. 'Let's hope they do.'

CHAPTER TEN

The tour drew to a close at the end of August. Alexandre was thrilled when Theo asked him to join him and Lena in Thessaloniki, worried that the impending two-month break would have consisted of him waiting on Horace in his house in London day in, day out.

The day before they were due at Victoria Station, Theo and Alexandre paid the circus director a visit. Horace sat at his desk, dressed pompously in one of his trademark suits. Alexandre couldn't fathom how the portly gentleman could wear such attire in the summer heat.

'Here about the bargain we made?' Horace clasped his hands together.

Theo nodded. He'd told Alexandre to let him do the talking. After nearly a decade of working for Horace, Theo could read him better than anyone, he said. But Alexandre wasn't so sure.

'I want to ensure he'll be free to return—'

Horace held up a hand, silencing the illusionist.

'I've been observing him. His hand-to-eye coordination and presentation skills need more work, but he's a quick study. How much longer until he can complete the types of tricks you do?' The circus director knew that the real money lay in the big-ticket illusions, the masterful grand finales that Theo was so good at.

'At least another year of practice for him to do it on his own.

But the boy's intuition coupled with his sleight of hand is an uncanny combination.' Theo knew a bit about mentalism, was fairly adept himself at reading people, but what Alexandre possessed, especially for someone so young, was nothing short of a miracle.

'What do you propose? A seance? A display of telepathy?' Horace twirled the pen in his inkwell around. The nib on the other end scratched the bottom, making an unpleasant sound. 'Dunninger made all those frauds fall out of vogue, you know. It's very unpopular.'

'He's not a fraud.'

'You don't have to worry about me letting the boy go, Theo. He's proven his worth. But even you must know that he's playing everyone for fools.'

'I'm not sure you understand. Even I can't figure out how he does it.'

Horace laughed. If he spent all his time trying to understand what went into each act he oversaw, he'd never sleep. 'You don't need an explanation.' He leaned back in his chair. 'You know it can't be real.' Horace turned his attention to Alexandre, who was standing quietly in the corner. 'Tell us, Alexandre. It's just not possible for you to know things that we haven't already told you, is it?'

In response, Alexandre said nothing. He'd learned that it was best to not engage in Horace's goading.

'You're not much different than the others here. A child whose mother didn't care enough about you to raise you properly,' Horace said.

Alexandre, silent in the corner, felt anger roil inside him. It was one thing for Horace to speak ill of him. It was an entirely different matter when he spoke ill of his mother. His eyes narrowed and he clenched his fists, but it was not brute force by which Alexandre struck his first blow.

'Your grandmother's name was Esther,' he said, evenly.

The smirk on Horace's face vanished. 'What did you say?'

'Your grandmother's name was Esther. She was the most important person in your life.'

Horace was fully alert now, watching Alexandre warily. 'Surely you overhead that from someone else,' he said, adopting a breezy tone.

Alexandre continued. 'Esther died, at some point between when we left Napoli and when we reached Palermo. You never got to say goodbye. You never got to show her what you created. You're worried it will haunt you forever—'

'Enough!' Horace strode out from behind his desk and grabbed Alexandre's collar. 'How dare you! What business is it of yours who my relatives were?!'

'Horace, that's enough. He didn't do anything wrong,' Theo said, wrenching Alexandre from his grip.

Horace sputtered, a tiny bead of sweat trickling down the bridge of his nose. 'Didn't do anything wrong? Why, he's marauded my mind! He's—' the circus director trailed off, regarding the young boy with a newfound fear. He hadn't told anyone his grandmother had passed away, not even Chadwick. He'd received a telegram in Napoli telling him about her illness and then another when they reached Palermo, telling him she was gone. But how this boy, who he'd barely had a passing conversation with, could know this, he couldn't comprehend.

'Was he right?' Theo asked Horace, gently.

Defeated, Horace took a seat on his chair and began fanning himself with a folded slip of paper.

'Yes.' He glanced at Alexandre. 'We look forward to having you on tour come autumn.'

Outside Horace's study, Alexandre turned to walk back to his room.

'Wait,' Theo said. 'There's still the matter of our contract.'

Alexandre shifted his weight from one foot to the other

uncomfortably. 'It's not necessary,' he started, but Theo held up a hand.

'We have an agreement. No arguments.' Theo held out a bulging envelope. Alexandre glanced around to make sure no one was watching, then reluctantly stuffed it into the pocket of his trousers.

'Say "Ahhhhh".'

'Ahhh,' Alexandre said, sticking his tongue out. Dr. Wilson placed a wooden stick on it and peered inside.

'Excellent. Now, if the phlegm returns, you'll need this.' Dr. Wilson removed a small bottle of liquid from his medicine cabinet. 'Take two drops upon rising and two before bed.' He screwed the dropper lid on tightly and handed it to Alexandre. 'Let me get you a bit more of that balm.'

As the doctor bustled around, Alexandre swung his legs up and down, striking them against the bed frame. 'Dr. Wilson? I was wondering . . . Lena said she had polio when she was really young and that's why she can't walk.'

'Yes, that's right,' Dr. Wilson answered. 'Her immune system's never been great – she was born premature, you know. Initially though, she could crawl and was starting to pull herself up and stand.' Dr. Wilson frowned, shaking his head sadly. 'Tragically she caught polio during a stay in England when she was barely a year old. Theo never forgave himself for exposing her to the disease.'

Alexandre frowned. 'So . . . he used to take her out more?'

'Oh, yes,' Dr. Wilson nodded. 'He's always been protective, mind you. But he used to take her to meet other kids in the cities we frequented, letting her crawl anywhere she liked.' He shook his head sadly. 'All that changed after she caught polio. It was touch and go. She spent months in the hospital in London. We really didn't know what would happen. Theo was bereft.'

'I see,' Alexandre said, considering this. 'Will she ever walk, d'you think?'

Dr. Wilson secured the lid of a small tin of methyl balm. 'Remember, just a penny's worth of this,' he said. 'After her stay in the hospital, we were simply glad to have her back here, safely. And Lena doesn't let it bother her as much as you might think. Yes, she was lonely before you arrived. But look at everything she does. She's self-sufficient, extremely capable, an excellent student. Her inability to move like the rest of us hasn't hampered her motivation.'

Alexandre cocked his head. 'But . . . just the same: How do you know she can't walk?'

Dr. Wilson laughed as he placed the items for Alexandre in a small bag. 'Why, it would be next to impossible at this stage in her development. She missed out on those crucial early years.'

'So,' Alexandre paused thoughtfully, 'you don't know, really.'

'Don't know what?'

'That she can't walk.'

Dr. Wilson stopped what he was doing abruptly and peered at the young boy like he was seeing him for the first time. 'What did you say?'

Alexandre brushed his hair out of his eyes as he took the bag, jumping down from the bed. 'I mean, how do you know for certain she can't walk, if she's never really tried in the first place?'

A few days later, Theo, Lena, and Alexandre docked at the mouth of the Thermaikos Gulf. Lena rolled herself across the footbridge as Theo and Alexandre followed, the latter turning and twisting his head at the sights and sounds of the Greek fishing port. A fisherman clad in muddied waders and a white shirt noticed the trio.

'Did you hear?'

They shook their heads. The fisherman was holding a freshly caught fish and a small sharp knife. As he spoke, he flicked the scales from the fish's body. In the glare of the sun, they had the

97

appearance of gigantic, shimmering sequins. 'Germany invaded Poland yesterday. The world is at war.'

Lena gripped her father's hand and watched the scales float briefly on the water before sinking to the depths of the Aegean Sea.

CHAPTER ELEVEN

The war, Theo told them, was a grave one, but it hadn't yet spread south. Greece declared neutrality and Thessaloniki, at least to Lena, still felt like the home she always returned to each year. Thessaloniki in September meant hot steamy nights and days spent sorting through the smoothed bits of broken glass her father collected for her each morning outside the tavernas in Ladadika. It meant bustling evenings in Aristotelous Square and day drives to Halkidiki, where she donned the striped and polka dotted swimsuits Martha hand-stitched for her each year. Her father would take her out of her chair and gently place her on the sand, where she'd lie for hours, letting the sun warm her belly.

She didn't have any more friends in the city than at the circus, and most of the children were busy getting ready to return to school just as she was starting her break, so she was doubly excited about Alexandre being there.

One day, after an afternoon spent skimming stones lazily by the Gulf, Alexandre, Theo and Lena ventured up to Aristotelous Square. The lifeblood of the city, it was always brimming with action no matter the hour. Though it was past lunchtime, Lena was pleased to see that the street food vendors were still out hawking their goods.

'Papa, can we have falafel?'

Theo chuckled. 'I think that can be arranged.' They moved

towards a falafel stand, where a crowd of people were waving their arms in the air impatiently, yelling orders as the owner and his son tried to keep up.

'While you're waiting, go see Mr. Nikitas,' he said, pointing to a drinks stall a little further up, 'and buy two bottles of whatever you and Alexandre want,' he continued, placing the drachmas in Lena's palm. 'And stay in one place!' Theo warned.

'We will!' Lena pocketed the money, then led Alexandre away from the throngs of people.

'What are you going to get?' Alexandre asked, as they came to a halt in front of the drinks stall.

Lena studied the rows and rows of colourful bottles peering back at her, unsure if she felt like a sour cherry *visinada* or one of the mixed colas that always filled her stomach with bubbles.

'*Portokolada*,' she said at last, pointing to a glass bottle filled with bright orange liquid. 'And you?'

'The same.' Alexandre grinned.

'Two please,' Lena said, handing over the money to Mr. Nikitas, who handed her two chilled bottles in exchange. Lena opened the tops and passed one to Alexandre. They drank in silence, gulping at the orange liquid, savouring the fizzy sweet taste.

Lena wiped her mouth with the back of her hand and surveyed the square. She noticed a group of cats congregating nearby and waved her hand to them, trying to bring them closer. An exceptionally bold grey one came forward and rubbed up against her bare leg and she bent down to stroke it.

'Helena Calista Papadopoulos.'

Lena froze. She wondered if she'd heard correctly and looked to Alexandre to prove her wrong, but he too had stopped drinking.

'Helena Calista Papadopoulos.'

There it was again. She glanced to her right and saw the speaker sitting a few feet away.

Adelpha Chatras. Lena had heard about Adelpha from a girl who lived two streets over from their house who was the same age as Lena. They'd sometimes played together as youngsters on the weekends during the months Lena was in town.

'Stay away from her. My *papou* says she's a witch.' The girl had said one afternoon when Adelpha walked by.

Lena remembered the comment now and felt her skin bristle. 'It's Adelpha,' she whispered.

'Who?'

'Someone I know told me about her. She said she's a witch. She said she's over one hundred years old.'

'How does she know your name?'

Lena shrugged. No one called her Helena. Not even her father. She handed her bottle to Alexandre and pushed her chair forward slowly.

When Adelpha saw the two children advancing, she pointed a gnarled fingernail in Lena's direction and smiled, revealing a set of yellowing, jagged teeth.

'Daughter of Gia and Theodoros.'

Lena stopped abruptly and Alexandre banged into her. A few drops of *portokolada* had spilled out of Lena's bottle onto the ground and she watched as a swarm of ants gathered round.

Adelpha sat hunched over a pile of random objects. Sharp pieces of a broken mirror that had lost their sheen, a cracked terracotta flowerpot, a few coins, a stray ruby earring with its backing missing. Adelpha was a human magpie. She noticed them eyeing her possessions and hunched over them protectively.

'How do you know my parents?' Lena asked.

Adelpha cocked her head. 'Cursed forever because of your father's betrayal.'

A cat darted in front of Lena's chair, and the two children jumped. Lena took a breath and continued. 'What did my father do?'

Adelpha blinked, her steel grey eyes looking lost. 'My secrets come with a price.'

Lena waited, but Adelpha didn't speak further. So she asked Alexandre for the leftover drachmas from the drinks and moved herself closer to the old woman, handing them over. She had to touch the old woman's palm to do so and this meant getting uncomfortably close. Lena tried to keep looking at the ground but it was hard not to stare at Adelpha's hands. They were ancient and gnarled, the knuckles resembling tiny knots in tree branches, the skin flaking off in dried, white bits.

'What did my father do?'

Adelpha's eyes gleamed and her mouth turned up at one corner. 'Do not fall for his act. He is a good showman, that Theodoros. Fooled everyone into thinking he loved Gia—'

'Stop!' Lena shouted. 'You're lying! My father loved my mother more than anyone.'

Adelpha cackled, her eyes rolling around lazily. Eventually the cough subsided and she stared back at Lena.

'He loved her, Helena. But in what way? We all have secrets. Some of us simply hide—'

'Lena!' Theo had arrived, clutching two paper bags, but the look on his face was not a happy one.

'Papa,' Lena began.

'I *told* you to stay in one place,' Theo said.

Alexandre frowned. They weren't that far away from their agreed upon meeting point.

Lena gestured to Adelpha, who seemed to have tired of her audience and was now arranging her assortment of objects into a semi-circle. 'This lady called for me. She knows my name. How does she know my name?' she asked, looking quizzically at her father.

Alexandre kept his eyes on Theo, watching the colour drain from his face. Normally so composed and charismatic, he actually looked nervous. Theo swallowed and shook his head.

'Of course she knows your name. You were born here.'

'But she was saying things about you and Mama. Things that sounded—'

'Enough,' Theo said, signalling for Lena to move away from Adelpha. 'Setting store by the words of a crazy old woman. What's next?'

The trio headed back to Persefonis Street in silence. Once they'd reached the house, Theo seated the two children in the kitchen and placed a falafel sandwich on each of their plates. He filled three glasses with water and sat down across from them.

'You shouldn't be talking to strangers.' Theo sighed, taking a sip of water.

'It wasn't our fault!' Lena stared glumly at the pita bread, poking at a puddle of hummus that had oozed out from one of the ends. 'She called my name—'

'It doesn't matter,' Theo interrupted her. 'Aristotelous Square is so busy, what if you'd gotten lost? What if someone had taken either of you?'

Lena and Alexandre sat in silence, neither of them hungry anymore.

'Who is she?' Alexandre asked eventually, his curiosity getting the better of him.

'Adelpha's lived here longer than most,' Theo said. 'And while I don't like to speak ill of anyone, she's getting old, doesn't remember things. You can't trust anything she says.'

'But she knew Lena's full name and yours, so obviously she remembers some things,' Alexandre pressed.

Theo shrugged. 'Everybody knows our names, this is where Lena was born – oh, darling, don't be like this,' Theo said, affectionately. Alexandre glanced at Lena, who had started to cry. Theo stood up and came round to comfort her.

'I wasn't going to go with her anywhere. Why don't you trust me?'

Theo softened. It was true he let what had happened in the past impact how he treated Lena, sometimes to the point that he forgot how quickly she was growing up. 'I'm not worried about what you would do, Lena. Of course I trust you. I'm worried about what *others* would do. You can't trust people. And you can't run away from them, so it's even more important to not engage with them in the first place.' He pulled her plate of food closer to her. 'Now come. Eat. I have it on good authority that there's fresh baklava waiting for you afterwards,' Theo said, gesturing to the extra paper bag he'd brought back.

'Really?' Lena brightened and picked up her falafel.

'Yes, really,' Theo said.

Alexandre watched Theo carefully as he unwrapped the sticky wax paper covering the baklava and placed it in front of Lena. Then he took his seat, picked up his water, glanced at Alexandre and smiled.

There it was, Alexandre thought. A flicker of concern, a shadow of a doubt, a tightened grip on the glass in his hands. The tell-tale signs of someone with something to hide. But Theo was a consummate performer and as quickly as the moment arrived, it was gone. To the untrained eye, it was nothing. But to Alexandre, it was everything. He knew something was off, but it would take more investigation to figure out the truth.

He opened his mouth to start questioning him again but stopped. He thought about the way Theo doted on Lena the way her face lit up when she was around him, and about all the sacrifices he'd likely had to make to ensure she had the best care. Alexandre had never had that.

In that moment, he decided to keep his mouth shut. Why worry Lena? Besides, he thought, remembering the night in the barn, when everything changed, Theo wasn't the only one with a past he wanted to keep buried.

Chapter Twelve

At the end of October, the performers headed back to London. Despite France and Great Britain declaring war against Germany, Horace insisted that the circus was buffered from the dangers of what was happening all around them, that the World of Wonders was a country unto itself, existing in a bullet-proof, conflict-free bubble.

Security had increased at border crossings and inspections conducted by the local police or the SS were not uncommon. However, the circus was granted special permission to move through the continent with little, if any, hassle. Horace understood the Nazis. He knew what they liked and didn't like, and so he commanded Johannes to scrub his face clean of any traces of lipstick at each checkpoint they passed through. The two Romani twins were forced to practise speaking with Italian accents. Fearing the SS would mistake her for a mulatto, Horace insisted that Nneka paint over the creamy patch of skin on her face. She was forced to sit for ages while the makeup artist covered her face and neck with a mixture of foundation and pressed powder.

Alexandre, though technically the one that endangered them the most, had been blessed by his father's looks. With his flaxen hair and ice-blue eyes, he warranted barely a glance from the officers who clambered into the train carriages at each border crossing, checking the passenger papers. Chadwick was quick to ply them with food, drink, and entertainment, and then, if everything passed muster, they were free to go.

During their first week back, Dr. Wilson pulled Theo aside at dinner one evening, asking him to come to the infirmary carriage.

'Have you noticed something wrong with Lena?' Theo asked nervously, taking a seat across from the doctor.

'On the contrary, I wanted to talk to you about some new research. I did a lot of reading over the break,' he said, pulling out a stack of papers and placing it on his desk. 'There's been talk of an unconventional, but promising treatment for polio survivors. It was pioneered by a bush nurse from Australia.' Dr. Wilson gestured to a pile of woollen rags next to him. 'The basic premise involves soaking rags in hot water, wrapping them around the child's legs and conducting a series of exercises designed to bring back life to limbs that have atrophied – or in Lena's case, never truly been used in the first place.'

Theo shook his head. 'Lena is fine the way she is. She doesn't need fixing.'

Dr. Wilson nodded. 'I agree completely. This isn't about anything being wrong with her. It's more that with the advances in treatments, it might be worth exploring options.'

Theo picked up one of the rags and eyed it dubiously. 'And this? This is your solution?'

'I'll admit many are skeptical. We've had success with plaster casts, braces and the iron lung,' Dr. Wilson continued. 'But this treatment is different. We'd be healing from within.' He paused. He didn't want to give Theo false hope, but at the same time, he was enthused about the prospect of what could happen. 'I think that if it works, it could change her life.' He proceeded to go over the details of the treatment, how long it would take, what it would entail and how it might feel for Lena.

'Do you think it would work for her?'

'I can't promise anything, but that boy made a startlingly frank point: If we don't try, we'll never know.'

That evening, before Lena went to bed, Theo told her about what Dr. Wilson had said.

'Let me be perfectly clear – this is your choice.' He patted the bedspread. 'No matter what you decide, we'll all love you just the same.'

Lena was quiet for a minute. She glanced down at her legs snuggled under her blanket. In her gut, she knew she'd be ok if things stayed the way they were. But there was no denying the truth – her life would be easier if she could walk. Not better. Just simpler. Besides, she thought, warming to the idea, she could look at this as her very own science experiment, with herself as the test subject.

'I think,' she said slowly, making sure she felt confident with her choice, 'I think I'd like to try,' she finished, a slow smile creeping across her face.

And so Lena began an experimental physical therapy protocol devised by Dr. Wilson. Each day, she'd arrive at the infirmary to find him boiling a set of woollen rags. Once hot, he'd wrap them around her legs and guide her through a series of exercises designed to build her lower limb strength and circulation – leg lifts, hip adduction, hamstring flexion, calf muscle raises and more. Dr. Wilson also insisted that Lena begin strengthening her abdominal muscles.

The treatment didn't come without pain or monotony. The rags were breathtakingly hot and the exercises, tedious. Sometimes, as she worked through them, Lena would bite her lip till it bled. More than once she'd shake her head after the rags had been applied, claiming she didn't want to do it anymore.

'It hurts,' she gasped, fighting back tears as the heat sunk into her limbs.

'Try not to think about the pain,' Dr. Wilson would say. 'Focus on the end result.' And she would close her eyes, whisper the word her father had told her in the Hungarian maze, *epiméno*, then continue on.

Slowly, Lena's legs began to show signs of life, hints of colour. After two months of steady therapy, she looked down at her limbs in a bath as they stretched out in front of her, hardly recognising them. Buoyed by signs of progress, she began attacking her exercises with the same enthusiasm she brought to her schoolwork, diligently repeating each painful movement until she'd mastered it. In the evenings, she recorded notes about her progress in a journal she kept by her bedside.

Alexandre would often keep her company, pointing out times when her form could improve or cheering her on when she grew weary. On a cool November day, they sat alone in the infirmary, waiting for Dr. Wilson to return.

'Those cloths smell awful,' Alexandre said, wrinkling his nose.

Lena threw a pillow at him. 'Not my fault.'

Alexandre tossed the pillow playfully back to her then stretched his arms overhead. 'I'm bored,' he announced. 'And hungry. Can we wait in the dining hall?'

'Dr. Wilson said to stay here.'

Alexandre thought for a moment, debating what they could do that wouldn't require leaving the carriage but also satiate their appetites.

'I know!' He snapped his fingers. 'Let's have a picnic.'

Lena laughed. 'We haven't got any food!'

'Leave that to me,' Alexandre said, already halfway out the door. Not ten minutes later, he rushed back in, basket in tow. 'Look,' he said, dropping the basket on Lena's bed.

'Where did it all come from?' Lena asked, taking in the feast. There were tiny rounds of cheese packed in red wax, packages of cream crackers, bottles of blackcurrant cordial, two packets of Garibaldi biscuits, Battenberg cake, a bottle of capers, a jar of mustard – and that was just what Lena could see on the top.

'Mario,' Alexandre replied, lining up all the items on the perimeter of the bed. 'Cheese round?' He offered her a small red ball, watching as Lena tore off the wax paper and bit into it.

'Delicious,' she said.

'Those ones are my favourite,' Alexandre agreed, tearing open a packet of crackers. 'I'd eat them all the time in Italy.'

'Tell me about your travels,' Lena said, taking another bite of cheese.

'What do you want to know?'

'Where have you been?'

'Where *haven't* I been,' Alexandre said wistfully. 'I've been to France, of course. Spain, Italy, Germany and Poland. Holland. Morocco.'

'Morocco! What were you doing there?'

Alexandre furrowed his brow. 'My father had a very special piece of art he was looking to sell. And there was a prospective buyer in Morocco. So we sailed from the tip of Gibraltar all the way to Morocco.'

Lena spread a dollop of mustard over a water cracker. 'What's it like?'

Alexandre thought back to the overcrowded *Jemaa-el-Fna*, a cluttered medina with people hawking everything from cheap trinkets to expensive leathers. His father had instructed him and his mother to stay busy while he visited the *Kutubiyya Mosque* in order to complete his deal. 'It was chaotic. Hundreds of people, everywhere. Easy to get lost.'

'What kind of art was your father selling?'

'A Velázquez!' Alexandre said. 'From Spain. Do you know who Velázquez was?'

'A king?'

'Not quite,' Alexandre popped a piece of pickled turnip into his mouth. 'Diego Velázquez. Born in Seville. Influenced by Caravaggio, he painted many, many works for the King of Spain. The painting my father was selling was *Las Meninas*. It's famous. So famous that the King insisted it hang in the *Museo del Prado* in Madrid, so that all the world could see it.'

'That's amazing.'

Alexandre paused, retracing the threads of the story he'd been weaving. He thought back to his father shaking him and his mother awake in the dark of the night in the Spanish capital, insisting they leave right away. He remembered wiping sleep from his eyes, stumbling out of the vacant flat and seeing the gigantic painting sitting in the open back of a wagon. He remembered the choppy boat ride and the hired help his father had contracted to move the painting, who leered at him anytime he got in their way. Then he looked at Lena and continued. 'One day, the King of Spain came to my father and said he wanted to sell it to an interested buyer in Morocco. But it was such a valuable painting that the King didn't trust anyone but my father to deliver it. So that's what he did, he took it right into the mosque and sold it.'

'Who was buying it?'

'Mmm . . . the Sultan of Morocco.'

'The Sultan,' Lena sighed dreamily, imagining what a sultan would look like. 'How much did he pay for it?'

Alexandre frowned. She was asking so many questions that sooner or later he was going to run out of answers. 'Not much.'

Lena raised her eyebrows as she sipped on an elderflower soft drink. 'Surely it was worth thousands!'

'It was,' Alexandre said carefully, 'the Sultan traded us priceless gifts to give to the King. Like . . . a beautiful tapestry from the walls of the mosque itself.'

'Wow,' Lena sucked in her breath. 'Was it incredible?'

Alexandre nodded. 'Magnificent. We needed ten men just to

move it. It was all shades of turquoise and blue and green laced with silver and gold and purple threads. Purple is a royal colour, did you know? And they'd hand-stitched the calligraphy right into it, this beautiful Islamic prayer.'

'I can't believe you met a Sultan.' Lena picked at a dollop of clotted cream she'd placed on a scone. 'Why was it so dangerous to bring the painting over?'

'Erm . . . the pirates.'

'No!'

'Yes! Barbary pirates. They roamed the coast, seizing anything of value. But my father was so skilled at avoiding them. There really was no one else who could have delivered such a valuable piece of art in one piece. In fact, the Sultan was so happy he even gave me a gift,' Alexandre added.

'Really? What was it?'

'Um, a jewelled dagger,' Alexandre said, thinking back to the toy trinket his father had tossed carelessly in his direction after the deal was complete. 'It had diamonds and emeralds and a huge giant ruby at the hilt.'

'Did you celebrate after?'

'Sort of,' Alexandre said. His father had come back drunk on red wine and announced he was spending the night at a harem in the centre of Marrakech. It was a celebration, at least for him. 'I went on a night picnic, with my mother!'

'Anja,' Lena said, proud that she remembered her name.

'We packed the plumpest pomegranate seeds, the ripest mangoes, the greenest pistachios and jugs of pure passionfruit juice. And we took a camel to the centre of the Sahara desert. There, we watched fire dancers twirl as we feasted into the night.' Alexandre stopped talking, remembering how it had really played out. He remembered how he and his mother had nearly frozen to death. The desert, so warm in the day, fell to near icy temperatures at night. He remembered going from stall to stall in the market,

111

pleading with one of the souk sellers to give him scraps of fabric, anything to help shield them. He remembered his mother wrapping her only shawl around him, sacrificing her warmth for his and the cold she caught with the cough that ravaged her body for weeks. All because his father wanted to blow the money he'd earned on women and drink.

'Your old life sounds amazing,' Lena said. 'I wish I had an international art dealer for a father.'

Alexandre gave her a half-hearted smile. 'Your father's an illusionist! Everyone must be jealous!'

Lena shook her head, her smile fading. 'I doubt it.'

Alexandre was silent for a moment. 'If you could do anything, anything at all. What would it be?'

Lena picked a few grapes off the bunch she was clutching in her hand, contemplating the question. 'I'd like to go to a boarding school, like Clara. Then I could study and be a scientist or a doctor or an astronomer.'

'Why's it called a boarding school?'

'Because you live there.'

'Sounds awful.'

'I think it sounds lovely. Clara said at St. Ives they have loads of dorm rooms all with beds lined up. The food's bad, but that's alright. And every Sunday, they'd get pocket money and use it to buy pudding or sweets. Clara's favourite was the Eccles Cakes. I've never had an Eccles Cake,' she said, enviously.

'You don't need to go to boarding school to try an Eccles Cake! Mario can make you one!'

'But I want to go,' Lena said, earnestly. 'Clara said they have every kind of subject you can imagine. And a huge library. Also, you live with loads of other girls who have to be your friends because there's no parents.'

Alexandre felt a pang of guilt, remembering what Theo had said about wanting to keep Lena close. But looking at her forlorn face, he wondered if her father was doing the right thing. 'If you want to go, why don't you?'

'My father would never let me leave.'

'Have you asked him?'

Lena hesitated. Her father indulged her love of learning to no end. But the few times she'd wondered out loud about boarding school and university, he'd abruptly change the subject. Still, Alexandre had a point. She'd never actually outright asked Theo, but it was mainly because she was certain of what he would say. She looked at Alexandre, her eyes flickering with pain. 'It's not that easy. I can't just walk out of here.'

'You don't need to be able to walk to study at a real school. Besides,' he said, pointing to her legs, 'look how much progress you've made.'

'And how am I meant to get there in the first place?' Lena challenged.

'Your father can drop you off in the autumn and pick you up in the spring. That *is* what boarding school is, isn't it?' Alexandre stuffed an olive in his mouth.

'It's not that simple,' Lena said, avoiding his gaze. Alexandre studied her. She'd gone quiet and was staring at her legs.

'I know it's not simple,' Alexandre said, treading carefully. 'All I'm saying is, your brain's not the thing stopping you, is it?'

The World of Wonders would traverse through nine more cities, over three more months before Lena finally mustered up the courage to broach the topic of attending a school outside the circus. They were in Munich and she was in the library, her lessons done for the day, quietly completing her homework. Across from her, Clara was reading a book. Lena had replayed that conversation she'd had with Alexandre many times in her head. *Your brain's not the thing stopping you, is it?*

'Clara,' Lena said, putting down her pencil. 'Do you think . . .'

She paused, not quite believing what she was about to ask. 'Do you think I'd be a good enough student? For St. Ives?'

'Oh. My.' Clara sat silently for a moment, processing her question. 'I must confess, I've never seriously considered boarding school for you, given the circumstances. But if I were to isolate your academic abilities, I see no reason why you wouldn't thrive in such a place. Your interest in and passion for science in particular, are impressive. I personally think you'd make a fine doctor.'

'Who'd make a fine doctor?' Theo had entered the library.

'Papa!' Lena jumped, startled to see her father. 'What happened to your workshop?'

Theo pecked her on the forehead. 'Young Klaus took ill with a poor stomach. Too many caramels, I think,' he said, chuckling. Clara glanced at Lena.

'Mr. Papadopoulos, I was just telling Lena that she's been performing exceptionally well this school year.'

Theo beamed, squeezing his daughter's shoulders. 'With the amount of time she spends studying, I would expect nothing else.'

Clara cleared her throat. 'Have you ever considered the possibility of additional schooling?'

'Extra hours on top of the regular sessions?' He looked at Lena. 'If you think she can handle it, I won't object—'

'No,' Clara interrupted him gently. 'Not here. At a boarding school. There are some excellent ones in and around London and I'm sure we could work out the arrangements. I'd never considered it before, but when Lena mentioned it to me, well, I actually think it's quite brilliant.'

Lena shifted uncomfortably in her chair. She wished Clara hadn't said it was her idea.

'Lena,' Theo said in a low voice. 'This is your idea? Are you not happy here?'

'Of course I'm happy! I love it here. I just,' Lena whispered, fiddling with her pencil. 'Thought maybe I could . . . do more.'

'Oh, Lena,' Theo said, his face full of sorrow. 'I can't let you live in a dormitory alone. I know you've made progress with these treatments, but suppose the nurses there don't know what to do. Suppose you hurt yourself and no one is around. Suppose the classrooms are all on different floors . . .' And on he went, rattling off a list of obstacles.

'It's fine, it was silly to suggest it.' Lena picked up her notebook, refusing to make eye contact with her governess or father. 'Forget I asked,' she said keeping her head down.

Theo stared at his daughter, his heart aching. He hated disappointing her, wished there was something he could do to make her feel better. He motioned to Clara to join him in the hallway, out of earshot, and she followed him outside.

Theo ran his hands through his hair, frustrated. 'Clara, while I respect your skills as a teacher, please don't encourage these kinds of ideas. You know very well how I feel about Lena being separated from me.'

'I understand, sir. But . . . if I may . . . we've never *asked* if there are schools set up for students with physical limitations, have we? Maybe there are ones that could accommodate her condition. Dr. Wilson's already experimenting with her treatments, why not try the same with her education?'

Theo's eyes flashed angrily. 'Even if she thrived academically, I don't see how I could keep her safe if she was off living in some godforsaken school miles away.' He ran his hand up and down the velvet covered walls. 'I think it best not to speak of this to her again. It will only end in disappointment.'

Clara nodded silently and walked away.

Later that night, Theo sat in his armchair while Lena dozed peacefully. As he watched his daughter sleep, guilt gnawed at his insides, Gia's dying wish refusing to leave his thoughts.

I want my child to have an education.

Restless, Theo rose from his chair and removed a faded envelope from his dresser drawer. He sat down at his desk and lit a candle, taking care to position it so that the light didn't disrupt Lena's slumber. He slid the letter out and began reading it, his mind drifting back to a happier time: That night in Madrid. The sun-soaked streets of Thessaloniki. His hand clutching hers, a promise to never let go.

Till we are together forever, my sweet Theo.

Yours, Isabella.

As the letter came to a close, a familiar feeling of dread swirled inside him. This was when the memories turned sour, the once-happy vignettes of joy now overshadowed by a heavy sadness at how it had all ended.

Theo glanced at the shelves crammed with Lena's books, the flickering candle giving everything around him a soft glow. There was nothing he hated more than disappointing Gia and Lena, but they didn't understand things the way he did. They didn't have the benefit of hindsight.

I'm sorry, Gia, he thought, stuffing the letter hastily back into the envelope. He got up, pulled open the dresser and buried it under a pile of thick, woollen sweaters. Theo took a deep breath as he curled his fingers around the dresser's cool brass knobs. *I can't risk losing any more than I already have.* Then he shut the drawer firmly and blew out the candle.

CHAPTER THIRTEEN

By the spring of 1940, Alexandre could do the cups-and-balls trick, the dove-pan illusion, the disappearing-penny act, and the French drop. At Horace's request, he appeared before each performance in the lobby, along with four other cast members. There was a contortionist painted gold and blue so that it looked like she was wearing nothing but a second skin. There was a water ballerina clad in a metallic blue mermaid's tale. She spun and floated gaily in her glass tank, gracefully executing pirouettes and somersaults as spectators gawped and pointed. A bare-chested fire eater stood imposingly near the entrance, his muscular limbs shiny with sweat from the heat of the flaming stick he brandished. But this flame wasn't the standard orange and amber. It began as a brilliant blue, but when he withdrew it from his mouth to the gasps of the crowd, it was pure gold. Lastly, there was the knife juggler, who tossed gold daggers with blue handles in the air and caught them with ease. He began with twelve daggers then swapped these for twelve golden swords that were so heavy, even Alexandre couldn't figure out how he managed to handle them. The knife juggler's hair was long and black with a streak of gold running down the left side.

Alexandre was thrilled to finally be contributing in a more meaningful way. With Theo's encouragement, he added in little sleights of hand to each of his manoeuvres, asking a bearded man to write down what colour he was thinking of on a blank piece of paper, before folding it and hiding it in his pocket away from Alexandre's eyes. When the young magician proceeded to make a silk scarf materialise out of the air that was the exact colour the man had written down, the onlookers went wild. They were not the big, majestic sweeping escapes that Theo pulled off, but, as Horace watched the crowd around the young boy from his perch on a balcony above, his mind began turning.

As spring gave way to summer, Europe became increasingly chaotic. Chamberlain had resigned only to have Churchill take his place. Paris fell and France surrendered. The blue and gold carriages were stopped more frequently, searched by an SS eager to inflict pain and find fault with anyone who wasn't like them.

'Would it be so bad, to stay in one place?' Theo asked during one of their searches. 'The *Cirque d'Hiver* is doing booming business in Paris.'

Horace sniffed. 'We are not *other* circuses, Theo. Part of our appeal is our scarcity. When you only have a short window to see something, you're more likely to go.' He gestured to the expanse around him. 'What incentive would people have to come if we set up a permanent place?'

Theo nodded warily. He understood the circus director's logic, but he couldn't help but wonder if it was the right choice.

There was also a growing concern among the cast, whispers about safety, allegiances, and money. Horace didn't let anyone see his books but as he studied his financial reports for June, he knew he had to act fast. A series of cancelled appearances in occupied Denmark, Luxembourg and Norway meant he had a deficit for the first time. But holding back in this climate was for the meek – and Horace was anything but.

'Do you know what people want, Chadwick?' Horace asked one evening as he puffed lazily on a cigar. Chadwick shrugged. Horace exhaled a thick ring of smoke, watching as it slowly disappeared into the air. He smiled. 'Exclusivity coupled with hedonism.'

Horace's Bath and Bubbles party was an invitation-only affair, reserved strictly for the very wealthiest. Fearing what could happen in London as the war escalated, Horace elected to set up on the grounds of sprawling private estate in Surrey.

As the guests arrived, they were greeted by cast members dressed as pool attendants and flapper girls serving drinks. Between trays of sidecars and mint juleps, they unleashed back-flips and cartwheels. The orchestra, dapper in their white and black tuxedos, played at the centre and the Mirage Maze had been decorated with sprays of pink, white and red English roses.

Inside, the stage and sets had been reconstructed around a giant Plexiglas swimming pool that was shrouded in black. When the show began, mauve and pink beams of light illuminated it from underneath with a fairy-like glow. The audience gasped as the full set came into view. There were diving boards that moved hori-zontally and vertically through a series of pulleys and rigs, tossing acrobats, trapeze artists, and divers clad in red and white striped swim attire out into the air. Behind the pool, a giant trampoline caught former elite divers, who rebounded back up, saluting the audience each time to rapturous applause. Following a synchro-nised swimming show set to music from the Cotton Club, Theo and Alexandre teamed up to do a double Chinese water chamber act. They came out onto the stage dressed as a copper and pris-oner. At the end, the copper, Alexandre, waved from the tank, his hands free of handcuffs while his prisoner, Theo, took a bow atop the twelve-foot tall diving board, before jumping into the pool as a pall of darkness fell over the place.

Afterwards, there was a reception on the lawn. The performers changed out of their costumes and donned ankle-length gowns and tuxedoes to mingle with the British aristocracy and society mavens. Mauve and pink champagne was served in glass coupes rimmed with real gold and the kitchen staff, kitted out in white, served trays of foie gras and water crackers purchased on the black market.

Lena, Alexandre and most of the other children elected to stay up late that night. The success of the show meant energy levels were at a season's high. With Alexandre's help and insistence, Lena participated in the milk can toss, blushing each time the other children cheered whenever she came close to getting a ball near one of the cans. When they grew tired of this game, they gathered at one of the long tables and ate lemon sorbet served to them in sugar-rimmed coupes.

From afar, Theo watched his daughter fondly. The benefits of Lena's therapy sessions extended far beyond the physical effect on her legs. The confidence she'd gained had spilled over into other facets of her life. In the last few weeks especially, Theo caught her laughing with great abandon and engaging with the other children. Even when she was sitting in her chair, she was no longer hunched over with her arms crossed, trying to hide herself from the world.

Seated with the other children, Lena settled back in her chair, enjoying the scene. It didn't matter that everything was crumbling around them. For the first time in her life, Lena felt like she was part of something, like she finally belonged to the exclusive club.

The party continued into the night. At two o'clock in the morning, Horace climbed up on a podium. The night had been an unabashed, roaring success. Already the Rockford family had confirmed that they would pledge part of their fortune to keep the show afloat, and other offers kept tumbling in.

'In times like these, many wonder how we can do what we do. Why this level of excess is still important when Europe is staring down the barrel of austerity.' Horace paused for effect. 'But I say no. In times like these, the World of Wonders is more important than ever. Where there is bedlam, we bring harmony. Where there is ambiguity, we bring assurance. Where there is darkness, we bring light.' At these words, the spotlights blinked, drilling home the point even more. The audience began to clap. Horace, in his element, raised his glass. 'A toast,' he said, merrily to the cheers of the drunk crowd. 'To all of you! And to what the World of Wonders will become!'

Two days later, the Battle of Britain began.

CHAPTER FOURTEEN

In August, Theo, Alexandre, and Lena returned to Thessaloniki for their annual break. The two children spent the lazy days of summer playing games under the shade of a cypress tree, shooting marbles on the wooden floor in the hallway and stuffing themselves with as much ice cream as they could. Alexandre continued his lessons with Theo, adding more tricks to his arsenal and Lena kept up her exercise therapy routine. Dr. Wilson had showed Theo and Alexandre how to soak and wrap the wet rags around her limbs and they took turns doing it. The progress in her legs was so exciting that thoughts of boarding school started to fade into the back of her mind.

Just before they were due back in London, Metaxas stood up to Mussolini, resulting in the Greek Army going to war against Italy. Theo sat in his kitchen, listening to the sombre voice of the BBC World Service reporter. He was torn. If they stayed in Greece, he would have to find some means of supporting his daughter and Alexandre. If they went back on tour, he risked putting their lives in more danger. Horace's telegrams were laced with a remarkable positivity, as though he was oblivious to the continent crumbling around him. Theo thought about what kind of work his skills would get him in Thessaloniki. A jobbing carpenter? A fix-it man for hire? No economy in Europe was thriving at the moment. As bizarre as it sounded, the world of make-believe was probably their safest bet, Theo concluded wearily, turning the knob of the radio off.

They arrived at Victoria Station only to be squirrelled away to a hired house in Epsom. It was only then that they started to see how much things had changed. Seven performers from the last tour hadn't returned. Three had made their way to Portugal, which they claimed offered neutrality. Others simply didn't want to leave their families. Two male acrobats took up arms with their respective countries.

London had become a war zone, Horace explained one evening at a cast meeting, but he added that it wouldn't affect them. But the reality told a different story. Theo was horrified to see barrage balloons lingering on the outskirts of the practice house where they were holed up. At night, Lena and Alexandre lay awake, listening to the strains of the RAF planes battling with the Luftwaffe. The air raids had nearly tripled in number and the *rat-a-tat* of guns firing was now as common as birdsong.

With a new tour came a new school year. On the second day of the term, Clara sat across from Lena, a serious look on her face.

'Did I do something wrong?' Lena asked. She glanced at the packet of holiday coursework she'd submitted the day prior.

'What I'm about to say must stay between us. I'm doing this at the risk of my career.'

'Doing what?'

'I met a man over the summer. A man who, within five minutes of our conversation, told me I was about as valuable as a bottle of spoiled milk – old, sour and no longer of any use to anyone.'

Lena frowned. 'He doesn't sound like a very nice man.'

'Indeed,' Clara said. 'That particular gentleman wasn't, as my mother said, fit for me. However, one good thing did come of it. It made me realise how little the world values the female mind.' Clara looked hard at Lena. 'You are bright, Lena. You're brighter than I was at your age. Lord knows it's a cruel benefit of spending your childhood isolated in this library and infirmary. But you have a gift and it would be a shame not to use it.' Clara reached underneath the table and took out a stack of fresh textbooks, all different colours with smooth covers and unbent spines that gleamed under the light. 'The holidays provided me with an abundance of time to think. And I've decided if you would like to, you should work towards studying for your examination for admittance to St. Ives.'

Lena blinked. 'Pardon me?'

'We can begin preparations immediately. You're studying as it is, so why not aim for a higher target? Mocks are in June and the real exams take place the following February.' Clara took the first book off the pile and slid it in front of Lena. 'You were right. Your brain is far from broken and you owe it to yourself to use it to the best of its' ability.'

Lena had already wheeled her chair around the table and now she reached up and threw her arms around her governess, burying her face in her hair. 'Oh thank you! I *promise* I'll be your best student!'

'You're my only student!'

Lena grinned, but just as quickly as her mood had lifted, it dropped. 'Are you quite sure we can't tell Papa?'

Clara paused, thinking back to the brief conversation she'd had with Theo last season. She understood where his hesitation came from, but she also knew she had to give the girl a chance. 'I don't want to lie, but I see no other way. Sometimes the people who love us most hold us back because they want to protect us. For now, I think you should focus on the work. If you end up being admitted, we'll cross that bridge together.'

Ten days before Christmas, Dr. Wilson asked Lena to meet him in the infirmary. Thinking that it was going to be a routine progress update, she wheeled herself down the hall. The past few weeks she'd made huge improvements, even feeling her reflexes, her mouth curling up into a delighted smile when she saw her knee move in response to the taps of Dr Wilson's tiny hammer. Perhaps he'd have a new set of exercises for her, or had discovered a type of woolen cloth that didn't smell.

When she reached the infirmary carriage, she rolled herself in, coming to a halt when she saw Alexandre standing beside her father and Dr. Wilson.

'What are you doing here?'

'We wanted him to be here when you opened your gift,' Dr. Wilson said.

'Gift?' Lena wrinkled her brow. 'It's not my birthday.'

'An early Christmas present! We decided it couldn't wait,' Theo piped up. He moved to one side and Lena saw a long package, lying on the bed she usually stayed in when she was there. It was about the width of the bed and was wrapped in brown packing paper with a huge red bow fastened around the middle. Looking at her father curiously, Lena untied the ribbon and ripped off the paper. Inside were a pair of industrial looking metallic rods. There were two thick straps of brown leather with buckles near the top and near the bottom.

'What are they?'

'They're leg braces!' Dr. Wilson said.

'For me?' Slowly, Lena looked at Dr. Wilson, not daring to believe it. 'Does this mean—'

'That you can try to start walking? Yes!' Theo shouted, unable to contain his excitement. And then everything happened so fast, her father leaning over to hug her, Alexandre picking up the braces and holding them out to Lena and Dr. Wilson launching into details of a new physical therapy plan.

'What do you think?' Dr. Wilson asked after he'd finished talking.

Lena burst into tears.

'I hate them,' she cried. 'Take them away.'

'Lena?' Theo's face fell.

'Give them back. I won't wear them.' Tears streamed down Lena's face as she rolled herself into the hallway. Theo tried to follow her, but Alexandre stopped him.

'Let me,' he said.

In the hall, Lena dried her tears, feeling guilty for her outburst. Dr. Wilson, her father, Alexandre – they'd been nothing but supportive.

'Need a friend?' Alexandre asked, joining her outside. He watched Lena glance at the infirmary door. 'It's ok. I told them to give us some time.'

Lena smiled appreciatively, wondering what to say next. How could she explain to Alexandre – to anyone – the emotions she was feeling? She traced her finger in a groove on her wheelchair, then glanced at Alexandre.

'It's not that I don't want to try,' she began carefully. 'But . . . I'm used to everything the way it is now. It's comfortable. And everyone's so used to me being in my chair. It's . . .' she trailed off, amazed at what she was about to say. 'It's so silly but now that it's real, I'm not sure I want it.'

'It's not silly,' Alexandre replied. 'It's hard to make a change.' His stomach churned as his mind raced to the money and stolen objects hidden in the empty hollow of his bedroom floor.

Lena nodded, grateful that he seemed to understand. 'Plus, they're ugly, aren't they? If I wear those, everyone will laugh.'

Alexandre grinned. 'Have you *seen* some of the costumes Martha puts people in?! If they laugh, you could easily laugh right back!'

Lena sighed. He had a point, although she didn't want to admit it.

'If you don't want to try to walk, that's your choice,' Alexandre said. 'But if you're afraid to try because the idea of becoming someone new is scary, or you're worried about what the others will say, well, I think you should give it a shot.' Alexandre glanced at the infirmary door. 'As for how they look, how about instead of thinking of them as ugly, you flip it. Think of them as beautiful.'

Lena laughed, convinced he was joking. There was nothing beautiful about the clunky metal contraptions she'd just seen.

'I'm serious,' Alexandre continued. 'They're beautiful because of what they can make you *do*. Imagine what it would be like to walk? Or swim in the sea in Greece? Or to kick a football. Or, to even walk into a boarding school,' Alexandre's eyebrows shot up as he said this last line. 'Plus, you said this was an experiment and that you can't have a proper experiment without consistent data. Can't stop now.'

Lena mulled this over. Using braces would open her world and the opportunities available to her a bit more. And she hated the idea of not completing her research because of fear of what others would say. That wasn't how any of the great scientists thought, she reminded herself. She glanced at the infirmary door, chewing thoughtfully on her lower lip. Then she broke into a grin and nodded at Alexandre.

'Alright. I'll give them a try.'

CHAPTER FIFTEEN

Following a successful new year run in Eastern Europe, the circus moved north, plunging towards Scandinavia. As the line of blue and gold carriages edged closer to Norway, Lena and Alexandre enjoyed a game of pinochle on a lazy Monday evening. Two seats over, Lena could hear her father singing with Nneka and Anna Maria as they drank from a bottle of retsina. Outside, delicate flakes of snow swirled around, and shards of ice clung to the windowpanes, enveloping the carriages in a white cocoon.

'Your turn,' Lena said, yawning as she felt the effects of her earlier therapy session with Dr. Wilson. After the initial fear over how she would look in her braces had worn off, Lena had attacked the challenge with renewed focus, forcing herself to work through the struggle of being on her feet. The feeling she'd had as she took her first tentative step, her father, Alexandre and Dr. Wilson cheering her on, had been indescribable. But the act of standing was strange and her hips, stomach and back ached at the end of each day. Though her progress was steady, it was tiring and she would often flop back into her wheelchair at the conclusion of her sessions. This evening, she'd kept her braces on, but had undone the clasps, allowing her legs some room to breathe.

'Ace of spades,' Alexandre smiled triumphantly. 'That's two for me and none for you.' He held out his hand to take Lena's cards, but just as she offered them to him with a little sigh of resignation, the train gave a sudden lurch and the screeching of brakes filled the carriage. The cards scattered onto the carpet.

Lena craned her neck and saw her father and Nneka. 'Papa, why are we stopping?'

Before Theo could answer, Chadwick appeared at the entrance of the carriage, a pinched look on his face.

'The SS want to carry out a thorough inspection of this train. If we pass, we move to Oslo. Everyone is to gather in the dining carriage in exactly thirty minutes. And remember,' he said, looking meaningfully at Nneka and Johannes. 'To make yourselves presentable.'

'They've never done an in-depth inspection,' Anna Maria said, frowning. 'Why now?'

'I don't make the rules,' Chadwick replied haughtily, before marching away to alert the rest of the cast.

As Lena secured her braces, she scanned the carriage, noting the worried faces of the other performers. Alexandre, who'd been basking in his victory just a moment ago, looked as white as a sheet. She glanced up at her father.

'Is it bad?'

'I'm sure it's nothing. Come, let's get cleaned up.'

Twenty minutes later, Alexandre stood in his compartment and studied his reflection in the mirror. Though the resemblance to his father was obvious, it had been two years since anyone had heard anything about Jacques Robichaud. Surely no one was looking for anyone or anything connected to him now. The damage was done and Jacques was gone. Besides, it wasn't as though the SS had a collection of faces they could draw from.

He'd chosen a pale blue shirt, grey slacks and donned a blazer to look more professional. He glanced over at the loose floorboard near the closet, wondering how deep this inspection would be. Surely Horace would have warned them if rooms were being searched. After all, he wasn't the only one with things to hide, remembering the absinthe and cigarettes he'd seen that belonged to other members of the cast. He closed his eyes, his father's words filling his mind.

Cover your tracks, Alexandre! They can't find you if you don't leave a trail!

He clutched the fake passport Horace had made for him in one hand and smoothed down the lapels of his blazer with the other. To the outside observer, he looked like an orphan boy who had joined the circus to make some money. It was just like his father said, Alexandre reasoned, straightening up. People couldn't see what they weren't looking for.

In the dining carriage, the performers lined up one by one. After passing Horace's checks, they waited, some laughing and chatting as if they didn't have a care in the world. Alexandre stared at them enviously, wondering what it would be like to have nothing to hide.

He heard the SS officers before he saw them, the steady click of their heels against the polished wood echoing in the hall. He watched as the head officer made his way down the line, followed by two lesser ranked officials. Every so often, he could hear the head officer speaking in English with a thick German accent. As the officer turned down their row, Alexandre recited a silent prayer.

'Your papers.' Suddenly the head officer was in front of him, holding out his hand. Alexandre placed his passport and contract in his palm and looked straight ahead, his expression unchanging, while the officer flipped through them. Alexandre hoped that he couldn't hear his heart beating three times faster than normal. 'You are from France?'

'Yes, sir.'

'For how long you have worked here?'

'Two years and three months, sir.'

131

The officer closed Alexandre's passport, tucking the contract in between its pages. He cocked his head.

'Are you nervous, Alexandre?'

Alexandre shook his head. 'No, sir.'

The officer held his gaze. Then, finally, he handed back his passport and moved.

After what felt like hours, Horace announced that everyone was allowed to return to their carriages. Alexandre let out a sigh of relief and began following the other cast members out.

'Alexandre,' Horace called. The officer was standing next to him. Alexandre felt his blood run cold.

'Yes?'

'You and Theo have been requested to keep the officers entertained.'

Throughout the dinner, Alexandre concentrated on executing each trick perfectly and studiously avoided the gaze of the head officer, who slurped his wine noisily, pausing every so often to wipe his lips with the back of his sleeve.

'You are good at hiding things,' he drawled, chewing on a piece of chicken. 'It is a skill that most don't have. Especially not at your age.'

'My father taught me.'

'Oh? And where is he?'

Alexandre flushed. 'He's dead.'

The officer picked out a scrap of food lodged between his teeth and smeared it on his plate, studying Alexandre with renewed interest. 'What happened?'

'I don't know,' Alexandre shrugged, his skin beginning to crawl underneath his collar.

The officer sipped at his wine slowly, his eyes never leaving the young apprentice. His lips curled as he drained the last of his glass, as though amused by some private joke. Then he stood up and clapped his hands twice. 'Gentlemen. That will be all.' He turned to Alexandre as he buttoned his coat. 'Until we meet again, Mr. Robichaud.'

Mario had come out to clear the plates and Alexandre knew the courteous thing would be to help, but he couldn't move.

'Join me for a meal?' Theo approached him with a plateful of leftover food.

Alexandre jumped. 'I'm not feeling well,' he said, rushing out of the dining hall.

Later that evening, Lena, who was back in her wheelchair after the long day she'd had, barged into Alexandre's room, but stopped abruptly. He was sitting hunched over on the floor, his head in his arms, crying softly. Embarrassed at seeing him in such a vulnerable state, she stared, frozen. She'd never seen a boy cry.

'Are you alright?' she asked, feeling stupid the minute the words came out.

Alexandre wiped his eyes. He wanted to say everything was fine, but the events of the evening had drained him and he couldn't muster up the strength to put on a show any longer.

Lena hovered in the doorframe and then rolled herself closer to him but remained quiet.

After a few minutes, Alexandre reached into his pocket and pulled out the golden star necklace, turning it over in his palm. He closed his eyes and pictured his mother's smiling face. He could smell the scent that she carried with her everywhere – of lemons and laundry soap. What he would give to have her here right now. What he would give to be able to bury his face in the thick folds of her brunette hair, always wavy from the salty Marseille coastal air. He hiccupped, fresh tears falling from his eyes. There were some things that only a mother could fix.

'They've gone. Papa saw them off,' Lena said kindly.

Alexandre put his head in his hands. For a second he thought about telling Lena everything. How good would it feel for someone to finally know who he was? But then he looked at Lena out of the corner of his eye, her innocent face stricken with concern and felt himself harden. His father was right. He couldn't let his guard down, lest the web of lies he'd concocted came back to haunt him.

'I'm scared too,' Lena continued. 'But—'

'*You're* scared? What do you have to scared about?' Alexandre snapped.

Lena flinched. Alexandre had never spoken to her like that. 'The guards. They're scary—'

'You have nothing to be afraid of!' Alexandre rasped. Anger seethed through him as he realised how close he'd come to revealing his past and he clenched his hand shut, covering the necklace.

Lena stared at him. 'I didn't mean—'

'Don't you know how lucky you are? You're protected from everything. The worst that'll happen is you'd get in a bit of trouble, but your father would save you, like he always does!' His words, normally so encouraging, cut her like a knife.

'My father's not perfect!' Lena retorted. 'He barely lets me do anything!'

'At least he loves you!'

'Well, I never grew up with a mother who loved me, so I guess we're even!' The words slipped out before she could stop herself.

'I think you should go,' Alexandre said gruffly, not meeting her eye.

'Gladly!' Lena yelled, pushing herself towards the hallway. She didn't bother closing the door.

Unnerved by her conversation with Alexandre, Lena spent the next few nights tossing and turning. What he'd said was true. She didn't know what it was like to be truly afraid. The war was in full force and yet Lena still felt a buffer between her and the real horrors, as though she existed in another dimension. She had no idea what it felt like to struggle for food or what it felt like to have to adopt an entirely new identity for fear of being found out. Even though she'd grown up without a mother, she'd always had her father, who loved her unconditionally. Her privilege made her feel guilty and that, coupled with her unease about Alexandre, added to her insomnia.

On the fourth night of sleeplessness, she hoisted herself into her chair, taking great care not to wake her father. Once she was safely outside her carriage, she rolled herself towards the dining cart, where she saw Nneka sitting next to a bottle of wine.

'What are you doing up at this hour?' Nneka's sultry voice was like molasses. Lena thought she was stunning. 'Have a seat,' Nneka said, getting up to move the chair opposite her out of the way.

Lena pulled her wheelchair up to the table. 'Alexandre's mad at me.'

Nneka let out a deep, throaty laugh and twirled the stem of her wine glass between her elegant fingers.

'I doubt that. You two are like glue!'

Lena frowned. She didn't like the way adults questioned her feelings. 'This time,' she insisted, 'is different.' She explained what had happened. 'I know he's afraid, but I don't understand why he would get so mad at me.'

Nneka took a contemplative sip of her wine. 'Do you know what happened to Alexandre's parents?'

'The police killed them.'

'Do you know which police?' Lena shook her head. 'We're quite certain it was the SS. The same people who stopped us last week.'

Lena shuddered thinking of the bruises she'd seen when she found Alexandre in the food supply carriage. 'So, he was afraid they came back for him?'

Nneka smiled sympathetically. 'Not necessarily, but try and think about it would feel if someone who had killed your parents showed up on your doorstep. Wouldn't you be afraid?'

'I guess,' Lena nodded. 'But he doesn't have to be afraid. He has us.'

'He may love us and be happy here, but old wounds linger. And Alexandre has nothing. Imagine what it's like to be in his shoes. To be abandoned in the most horrific way possible, and then have to figure out what to do, as a child? Do you think it's easy to get over that?'

'No,' Lena admitted. 'I tried to help him feel better but he got cross with me.'

'Give him time. Boys don't always like to talk about what they're thinking, you know?' She laughed. 'It makes it hard for us girls, but that's the way it is.'

Lena nodded but her stomach was still churning uneasily. 'What if he never wants to be my friend again?'

Nneka burst into laughter. 'You don't worry about that. I guarantee you that's never going to happen.' She paused. 'You really like him, don't you?'

Lena stared at Nneka, exasperated. 'Of course I do! He's my friend.' Nneka smiled broadly, which only served to infuriate Lena more. 'What?'

'Nothing,' Nneka said, pushing her chair back. She deposited her empty wine glass on a dish tray. 'Come on. Let's get you back to bed.'

In the rare moments she wasn't tied to her desk or holed up in the library with her books, Lena continued to work at her physical therapy exercises and practised walking in her braces as much as she could. After a slow start, she'd had a miniature break-through of sorts in February when she'd overheard a ballerina complaining about leg pain in the infirmary to Dr. Wilson.

'You must strengthen your feet,' he'd said, in response. 'Your leg hurts because your foot muscles aren't strong enough.' He went on to explain that the foot was comprised of a complex mix of bones,

136

joints, muscles, tendons and ligaments. There were, he said, over one hundred of these in total. He'd prescribed a treatment of foot strengthening exercises for her to do each morning and evening.

After the ballerina had left, Lena asked Dr. Wilson if he could show her how to do the same routine.

'I'll try anything if it will help,' she said. 'And I promise I'll work hard.'

Dr. Wilson laughed, charmed by her dedication. 'I'm not worried about that part,' he answered, showing her through the routine.

Over the next month, Lena dedicated herself to repeating the exercises, night and day, carefully going over them in the quiet of her room. The consistent act of massaging, strengthening, pointing and flexing strengthened her feet and accelerated her movement abilities. By the end of March, she was taking eight, nine, then ten steps in a row before having to reach out and grab at the chair Dr. Wilson kept in front of her. Buoyed by her achievements, Lena visited Dr. Wilson at the start of April with a special request.

'Do you think I can do it?' she asked, after explaining her idea.

'You've proven me wrong twice now. So, yes. I think it can be done and I'll help as much as I can,' he replied fondly.

'Thank you!' Lena threw her arms around the doctor. 'But you can't say anything to Papa!'

'I promise,' Dr. Wilson said.

By the time Theo's birthday rolled around at the end of the month, Lena was ready. After a dinner consisting of all his favourite foods, Theo blew out the candles on a Black Forest cake, surrounded by cast and crew in the dining carriage. He had just begun slicing the cake into small squares to share with everyone when Lena announced she had a present for him and insisted he sit on a chair a few feet away from her.

'The cake can wait. This is more important,' she said.

Amused, Theo took a seat, curious about what she had planned. Over the years he'd received a great many gifts from his daughter, mostly homemade. A necklace made from dried pasta shells. A drawing of him performing. A diorama she'd made out of an old shoe box. Once, she'd insisted on Mario letting her bake her father's cake and he'd watched, touched, as she carried out a misshapen pile of dough, complete with wonky frosting and candles, proudly singing 'Happy Birthday'.

But as he looked around today, he couldn't figure it out. 'Is this some sort of magic trick?' Theo asked.

Lena shook her head while the cast members around her fell quiet. She glanced at Alexandre and Dr. Wilson, who were on either side of her.

'Ready?' Dr. Wilson asked. Lena nodded. Taking a deep breath, she pushed herself up, steadying herself on her braces. Keeping her focus on her father, she moved one foot forward and took a step. Then another. Then another and another and another. She paused for a second, stopping to regain her balance. She was staring straight past her father now, intent on remaining focused on the task at hand and not getting distracted by him. Her goal was thirty steps. She'd done it in practice, rehearsed it in her mind, imagined it when she went to bed every night for the last month. She could do this. Slowly but surely, she started again, placing one foot in front of the other, never slouching, or stumbling, but staying firmly upright, her end goal in mind.

'Twenty-nine . . . thirty. ' Lena let out the last number with a gasp, falling into her father's arms. He squeezed her tightly, overcome with emotion. When she'd caught her breath, Lena jiggled one of the braces.

'Did you see the ribbons? I chose blue and yellow because those are your favourites.' It was only after she looked up that she realised her father was crying. 'Papa,' she said, her voice tender. 'Don't cry.'

Theo laughed, dabbing at his eyes. When he'd composed himself, he looked down at his daughter.

'Just thinking your life could be a bit easier, for your sake ...' He turned to Dr. Wilson and shook his hand earnestly. 'James, I don't know how to begin to thank you.'

'Don't thank me. He planted the seed,' Dr. Wilson replied, gesturing to Alexandre. 'And Lena,' he continued, 'is the one who's been doing the work. I'm merely an overseer.'

Theo squeezed Lena's hand affectionately, then turned to his apprentice. Unaccustomed to praise, Alexandre shoved his hands in his pockets and looked at the floor, but Theo reached out and gently raised his chin. Then he grasped his shoulders and pulled him into a hug.

'Thank you, Alexandre. From the bottom of my heart, thank you.' Theo stepped back and waved his arms, addressing the large crowd. 'Who's hungry for cake?'

CHAPTER SIXTEEN

That summer, the World of Wonders extended its tour across a bullet-ridden France, but the crowds were beginning to thin as fast as the hair on Horace's head. To her credit, Lena had remained focused, studied incredibly hard and, in June, wrote what she thought was an excellent mock exam. The results, Clara told her, would take a few weeks to arrive, so for the weeks after the exam, Lena busied herself reading novels, watching Alexandre rehearse and even began walking outside of the circus hallways, traipsing slowly and methodically through the lush grounds. She'd worked her way up to over 200 steps before having to take a break. Her back no longer twinged with pain and she felt a flutter of delight each time she was able to walk a bit further, her legs and confidence growing stronger.

During the final days of that season's tour, Lena sat in the library, making a list of all the things she wanted to do with Alexandre in Thessaloniki when Clara burst through the doors.

'I've been looking everywhere for you! Is your father here?' When Lena shook her head, Clara locked the door and hurried to take a seat opposite the young girl, her brown eyes shining. 'The mock results are here!'

Lena's eyes widened 'And?'

Clara grinned. 'You've scored very well.' She handed her the envelope and Lena began scouring the pages within. 'So well,'

Clara continued, 'that they've agreed to let you sit the full examination in February.'

'Really?' Lena squealed, joy bolting through her. It was one thing to have your teacher and father say you were talented. It was entirely different to have an impartial third party recognise your achievements.

'Really.' Clara held up a thick manila envelope. 'I've managed to gather a series of past examinations. Six months is plenty of time to prepare.' Clara took a deep breath. 'Now, you don't have to write it if – Lena?' Clara asked, noticing the dip in her mood. 'Are you alright?'

'I wish I could tell Papa,' Lena replied, shaking her head sadly.

Clara softened. 'Would you like me to speak with him? Now that we've got proof of your ability, perhaps he'd be more receptive to the idea?'

Lena sighed. She hated lying to her father, the one person who'd supported and nurtured her throughout her life. But she knew what he was going to say.

'No,' she replied. 'Don't tell him. But can I tell Alexandre? He won't say a thing to anyone!'

Clara eyed Lena skeptically. The two children had grown awfully close, but that didn't mean that he could be trusted with a secret this big. But seeing the look on Lena's face, Clara relented. 'If you're absolutely sure he'll stay quiet, then yes. You may tell him.'

Lena's face brightened. 'Thanks. And I've already made up my mind,' she continued, gesturing to the results page. 'I want to write it.'

'Splendid! This is splendid news!' She looked lovingly into the young girl's eyes. 'I'm deeply proud of you, Lena.'

As the day wore on, Lena waited impatiently for Alexandre to finish his meetings. He'd been cooped up all day with the other performers in the dining hall, plans and proposals for the next tour already well underway. She busied herself in her room, picking out the clothes she wanted to bring back to Thessaloniki for the holiday break. As soon as she heard a knock on the door of her compartment, she yanked it open.

'Were you standing there waiting for me?' Alexandre teased.

'I've got news!' Lena urged, poking her head into the hallway to make sure no one else was around. 'Big news.'

Alexandre grinned. 'Go on!'

'Remember how you said I could go to boarding school if I really wanted? That my brain wasn't the thing that was broken?' She could hardly contain her excitement. 'You have to promise not to tell anyone – especially not Papa – but I spent the past year studying for the mock exam to St. Ives. I wrote it in June.'

'And?'

'I've just been told I did so well that I can write the real exam! It's not until February and it takes months to prepare,' she continued, picking up a skirt and folding it, 'but can you believe it?'

Alexandre enveloped Lena in a hug and Lena felt her stomach flutter strangely. 'See?' he said, his voice loud in her ear. 'You see what you can do when you believe in yourself? Let's celebrate. We both have so much to be happy about.'

'We?' Lena asked.

Alexandre nodded, a grin spreading across his face. 'I'm getting my own act on the main stage.'

'What?!' Lena dropped the skirt.

'Horace just told me! He said I'd shown exceptional improvement and that it was time for me to go solo.'

Lena let go of her brace handles and threw her arms around Alexandre. 'That's wonderful!' She felt her face flush as Alexandre squeezed her and quickly pulled herself away, smoothing out her top. 'I'll help. We'll set up rehearsal space in the garden. And we can even put on a small show, down by Ladadika.'

Alexandre raked a hand through his hair. 'The thing is ... I can't come back with you. Horace said I have to stay here and rehearse with the other performers.'

'That's silly. I'll tell Papa to speak with him. He'll—'

'Lena . . . I want to stay,' he said finally, his tone apologetic.

'Oh,' Lena answered quietly. 'Right.' She turned away and picked up the skirt she'd so hastily dropped a few moments ago.

'Lena.'

'You don't have to explain.'

'It's only two months—'

'It's fine. Have fun.' Lena shot him a brief smile and looked away as he slumped out of the room. But as soon as she heard the door close, she dropped the skirt and fell on her bed in tears. She took out the list she'd spent all morning working on and tore it up into tiny little pieces, letting the white bits of paper flutter to the ground. Why was he abandoning her? And why was she so upset? *Stop it. Stop crying!* she whispered, brushing away the dampness that clung to her cheeks. *It's just a few weeks.*

When Lena arrived in Thessaloniki, it was to a city under occupation, vastly different to the one she'd left a year ago. The famine sweeping Greece had left its mark on the once-grand metropolis. Everywhere she went, she saw outstretched palms and heard parched voices pleading for a few drachmas. She tried not to notice the horrifying contrast between the rail-thin arms and distended bellies that bloated out like balloons. At first, she gave away the few coins jingling in her pocket, but she quickly realised she couldn't give to everyone who asked, and so she stopped giving at all.

With no Alexandre around, Lena felt adrift, like a rudderless ship. She thought about him constantly, wondered what he was doing and who he was doing it with.

Things with her father were strained too. She'd become less and less open around him. She refused to hug him tightly anymore because she was afraid of what her body had become. At night, she lay awake, wondering if Theo noticed. Surely he had seen the extra curve in her hips, the roundness of her breasts and yet, he continued to say nothing. When he asked her why she no longer wanted to accompany him on his outings to Ladadika, or lie on the sand in her swimsuit when they travelled to Halkidiki, she lied and said she wanted to protect her skin from the sun.

One evening, after Theo had asked Lena why she didn't want to join him for a night of cards at the neighbour's home, she snapped.

'I don't want to spend all my time with old people!' she yelled, getting up from the table.

Theo winced as he heard the door to his daughter's bedroom door slam shut a few seconds later. He'd noticed Lena becoming increasingly moody, but he was too preoccupied with bigger problems to give her the attention he knew she needed. With each passing month, the war grew worse. His beloved Greece was now occupied not just by the Germans, but by the Italians and Bulgarians too. After they'd seized power, it hadn't taken long for King George to flee. He was now somewhere in Egypt, reports stated, and although a Greek parliament 'ruled' from Athens, the country was essentially out of their control. In the face of the growing hold that the Axis powers had over Europe, his main priority was keeping Lena and Alexandre safe.

Theo buried his head in his hands, his heart laced with conflict. It was not often that he felt alone, but today, he wished that Gia was there to help.

CHAPTER SEVENTEEN

On the journey back to England, Lena thought about what she would say to Alexandre when she saw him. She wondered what he would think of the new dress she'd purchased from the Turkish seamstress on Platonos. She fingered the yellow hem and fiddled with her hair. It had been nearly two months since they'd spoken and Lena hoped that he'd forgiven her for the way she'd acted the day he'd told her about his promotion.

When they disembarked at Victoria, she scanned the crowd hopefully, but it was Chadwick who had come to receive them. He ushered them into a waiting car, and she settled in for the long ride to Epsom.

When she finally saw Alexandre, her fear was replaced by shock. He'd sprouted at least three inches. He greeted her with an awkward hug, taking great care to keep an inch of space between them.

'You cut your hair,' she said.

Alexandre sheepishly ran a hand through his trim locks. Lena's eyes took in the stubble on his face before scanning the rest of his body. She was embarrassed to notice new muscles, defined arms, and broader shoulders. She had never thought to look for these things before. Her face turned red when she thought about him hugging her tightly and she pretended to have something stuck in her eye so that she could turn away.

'So did you,' he replied, and Lena touched her hair as if this was news to her, too. She stared at him, stunned. His voice had gotten lower. He no longer sounded or looked like a boy.

'Yeah.' Lena paused, her voice caught in her throat. All those hot summer nights she'd spent holed up in her room in Thessaloniki, wishing she could talk to him. And now, she had absolutely nothing to say. 'I should unpack,' she said, relieved when he didn't try to stop her. 'See you later.'

Except she didn't. Between studying and her physiotherapy sessions, it was easy to avoid Alexandre. She missed him, but she was more terrified of standing there, staring at him, with nothing to say.

A week before they were due to start the new tour, Lena spotted Alexandre in the dining hall, hunched awkwardly over his plate, his elbows splayed widely on the table as he reached for his food.

Suddenly he looked up. His face lit up and he waved his arm, signalling for her to join him. Lena scolded herself for getting caught looking at him and thought about pretending she hadn't seen. She hadn't brushed her hair before coming to dinner and was wearing an old cotton dress. But this was Alexandre, her best friend. She swallowed her pride and went over to him.

'Lena!' He sounded happy. 'Where've you been,' he asked, as she took a seat across from him.

'Studying,' she answered, stirring chunky flakes of parmesan through her risotto.

Alexandre nodded, shovelling a spoon of spaghetti into his mouth. 'I guessed as much.'

Lena concentrated on creating a swirl pattern in her bowl, her nerves mounting. The two sat in silence, eating. Grasping for a topic of conversation, Lena surveyed the spread of food on Alexandre's tray. In addition to the spaghetti, he'd grabbed two slices of olive focaccia, a bowl of the same risotto Lena was eating, a chicken breast and a giant plate of spinach doused in olive oil.

'Are you going to eat all that?' she balked.

'I'm hungry,' he protested.

Lena laughed and for a minute, it felt like they were back to their normal selves.

'Your walking's improved,' Alexandre commented.

'I know. Dr. Wilson says I might be able to use just a cane one day,' Lena said, gesturing to the braces. 'Can you believe it?'

Alexandre beamed. 'I believe I was the first,' he added, winking. 'Well, I hope you're not going to be so busy that you can't come to opening night.'

It was more of a statement than a question and yet Lena didn't want to seem too keen. 'I'll come if I'm free.'

Alexandre straightened up. 'You have plans?'

'Might be playing cards with Clara,' she lied, eating a mouthful of risotto. She had no intention of playing cards. It was tradition for her to watch from backstage.

'Oh.' Alexandre stabbed at a piece of spinach with his fork.

'Is this seat taken?'

Lena turned around and came face to face with Pari, the girl Horace had found in the orphanage in Persia. Now a woman of eighteen, Pari had morphed from a tiny child with aquamarine eyes into a beautiful dancer and contortionist. She stood before Lena, her white teeth sparkling.

'Of course,' Alexandre beamed at Pari as she set her tray down next to them.

'Lena *jaan*, how are you?' Pari asked.

'Fine,' Lena answered, wishing that Alexandre hadn't invited her to sit with them. They'd only just begun to get back into a familiar groove.

'You must be coming to the show? Alexandre and I have been working so hard on the Levitation Trick.' There was a slight exotic lilt to Pari's speech and the way she addressed Lena made her feel like a child.

149

'I'm not sure I have time,' she murmured. Her gaze fell on Alexandre, who looked disappointed.

'Please? It won't be the same without you.'

Lena's heart softened. After everything that had happened between them, he was still her closest friend.

'Alright. I'll be there,' she promised.

The following week, Lena waited backstage, thumbing through the programme she'd swiped from Chadwick's pile when he wasn't guarding it. The show, she read, was inspired by Petipa's *La Bayadère*. But of course, Horace being Horace, he'd put his own whimsical spin on things, adding in extra acts and taking artistic license where he deemed necessary. The Levitation Trick that Alexandre and Pari would be performing was the penultimate act of the night. In Horace's incarnation of the classic story, Pari played Nikiya, a temple dancer who pledged her eternal love for the warrior Solor, played by Alexandre.

Lena bit her lip as the lights dimmed. She hadn't seen Alexandre or Pari anywhere and wondered what they were up to. But her mind was soon focused on what was happening on stage. Horace never failed to impress her with his ingenuity. He'd dreamed up celestial delights in the form of magical sets drenched in fabrics of sea-foam green, arctic blue, and silver grey. Horizontal platforms floated effortlessly in a choreographed fashion, laddering up to the theatre's roof. Along the way, aerialists clad in pearl-studded ecru leotards twirled around thick drapes of frost-coloured silks, descending in a dazzling manner. Watching a World of Wonder's performance truly did take her breath away.

When the water ballerinas came offstage and towelled off around her, Lena slipped out quickly to use the washroom. When she returned, she was startled to see Pari and Alexandre standing backstage where she'd been all night. Her heart plummeted as she took in Pari's gold headpiece, thickly braided hair that fell to her waist, pale blue silk jodhpur pants and golden-coloured bra made entirely out of topaz and agate.

'Oh! Lena! So pleased you could make it!' Pari said brightly, leaning down to hug her. Lena noticed that her hands were covered in henna, a labyrinth of curlicues and swirls that snaked all the way up to her elbows. She was wearing a lot of makeup and her eyebrows were shaped into two elegant arches over her aquamarine eyes. Lena thought she looked like a sparkling, magical creature, but said nothing for fear that Alexandre might feel the same.

'Thanks for coming,' Alexandre said, hugging Lena, his eyes rimmed with excitement and kohl. She wanted to respond but her voice was firmly lodged in her throat as she took in his uniform. Martha had dressed him in a midnight blue *sherwani*, gold drawstring pants, shoes that curled up in a satisfying point at the toes and a turban that matched the colour of Pari's headpiece.

Lena glanced at her programme. The next act was the one where Alexandre raised Pari, who'd been poisoned by a jealous maiden named Gamzatti, and brought her back to life.

'That's our cue!' Alexandre whispered loudly. He gripped Pari's hand, leading her onstage. As the crowd clapped, Lena tried to focus on the act. But she felt sick each time she saw Alexandre place a hand on Pari's bare back, or her stomach, or her small feet that were graced with thin, gold anklets.

When the illusion was over, Alexandre wrapped Pari's tiny body in a hug, clinging to her far too long, before they joined hands and took their bows. Over the applause, Lena could hear Pari laugh, light and carefree. Lena knew Pari had struggled, that she had lost her mother too, but this shared commonality had never bonded them. Pari had the strength of an athlete combined with the daintiness of a fairy. She was, in Lena's eyes, perfect.

'What did you think?'

Lena snapped out of her daydream. Alexandre was in front

of her. She blinked, stalling for time and failed to notice the hope in his voice. Instead, she saw the way Alexandre clutched at Pari's delicate hand. The henna made it look like Pari had captured him, entwined herself with Alexandre, that he was hers forever.

'She doesn't live.'

Alexandre's face flickered. Next to him, Pari's glow faded. She cleared her throat, adjusting the headpiece that still managed to glitter even though she was partially covered by the folds of the curtain.

'What do you mean?' Alexandre frowned.

Lena shook her head. 'I *mean*, that's not how the real story ends. Nikiya doesn't live. Gamzatti kills her.' She spun on her heels and walked away as fast as her braces would carry her.

Lena skipped the rest of the show, preferring to hide in the Mirage Maze. Tucked away behind the mirrored panels, she looked down at her body and cried. It wasn't fair. No matter how much physical therapy she did, she knew she would never be able to do the turns and jumps that Pari managed so effortlessly, like she was spun from silver thread and air.

Back in his carriage, Alexandre was fuming. He was furious with Lena for taking a moment that was meant to be wonderful and turning it into another bad memory. But after he'd changed out of his costume and settled into bed, he sighed. Most of his anger was directed at himself. He'd been so shocked at seeing Lena's transformation and still hadn't figured out a way to properly articulate what he felt. Time apart had only made his feelings for her stronger and added to his confusion.

Fool, Alexandre – letting a girl control your emotions!

He groaned thinking about the evening's events and squeezed his eyes closed, trying to shut out his father. He hadn't believed Pari when she'd told him that Lena was jealous.

'Just tell her I'm with Alexei,' Pari urged him, referring to the

Russian strongman she was dating. 'I promise things will be better if you do.'

He'd replayed all the interactions he'd had with Lena in the past few weeks, analysing them over and over again in his mind on an infinite, exhaustive loop. Was there something she had done, something she had said, where she alluded to feeling the same way? But it was no use. Where matters of the heart were concerned, his ability to read Lena was useless. Frustrated, he thumped his pillow one more time, rolled over and tried to sleep.

Chapter Eighteen

By January, Horace was drowning in debt. His *La Bayadère* idea wasn't bringing in the money he needed and the number of cities they were slated to visit had been cut in half.

On an early February evening, they crossed the border from Czechoslovakia to Hungary. Used to providing the SS with the usual bits of sustenance, then sending them on their way, Horace was surprised when one of the high-ranking officials returned the next morning. Fearing he'd been found out, he put on his best facade.

'Good evening, Officer.'

The officer saluted him in response. He stood over six feet and was solidly built, the smattering of badges dotting his grey-green uniform a stark reminder of who Horace was dealing with. He stared at the circus director with his piercing green eyes.

'I know you,' Horace began, trying to place the face.

'From the Norway checkpoint,' the officer answered in accented but clear English. 'I have been following your circus with much interest, Mr. Beddington. Is there somewhere we could chat?'

The evening before she was to write her entrance examination, Lena sat with Clara in the comfort of the library. Outside, a storm covered the carriages in windy blankets of ice and snow as they sped through the war-torn continent. Lena sipped on the hot cocoa Mario had for made her, and stared out the window, mentally going over everything she'd spent revising for the past few months.

'Nervous?' Clara asked.

Lena shook her head. She felt oddly at ease with herself. Clara had run her through so many practice examinations, going so far as to imitate the conditions of the real thing (in the library, from 9am to 12pm, no breaks), that she didn't feel like anything would be different tomorrow.

There was a knock at the door. 'Who is it?' Clara asked, rising from her chair, pulling her long skirt up slightly so that she wouldn't trip.

'Alexandre. I'm alone. Is Lena there?'

Clara glanced at Lena, then unlocked the door. As Alexandre slipped in, Lena did her best to stop her face from turning red. He made small talk with Clara for a few moments and then walked over to Lena. She crossed her arms and blushed.

'I wanted to wish you good luck for tomorrow.'

'You remembered,' Lena said, lowering her arms slightly.

Alexandre shrugged, a hint of his boyishness coming through. 'Course I did.' He stuffed his hands into his pockets and began swaying from side to side.

'Well, thanks,' she replied, wishing she could leap up and hug him, and have everything strange between them disappear.

'Ok then. I guess I'll go,' Alexandre started, but he didn't move. He closed his eyes for a second and took a deep breath. 'Lena,' he said, looking directly at her. 'No matter what happens, what you've done to get here is amazing. I thought you should know.'

He turned around before Lena could respond, mumbled something to Clara about the show and left. *I only did it because you made me think it was possible*, Lena wanted to say. She wished she could pull his arms around her and feel the warmth of his body rising and falling next to hers. But that was never going to happen, she frowned, remembering the way he'd looked at Pari.

'I haven't seen you two together much,' Clara observed.

'We've both been busy,' Lena said, gesturing to the books on the side table.

'As long as that's the only reason.'

For a minute Lena thought about telling Clara everything. The way her feelings for Alexandre had shifted, the pain she felt when she saw him looking at other girls. And that tiny sliver of hope that maybe one day he'd feel the same way she did.

'Is there something you want to talk about?'

Lena shook her head, refocusing her thoughts on the examination. 'So, I write tomorrow but won't know the results for a few months?'

Clara regarded her intently for a moment, but then said. 'That's correct. We'll get word in late spring or early summer about the results. And Lena?' She smiled reassuringly. 'Don't worry. You're ready.'

Lena smiled back at her governess. With all the tumult and uncertainty around her, at least she could be confident about one thing. She'd done the work and knew with conviction that she was prepared for whatever was going to happen in the morning.

Back in the safety of his own carriage, Alexandre crouched on the ground and levered up the loose floorboard. For a moment he sat there, staring at the collection he'd amassed over the last three years.

I'm telling you, he wouldn't survive a day in the wild alone!

Alexandre felt his jaw stiffen. It wasn't nearly as impressive as any of the hauls his father had done in his heyday, but it was an accomplishment, nonetheless. He reached down into the hollow cavity and removed a golden medallion, depicting a portrait of Empress Maria Theresia, of the Hapsburg Empire. He'd got it in

Vienna, sliding it out from under the glass case where it sat and slipping it into his pocket with ease.

Next, he picked up a piece of fabric and carefully spread it out on the ground. This was one of three items he'd taken from the Victoria and Albert South East Asia collection. It was a wall hanging crafted from the finest silks and satins, all varying shades of pink, cream and gold.

'It was handwoven by a group of artisans in Gujarat,' he recalled the museum curator boasting, as he led the cast on their private tour two years back. 'Once they'd finished weaving it, the prince who'd commissioned it cut off their hands, because he never wanted anyone else to make anything as beautiful.'

One by one, Alexandre took out the various objects, miniatures and fabrics he'd acquired, laying everything out neatly on the floor around him. When he'd finished, he frowned.

'A *weak, useless boy! Being sensitive will get you nowhere, Alexandre!*'

He clamped his hands over his ears, trying to quiet his father's voice. Lena had taught him that people could change. She'd pushed through her own doubts and was on the cusp of her biggest achievement yet.

Alexandre leaned his head against his bed, staring at the dresser drawer above that held his wages. Never in his life had he expected to make an honest living. Not after everything his father had taught him. He cursed him now, for what he'd made him do, what he'd turned him into.

You cannot outrun who you really are. His father's last words to him rang through his ears.

No, Papa, he said, steeling himself. *You are wrong. People can change. I'll show you.* Reaching up to his bedside table, he grabbed a pen and notebook and ripped out a sheet of paper. He began writing down the name of each of the items surrounding him, followed by the place he'd picked them up. At some point over the next year, the tour would hit each city that had every single museum, gallery, library and vault he'd ever been to, and he would use those visits to make everything right. He would return everything and, in doing so, expunge himself of his sins. He couldn't take back what he'd done, but he knew now that he could change who he was meant to be.

In March, the cast travelled to Monaco to perform at a private show for the House of Grimaldi. Though they were not the most enticing audience, private shows provided a stable stream of income and an outlet for the performers to keep their skills sharp.

Afterwards, Theo bowed out of the cast party, telling others that he was heading to the casino to try his luck at baccarat. On the way, he told the driver to make a detour. He looked outside the window at the grandiose millionaire's playground that had come under occupation by the Germans. As they drove by the coast, boats dotting the sparkling blue waters, Theo sighed wearily, wondering if this was the last jewel left in Europe. He was tired of fighting. Countries were disintegrating, defeated from the blows the Axis powers repeatedly doled out.

The car pulled up outside the American Embassy, and Theo, his thoughts on the future, got out.

CHAPTER NINETEEN

A few weeks before her thirteenth birthday, Lena noticed a rust-coloured stain on her underwear, her stomach plummeting at the sight of it. She wondered if anyone could tell, wondered if the world would know that something fundamental about her had changed. She was a woman now.

Feeling awkward about asking her father for help, she told no one. But on the third day, Clara noticed a linen handkerchief that was coloured reddish-orange slip out of Lena's skirt while she was heading back to her carriage.

'What's that?'

Lena saw the blood-soaked handkerchief on the floor, then looked at Clara, who, judging from her facial expression, had quickly pieced together what was going on. Exhausted from the exam, her confusion about Alexandre, and now this, Lena burst into tears.

In the safety of the Clara's carriage, Lena told her what had happened between sobs. Her governess hugged her and told her that everything was going to be ok. But, she added, it was important that they tell Lena's father so that he could get her the supplies she needed. Lena nodded reluctantly, then asked Clara if she could tell him for her. Lena didn't know how to speak to her biggest hero about this.

Clara agreed and told her to wait in her carriage. About

twenty agonizing minutes later, there was a soft knock. Then Clara opened the door and Lena saw Theo was standing behind her, his face tense with worry. Clara whispered something to him and he nodded, walking into the carriage and closing the door.

'Papa. I'm sorry I didn't tell you,' Lena began. And then it happened all at once, Theo rushing over to her and taking her in his arms. She began to cry again, all the months of pent-up frustration flooding out of her.

'You have nothing to be sorry about.' He held her, letting her cry until she had got it all out. 'I'm the one who should apologise. You were growing up right before my eyes and I . . .' He looked away, upset. He couldn't tell her the truth just yet. Feeling guilty, he hugged her tightly. He'd been so preoccupied with his own planning that he'd barely been present as a father.

Lena sniffed and told him it was ok, but Theo shook his head. 'You are everything to me, Lena. Nothing will change that.' His eyes filled with concern. 'You must tell me when things like this happen. Clara has already offered to help you get what you need. But I also need to know. I *want* to know,' he added.

Lena nodded and smiled, feeling like a weight had been lifted off her.

Theo pinched her cheeks. 'Now. I believe someone has a thirteenth birthday approaching. It's a big one,' he said, his eyes beginning to twinkle. 'I was going to wait until the actual day, but I think now's the right time.' He reached into his pocket and took out a blue and gold leather keychain, a brass key dangling from the middle.

Lena stared at the key, not daring to take it. 'Is this . . .'

Theo nodded, breaking into a laugh. 'It's time you had your own carriage.'

Lena threw her arms around her father's waist, hugging him tightly. 'Thank you, Papa!' She pulled back and took the key from him, turning it over in her hands. The leather smelled new and fresh, like it had been recently cut for her. 'Can we decorate?'

'Any way you like,' Theo said. 'But first, we have to get your party sorted!'

'I'm too old for parties.'

Theo let out a booming laugh. 'No one is ever too old for parties! What do you say we do a dinner with the whole cast?'

Lena's gaze wavered. She wasn't sure how she was going to ask Alexandre, but the idea of celebrating with everyone was a welcome change to the strife that had clouded the world.

'Ok,' she agreed.

Two days later, Lena spotted Alexandre in the games parlour and began fretting over her party again. As she hovered near him, trying to remember how she used to speak to him, Alexandre lifted up the mahjongg box. Someone had failed to secure the clasp and the case sprang open, causing a mountain of ceramic tiles to cascade out all over the floor.

The sudden noise was such a surprise that Lena burst into giggles. Alexandre whipped his head around and saw her there. She halted for a brief moment, covering her mouth, but their eyes locked and they both succumbed to gales of laughter, until they were almost in tears. Lena stooped down and began helping him pick up the pieces. As they plonked the tiles back into the box, the quiet between them began to grow. Lena began to fret over what she was going to say. She racked her brain for the perfect phrase to break the ice. But before she could get to it, Alexandre cleared his throat.

'I heard you're having a birthday party?'

'I am,' Lena said, smiling. 'I heard you're coming?'

Alexandre broke into a grin.

Lena's party took place on a Monday night when they were stationed in Seville. Spain had remained neutral during the war and Horace had made the decision to stay in the country for at least two months, citing it as one of the last remaining safe spots to generate revenue.

Theo asked for the cast members to gather in front of the dining carriage, whereupon they would begin walking to a nearby restaurant he had rented for the night. Mario had gone ahead and, with the help of the two chefs there, taken it upon himself to create a menu full of Lena's favourite foods from Thessaloniki spliced with the typical tapas offerings native to the Spanish city.

It was nearly time to meet everyone and Lena hurried to finish dressing in her carriage. She sucked in her stomach and tugged the pale blue dress her father got for her down over her hips. He'd given it to her that morning, his eyes shining.

'I asked Martha to design it,' he'd explained, pointing out little details, like the silvery thread that formed a thin band around the hem. A tiny strand of crystals circled the neckline and the dress fell just above Lena's knees. It was the first grown-up thing she'd ever owned. 'I told her to use the measurements on file,' Theo said, proudly. Lena didn't have the heart to tell him that in the eight weeks that had elapsed between those measurements and today, she'd grown half an inch and added a pound or two to her waistline.

But it was the thought that counted and she saw that her father had Martha design it so that her braces could be worn comfortably underneath without disrupting the fall of the dress. She smoothed the dress over her hips, checking the inside seam and noticing, with relief, that Martha had left a few extra inches of material with which to let it out.

Satisfied with her outfit, Lena picked up a brush and began raking it through her hair, trying to untangle the knotted ends. With a glittery clip in one hand, she gathered a section of strands. But when she tried to close the clasp, it sprung back uncooperatively. Lena tried again, but it popped out and sailed to the floor.

Exasperated, she shoved the clip in her drawer, and began scraping her hair back into a ponytail.

'Leave it down.'

Alexandre was standing in the doorway of her carriage, clutching a huge box. He was wearing shirt and pressed trousers, his hair slicked back with styling creme.

'It looks nice down.'

Without losing his gaze, Lena let her hair fall across her back.

'Thanks,' she said, checking her watch. 'We should go.'

'Wait.' Alexandre's eyes shifted to the box. Lena thought he looked nervous. Briefly, she allowed herself to wonder if his nerves were a result of his feelings for her, but she quickly brushed it out of her mind. Alexandre was fifteen, practically a grown man. What could he possibly see in her?

'Happy Birthday.' He placed the box on her bed. 'I didn't know what you wanted,' he continued, 'but I thought you might like this.'

'Thanks,' she said, surprised. He'd never given her a gift. 'Can I open it?'

He shrugged, failing to hide the fact that he was dying to see her reaction. No one was calling for her yet, so she sat down on her bed and motioned to Alexandre to join her. The box was wrapped in brown paper and tied together by uneven lengths of string.

'Sorry,' Alexandre muttered when he noticed her studying the package.

'It's ok,' Lena said, touched that he made the effort to wrap it in the first place. Her fingers trembled as she unwrapped it and looked inside. What she saw made her jaw drop.

It was a miniature orrery, and from the looks of it, a very ancient one. She lifted it carefully out of the box and placed it on her bed, marvelling at its beauty. Then she looked back in the box and saw a series of smaller packets wrapped in newsprint. She slowly unwrapped each one to reveal the sun, an assortment of moons, and the nine planets all crafted from semiprecious polished stones. The orrery's framework was formed from solid brass, and a ring engraved with the zodiac divided the upper and lower sections. She sat, staring at the contraption in front of her, running her finger around the rim of its circumference. Then she picked up a citrine Jupiter, an agate Mars, and a malachite Earth, clutching each one in the palm of her hand.

'There's one more thing,' Alexandre said.

Lena peered inside the box. Right at the bottom was a tiny drawstring bag, no bigger than a deck of cards. If Alexandre hadn't mentioned it, she'd have missed it, she thought, as she took it out. She tugged at the strings and tipped it upside down. 'Oh!' She exclaimed, a delicate bracelet falling into her palm. It was made of fine silver and had a tiny dove-shaped moonstone charm at its centre.

'I found it in Milan,' Alexandre explained. 'The dove reminded me of the constellation Columbae. Do you know it?'

'Mmm, no I don't think you've ever told me about that one.'

'It's below Orion, but it's very faint. If you weren't looking for it, you'd miss it. You have to be a keen stargazer to know it's there, but once you see it, it's incredible. Do you like it?'

'It's beautiful,' Lena replied. 'I love it.'

'The entire solar system. In your room,' Alexandre said, beaming at her. He paused and then inched closer to her. 'Lena,' he whispered. He took her right hand in his left. Lena could feel her heart beating so fast but didn't know what to do. She tried to speak but no words would come out. She waited for him to say something else, but all that came was a kiss. His lips, slightly chapped, on her right cheek, and then a turn of her chin to face him. How long had she wished for this moment? How many times had she played this scene out in her head? She closed her eyes and thought back to the time she overheard a young cast member explaining to another that you had to keep your eyes closed if a boy was about to kiss you if you wanted to do it right. A moment passed and then, ever so lightly, she felt Alexandre's lips brush against hers, the cool touch of his fingers on her cheek.

It was over within five seconds, but every fibre of her body felt like it was on fire. She pulled away, opening her eyes. The expression on Alexandre's face told her that the same mixture of embarrassment and excitement was running through him as well. Lena smiled, unable to hide her happiness. He liked her. If she wanted proof, here it was. At that moment, she felt like she could do anything.

'Lena!' Theo's voice cut through the moment and both Alexandre and Lena jumped.

'Don't tell anyone!' she whispered loudly, her face darting back and forth between the door and Alexandre. He smiled and took her left hand in his, kissing it softly.

'I won't.'

Lena checked her appearance one last time then hurriedly did up her braces as she smiled at Alexandre. As they exited her carriage, he placed a hand on her right shoulder, a gesture that made her stomach flop.

'Lena, you look beautiful,' Theo said when he saw her. He glanced at Alexandre. Lena felt a sudden shot of embarrassment. Did he know? Could he tell that she'd been kissed? Lena didn't have time to think about it because Theo pulled her forward. 'Come,' he said, directing her down the hallway to the exit. 'We don't want to keep everyone waiting.'

The *El Rinconcillo* had been owned and operated by the De Rueda family since the 1600s and was a favourite stop for the cast members each time they were in Seville. Lena could smell the *tirokroketes* hissing before she'd even entered the restaurant. The thought of the sizzling cheese oozing out of the crisped exterior made her mouth water.

'Lena! Happy Birthday!' Anna Maria and a few others had arrived ahead of them. Jussi popped a *tirokrokete* in Lena's mouth before she'd taken her coat off and she savoured the salty taste of the fried pastry, grabbing at the stringy strands of cheese. As the rest of the cast clambered into the space, the rioja and cava began to flow. Lena sat at the head of the table, surrounded by the people she loved and beamed as plate after plate of Iberian ham, gordal olives, and tortilla bites were placed before her.

After the appetizers, the games started. Lena didn't know if it was because everyone had made a point to not speak of the war, or if everyone was genuinely happy to have something else to think about, but she couldn't remember a more fun birthday. Nneka began a game of charades. Lena's stomach ached from laughing, as she watched Johannes pretending to be a giraffe. Theo and Alexandre paired up to perform a few tricks, culminating in Theo pulling a tiny jewellery box out from behind Lena's ear.

'Open it,' he said. Inside, Lena found a tiny strand of pearls held together by a silver clasp on a bed of velvet. 'It was your mother's. I was saving it for your thirteenth birthday,' Theo said, fastening the necklace around her throat. 'Happy Birthday my darling girl!' He kissed her on the cheek. 'And may you have many more!'

After the games, the main courses arrived, for which the chefs had gone completely Greek. They feasted on platefuls of souvlaki, tore through flatbread seasoned with spices and oil and followed it with the fluffiest grains of rice Lena had tasted in ages. Mezedes were passed around and the adults drank glass after glass of ouzo, growing looser and louder by the minute. Around 11 p.m., one of the orchestra members brought out a Spanish guitar and they played late into the night, accompanied by Nneka's singing and the stamping of feet from the band of revellers. For dessert, Mario made a passionfruit cake with lime cordial and piped the number 13 acrosss the top in mascarpone and vanilla bean icing. There were also fresh *loukoumades*, Lena's favourite Greek treat from Thessaloniki. Everyone sang 'Happy Birthday' as Lena sat grinning, preparing to make a wish. As she blew out her candles, she caught Alexandre's eye and grinned. She'd never felt so absurdly content.

CHAPTER TWENTY

Over the next few weeks, Lena awoke each morning, expecting the buzzy feeling flowing through her body to have disappeared. But it didn't go away and she revelled in the elation, thankful for a kind of joy she'd never experienced. After her birthday, she and Alexandre had spent part of every day together, a love that had been building for years finally blossoming between them.

Of course, not everything was perfect. As happy as they were to have reached this new understanding, they didn't want others finding out about them. The thought of bringing up the subject with her father made Lena feel queasy. She'd never had cause to talk to him about boys in the past and wasn't sure how he'd react. He loved Alexandre like a son, but whatever Lena and Alexandre had was too new, too fresh for either of them to want outside opinions just yet. So they had to take care to not let their feelings slip whenever they were around Theo, which, between Alexandre's practice sessions and their weekly group outings, was proving to be difficult. To make things easier, they began meeting in empty carriages, lurking in their rooms, or hiding in the maze.

On their day off in Barcelona, Lena sat in her room waiting for Alexandre when she heard Clara in the hallway.

'Lena?'

'Hi,' Lena answered, opening her door and stepping aside so her governess could come in. 'Is everything ok?'

Clara looked as though she might burst from happiness. 'It's here!' She waved a letter around excitedly.

Lena's eyes grew wide. The results from her examination for St. Ives. She'd been so preoccupied recently that she hadn't noticed the time slipping by. Holding her breath, Lena opened it and began reading. *We are delighted to inform you*.

'They've accepted me!'

In response, Clara threw her arms around her young student and planted a kiss on her forehead. 'I knew you'd do it. I knew it! Oh, this is a massive achievement! I want to shout it from the rooftops! But ...' she stopped, noticing Lena's smile wavering. 'Don't worry. We'll talk to him. You should be very proud, Lena.'

Lena sat quietly, re-reading the letter. She knew she should be worried about the impending argument with her father, but for a few minutes she wanted to enjoy what had just happened. Something that had only ever existed between the pages of the novels she read and in her dreams at night was now a real possibility. *Delighted to inform you ... Very much hope you will join us*. And on and on. She'd done it. She'd taken a risk and she'd succeeded.

'Do you think you'll go?'

Lena looked at her governess. 'I desperately want to. But what if he doesn't let me?'

'Lena Papadopoulos,' Clara said firmly. 'Where there's a will, there's a way. I'll speak with him. In the meantime,' she said, pointing to the letter. 'I have a feeling a certain young man will want to celebrate.'

'Celebrate what?' Alexandre asked. He was hovering in the doorframe.

'Perfect timing!' Clara ushered him into the room. 'Lena was accepted to St. Ives.'

'What?' Alexandre couldn't restrain himself and scooped Lena up in a hug. 'That's fantastic!'

172

'Thank you,' Lena said, blushing, as he put her back on the ground. Clara turned to Lena.

'I'd love to stay, but I'm headed into town. First thing tomorrow, you and I will sit down and sort out a plan.'

Lena grinned and nodded. Clara hugged her one last time. After she'd gone, Alexandre clasped Lena's hands in his.

'How do you want to mark the occasion? Ginger beer and cheesecake? A chocolate cherry pie?'

'No,' Lena replied thoughtfully. 'I want to do something different.'

'Like what?'

'Let's go out.'

Alexandre frowned. 'In the city?' He watched Lena nod eagerly. 'It's too dangerous. What if someone sees us?'

'They're not going to. I'll tell Papa I'm going with Clara. He won't know any better and she'll be gone by then.'

Alexandre looked troubled. 'I can't lie to your father.'

'You're not lying to him. I am.' Lena wasn't sure where the sudden brazenness had come from but she didn't care. She'd worked so hard for this moment and she wasn't about to let her father's rules about what she could or couldn't do stop her from enjoying it.

After telling her father she was joining Clara on her day out, the two children hailed a taxi to the famous Parc Güell where they spent a magical afternoon together, kissing against the backdrop of the blue and green tiled benches. Alexandre would stand next to her, helping as she climbed the colourful spiralling staircases, stopping and turning around every few minutes to take in the magnificent views of the city. Everything, Lena thought, looked new through the blurry eyes of love. Following the park, Alexandre treated her to a cold coffee at Casa Almirall in the Ciutat Vella district. Afterwards, they walked the ancient streets, darting in and out of doorways and up and down corridors, laughing and kissing.

173

When they finally arrived back at the circus grounds, the damp scent of sweat and fresh air mingling on their clothes, everything around them was dark.

As they walked softly through the carriages, Lena smiled sleepily. A full day out had drained her but she didn't want it to end. 'I'm thirsty,' she announced, dragging Alexandre into the food supply carriage. She glanced around, her eyes eventually falling on a crate of champagne. Grabbing one of the bottles, she held it out.

Alexandre looked around nervously. 'We can't.'

'We're celebrating! Open it!'

Reluctantly, Alexandre took the bottle. 'Just a few sips, alright?' He held the bottle away from him and pushed at the cork. It shot off with a satisfying pop, and the sweet smell of alcohol tickled Lena's nose. She'd had a taste of retsina and raki, but never champagne. She grabbed the bottle from Alexandre and took a long swig. The bubbles fizzed down her throat and into her belly, causing her to hiccup.

'Shhh!' Alexandre hushed her. 'We can't stay here. I've seen Johannes sneaking in and out, taking sweets when he thinks no one's awake.'

'Hah!' Lena sang, suddenly buzzy with adrenaline, drunk on her newfound independence. 'I knew it!'

Alexandre took hold of her elbow and guided her down the hallway, the two taking turns sipping the champagne. By the time he'd steered her into the costume carriage, she was drunk.

Lena took her hands off her braces and tipped forward, draping her arms around Alexandre's neck. At one point, she was so off balance that he had to steady her as she stumbled forward, lest she tumble right to the ground. He let out a laugh, the alcohol starting to go to his head, and she put a finger to her lips, her eyes wide. Scooping her into his arms, he carefully lowered her to the ground. She yawned and gazed up at him, her eyes feeling heavy.

'Time for bed,' he said.

174

In response, Lena reached an arm up and twirled it around. 'Stay,' she insisted.

Alexandre hesitated but then grabbed a roll of sequinned blue material that was sitting next to him and unspooled it over her. He sank down next to her, taking care to keep his body above the makeshift blanket he'd made. Lena giggled as she lifted her head to kiss him. He tasted like chocolate and champagne.

'Lena,' Alexandre said, pushing her away. 'We have to get back.'

Lena sat up lazily, leaning back on one elbow. She caressed Alexandre's hair with her free hand. 'Five more minutes.'

Alexandre glanced around uneasily, but the entire circus was quiet. 'Fine,' he said. 'Five minutes.' He wrapped his arm around Lena's waist as she settled back onto the floor. He didn't remember falling asleep.

'They're here. I found them!' The sound of Johannes' triumphant voice pounded in Lena's ears. She squeezed her eyes shut wondering why he was here. What was he doing in her carriage?

All around her she felt movement. Yelling. Scuffling. She opened her eyes briefly and saw the blurred lines of concerned faces hovering above. A sharp pain stabbed at her head and she moaned, wishing that everyone would stop talking and leave her in peace. She rolled to one side and squinted. Alexandre lay next to her and she smiled, the events of last night coming back. But her smile quickly turned to a frown when she noticed other cast members coming into focus. In a flash, Alexandre was up on his feet and she heard yelling. Why couldn't everyone be quiet she thought, her eyes fluttering open and shut. And then she saw him.

'I assure you nothing happened.' It was Alexandre's voice, pleading with Theo. Lena squinted through one of her eyes. Her father looked angrier than she'd ever seen him in her life. 'I wanted to make sure she was ok.'

'What were you doing here in the first place?' Theo's voice

was cold, authoritative. A hush fell over the carriage. Anna Maria arrived and began shaking Lena gently.

'Lena,' she said, calmly. 'Let's get you up.' But Lena brushed her off. Her father was livid and looked like he might strike Alexandre any second.

'Stay away from her! Do you hear me?' His voice was like ice.

'Sir, if I could just explain—'

'You've done enough. Go.'

When Lena was finally taken back to her father's carriage, she felt like the line of questioning would never end. Her head ached and she just wanted everything to stop, she thought, sitting hunched over on his bed.

'Papa,' she said, her voice hoarse. 'I'm sorry.'

'You have nothing to be sorry about. This is all that boy's fault!' Theo said, frustration in his voice. 'After everything we've done for him. And Clara pretending to be taking care of you—'

Lena flared up, angry that her father was attacking the two people she loved most next to him. 'It *was* my fault. I *wanted* to stay out. Alexandre tried to get me to go back to my room. The trip into town, the champagne – all of it was my idea! Clara had no clue we were gone.'

Theo looked at her, hurt. 'But why were you running around the city and drinking?'

Lena bit her lower lip. He was going to find out sooner or later. 'We were celebrating.'

'Celebrating?'

'I asked Clara if I could write an exam. For boarding school. I got the results yesterday and ... I was accepted,' she said, lifting her chin. Despite the circumstances, she was proud of her achievement.

'What?' Theo asked softly.

'I was accepted,' Lena repeated. 'Into St. Ives.'

'How did you write this exam without anyone knowing? Who gave it to you?'

'Clara.'

Theo's face darkened and before Lena could stop him, he was gone. A few minutes later, he strode back in, Clara in tow, her face pale and her hands shaking.

'Tell me exactly what happened.'

Lena sat helplessly as her governess explained everything. How Lena had brought up the idea of the exam that day in the library, right before Theo had walked in on them. How she'd said 'no' at first, but then relented. How she'd helped her prepare in secret, for months and then administered the actual examination that past February.

'Yesterday morning I received the results.' She stared at the ground, silence hanging between her and Theo.

'How could you lie to me? I trusted you,' Theo said, disappointment hugging the lines on his face.

Clara was silent for a minute. 'I regret that Lena and Alexandre were in a position that might have endangered both of them last night. I had no idea she'd said she was coming with me.' Clara raised her face. 'However, I have no regrets about encouraging her to write the examination. It's wrong of you to keep her from pursuing something she's clearly brilliant at because of her physical limitations—'

'Thank you, Clara,' Theo spat. 'But only I know what's best for my daughter. Given what's transpired, I have no choice but to terminate your employment immediately. Please, pack your things and await further instruction in your room. You are to speak with no one and leave a forwarding address where your final monies can be sent.'

Lena stared at her father, horrified. This couldn't be happening. He couldn't be letting her beloved governess go. She looked at Clara, who seemed stunned but quickly collected herself and swallowed.

'Yes, sir. I apologise for any harm I've caused.' She glanced at Lena sadly, a brave smile on her face. 'Stay well, Lena,' she said, turning to let herself out of the room.

'Papa,' Lena said, her voice trembling as she scrambled for her braces. 'You can't be serious.'

'You think this is a joke?' Theo yelled. Lena had never seen him so angry. 'You deliberately defy me to write an exam for a school you will never be able to attend. You're out drinking, wandering the streets. Then, I find you sleeping next to a boy! How could you?' Theo's eyes simmered with pain.

Lena thought about the years of history she'd shared with Alexandre. She thought about the way her father had tried his best to encourage her academic interests, always reacted so proudly whenever Clara told him she'd performed well on yet another test or quiz. It wasn't fair that he was now acting like this. She stared down at her lap, fat tears falling from her eyes, unable to respond.

'I have nothing against Alexandre.' Theo said. 'But God forbid anything happens to you. You are a woman now. It's simply not safe!'

'We didn't *do* anything!'

But Theo wasn't finished. 'Then there is the matter of his background. He is a Jew, Lena! A Jew! Suppose someone found you. Suppose his cover was blown! You could have been killed!' Theo's voice rose but all Lena could do was sob. 'You are to stay away from him. Do you understand?'

'Papa,' Lena pleaded. 'We'll go back to being friends—

'I mean it! You could have been seriously hurt—'

'But I wasn't! I'm fine! My legs are fine! My lungs are fine,' Lena screamed, as she pushed herself up. She thumped the ground hard with one of her braces. 'Just once, I wanted to be like everyone else! I wanted to be normal.'

Theo sighed. 'You truly are your mother's daughter, aren't you?'

'What does that mean?' Lena asked, confused.

Theo shook his head. 'There's no need to be dramatic. I'm doing all of this for your benefit.'

Lena laughed bitterly. 'By taking away everyone I love? You never let me do anything! You said I couldn't walk and look what I can do now. You said I couldn't go to boarding school, but look what I did. I'm sick of you telling me how I'm meant to live my life!'

'You are not to leave your room for anything but meals or physical therapy until we reach London.'

Lena balled her hands into little fists. 'You can't do this!'

'I am your father,' Theo bellowed. 'And I will discipline you however I see fit.'

'I hate you!' Lena screamed, rushing from the carriage as quickly as she could. She didn't stop until she reached the Mirage Maze, where she curled up in a ball and cried.

In the quiet of his room, Theo slumped into his armchair, weary with exhaustion. After finding Lena's bed empty that morning, time had stopped, his mind racing through all of the horrible things that could have happened to her. The thirty-two minutes that had elapsed between discovering she was missing and finding her sleeping like a baby were the longest of his life. He wiped his brow and wondered what to do. He deeply regretted having to fire Clara, but it was for the best. They wouldn't be around in a few weeks' time, and he'd see to it that Horace paid her enough until she was able to find another job.

Theo sighed. Everything had become such a mess. He wanted to run to Lena, to take her in his arms and tell her that all she had to do was wait a few more weeks. He had no intention of keeping her apart from Alexandre forever, but he couldn't risk anyone finding out about his plan. Just a few more weeks and they'd be free. In time, Lena would thank him for what he'd done.

CHAPTER TWENTY-ONE

As the circus pulled away from Barcelona, Lena tried her best to adjust to a new pace of life. So accustomed to spending her days and nights with Clara and Alexandre, she now spent the bulk of her time holed up in her room or in the infirmary, grateful that she at least had her books and the company of Dr. Wilson. She'd heeded her father's orders and stayed away from Alexandre, but it wasn't like it had been difficult. He'd taken Theo's warning to heart and immersed himself in practising. Once inseparable, their paths now barely crossed.

On an early June morning in Zaragoza, Dr. Wilson arrived at one of Lena's daily exercise sessions with more vigour than usual.

'I've been doing more research.' He waved around a file folder with her name scrawled in black ink on the tab. 'And I believe you'll be able to walk unaided! What I think has happened is that all of the exercises you've done have created new connections. Your brain has formed new neural pathways – paths that never existed, because you'd never had to use those muscles. In short, it means you're capable of much more than we ever thought possible.'

Lena hesitated. A few months ago, she would have jumped at the chance to walk with no help. But the heartache clawing at her insides made it tough for her to focus on little else than all she'd lost.

'We'd first focus on moving to a cane,' Dr. Wilson continued. 'Once you've mastered that, we can aim for you to be free of any aids.' He glanced at Lena. 'My dear I thought you'd have been a bit more excited than this.'

Lena picked at the strap of her leg brace. 'Everything's such a mess.'

Dr. Wilson sat down next to her. 'I know you may find it hard to believe, but you were both overdue for an argument! Up to now you've never argued. There's not a father and daughter I know of who hasn't quarrelled.'

'Things won't ever be the same.'

Dr. Wilson shook his head. 'No, they won't – they'll be better. All relationships evolve and you're growing up. That old adage "time heals all" is true. In the interim,' he gestured to her braces, 'why not focus on something you can control?'

Lena eyed the cane warily. 'How much time will it take?'

'Until you're free of the braces? With a positive attitude and consistent efforts, I would say in as little as two or three months.'

Lena rubbed the dampness from her eyes. She thought about what her father had told her in the maze. *Epiméno*, Lena. You must endure. She lifted her chin towards the doctor. 'We'll start tomorrow?'

And so she began working towards yet another milestone goal. She'd take one step using the cane and then two. Often she slipped and had to grasp for a nearby wall to steady herself. But her steely resolve and lack of any other distractions meant she saw improvements quickly.

In the evenings, while the cast performed and mingled at parties, Lena stayed in her room. Clara had kept her promise to stay in touch. She was staying with her parents in Fulham until her job as an English teacher started at a boarding school in Dorset. Most nights, Lena snuggled into bed with Clara's letters, relishing the miraculous love story that was unfolding hundreds of miles away.

15th June, 1942

Dear Lena,

Thanks for your letter, it was lovely seeing it waiting for me when I arrived home. How are you feeling? Did you finish reading 'The Count of Monte Cristo'? It's one of my favourites!

Forgive my selfishness for the remainder of this letter but I couldn't wait to tell you. Remember how I mentioned I'd been frequenting a small, cosy café – the one that serves those delicious fruit crumbles? Well, who should walk in yesterday but a but a well-dressed RAF officer! He was on leave for all of 36 hours to visit his sister, who'd just given birth, and had got lost while looking for the local off-licence. It was pure fluke that he wandered into the café.

We got to speaking and he asked if I'd meet him today. He said normally if he was courting he'd have rung up on the telephone but given the circumstances, he had to make an exception.

I was frightfully worried as I walked back this morning. I'm so used to being disappointed where matters of the heart are concerned. But when I walked in, there he was, sitting at my favourite table – the one I've only ever sat at alone – with two slices of almond cake, two mugs and a freshly brewed pot of Twinings.

His name is Fitz. He's got brown hair, brown eyes and the kindest smile. I feel silly writing to you just hours after he's left, but there's something about him.

Lena beamed as she tucked the letter away, rifling through her stack to the one holding the inevitable.

20th July, 1942

Dear Lena,

I apologise for my silence. I've no excuse other than I fear I have fallen hopelessly in love! I've caught the disease that drives men and women mad.

Since my last letter, things have accelerated with Fitz. He doesn't know when he'll be back and I obviously can't visit him, but it doesn't matter. We've something special, something permanent. It's almost as though all of those dreadful dates were worth it. We've already discussed marriage. You may think this an irrational decision, especially for me, but this war has put everything so drastically in perspective. One never knows how much time one has left.

My dear girl, I hope this serves as some kind of inspiration. I couldn't have known this would happen when I was let go from the circus, but had that horrible event not happened, I would never have met Fitz. I know everything feels a bit hopeless right now, but don't lose faith. Your greatest achievements often grow out of the worst circumstances.

All my love,
Clara.

CHAPTER TWENTY-TWO

The circus rolled into Rouen in the mid-August heat, the richness of the blue and gold carriages looking out of place in the sleepy provincial French town.

In his study, Horace noticed a tear in the once-sumptuous leather fabric of his chair and resolved to purchase a new one with his upcoming windfall. He'd agreed to loan Alexandre to the SS officer who'd come to see him earlier that year. The officer wanted to see if there was a way to use the boy's skills of deception in their own war efforts. Knowing that Alexandre would never willingly fight for the Axis powers, Horace and the officer decided to make it look like he was captured. Though he loathed to think what Theo and Lena would say once they found the boy was missing, no one was stupid enough to go after the SS. Besides, he thought, Theo wanted this for the girl. The rumour mill circulated fast in such small confines and it had taken less than an hour for Horace to find out what had happened between Alexandre and Lena that day in Barcelona. Theo wanted them to be apart. It was, he told himself, for the best.

'Sir?' Chadwick was stooped over a drawer filled with files on each cast member. 'It's not here.'

Horace frowned. 'It must be.' He tipped his chair back up and stood up. 'Perhaps your lack of organisation is to blame?' Horace pushed his assistant out of the way and thumbed through the

185

files for Alexandre's information. But his search revealed nothing. Chadwick cleared his throat.

'There's something else. Theo's and Lena's files are also missing.'

Horace's eyes narrowed and he hit Chadwick squarely on the side of his head. 'How many times have I told you to keep things in order! Look through them again!'

'But there are over one hundred performers—' Chadwick noticed Horace's expression and sighed. He knelt down and began laying the files side by side on the midnight blue rug.

'I'll be in my quarters.' Horace swept his jacket over Chadwick's head as he left.

The tentative knock that came just before midnight told Horace all he needed to know. Alexandre, Horace thought, as Chadwick opened the door and stood before him, his hands trembling, was not the only one who could read people.

'They're not there.' Horace stubbed out the end of the cigar he was smoking.

'Tomorrow. When they're rehearsing. Search their carriages.'

Chadwick nodded and left. Horace stared at the blue velvet edging on his bedroom door and pondered the situation. He hoped that it was simply an error, an honest man's mistake. But something told him he'd been made a fool, and that angered him more than anything.

The next evening, Chadwick returned with a far different demeanour, rapping loudly on the oakwood panelling. Horace ushered him in, offering him a seat on a blue ottoman. But Chadwick was too excited to sit.

'These,' Chadwick said, holding up three separate files, 'are the original documents taken from your office. And these,' Chadwick pointed to another set of documents, 'are papers requesting asylum to America.'

Horace felt the colour drain from his face. He imagined how financially disastrous it might have been had Theo been able to get away with this. He was furious that the masterful illusionist had almost pulled this off, had tried to slip away in the night without even telling him. After all Horace had done for him.

'Call the SS. Tell them we've got the boy's papers.'

'Wait.' Chadwick held up a letter. It was fraying at the edges and the ink was barely visible, but the words were still legible. 'Look,' he said, handing it to Horace who read it once, twice. A smile crept across his face.

'And you're positive it belongs to him?'

Chadwick nodded gleefully. 'It's his name and address.'

Horace shook his head. 'All this time.'

'There's one last thing.' Chadwick held out another stack of documents. Horace snatched them out of his assistant's hands, his eyes growing wider as he read them.

'Well, I could never expected this. Do you think she knows?'

'Of course not!' Chadwick crowed, clapping his hands. 'I'll notify the SS!'

Horace held his hand up. 'Not yet.' A wicked look flashed in his eyes. 'Do you know what would make Theo even more sad than losing the boy?' Chadwick shook his head. Horace smiled as he tucked the contracts and letter into his breast pocket. 'Losing his daughter.'

When Horace singled Lena out the next morning at breakfast, she was not in the mood. She'd grown weary of avoiding Alexandre and tiptoeing around her father and the appearance of Horace only added to her frustration.

'What do you want?' she asked icily.

Horace adopted a wounded expression. 'Is that any way to speak to your uncle Horace?'

'You're not my uncle.'

Horace removed the sheets of paper from his pocket and fanned them out slowly. 'Have you seen your father?'

'No.'

'It's just. It seems he's lost these and I wanted to return them to him.' He slid the sheets her way: 'I know these past few weeks have been difficult for both of you. But he *is* your father. And I wouldn't want these falling into the wrong hands.'

Lena smiled sarcastically, making a big show of picking up the pieces of loose-leaf. But as she folded them over, she recognised her father's name on the yellowed piece of paper..

May 14th, 1929. It was dated nearly two weeks before her birth. *My dearest Theo,* it began. As Lena read the letter, her mouth went dry. It was from a woman named Isabella and, from what she'd written, it seemed like she was in love with her father. But that didn't make any sense, Lena thought. Theo was married to her mother, about to become a father for the first time.

I do hope Gia won't be too sad about losing you.

By the time Lena reached the bottom, her eyes were glistening. Quickly she scanned the contents of the remaining sheets of paper, five in all, her eyes widening. She looked up and saw that Horace was no longer in the dining carriage. Moving as fast as she could, she rushed out into the hall where she almost bumped into him.

'Where did you get these?'

'Why? Are they important?'

Lena glared at Horace, her thoughts spinning, trying to account for too many things at once. Her mind flashed back to the day in Aristotelous Square. She thought of Adelpha's words, of how dismissive her father had been of the elderly woman. Then she thought of Alexandre, how quickly and easily he'd befriended her. How, despite all her shortcomings, he never once chose to spend time with any of the other children.

'My dear, you're looking slightly pale. Should I call Dr. Wilson—'

'Stop. I don't know how, but you did this. These *contracts*, are fake. As for this, I don't believe a word of it,' she said, waving the letter in the air.

Horace chortled. 'I can assure you I've never seen any of those documents in my life.'

'You forged them.'

Horace raised his eyebrows. 'Why would I forge anything? How would it help me?'

Lena considered this. She hated to admit it, but he was right. Horace didn't do anything except for personal gain, but there was something about the way he was looking at her that made her feel unsettled. 'I don't believe you,' she said at last.

Horace cleared his throat. 'Perhaps you'll believe the source.'

As if on cue, Theo entered the hallway. 'Horace. Chadwick said—'

But Lena jumped in, thrusting the letter in front of her father before he could finish.

'What on earth . . .' Theo took the piece of paper. The reaction was immediate. Before he'd even had a chance to read it, Lena could sense that he knew exactly what it was.

Lena watched her father read the letter, then shoved the contracts his way. 'Well? Are they yours?' she demanded.

Theo's face was pale. 'Where did you get these?'

'Are they yours? That's all I want to know.' Lena was surprised by the strength of her voice and heartbroken at how quickly things could change, how fast trust could be shattered. Theo nodded reluctantly. Lena shook her head, tears pushing at the corners of her eyes. 'How could you?' Her voice cracked as she turned and took off down the hallway.

'It's not what you think—' Theo started after her.

'No!' she yelled, turning around. Theo stopped, sadness stabbing at his heart as his daughter faced him tearfully. 'Leave me alone.'

'Lena,' he continued. But she shook her head and kept walking.

'Children,' Horace sneered.

Narrowing his eyes, Theo walked right up to him and jabbed his finger in his chest.

'We need to talk.'

Blinded by the tears in her eyes, Lena rushed to Alexandre's room, banging on the door with the bottom of her brace. When no one answered, she rattled the handle, relieved when she heard it click open. She pushed it open, only to find it empty. Lena hesitated. She didn't know where Alexandre was but rather than wander all over the train looking, she decided to wait. She had to know that at least part of what she'd seen wasn't true. It couldn't be. Alexandre loved her. She could feel it in the tension between them whenever they passed each other in the dining hall, she could see it in the gaze he gave her whenever their eyes met across a room. He loved her, she thought.

Lena looked around, glancing at the clock on Alexandre's bedside table. Anxiety coursing through her body, she began pacing up and down the small space, losing herself in her thoughts as the minutes ticked by.

'Ow!' Lena tumbled forwards and banged into the closet door. She glanced behind her, noticing a slight elevation in one of the floorboards. As she rubbed her knee, she took a closer look at it. It had a small nick on one side. Using the back of her fingernail, she pried it up, surprised at how easily it moved and looked down. Inside the hollowed-out cavity was a treasure trove full of small objects. Puzzled, she reached in and pulled out the closest one, an old music box fashioned out of pale blue ceramic with delicate filigree work. Lena looked closer and took out a tiny scroll, then a set of silver spoons.

'Lena?' Alexandre's voice was thin. Lena turned around, still clutching the spoons. Alexandre went white when he saw them and he rushed forward, grabbing them out of her hands. 'Haven't you heard of knocking?'

'I did. You weren't here. I didn't think you'd mind if—'

'If you started going through my things?'

'I wasn't – I tripped over the floorboard.'

'I thought your father told you to stay away from me,' Alexandre said gruffly, picking up the objects she'd removed from his hiding spot and tossing them on his bed.

'I came here to tell you something. He lied,' Lena said, anguish creeping into her voice. 'My father lied to me. He had an affair.'

Alexandre's eyes widened and for a brief moment he forgot about what she'd just found in the floor. He thought back to the day they'd met Adelpha in Thessaloniki. Alexandre had known even then that something was off, but he'd never thought the truth would be as devastating as this.

'Are you sure?'

Lena nodded. 'Horace found a letter my father's lover wrote to him. It was dated two weeks before I was born. I guess he never returned to her . . . but still. I can't believe he would do that to my mother or that he might have left me, too.'

She looked so crushed that Alexandre couldn't help himself. He put his arm around her and patted her back affectionately. After a moment, he felt her body stiffen.

'There was something else he found,' she said, smoothing out the papers in her hand before handing them to Alexandre.

Alexandre felt his face flush and his hands began trembling. There, staring back at him, was the pile of contracts Theo had made him sign over the years.

'I thought they must be something Horace made up,' Lena continued, her voice hopeful.

For a brief moment, Alexandre thought about keeping up the charade. He'd spent so long lying to her about who he really was, what did it matter if he continued? But as he looked at Lena's wide eyes brimming with innocence, something in his stomach told him he couldn't do it anymore.

'They're not real, are they?' Lena asked. When Alexandre didn't respond, she spoke quietly, her voice oddly calm. 'Did my father . . . pay you to be my friend?'

Alexandre stared at the contracts. 'I'm so sorry.'

Stunned, Lena stood up abruptly and took a step back. 'You've been lying to me all this time?'

'No! I mean yes. But,' Alexandre tried to compose himself. 'I never wanted to sign them! It wasn't my idea.'

'Then why did you?'

'Your father insisted! And I needed the money, at least at first,' Alexandre said, trying to justify his actions. 'I didn't know you. Everything was so new. But I never liked it and I told your father many times to stop. I never spent any of the money, either.'

'I don't believe this,' she whispered. 'Do you even like me?'

Alexandre tried to take her in his arms. 'Lena! I love you.'

But she was too far gone, shaking with anger, and didn't hear him. 'Is this all I ever was? A way for you to make extra money?' She brushed tears from her eyes.

'I promise, I never asked for anything! It was all your father!'

'I don't know who to believe,' she yelled, exasperated. She pointed at the objects lying on the bed. 'What about those?'

Alexandre stared at the artefacts and then at Lena. He wanted to remember in exact detail the way she looked at him before she found out. Even when she was upset, he could see the hope in her eyes. He could hear the tenderness in her voice and feel the love radiating off her. He wanted to remember all of these things, because he knew that once she knew the truth, the whole truth, everything would change. He rubbed the charm of his mother's necklace in his pocket and swallowed.

'I can't do this anymore,' he said, looking wearily at her. 'You deserve to know who I really am.' He took a deep breath and sat down on his bed, dropping his head in his hands. 'Let me start at the beginning. My father wasn't an international art dealer.

He was an art thief. One of the best. I spent my life moving from place to place with him and my mother, trying not to get caught. He was grooming me to follow in his footsteps. That's why I'm so good at manipulating objects, at reading people. That's why I had so many stamps in my passport and why I never stayed in a real school long enough to make any friends.' He paused, lifting his head, his face stony. 'As I got older, I began to realise that what my father was doing was wrong. But my mother had nothing – no job, no savings. We didn't know what else to do. And it's hard to leave that life, once you're in it. It's such a rush, taking something, earning a month's salary in the space of a few hours. Still, I knew it was wrong and I told my mother, many times. At first she was afraid to leave, but finally she relented. She didn't want me to end up like him, so she promised she'd do what she could to get us to a safe place.'

Lena shook her head, her brain working on overdrive. 'How did you end up here? Are your parents even dead?'

Alexandre's shoulders slumped and he nodded. 'Yes. They are. The night my parents died, we were staying in an abandoned barn in Volmeden, just outside Amsterdam. We'd arrived there after fleeing Germany, because it wasn't safe anymore.' As he spoke, Lena remembered the stamp on the passport she'd found on him in the food supply carriage. 'My mother and father got into a fight, because of me. I'd told her again that I wanted to go to a proper school, have a proper life. She'd been hiding small amounts of cash every time we completed a job, hoping to build up enough for us to go. But that night my father found her stash and got so angry. They'd had fights before, but this one was bad.' He stopped, shivering at the memory. 'I was worried he was going to kill her. So I ran to the nearest house and begged the couple inside to get help. Then I ran back to the barn to try and save my mother.' Alexandre nearly choked on his next words. 'My father had already hit her a few times but he was getting more aggressive

193

and was holding a butcher knife. When he saw me, he came for me. I would have died for her, Lena,' he said, his face twisting into a horrible shape. 'I *tried* to die for her. But she shoved me out of the way at the last second, just in time for him to strike.' He closed his eyes, feeling sweat gathering on his hands. 'The blow that was meant for me killed her.'

He felt tears creeping into the corners of his eyes but brushed them away, forcing himself keep going. 'And then something came over me ... I grabbed the knife. I didn't mean for it to be so bad. I just wanted to hurt him, for what he'd done to her.' Alexandre's eyes glazed over. Lena had the impression that he was looking through her rather than at her, as though she were translucent. 'Then I heard the sirens wailing. There was blood all over my hands. I didn't know what to do. I grabbed my mother's necklace, and sprinted out the back. I ran and ran with no destination in mind. The next morning, I cleaned myself up in one of the streams I'd found on the way and then kept running. About a day after, I saw the circus carriages and thought I would take shelter briefly, until I figured out my next move.'

Alexandre glanced at Lena who was staring at him with a horrified expression. 'I wasn't supposed to stay here. I was supposed to take what I needed to survive and move on. But then I collapsed and you found me and ...'

'So you used us?' Lena asked quietly. There was an edge to her voice that made Alexandre's heart burn.

'No. Well, yes, at first,' he replied, uncomfortably. 'I didn't know if I could trust you. But I ended up loving it here. I loved spending time with you. I *wanted* to stay. I'd never felt like I belonged anywhere before.'

'You stole that magnifying glass from the planetarium,' Lena continued, slowly piecing together bits of Alexandre's story. 'And you've stolen all of those, haven't you,' she said, pointing to the objects on his bed.

He nodded, his face full of remorse. 'But I've changed! There were more, but you inspired me.' His voice grew calmer. 'Lena, whatever you set your mind to, you somehow achieve it. You showed me what's possible when you believe in yourself. So I started returning them. See?' He pulled a sheet of paper out from his drawer.

Lena took it, scanning its contents quickly. It was a detailed list of every object he'd taken and where he'd taken it from. Most of them had been crossed out.

'I've been keeping a record. The ones with no line are what's left.' He shook his head, pleading. 'I'm not the same boy I was. You have to believe me.' He looked up and saw the pain in her eyes. 'Lena—'

'Don't.' Her voice was beginning to crack.

'We can start over, together, now that you know.'

'Start over? How can I *ever* believe anything you'd ever say to me again?' Lena screamed. She flung open the door. Alexandre leapt up to follow her, but she whirled around. 'Stay away from me,' she said, her voice cutting him like ice splinters. And then she turned and raced away from Alexandre, from her father, and from the jagged shards of her shattered world.

CHAPTER TWENTY-THREE

Furious with Horace for what he'd done, Theo decided he was finished. He headed to his dresser and found the asylum papers gone, along with all their other documents, then rushed to Alexandre's room.

'Alexandre! Thank goodness you're here. Are you alright?' he asked, noticing his apprentice's red eyes.

'Fine,' Alexandre replied. It was only when he looked up that he noticed the panic on Theo's face. 'What's wrong?'

Theo explained the situation as quickly as he could, detailing his plan to go abroad. 'We have no choice but to go. I don't trust Horace anymore.'

Alexandre sat on his bed, deflated. 'Wait. You weren't trying to keep me and Lena apart?'

Theo softened. 'I wasn't happy about finding you sleeping next to her. But I know you'd never hurt her.' He glanced down the hallway outside Alexandre's room nervously. 'Now please! We must act fast!'

Alexandre shook his head. 'Wait. There's something you need to know first.'

Lena walked as quickly as she could through the halls, not stopping until she reached the library. Bereft and still in shock from Alexandre's confession, she sank into one of the armchairs, tears rolling down her face. How had it come to this? How on earth had the two people she loved most ended up being the ones who'd betrayed her trust?

Lena fingered the bracelet Alexandre had gifted her for her birthday. At the time, she'd thought it represented something more, the start of a new phase in her life. She realised how little she knew about the boy she'd found lying in the food supply carriage all those years ago. She'd always thought it was simply too painful for him to talk about his past. How silly she was to have thought that he might have wanted to willingly be her friend, let alone love her. *Look around you, Lena,* she thought, her eyes glistening. *This is who you are. It's you and your books and your useless legs. You have no friends. You never did.*

'That's all you need to know,' Alexandre finished quietly.

Theo looked at his apprentice, who suddenly seemed so young and vulnerable. 'Alexandre—'

'If you're going to tell me how terrible I am, save it. Lena's already done that.'

Theo shook his head. 'I don't think that. I think you were a scared boy who did what he had to in dire circumstances.'

Alexandre wiped his nose. As hard as it had been to tell them, at least he didn't have to lie anymore.

'There's more to say, but time is of the essence.' Theo glanced at the clock.

Alexandre looked up. 'You still want me to come with you?'

Theo nodded. 'Everyone has a past. And you've shown you can change. Now hurry,' he said, standing up. 'We must move. Where did Lena go?'

Alexandre shook his head. 'She left, told me not to follow her. She was so upset.'

'Get everything you need and meet me at Horace's office in twenty minutes. I'll pack some of her things and we'll find her after we get our papers back. I'll hire a car to get us to London. There's no point staying here.'

After they'd shoved what they needed into their bags, the two illusionists headed to Horace's office, Theo determined to close this chapter of his life and start anew.

When Chadwick opened the door, Theo stopped short. Horace was sitting directly opposite them, his hands folded. Theo felt an eerie chill run through him, but kept calm.

'How dare you,' Theo said to the man he once regarded as, if not a friend, at least someone he respected. Horace had done so much for him that it made him sad to think their relationship would end this way.

'How dare I? How dare *you*. What did you think was going to happen? That I wouldn't figure it out?' Horace's voice dripped with anger and he leaned forward to light a cigar.

'I was doing it for the children!'

Horace let a ring of smoke float from between his chapped lips. 'Why should I believe you? You would have taken *everything*. My ideas. My secrets. You would have set up your own show and profited from all of my hard work.'

'For heaven's sake, can't you see how dangerous Europe's become?'

'You once told me that timing was everything, Theodoros.' Horace leaned back and exhaled a lazy ring of smoke again. 'How right you were.' He nodded to Chadwick, who opened the door. Four SS guards and a head officer stepped in, clad in khaki grey uniforms. When Alexandre looked at the head officer, he felt his blood go cold. It was the same one from the checkpoint dinner in Norway. Panicking, Alexandre tried to catch Theo's attention, but the illusionist wasn't looking at him.

'Officer,' Horace said. 'As you know, I do everything I can to keep those who don't belong away from my establishment. But alas. It's not always possible.' Horace sighed and signalled to Chadwick who brought him a stack of papers. 'It pains me greatly to have to do this, Theo. You were one of my best.' Horace held up a passport, stamped with the letter 'J' in red. Alexandre felt his heart stop. His old passport. The one he thought was destroyed. He never should have trusted them. He moved to run but the guards were standing by the doors and showed no signs of getting out of his way. Horace handed over the passport and the papers to the officer standing before him.

'You'll find evidence of the fugitive and the man who hid him in there. They were planning to leave for America, under a false identity he created for the boy,' Horace said, pointing at Theo. 'Do what you will with them. They no longer concern me.'

Back in the library, Lena was starting to get hungry. In her emotional state, she'd forgotten about lunch and realised she hadn't finished her breakfast after Horace had interrupted it. Although she didn't feel like facing anyone, Mario would let her eat alone in the kitchen, she thought, unbolting the library doors and heading in that direction.

Back in Horace's office, Theo was doing his best to stay calm. 'Sir,' he stepped towards the officer leafing through their papers. 'This man is a liar.'

'No more of a liar than you are!' Horace yelled.

'Sir, if you could please let me explain—' But Theo couldn't finish his sentence because at that moment, he saw the guards to his left grasp Alexandre's arms. Thankfully Alexandre was too fast for them. He'd slunk towards the door when all the attention was on Theo.

'Theo! Go!' Alexandre yelled as he ducked and began to sprint down the hallway. Theo reacted immediately, flipping over Horace's armchair and taking off in the opposite direction. Alexandre moved swiftly, but he hit a dead end. When he turned, two guards were right behind him. One of them raised his fist, punched Alexandre squarely on the side of his head and watched, snarling as the young apprentice slumped to the ground.

At the opposite end of the hallway, Theo managed to head off the guards chasing him, but was now embroiled in a struggle with the head officer.

One hallway over, Lena was just about to enter the kitchen when she heard yelling. It sounded like German. Were they being searched again, she wondered, fear rising when she thought of the stolen items hidden in Alexandre's room. Panicking, she let the kitchen door bang shut and followed the noise.

Hearing the commotion outside, other performers had begun to emerge cautiously from their carriages. As Lena drew closer to Horace's office, her father's voice became unmistakable. Her heart raced as she walked as fast as she could.

'Papa?'

She rounded the corner only to see Theo in the grip of a uniformed guard. 'Papa!' she screamed. Theo's eyes met hers.

'Lena! Get out of here!'

Lena stood frozen to the spot. Her father's lips moved again but she couldn't hear anything. This couldn't be happening, not to Theo. Her father was the one who stuck his neck out for an orphan when no one else would. Her father was the one who, despite his transgressions while married, had never abandoned her. Her father was the one who had brought the entire universe to her, when she wasn't able to go out on foot and see it for herself. In that moment, she saw him clearly, and knew her love for him would overcome her temporary anger. She squeezed her eyes shut, hoping that when she opened them again, the hallway would be empty, the guards gone, her father free.

But the guard remained, clutching Theo tightly. Hearing the sounds of another struggle behind her, Lena turned and saw Alexandre slumped in a corner at the opposite end of the hallway. She rushed towards him. 'Alexandre, get up!'

He moaned groggily. 'Lena?'

Lena tugged desperately at his sleeve. 'We have to get out of here!' She slapped his face. But it was no use. From the corner of her eye, Lena saw a sharp movement. A guard had spotted her hovering over Alexandre and was now making his way towards her. 'Alexandre. Move!' she shrieked.

'Lena!' It was her father. He could see the guard advancing. Lena locked eyes with her father and he yelled with more urgency than she had ever heard. 'Lena. Go!'

Lena's face crumpled as she took one last look at Alexandre. She slipped off her dove bracelet and quickly shoved it in his pocket, tears spilling down her face. 'Alexandre. I'm so sorry.' And then she turned in the opposite direction, ignoring the pain in her legs and took off, her mind going into survival mode. She knew she couldn't outpace the guards, so she twisted back on herself and quickly sidestepped into a parallel hallway, away from Horace's study. From there, she ducked into one of the side rooms, closing the door quietly and locking the door. She leaned against it, breathing heavily. The guards may be fast, but she knew the circus and its hallways like the back of her hand. From outside, she heard the sound of guards rushing past and her father's voice.

'Don't be scared, Lena! I will find you. I promise!'

Closing her eyes and fighting back tears, Lena waited. She knew where she had to go. When she ceased to hear voices on the other side, she unlocked the door and peeked outside. She knew they'd still be looking for her. Once she was sure the way was clear, she took off again, darting in and out of crevices, alcoves, and curtains, until she arrived at the entrance to the Mirage Maze.

Once inside, she turned left and right and left and right, moving at a pace accelerated by the fear clawing at her insides. She didn't stop until she arrived at the Proteus cabinet.

Flinging the mirrored panels open, Lena limped in and collapsed, her legs throbbing, and carefully pushed the panels together until they were flush with each other. She waited, trembling, worried that the guards would be able to detect the beating

202

of her heart, the panting of her breath. She heard footsteps run past her once. Twice. She could hear more guards entering the maze, shouting at each other in German.

Terrified, Lena tore off her braces and clutched her head in her hands. She closed her eyes and began reciting a prayer over and over in her mind. *Please. Let them be ok. I promise I'll forgive Papa. I promise to never ask for things to be different again. I promise to be happy with what I have. I promise to stay away from Alexandre. Please!* She prayed and prayed as her father's words *I will find you. I promise*, echoed in her ears.

CHAPTER TWENTY-FOUR

Lena didn't know how long she stayed inside the Proteus cabinet but at some point, she drifted off to sleep. When she awoke, night had fallen and a fine drizzle was coating the panels that shielded her. Shivering, she listened for the sounds of the Germans, but all she could hear were members of the cast calling her name. She closed her eyes, wishing she could hide in the maze forever. But she knew she had to face whatever was on the other side, so she fastened her braces, pushed apart the mirrors and began walking towards the exit.

It was Anna Maria who spotted her first. She cried out, rushing to Lena's side and wrapped her arms around her tightly.

'Don't worry. We'll find them.'

Lena's heart lifted when she heard Anna Maria's words. If she said they would find them, it meant they were still alive. It meant that there was a chance.

At the demands of the cast, Horace extended the circus' stay in Rouen. The performers had abandoned their duties, and instead spent their days walking the streets of the small town, asking around for Theo and Alexandre. Jussi took Lena to the local police station, but as they walked away after filing their report, Lena felt her stomach drop: she knew the police were too afraid to go up against the SS. They'd do whatever they had to keep themselves safe.

Through all of this, Lena was comforted by the performers, who tried to keep her spirits up. Mario made her favourite foods, ensuring a plate was delivered to her room at each meal. Jussi, Anna Maria and Nneka took turns sitting by her bedside each evening, waiting until she'd fallen asleep. Dr. Wilson encouraged her to continue with her therapy sessions, knowing that having something to do would be good for her. Even some of the younger performers were going out of their way to check in on her, inviting her to take part in their games.

Yet even with all the extra help, Lena struggled to see past the fear enshrouding her. It felt like her whole life had been put on hold indefinitely and that she wouldn't be able to think about anything else until her father and Alexandre were found.

A week of waiting turned into two. With each passing day, Lena sank deeper into a pit of despair, terrified of what the next day would bring.

After hearing nothing for almost three weeks, Jussi and Anna Maria called Lena into the library one afternoon.

'What is it?' she asked, anxiety rising in her when she saw their facial expressions.

'Lena,' Jussi began. 'One of the townsfolk said they'd seen uniformed officers going in and out of an old house on the outskirts of town.'

Lena brightened. 'You found them?'

Jussi paused, struggling to get his next words out. 'There was a fire. It doesn't look like there were any survivors.'

'What?'

'The house burned down,' Anna Maria said gently.

'But, we don't know for certain they were there!' Lena exclaimed. Anna Maria and Jussi exchanged a glance and then Lena watched as Jussi unfurled his fingers to reveal Alexandre's mother's necklace. Charred on the tips, the once bright diamond star shone no more. She felt her voice catch in her throat. 'No,' she whispered.

'The remains of six male bodies were found—'

'No,' Lena wailed. 'He told me he'd come back!'

'Lena,' Anna Maria tried to embrace the young girl, but Lena pushed her away fiercely. She rushed out of the library, walking as quickly as she could to Horace's study, and barged in without knocking. When Horace looked up from his desk, Lena could tell from his facial expression that he'd heard the news.

'My dear, I'm so sorry. I never meant for this to happen!'

'Didn't you?' Lena yelled. 'You planned this! You wanted them gone.'

Horace rose from his desk. 'I wanted no such thing! But my circus was at risk! Your father was going to leave me with nothing. I did what I had to do!'

'My father would never betray you the way you betrayed him,' Lena spat. 'He was a trustworthy man!'

'Then why was he planning to leave the country?'

Lena frowned. 'What?'

'Chadwick found asylum papers to America amongst his belongings,' Horace said, stepping out from behind his desk, his eyes narrowing.

'But, he never said anything.'

'That's how lies work, Lena. A secret escape, a hidden affair.' Horace watched the young girl like a hawk. 'It seems even you didn't know your father as well as you thought.' He knew he was rubbing salt in her wound, but he was sick of everyone blaming him for the tragic turn of events. If Theo hadn't been trying to leave in the first place, he would still be safely on board.

'You're a liar!' Lena choked, unwilling to believe him. She began pulling at the books lining the opulent shelves, throwing them on the ground in a fit of fury when Anna Maria and Jussi burst into the study.

'Lena!' Anna Maria said. She rushed over to her and grabbed her by her shoulders. At first, she felt the girl resist but then Lena

207

collapsed against her chest, weeping. 'Come. You shouldn't be here,' she said soothingly as Jussi hoisted Lena into his arms. Horace watched as the trio left, the girl looking like a tiny, helpless baby bird, crying for a parent that would never return.

Years ago, Lena remembered asking her father what he did after her mother died.

'In the Greek Orthodox church,' Theo said, 'we mourn the deceased for forty days.'

'What does "mourn" mean?'

'It means you allow yourself to be sad. It takes time to process losing someone you loved.'

'Did I mourn?'

'You were so little, but yes, I'm sure you felt some part of her leave.'

'I don't remember.'

'It's ok. The important thing is after you finish mourning, you have to keep living. Your mother wouldn't have wanted us to be sad forever, only looking to the past.'

Lena thought about that conversation now, as she sat in the dining hall surrounded by cast members who'd come out to remember her father and Alexandre. Death, she'd quickly realised, brought out different things in different people. Some of the performers wore their emotions publicly, unashamed to cry. Others dealt with it by reminiscing about the good times they'd had. Still others mourned in private, taking care to avoid Lena because they felt uncomfortable in her presence.

Lena didn't know what she felt. She moved through each day as though stuck in a fog, repeating the same stock responses to everyone who asked how she was feeling. She spent most of her time in her carriage alone, staring up at the ceiling, an ache permeating her gut that she was sure would never fade. She'd completely lost her appetite and turned her nose up at meals.

'Lena,' Mario would say, looking sadly at the plates gathering in the hallway. 'You must keep your strength up.' But it was no use.

The only time she felt any kind of peace was when she slept and even then, it was fleeting. She'd wake up each morning, the tiny gap between dreaming and reality setting in providing the one moment of respite in her days.

'I can't do this anymore,' Lena whispered during a physical therapy session, her face crumpling as she finally admitted defeat. She sent her cane scuttling across the ground as she slid to the floor, cradling her head in her hands.

'You're doing marvellously,' Dr. Wilson coaxed.

'Everyone who loved me is gone,' she said, beginning to cry, as if only realising it for the first time.

Dr. Wilson knelt down. 'That's not true. I'm still here. And so is Anna Maria and Jussi and a whole host of people who love you.'

Lena pointed to her legs, tears streaming down her face. 'What's the point?'

Dr. Wilson's face softened. 'The point,' he said gently, hooking his arms underneath hers and hoisting her up like a puppet, 'is that you must continue to live your life.'

'I can't.'

'Perhaps not this second, but you will. Think about what kind of person your father would have wanted you to be. Then be that person. Even though he's not here, you can still make him proud.'

In September, a month after Theo and Alexandre had disappeared, Horace decided it was time to move on and the circus set off for England. As the train drew closer to London, Lena stared out the window, shivering. The day was cold and grey, not unlike the atmosphere onboard the train, she thought. Whereas the arrival at Victoria usually meant the start of rehearsals for the new tour, Horace had postponed the upcoming season, citing a need to 'refocus his creative efforts' as the reason. But Lena knew it was because the cast no longer trusted him. A third had resigned and among the performers that remained, whispers circulated every day about who would be next. She knew she should try to figure out her own way forward, but she was finding it difficult to settle back into her old routine. How could she, when there was nothing from her former life to go back to?

One evening, as she rummaged through her cupboard trying to find an extra blanket, she caught sight of the planets from the orrery Alexandre had gifted her. She'd dismantled it soon after his death, finding it unbearable to look at. But now the smooth malachite rock of Neptune gleamed like a beacon of light and she felt something catch inside her. Stumbling backwards, she curled up next to her bed, shaking. She dared not tell anyone what she was thinking for fear that they would dismiss her feelings as child's play. But in the solitude of her carriage, she knew that her feelings for him were true and pure. She'd loved him. It was a big word, *love*, and not one that she would toss around carelessly. But no matter how hard she tried to deny it, the person she had loved was gone and now she'd have to live with the weight of how she'd treated him for the rest of her life. Regret, she thought, forcing herself to stand up and climb into bed, was a terrible thing. As she tried to sleep, she wondered if the sadness weighing her down would ever lift.

Then one morning – she wasn't quite sure which, because she was no longer keeping track of time – she woke up and didn't feel quite as bad. She waited in bed, waiting for the sinking feeling she'd come to know so well to resurface. But a few minutes passed and it still wasn't there. She removed her covers and sat up.

Not wanting to push things, she went about her day as normal, only this time, she finished the meals Mario had left outside. In the afternoon, she cracked a book open and read a few pages.

The next day, she did the same. At the end of the week, she ventured into the kitchen, blushing when everyone turned to look at her as she entered.

'Ai, Lena! There is colour in your face!' Mario said warmly, as he steered her towards the pot of pasta he'd been fussing over. 'Try this,' he said, holding out a wooden spoon.

Lena spooned some of the food into her mouth and chewed on it thoughtfully. 'It's good,' she said, nodding. 'Very good.' And then she smiled.

Later that afternoon, as she sat at her desk re-reading some of her old exam notes, she caught sight of her cane.

Think of the person your father would have wanted you to be. Then be that person.

Lena bit her lower lip. And then, before she could change her mind, she fastened her braces, grabbed the cane she'd been using in her therapy sessions and set off for the infirmary carriage.

She found Dr. Wilson hunched over an assortment of ointments he was labelling.

'Lena?' he asked, upon seeing her.

Lena gripped the doorframe with one hand and held out the cane with the other. 'Are you busy?'

A few days after resuming her therapy sessions, Lena felt brave enough to venture into her father's carriage, which had sat untouched since his capture. As she entered the space she'd shared with him for so many years, a lifetime of happy memories came flooding back. Her father had never been the neatest person, but now she looked upon the stacks of papers and unfolded clothes with affection. She plucked a sweater off a chair and lifted it to her face, rubbing it against her cheek, before folding it.

After she'd done the same with all the clothes, she opened his dresser to put everything away. As she made room for the sweaters, she glimpsed a bulky envelope tucked at the back.

Curious, Lena pulled it out and dumped the contents on his bed. The first paper she picked up had a heading that read 'St. Ives School for Girls – Application for Admission.' She scanned it, then

211

flipped it over to see a list titled 'Alternative Schools in America'. As she read the list, it dawned on her that Horace wasn't lying. Her father was planning to leave the circus. Theo knew Lena wasn't going to be able to get the education she desired and even though he'd tried to stop her from going to boarding school, if this list was any indication, he'd changed his mind. He also knew how dangerous it was for Alexandre to stay in Europe, so he'd made the ultimate sacrifice and had been preparing to give up his life's work for them.

In a thick, smaller envelope, Lena found a stack of bills with a note in Alexandre's handwriting:

I don't need your money to be her friend.

Feeling her stomach lurch, she counted out the bills one by one. It was all there. He hadn't spent a penny.

Her heart thumping, Lena flicked through the remaining documents. When she found the letter from Isabella to her father, she re-read it, waiting for the resentment to grab hold of her. But all she felt was sadness. Because her father had done the right thing when it counted. He'd chosen her and her mother over this woman.

I will find you. I promise. The last words her father spoke flooded her ears. Frowning, she scanned the room, wondering if there was more to what he'd said than she initially thought. Perhaps there was a hidden meaning, something he wanted her to find, or do. She was the straightforward one, forever taking things at face value. But her father was never like that.

She began tapping at the floorboards and pulling open cupboards, hunting for something unseen. She willed herself to find a note, a reminder, a talisman – some kind of sign that her father was going to come back to her safely. She wanted to believe that the past month had been a terrible trick and that with the snap of her fingers, everything would return to normal.

And so she looked. And looked. But it was no use. He was a master and had vanished, without a trace.

PART II

Nothing must be left to chance in a magical performance.

—DAVID DEVANT

CHAPTER TWENTY-FIVE

September 1942 – Theresienstadt, Czechoslovakia

'Go on, keep moving.' The Czech gendarme pushed the young woman standing a few feet in front of Alexandre.

'Please, sir,' she whispered, stumbling forwards. 'Some water?'

'Up there.' He nodded towards a set of wrought iron gates ahead. The woman turned around and addressed the line that snaked back at least fifty feet.

'Does anyone have any water?'

Alexandre craned his neck and saw that she was cradling a tiny baby in her arms. That did it. He pushed through the crowd, removed a small flask from his bag and pressed into her palm.

'Bless you,' she shot him a grateful smile. 'We were crammed on the trains. Four hours of standing. Nothing to eat or drink.' She shook her head as she cradled her baby, her black curls bobbing delicately around her face.

Alexandre opened his mouth to respond but before he could do so, a hand on his shoulder whirled him around. It was the gendarme. 'No talking until you register,' he ordered.

'Ok,' Alexandre conceded, falling back in the queue as they passed under a passageway with the words *Arbeit Macht Frei* arcing in dark block capitals over the top. Alexandre shuddered and stole a quick glance at Theo, standing a few feet behind him, but failed to catch his eye. The line was snaking forward at a glacial pace. While he waited, Alexandre replayed the events that had led them to this point.

After the guards had barged into Horace's study that day, Alexandre thought they were done for. He prayed that the bullet they were going to put in his head would be spot on target and that he wouldn't suffer. But then he had overheard a conversation between two of the guards, and the nature of Horace's initial deal became clear.

After their capture, they were held in a house on the outskirts of Rouen while a suitable punishment was discussed. Harbouring a Jewish fugitive was a crime, the officer had pointed out, and repercussions would be severe. But over a night of card magic and port, Theo managed to convince the guards that hiding Alexandre had been Horace's idea, not his, and would the guards give the two illusionists one last chance to prove themselves? In the end, the officer agreed to spare their lives in exchange for a year of hard labour and performances in a spa town being built in Czechoslovakia for prominent Jews.

'We've a selection of fine opera singers, a few artists, some poets and a very talented children's choir. But a pair of illusionists would really make it stand out.'

If after a year, the guard continued, they completed the contract he'd written up in a suitable manner, they'd be free to leave.

They weren't meant to leave Rouen until the end of September, but one night, a fire broke out, hastening their leave. Alexandre remembered waking up in a panic, images of that night in the barn flashing frantically in his head. It was only after a guard rushed in, screaming at them to run, that he realised it was real. He'd grabbed for Lena's bracelet, but couldn't find his mother's necklace in time. A moment later, he was standing in a field with Theo and some of the guards, watching the house and the guards who hadn't made it out go up in flames. He looked up to see the stars that always brought him so much comfort. But the fire had spread its smoke and ash across the sky, blocking his view, and he shed a tear, having never felt so alone.

Soon after, they were crammed on a train heading east and now they found themselves here, ready to begin their contract. It seemed like a brilliant deal at the time – but as Alexandre scanned the town, taking in the derelict buildings and the unreasonably high level of security, he began to wonder what they'd gotten themselves into.

'This way to the *Sluice*,' the gendarme said, pointing to a grey-ish building. 'For check-in.'

Alexandre shuffled forward and surveyed the scene unfolding around him. The place was grey, distasteful and unwelcoming. Ahead of them, a line of guards searched through each person's bag, taking what they wanted, before sending the residents on their way. Alexandre stopped in front of an SS officer who towered over him.

'Bag,' he ordered, passing his hand over the gleaming barrel of his gun. Alexandre slipped his bag off his shoulder. 'Jacket.'

Alexandre shook his head. The money he'd earned from the World of Wonders was rolled up safely inside his front pocket.

'It wasn't a question,' the guard snarled.

Reluctantly, Alexandre took off his jacket, watching as the guard turned out the pockets until he found the roll of bills. He unfurled it and counted the bills out one by one, then turned to leave the building.

'Hey!' Alexandre shouted. 'That's mine!'

'Exchange,' the guard said, by way of explanation.

Alexandre waited until he was out of sight, then reached into the pocket of his trousers, taking out Lena's bracelet. He didn't remember her doing it but Lena must have slipped it to him during the capture outside Horace's study. When he'd found it two days later, he'd nearly cried. He wasn't about to let it get away from him, so he slipped it under his tongue.

217

When the guard returned, he handed Alexandre a stack of what looked like play money

'*Ghetto gold*,' he said. 'For shops.' He pointed to the town square. Alexandre craned his neck, his eyes roving over the buildings, searching for a storefront.

'There are no shops.'

'You build. Now go.'

Outside, Alexandre waited until Theo had finished with the guards. 'They take all your money too?'

Theo pursed his lips and nodded grimly. A shrill whistle pierced the sky, silencing the murmuring crowd. A guard held up his hand.

'All women and children will follow me. Men,' he pointed to another guard who stood at the far corner of the courtyard. 'Follow him.'

Theo shifted his bag. 'Come on.'

The guard led the men to a group of buildings known as barracks. The town had a number of main housing units, he explained. The bulk of the residents stayed in the Dresden, Magdeburg or Sudeten barracks. Theo and Alexandre would be in Hanover. 'It's where most of the performers live,' he said, leading them up a flight of stone steps and coming to a halt in front of a room with no door. 'A tour of the town, followed by a list of work assignments will start in ten minutes downstairs. Don't be late.'

The two illusionists peered into the doorframe, surveying their new living quarters. The room was tiny, Alexandre thought, as he stepped inside. It had no cabinets, no chairs, and no storage facilities. In one corner, a crude table constructed out of scraps of wood held four filthy mattresses rolled up on top. There were no windows and no main source of lighting, save for a cracked oil lamp that sat woefully on one side. The whole place was eerily reminiscent of the squalid shacks and dilapidated hovels

Alexandre used to stay in with his parents, and for a moment he felt like he had regressed back in time.

'It's not so bad,' Theo said, putting on a brave face as he inspected the walls. 'A year will go by fast,' he said, noticing the horrified look on Alexandre's face. 'The important thing is we have each other.'

A few minutes later, Theo and Alexandre joined the rest of the new residents outside for their tour. As an SS guard led them around the town, Alexandre struggled to keep pace. According to the guard, Theresienstadt spanned roughly a kilometre and in addition to the barracks, housed a school, library, kitchen, hospital, vegetable garden, workshops and space for cultural performances. Alexandre's eyes widened as he tried to take in everything the guard was pointing out. He noticed a few shops and made a mental note to ask the guard about the proposed coffee shop being built later.

'We try to uphold a high standard of living for our residents,' the guard said proudly. Alexandre frowned, thinking back to the mattresses in his room and the sunken faces he'd glimpsed from some of the residents he'd passed during the tour. So far, Theresienstadt felt more like a prison than a growing cultural town for Jews.

As they approached what seemed to be the central area of the town, Alexandre shook Theo's arm. 'Look!' he yelled, pointing to a large circus tent dwarfing the main square. 'Is this where we'll perform?' he asked, excited at the sight of something familiar.

'No – it's being used as a workshop. Come this way.' The guard led them around the main square circus tent and out into an opening. On one side, there was a small, raised platform surrounded by a few chairs.

'Rehearsals and shows will take place here, thrice per week. You will be monitored for performance content. Nothing too political or outlandish,' he said. 'Shows happen in the evenings and you're expected to be at every single one. Occasionally there will be special events or additional shows in other venues across the town, but mostly, it will be the residents of the town watching. Try to keep morale up,' he said, as they moved on from the rehearsal area. 'It's important.'

Once the tour had finished, the guard explained what each of their work assignments would be. Both Theo and Alexandre would be placed in the *aufbaukommando*, he explained, walking them to the carpentry workshop known as *Badhausgasse*. Alexandre peered in the splintered doorway, taking in the mainly elderly faces, drawn with exhaustion, staring back at him. When he turned back, the guard was holding out two uniforms.

'Put these on. Your contract begins now.'

Later that night, Alexandre sat on the floor of his new room, massaging his hands. He'd spent seven hours hunched over a lathe, trying to smooth a wheel in less than ideal light. He'd never used a lathe before, but luckily Theo had shown him the basics, coming over every half hour to check on his progress. His back ached and his eyes were burning from concentrating all day and a lack of food.

He sighed, trying to recount all the information the guard had thrown at them earlier. The men couldn't socialise with the women after hours and were forced to sleep separately at all times. Children got to eat first in the mess hall. Work was to be completed during the hours of 8 am and 7 pm, every day. Curfew was at 10 p.m. If they were found wandering around after that, there would be repercussions.

'Hello.' A man with a thick Russian accent had entered their room. He was followed by another man who was eyeing Theo and Alexandre suspiciously. 'You are new? I'm Vasily.' He had sandy blonde hair, a chiselled nose, ruddy cheeks and striking blue eyes that matched Alexandre's. He was about the same height as Theo and very fit. He walked forward gracefully and shook Alexandre's hand. 'I'm from Leningrad. My sister, Natalia, she's living in Magdeburg. We are dancers. And you?'

'Illusionists,' Theo said.

Vasily brightened. 'Wow. Magic! This is Attila,' he pointed to the other man. Attila grunted a hello to the new arrivals but didn't extend his hand. He was squat, but built like an athlete, Alexandre could see the compact muscles that bulged underneath the dirty white vest he wore.

'Where are you from?' Theo asked.

'Hungary,' Attila answered. 'I gymnast. I trying for Olympic medal in Berlin. Training eight hours a day. And then?' He made a fist with one hand and punched his other palm. 'Germans crush dream.'

'Attila always angry. But excellent athlete,' Vasily explained. He glanced at the bags Theo and Alexandre had brought in earlier. 'You bring food?'

'We did, but they took all of it,' Theo replied.

'I managed to save something,' Alexandre said, pulling out a bar of Cadbury's chocolate from his bag. Vasily's face lit up.

'Cadbury!' He snatched it out of Alexandre's hand, holding it closer to the oil lamp. 'You share?'

Alexandre shrugged. 'You can have it.'

'Thank you!' Vasily tore open the bright purple paper, running his hands over the shiny gold foil inside. He broke off a tiny square and, with trembling hands, put it in his mouth. He closed his eyes, savouring the taste.

'I guess you don't get much chocolate around here,' Alexandre said. He pointed to the mattresses in the corner. 'Are those ours?'

Vasily nodded. 'Yes, but you only open when you lie down. Otherwise bugs coming in.'

Alexandre made a face. 'How long have you been here?'

'Maybe . . . six months? Attila here almost one year,' Vasily said, nibbling on another piece of chocolate.

'And you perform?' Theo asked. The two men nodded. 'Every night?'

'Two, three nights a week. Maybe more. In between work, we rehearsing with everyone, but most people do solo acts,' Attila said.

'When is your contract over?' Alexandre asked.

'Contract?' Vasily frowned. 'What is contract?'

'You have contract?' Attila demanded.

'No,' Theo replied smoothly. 'We simply wanted to know if there was an end in sight for the performers. We certainly wouldn't want to be out of work.'

Attila, who had taken a square of chocolate from Vasily, suddenly seemed very interested in the illusionists. He unfurled their mattresses laying them on the floor. 'You sit. Must be tired.'

Alexandre scrunched up his face and scanned the room again. 'Does anyone else live here?'

'So many come in – opera singers, writers, artists – but they all dead,' Attila said. 'Typhus, sometimes consumption. Maybe fifty people dead from this room since I arrive,' he added. 'But this place good,' he said, noticing the alarmed looks on Theo and Alexandre's faces. 'Some rooms? Twenty, thirty people. In same size.'

Alexandre's stomach lurched. What kind of living conditions had they walked into? The four men sat crouched around the lamp, Vasily and Attila explaining everything they'd learned the past few months. The rooms were tiny, but they never complained. As performers, they were given extra perks that the ordinary residents didn't get. The most important thing, apart from not irritating the guards, Vasily said, was to stay healthy. Residents got sick all the time and died. Alexandre was hardly surprised. Grit collected on the stone floors and tiny bugs scuttled across the walls and hallways. The rooms stank but then, so did everything else. As for personal hygiene, Vasily had said they could shower in groups, but there was only ever cold water available and rarely any soap.

'Have the guards ever hurt you?' Theo inquired.

Vasily and Attila exchanged a glance. 'So far, we lucky. Some people, not so lucky. You . . .' he took a deep breath, trying to find the right words, 'you follow rules. Less chance of being hurt.'

'Do people leave?' Alexandre asked.

Vasily considered this. 'People go to town. But they need guard. And always returning. Except when big group leaves.'

Theo frowned. 'What do you mean?'

Vasily shrugged, sucking on another piece of chocolate. 'Sometimes big group leaves on train. Thousands of people, walking out in big group. Guards say going to different town and start building place like this.'

'People promise to send postcards, but I never get,' Attila lamented.

A ripple of cold fear shot through Alexandre's spine. 'But they come back, right?'

Vasily shook his head. 'No. If big group leave, they never coming back,' he said, licking a bit of chocolate that had melted on his fingers. 'We never seeing them again.'

CHAPTER TWENTY-SIX

October 1942 – London, England

In the hazy glow of his study, Horace spun the globe that sat on his desk and watched it twirl. He'd had it commissioned by Hawksbury & Co. Globemakers after his first year in business. It was the only one of its kind in the world. With a traditional map done up in various shades of grey as its base, the globe tracked the inaugural journey of the World of Wonders across Europe. The painter had customised it with tiny details – a miniature acrobat in Minsk, an arc of tiny juggling balls shining over Italy – all hand-painted in gold and blue watercolours.

'Chadwick,' he said. 'The time has come for a new chapter.'

Chadwick, who'd been struggling to beat the dust out of the velvet draperies, immediately dropped the cane and scrambled to the ottoman across from Horace. 'New chapter?'

Horace nodded, his gaze narrowing as he thought back to the last few weeks. His cast had been at a standoff. A group of them had left and the ones who did stay were refusing to work or rehearse. Horace had presumed it a temporary matter, but four weeks in, things showed no signs of improving. With his reputation in tatters, he needed to make a big change.

He took a sip of his whiskey and dragged his finger across the globe, forcing it to stop at Asia. China. Japan. Thailand. India. As he looked at the countries, he felt a familiar surge of energy bubbling inside, the same kind that had taken hold of him when he was launching the World of Wonders. Yes, he thought, grabbing a blue velvet notebook to write in. He would create a new tour. A magical journey through the Far East. He could even redo the carriages in gold and red to match the exotic climate of their new destination.

'We're going East. To the land of spices and tropical birds and beaches.'

'How will we transport everyone?'

'Forget them. I'll find new performers. Thai acrobats and Sri Lankan fire walkers,' his voice swelling as he dipped his pen in Indian ink. 'Malaysian ballerinas. And animals! We'll have an exotic menagerie for the first time!' Horace scribbled notes at a breath-taking pace as the ideas came to him. It was all coming together. It would be bigger and better and reach an entirely new, untapped audience. Any circus could be successful in Europe. The real power nowadays lay outside the continent and Horace was going to see to it that he succeeded first.

'What about Lena?' Chadwick asked.

Horace frowned. In the weeks since the incident, he'd done his best to avoid the girl. 'Someone will take her.'

'But no one's offered!'

Horace swirled the last of his whiskey, watching the tawny liquid sloshing around. 'We'll wait a few weeks, put out some requests. If no one here will have her, we'll deposit her in an orphanage.'

Outside Horace's study, Lena felt her face go red. After weeks of emotionally challenging work, she'd finished organising her father's carriage and had come to return the key. But having heard Horace's plan, she slipped the key into the pocket of her jumper. Grasping her cane, she walked back to her carriage as quickly as she could.

Once inside, she curled up on her bed, pulling her blanket around her, Horace's words burrowing deep into her brain. She didn't care what he thought. But was he right about everyone else? Was that how the cast saw her, as nothing more than a burden? At 13, she was still too young to be without a legal guardian, but far too old to be adopted by a family who would want her. She had hoped that someone from the circus – Anna Maria or Dr. Wilson – would take care of her if that's what it came down to, but Horace was right. No one had explicitly offered and Lena didn't want to be seen as a charity case.

She glanced at her cane and thought back to something Clara had written in one of her letters. *Your greatest achievements often grow out of the worst circumstances.* Then she lit a candle and got to work.

The train ride from Victoria to Dorset was long. Lena had never taken the train alone and the sheer crush of people with harried looks on their faces unnerved her. By the time she folded herself into the taxi towards her final destination, all she wanted was go to bed.

She thought back guiltily to a few hours earlier, when she'd left the circus as dawn broke, with little more than a bag of clothing and a few necessities and keepsakes – the necklaces from her father and Alexandre's mother, money, and the planet Neptune from her orrery. She hadn't said goodbye as she'd made her way to the bustling central station in the heart of the British capital and she ached now, thinking of Anna Maria and Jussi rushing to and fro, looking for her. But she couldn't say goodbye. Farewells were too painful, too long-drawn out, she thought, gazing out the window at the passing English countryside. And if there was one thing she was certain of, it was that the only way she was going to move on from what had happened was to leave.

'Nearly there,' the driver announced and Lena perked up as they turned down a gravel road and approached the stately boarding school. The driver steered the taxi around the circular driveway, coming to a stop in front of the main doors.

'Now you's run inside,' he said, 'and I'll get your bags.'

Lena lifted her cane off her lap and stepped onto the gravel driveway. The Briarwood School was exactly as she'd imagined. An old-fashioned manor house with ivy creeping up the walls, perfectly manicured fields that sprawled for days and neatly trimmed rose bushes dotting the front lawn. On a tennis court across the way, two girls in green and grey uniforms practised their serves. Suddenly she didn't know what she was doing. Why had she thought this was a good idea? What if Clara didn't want her?

'Alright, love?'

'Yes,' Lena said. She clenched her fists and took a deep breath as she walked forward. Once inside, she approached the administration office. 'Hello,' she said, trying to sound authoritative. 'I'm looking for a Miss Clara Smith.'

The secretary peered at the young girl standing before her. 'Have you got a mother or father?'

'No,' Lena replied. 'Only me.'

The secretary looked at her with a pregnant pause. 'Whom should I say is calling?'

Lena hesitated. 'A good friend.'

'One moment.' The secretary walked away, turning around to look back at Lena before she disappeared up a staircase. Lena waited, drumming her fingers on the desk. After a few minutes, she heard footsteps approaching and suddenly, there was Clara, wearing a brown and red tea dress, her hair pinned up, her face free of makeup save for a slash of bright red lipstick. Lena immediately felt a wave of relief wash over her upon spotting her old governess.

'Yes?' Clara said, before registering who was standing in front of her. 'Lena? My goodness! What are you doing here?'

'Hello,' Lena replied in a small voice. And then she crumpled into Clara's outstretched arms, the weight of all that she'd lost finally hitting her.

CHAPTER TWENTY-SEVEN

February 1943 – Theresienstadt, Czechoslovakia

The girl was here again, the same one Alexandre had seen at yesterday's rehearsal. He recognised her instantly because of her hair – thick, shiny waves that cascaded across her back, with strands shimmering like gold whenever they caught the light of the harsh winter sun. That hair, he thought to himself the minute he saw it, did not belong to someone who had been in Theresienstadt more than a week, and it sparked something within him, a tiny bit of hope that had long gone dormant.

In the five months since he and Theo had arrived, there'd been very little to be hopeful about. Living in the garrison town was like being in a sweat shop. The work in *Badhausgasse* was gruelling and made worse by the dip in temperatures a month in. Alexandre often shivered as he sat hunched over his workbench, rough calluses lining his once smooth hands, the smell of sawdust permanently a part of him. Although he was grateful to have the chance to perform in the shows, the lack of freedom to innovate had begun to temper his motivation. For the past month, he and Theo had resorted to doing cheap parlour tricks, garnering lukewarm applause from the audience who had grown tired of seeing the same thing. But what could they do? They weren't allowed to send for any equipment or costumes. There were only so many times one could pull a scarf out of a hat before it became routine.

Even though he played in weekly football matches in the Liga Theresienstadt, ate regular meals (if one could call the stale bread and mouldy vegetables they were served 'meals'), and visited the town café and shops, the entire set up was far too controlling for his liking. Every week, hundreds of new residents arrived, but they weren't doing anything to increase living capacity. The hygiene practices were non-existent. At least a hundred people Alexandre had met since he arrived had contracted tuberculosis and died since he'd arrived. Yes, a lot of the residents were elderly, but still, there were times when it felt like he was living in a cemetary.

A few weeks in, he'd tried to get a letter out to Lena, but heard nothing back. But he kept writing, hoping that one would reach her. It was only after a resident mentioned they monitored every letter that left the place, ensuring that only good things were written, that Alexandre realised his correspondence had likely never made it past the fortress walls.

The bitter winter that set in soon after they arrived had done little to help matters, the cold and grey dulling what little spark he had left. And he wasn't alone. Everyone underwent a transformation as they walked the long trek from Bohusovic train station to the town, as though marching to their eventual demise. It wasn't uncommon for Alexandre to see someone a few weeks after they'd first met, now sporting a listless, hollow expression, like they'd resigned themselves to their fate.

So it was easy to spot the new girl, her whole demeanour shining like a beacon in a sea of darkness.

'Let's go again,' Theo said, tapping Alexandre on the shoulder. Alexandre turned his attention back to the trick he and Theo were practising, but found he couldn't concentrate. When Theo finally excused him, Alexandre jumped off the rotting wood stage and pushed through the crowd of people all walking back from their

230

daily tasks, trying to catch a glimpse of that golden hair. But by the time the crowd had dispersed, the girl was gone.

Later that evening, Alexandre forced the cold soup they were served each day down his throat, lamenting the fact that he'd ever complained about Mario's potato chowder at the circus.

'May I sit please?'

Startled, Alexandre glanced up. The girl he'd been looking for earlier was standing in front of him, holding a meal tray.

'Of course,' he replied, feeling his heart speed up.

'Thanks,' she said, smiling as she sat. 'I'm Leike.' Her voice was soft and sounded like dew drops falling on fresh cut grass.

'Alexandre,' he replied, unable to take his eyes off her. Up close, she was even more beautiful. She had clear, fresh skin, not yet marred by the drudgery of the town. Her eyes were like tiny pools of green, with hazel swirls that danced brightly when she spoke. And that hair – thick, caramel-flecked hair, that bounced every time she moved her head. Alexandre tried to cover his hands with the edges of his ragged shirt sleeves. He hadn't had a haircut, a nail trim or a proper shower since he'd left the circus, and he was suddenly embarrassed by how he must look to her. 'Did you just arrive?'

She nodded. 'Yesterday. I'm in Schneider group, for sewing. I saw you rehearsing. Is it for the show?'

Alexandre nodded, pleased that she recognised him. 'That was me and Theo, the other illusionist.'

'You were amazing,' she said. 'I can't wait to see it.'

As they ate, Leike told him that her parents were killed by the SS after a raid on their street in Vienna. Her younger brother got lost amidst the scramble to flee, but Leike was caught. She had no idea where her brother was now, or if he was even alive. She'd spent a few months in another town before receiving word about an opening in Theresienstadt for a violinist.

231

'At first, I was relieved,' she said, her eyes brightening briefly. 'But when I got here,' Leike glanced around uneasily, 'I don't know why, but something feels off.'

Alexandre's stomach churned as he grappled with whether or not to be honest with her. After Lena, he'd promised himself he was done with lying, finished with constructing half-truths. He contemplated telling Leike about all the horrors he'd witnessed: the merciless deaths, the controlling manner in which the residents were forced to live their lives and the thousands of townsfolk who mysteriously disappeared every few weeks, never to be heard from again. But what good would it do? It wasn't like she could leave now that she was here. Being realistic would only frighten her, Alexandre reasoned. It seemed cruel to dampen her bright spirit. In time, Alexandre thought grimly, the town would blow out the light that appeared to beam from within.

Instead, he told her about his journey from the coastal towns of Europe to the World of Wonders, enjoying the way her eyes lit up each time he spoke of the spellbinding circus. By the time they'd finished eating, Leike looked considerably more relaxed and Alexandre had momentarily forgotten where he was. The way Leike looked at him, not bothering to hide her admiration, made him feel alive again and restored a bit of the hope that he thought had been lost forever.

'Shall we eat tomorrow?' Leike asked, her green eyes crystalline and hopeful as they rose to return to their rooms.

Alexandre's smile faltered as he observed her body language. What was he doing? He loved Lena and after what had transpired at the circus, would never do anything to jeopardise her trust again. He pursed his lips as he clutched his tray. 'The thing is, I have a sweetheart back home.'

Leike stared at him wistfully. 'It must be nice, to know someone's waiting for your return.'

'It is,' he said, feeling a pang of guilt.

'Well. It was lovely to meet you, Alexandre,' Leike said, her voice graceful even in defeat, as she walked away.

'Wait,' Alexandre called. Leike turned back. 'You'll need someone to show you around, explain how things are done,' he continued. 'Meet me in the main courtyard tomorrow before work?'

'I'll be here,' Leike said, beaming.

CHAPTER TWENTY-EIGHT

April 1943 – Dorset, England

'You win again,' Olivia Anderson said. She pushed the checkerboard away with the tip of her stockinged foot, then walked to the record player to put her Bing Crosby record on again.

'That's what happens when you listen to Christmas songs in April,' Lena joked, removing the red and black pieces from the board. The two girls had been holed up in Briarwood's library all afternoon, enjoying the quiet that came with the Easter holidays. Most of the girls had gone home but Olivia's mother didn't have enough money for her to come back only for two weeks.

'Or so she claims,' Olivia had said, rolling her eyes.

Clara had invited Lena back to her parents' house in Fulham but Lena had opted to stay in the dorms. She liked the idea of being there when no one else was around and wanted to keep Olivia company.

'It's a perfectly decent song!'

Lena smiled as she looked at Olivia appreciatively. The past few months had gone by in a whirlwind. After showing up at the Briarwood School unannounced, Clara had promptly taken her in, no questions asked, and ensured she got a spot in the school.

Though she'd never been in a formal educational institution, Lena didn't waste any time. She threw herself into her studies, relishing the opportunity to have something to focus on. Due to the fact that she had no legal guardian, she was granted permission to stay with Clara until she'd settled in. After her own classes ended, she'd wait in the canteen for Clara to finish teaching. Together, they'd walk back to the tiny cottage Clara shared with two other teachers discussing the events of the day. In the evenings, Lena would lie on her stomach on her cot, propped up on her elbows and listen to Clara gush about Fitz as a small fire glowed from the hearth.

With Clara's help, Lena also continued making progress with her physiotherapy treatments. After seeing her arrive at the school with nothing more than a cane, Clara had excitedly arranged for a therapist from London to come and plan out a daily regimen for Lena to follow, which she did diligently and now had progressed to a point where she was walking entire hallways and staircases without the use of any aids.

In January, Lena had felt ready to move into the dormitories with the other girls. She took up residence in bed 4A on the upper years floor and that was how she came to know Olivia.

Olivia was in the same year as Lena and slept in the bed next to hers. They quickly struck up a bond over their shared hatred of the icy water that filled their wash basins each morning and the scratchy sheets that itched to no end. Their nascent friendship was cemented when Lena learned Olivia had lost her father in a mining accident a year prior.

'Mam didn't know what to do with me,' she'd told Lena as they lay awake whispering in their beds one evening. 'Luckily Pa had the brains to put money for tuition in a trust. If Mam got her hands on it, she'd have taken it round the pub,' Olivia explained. That was how Olivia had ended up at boarding school. 'Mam wanted me out the house,' she'd said. 'It's better this way.'

They looked an odd pair, Lena with her tan skin, curly dark hair and short stature and Olivia, with hair so blonde it looked white and skin as pale as milk. At 5'11', she towered over Lena. They differed too in their aspirations. While Lena thrived in Briarwood's academic environment, regularly taking on extra assignments, Olivia spent her free time on more practical matters: sewing, make-up application and hairstyling. But these differences only served to strengthen their bond. Lena helped Olivia with her coursework and Olivia taught Lena how to apply eyeliner and press her hair with an iron if she fancied a sleek look. Though she missed her father and Alexandre terribly, Lena couldn't have asked for a better alternative than what she had now.

Back in the library, Olivia flipped through a pattern catalogue. She'd learned to sew out of necessity, because it was nearly impossible to find clothes that fit her tall frame.

'This is what I'm going to make next,' she held up the catalogue, pointing to a grey and red checked pinafore. 'Oh!'

Lena was standing in front of the games cupboard, stacking the checkers board. She frowned. 'What?'

Olivia was at her side in two strides. She pushed her stringy hair out of her face, grinning. 'You did it again!' She pointed to Lena's cane, perched at the side of the sofa.

Lena looked down at her legs, blinking. This was happening more and more, her standing up and walking without thinking about needing the cane. 'I suppose I did.'

'It's brilliant, just brill! Next thing I know, you'll be joining me on the field hockey team.' Olivia's smile faded when she noticed a tear rolling down Lena's cheek. 'I was only joking!'

Lena shook her head and walked back to the sofa, where she hugged a green corduroy cushion to her chest. 'It's not that,' she said, as Olivia joined her, a concerned look on her face. 'I just walked from here to there. How could I not notice?'

'It's a good thing,' Olivia pointed out. 'Means you're not thinking about it as much.'

Lena sniffed. 'I don't want to not think about it! I don't want to be ungrateful. This was ... this was only ever a dream and the people who believed in me, they're not here.' She trailed off, wiping tears from her eyes. 'Sorry.'

'Don't be. Is it your father?'

Lena nodded, trying to swallow a lump in her throat. 'I miss him,' she whispered. She was wary of letting people in, careful of who she was vulnerable around, but she trusted Olivia.

'Course you do. It never really goes away, the missing them part.'

Lena hugged the cushion tightly, 'I feel bad when I don't remember him every minute of every day. Like now. He would've loved to see this, and I didn't even think twice about it.'

'You can't be expected to live in the past every second. And no one thinks you're not appreciative.'

Lena dabbed at her eyes. 'Sorry to bring it up.'

'You can always bring it up. Mam never wants to talk about anything, so it helps me, too.' Olivia grinned and held her hand out. 'Right. We've one week 'til cook comes back to haunt us with her boiled veg. Shall we raid the pantry?'

Just then, matron appeared at the library doorway. 'Lena! There you are! Telephone from Clara.'

Lena and Olivia exchanged glances. 'Go on,' Olivia said. 'I'll wait.'

In the administration office a minute later, Lena cradled the phone in the nook of her neck and collarbone.

'Hello?'

'Lena?' Clara sounded out of breath. 'Fitz proposed. I'm engaged.'

CHAPTER TWENTY-NINE

July 1943 – Theresienstadt, Czechoslovakia

'Get foot away from face!' Vasily hissed at Natalia. His left arm jerked and Natalia shrieked as she slid ungracefully out of the position Vasily was holding her in. He set her down awkwardly on the dusty ground, whereupon she extricated herself from her older brother's grip, put her hands on her hips, planted her stockinged feet in their trademark turned-out stance, and glowered at him.

'What is wrong?' Natalia waved her thin arms around animatedly. She had a fairy-like, delicate quality to her, but not in an attractive way. Alexandre thought it had something to do with the puckered look she always wore like she'd been forced to suck on a lemon.

'I can't see!'

'Clumsy! That's what you are!' And on and on it went. They would switch to Russian soon, which Alexandre didn't understand. Not that it mattered. Whatever the language, it was obvious that whenever the Dimitrov siblings spoke, ninety percent of the time they were quarrelling.

Alexandre slumped in his wooden chair. They'd been in rehearsals for over two hours and his patience was waning. His body felt like it was broken, his bones and joints aching far too much for someone his age. They were a little more than two months away from finishing their contract and he'd thought his mindset might have improved. But morale in the town had taken a turn for the worse with the arrival of the new Commandant of Theresienstadt, Anton Burger. Hailing from Austria by way of Belgium and Poland, Burger was even more ruthless than his predecessor. At over 6 ft tall, his presence was imposing but it was the cruel way in which he spoke to the residents that really frightened Alexandre, doling out punishments so severe that rumours had begun circulating about him being a murderer. He didn't think it was possible for living conditions to deteriorate any further than they already had, but he was wrong.

After Burger's arrival, the administration closed one of the main housing complexes, which meant hundreds of residents had to be moved into other already overcrowded living quarters. It was not uncommon to see forty residents crammed into a room meant for no more than six, and every day Alexandre thanked his lucky stars for the preferential treatment he received on account of his and Theo's status as illusionists.

With people living closer together than before, cases of typhoid, scarlet fever, diphtheria and tuberculosis rose, while sanitation practices fell even more, resulting in daily death counts that soared into the hundreds. With graves overflowing, the crematorium was put to full use, and the stench of burning flesh was now a constant presence, hovering in the air at every turn.

Alexandre and Theo had both lost more weight, the scant diet of watery soup and mouldy potatoes making it nearly impossible to stay healthy. Alexandre wasn't even sure he remembered what being in good health felt like. He was simply trying to survive.

His work schedule shifted too. Already accustomed to putting in long hours, Alexandre's endurance was tested when he'd learned they were now required to rise at six and report to work an hour later. At the end of their shift, no one was to leave until a guard had checked their work, and if they were unhappy with any detail, the entire unit was required to stay until the work completed was satisfactory.

He closed his eyes and tried to imagine being anywhere but here. Somewhere clean. Somewhere free. Cleanliness and freedom were two recurring thoughts in his dreams. He felt as though he'd been running on a track that went nowhere for the last ten months, waiting and hoping. Hoping and waiting.

Alexandre heard muttering behind him and groaned. Attila had arrived, once again, to argue with Theo. The two illusionists held the final spot of the summer show. But for the past few weeks, Attila had been gunning for the finale and had now taken it upon himself to attend every single one of their rehearsals, just so he could reiterate his desire to be last. Alexandre watched as the gymnast lumbered on stage where Theo stood, assembling a box for his routine.

'Last again?' Attila snarled. He poked a finger into Theo's right pectoral muscle. Alexandre rolled his eyes. Attila was becoming an increasingly difficult person to be around. All he did was complain. About the food, the performances, the bunks.

Alexandre watched Theo trying to stay diplomatic, explaining patiently why the performances were structured the way they were. It was like observing a verbal game of tennis, Theo delivering calm groundstrokes and Attila returning them like sharp, biting hits. Alexandre wasn't sure why Theo bothered with this every single day. He was never going to win unless he gave up his finale spot. Sure enough, Attila shouted a Hungarian obscenity (Alexandre was now fluent in swearing in five different Eastern European languages), spat menacingly on the ground, and stalked off the stage. Alexandre stared up, watching the constellations emerging as a blanket of darkness cloaked the vast summer sky. He thought back to the moment when he knew he and Theo didn't have a chance. There was the constant monitoring of the residents by the guards, the cruel beatings he witnessed out in the open, the abhorrent living conditions, the gruelling work schedule. But the fear settled in firmly when Fredy, the boy who'd recruited Alexandre to the town football league, failed to show up for practice one day. Then the next. After the seventh day, Alexandre asked the guards where he was and they shrugged and said he'd left. He knew then that they were lying. There was no deal. It was a trap and they had walked right into it.

'Alexandre?'

Alexandre opened his eyes to see Leike smiling down at him. He blinked twice, slowly lifting his head and looked around. He must have dozed off, he thought, noticing that Theo had finished his routine and the rest of the performers were packing up.

'Sorry. I think I was dreaming of what a proper bath feels like,' he replied, watching Leike curl up on the chair next to him, tucking her violin case underneath it for safekeeping. 'How was rehearsal?'

'Good. The new viola player is quite skilled, and we've made progress on the piece,' she explained.

As she spoke, Alexandre studied her. Her hair, once so full and shiny, now hung in limp, dull strands around her face. Her skin was dry and patchy, devoid of the fulsome glow and bounciness it had when she'd first arrived. Her eyes still sparkled though, with tiny drops of green and hazel shimmer. Over the last five months, he and Leike had grown close, brought together by the horrors of the place.

'Oh!' Alexandre shook his head. 'I've something for you.' He rummaged around in a torn bag he used to store his tools, eventually pulling out a small rose he'd carved from a piece of scrap birchwood. He'd drilled a tiny hole in the middle and threaded a piece of thick twine through it. 'Here,' he said, presenting it to Leike. 'Happy Birthday.'

Leike's face brightened as she reached for the necklace. 'Alexandre!' she exclaimed, fingering the pendant. 'You remembered.' She held it up to her neck, quickly fastening the piece of string into a knot.

Alexandre shrugged modestly, toying with the ripped cuff of his shirt.

'It's beautiful,' she said, running her fingers over the petals. 'Thank you.' Leike leaned over and pecked Alexandre on his cheek. Then she gathered up her violin and skipped back to her room.

Alexandre felt a stab of guilt as he thought about leaving her. A part of him knew he shouldn't have given her a gift. It would only make their eventual parting harder. But it felt so nice to know there was someone here who cared about him. Lately, it didn't even seem like Theo did, Alexandre thought, scuffing the gravel as he walked back to his barracks. Uncertainty flared up inside him as he tried to recall the hundreds of people who'd mysteriously disappeared. But Theo had insisted they stay.

'We've a legally binding contract to prove it,' Theo said, reminding Alexandre of the paper the SS officer in Rouen had signed and given to Theo before they arrived. 'Just follow the rules and we'll be fine.'

Trust no one, Alexandre! You must look out for yourself!

As his father's words rang through his ears, Alexandre's eyes narrowed.

A few minutes later, Alexandre watched Theo kick off his boots, which were caked in mud. Tiny bits of dirt flew across the floor, but Theo made no attempt to clean them up. Alexandre couldn't see his face, but his slumped shoulders suggested he was tired.

'Attila told me three boys escaped earlier this year. It's worth a try.'

'Too dangerous.' Theo arranged his boots in the corner and started rolling out the lumpy mattress on the cold stone floor.

'No more dangerous than staying.'

'Alexandre.'

'You can't honestly tell me you trust them.'

'We're almost done. Why risk it now?'

'Because these people are monsters! Don't you see?' Alexandre asked, as Theo took off his shirt. 'They're telling you what you want to hear. You think we have a deal, but just wait. In September, I promise, we'll still be here. Unless we've already died.'

Silence. Alexandre didn't know if it was the hunger in his stomach or the fatigue in his bones, but he was growing more and more agitated. He leaned in over Theo's shoulder.

'Where do you think all those people who leave, go? The Czechs that come in and "move on"? And Fredy? Where do you think they sent Fredy?' He hesitated before saying what he was thinking next but he was so fed up with being here, he couldn't help himself. 'You know, if you truly cared about Lena, you'd have tried to get out the day we arrived.'

'That's enough!' Theo snapped, his dark eyes glittering. He strode towards his apprentice until their noses were almost touching. 'You think I don't care about my own daughter? Alexandre, why do you think I haven't tried to escape?' He laughed bitterly. 'It is *precisely* because of Lena that we are still here! They know where she is! They could obliterate that circus and everyone in it if they wanted to. So I stay, and I do what they ask because I don't want to return and find her gone!'

Alexandre looked away. He knew he shouldn't have brought up Lena, knew that Theo was often sick with worry. And he had a point – the Nazis were ruthless and knew exactly where to find her – but he wasn't in the mood to agree with him. He took a few steps back and sat down on his mattress.

'While we're on the topic of Lena,' Theo continued. 'Why don't we talk about Leike?'

'No,' Alexandre said in a low voice.

'You two seem to be getting very close.'

'She's only a friend.'

'And what about after we leave?' Theo shook his head. 'Have you even thought about how Lena would feel if you showed up with another girl?'

'Forget this,' Alexandre shouted, getting up in a huff and heading for the hallway.

'This isn't like you, Alexandre,' Theo said, in a measured voice. 'You're not someone who leads people on.'

Alexandre turned around and snarled. 'Maybe it *is* me! After all, I am my father's son!' Without waiting for a response, he stomped down the stairway. The only good thing about being held by the Germans was how regimented they were. Though their rules were overbearing, it also meant things happened when they said they'd happen. For that reason, figuring out how to take advantage of the security lulls was easy once you knew the drill.

He hurried to the ground floor. Holding his breath, he waited under an archway a couple of feet away from the exit. Erik, the guard who stood watch over this corner of the courtyard, was the worst guard Alexandre had ever seen. He was lazy, gave into temptation too easily, and was predictable to a fault. At exactly 8:30 p.m., he'd be joined by Friedrich, the only other guard who could rival Erik when it came to stupidity, for a cigarette break. Friedrich watched the front gate, monitoring people moving between the small and big fortresses.

Alexandre flattened himself against one side of the arches and peered around the corner. As predicted, Erik was waiting. He sniffed, picked his nose, and wiped his hand on his uniform. With his other hand, he plucked a cigarette out of his pocket and lit it. Alexandre started counting in his head *one, two, three* ...

Twenty-seven, twenty-eight, twenty-nine ... Erik puffed away steadily and then tossed his cigarette on the ground, crushing it with the heel of his boot. Alexandre listened out and a second later, he heard the steady crunch of Friedrich's bike on gravel growing louder. Holding his breath, Alexandre inched forward and looked. Friedrich had arrived and the two guards were exchanging pleasantries in low voices.

Alexandre gave them another minute to get out of the fortress. They always met just outside the sweeping yellow archway that welcomed new residents, but out of clear view to anyone watching from above or roaming the courtyard. They used to smoke near the vegetable garden but when a stray cigarette butt ignited half the spinach crop, they were reprimanded and told to stay away.

120, 121 ... Theo had trained him well to keep time. Alexandre calculated that he had about ten minutes before they returned. He scurried out from the protection of the archway, darting behind a bin near the entrance. Crouching down behind it, he curled his knees close to his chest. The still-warm butt of Erik's cigarette lay next to him, letting off thin curls of smoke, the orange-red ember faintly aglow. He picked it up, placed it to his lips and inhaled, feeling his body relax. The first time he smoked, he almost got caught, his coughing was so loud. He'd since learned to inhale more slowly and now relished the ashy taste and the burning in his lungs. It felt good to feel something other than hunger, anger, and hopelessness – the three states that competed for his attention day in, day out.

To his left, he could make out the archway to the road that led to freedom. He blew out a curl of smoke, watching it fade to nothing in the moonlight. He estimated how much time he'd have if he was to make a run for it. It was nearly two kilometres to Bohusovic. He had no money, but he had skills. He was sure he could pick up enough work to cobble together the funds needed to get him back to London, to find Lena.

He thought of Theo. Of what he'd sacrificed to save him. Of what he owed to him. Two weeks earlier, he'd pointed out that the men from AK 1, who helped build the first ghetto when they arrived at Theresienstadt, were promised freedom, too. Two years later, they were still waiting.

Alexandre doubled over, suddenly feeling trapped. Trapped by Theo's unwavering faith in a piece of paper proclaiming their freedom, trapped by Leike, and trapped by the SS and Czech gendarmerie, who watched over them like hawks. He churned the cigarette butt angrily into the ground and watched the orange embers fade. He glanced at the gates. Fifty feet to freedom.

What are you waiting for, Alexandre? Jacques's voice flooded his ears as Alexandre stared wistfully at the cold metal bars.

Then he turned and walked back to the barracks.

CHAPTER THIRTY

August 1943 – London, England

Lena stared up at the magnificent arched ceilings surrounding her. St. Peter's Church on Black Lion Lane was the perfect place for a wedding, she decided, a feeling of calm settling over her as the rich strains of the choir boys' voices filled the cavernous space.

She shifted her attention back to the ceremony at the front, smiling as she watched Clara and Fitz recite their vows. That morning at breakfast, Miss Smith's father, George, told Lena that Reverend Montgomery wasn't even available to officiate when he'd enquired two weeks back. But, George said, waving around a piece of dry toast, crumbs flying everywhere, he'd put in a phone call, plugged his years of volunteer work and service and made mention of the fact that poor Fitz was only allowed four days leave and would the Reverend please be so kind as to make an exception and marry his daughter on that Saturday in August?

And here they were, at a wedding short on guests but long on love, cobbled together in the space of a fortnight with the help of family and friends. Lena glanced around, still finding it surreal that she was even present for this moment. The past two months had gone by in an absolute whirlwind. She'd been staying with Clara's family over the summer holidays in Fulham. Clara and

Fitz had been trying to set a wedding date since their engagement but hadn't had much luck given how little notice Fitz got when it came to taking leave.

When he rang Clara up saying he'd have a full four days off and could they try and put a wedding together with little more than two weeks' notice, Lena had been sceptical. But as Clara said, there was nothing like the promise of a celebration to spark movement in people. In no time at all, a dress was a found, a venue secured, drinks procured. Even the neighbours rallied around the Smith family, diving into their stores of pickled beetroot and cabbage, calling in favours to farmers and procuring enough chicken, potatoes and swede to feed the guests who could make it. In Bristol, Fitz's mother found fresh eggs and butter just two days out from the wedding ceremony and managed to whip up a gorgeous lemon buttercream cake.

Clara's older sister, Franny, had put a dress on hold for her at a shop in Soho.

'She used her last ration coupon to secure it,' Clara said of her sister, as she changed behind a clothing screen while Lena waited. 'But that's what Franny's like. Always thinking of others.' She stepped out from behind the screen. 'Well,' she announced, standing proudly. 'What do you think?'

Lena took in the ivory-coloured dress, at first thinking it was a little plain. The top resembled a feminine suit jacket. It had white buttons and a slim skirt that stopped just below Clara's knees.

'It's a bit short, but that's how all of them are these days,' Clara said, laughing and twirling around in front of the mirror. 'Franny said she'd lend me her pearls and white pumps to match. Plus, we'll have our silver horseshoes. And I'll have flowers and Fitz will look positively regal in his uniform.' Clara looked so happy that Lena couldn't help but agree.

'It's perfect,' she answered, meaning it. 'It's the perfect dress for the perfect wedding.'

And the perfect wedding was precisely where Lena sat at present, in a baby pink dress with a wreath of lilies in her air, watching her governess marry a man she'd fallen deeply in love with. As the happy couple kissed at the front, a huge smile spread across Lena's face.

'Doesn't she look stunning?' one of Clara's aunts whispered.

Lena nodded. 'She certainly does.'

'For he's a jolly good fellow, for he's a jolly good fellow. For he's a jolly good fellllooooow. That nobody can deny!'

The merry crowd of tipsy revellers clinked their glasses together as Fitz and Clara applauded. The ceremony had ended hours ago and the reception was well underway. Defying all expectations of what was possible in a terraced house, Lena looked around, amused as the scene at Clara's parents' home grew more raucous by the minute. Some of the guests had spilled out into the patch of green at the front, and still more had begun migrating up the carpeted stairs, balancing their plates of chicken and boiled carrots on their knees, trying not to spill their precious liquor.

Lena had positioned herself in an armchair in the sitting room with a plate of cake. From her spot, she could see the stairs, the kitchen and the dining room and decided it was the perfect place for observing. She leaned forward and took a bite of her cake, thinking back on the day. She'd been thrilled that her governess had found the love she'd always deserved. But for Lena, the day had been bittersweet. Each moment, from choosing the dress, to the ceremony and now the reception, cemented a painful truth. Even if she was lucky enough to get married, Lena's father wouldn't be there to witness it.

'There you are!' Clara and Fitz stumbled in front of her. Her teacher's cheeks were flushed pink and a crown of flowers fashioned out of the bouquet she'd carried during the ceremony adorned her head. She'd removed her pumps and was standing next to Fitz in her stockinged feet, pointing to the cake. 'I'm afraid after Mario, this won't taste like much.'

'It's delicious,' Lena answered, taking another bite.

'We had the most magnificent chef at the circus,' Clara explained to Fitz. 'He'd make the loveliest desserts – Italian biscuits from ground pine nuts and almonds, cakes filled with the richest mascarpone, buttery shortbreads.'

'I daresay we're lucky he's *not* here!' Fitz patted his belly. 'Did you enjoy the ceremony?'

'It was beautiful.' Lena placed her fork on her plate.

Clara exchanged a glance with Fitz, who nodded. 'Lena. There's something we've been meaning to discuss with you,' she said, taking a seat next to her. 'Fitz and I, we've been talking. And we wanted to know if you'd consider letting us adopt you?'

Lena stopped chewing, her mouth full of cake. 'Adopt?' she mumbled.

'The thing is,' Fitz began. 'We're happy being guardians, if that's what you want. But thinking about the future, wouldn't it be nice to have something more permanent? We considered asking you if you wanted to move to Thessaloniki first. Clara always said you loved it there. But to be honest, we'd much rather you remained here, with us.'

The shattering of glass followed by a rousing cheer could be heard from the next room but neither Lena nor Clara nor Fitz moved.

'I hadn't thought about you adopting me,' Lena said.

Clara jumped in. 'I'm not suggesting we'd be replacement parents. But you could stay with me at Briarwood for however long I'm there. And when Fitz returns, you'll live with us. We can talk about other arrangements in the future.' Clara took Lena's hands in hers. 'You don't have to decide now, but at least consider it.'

Lena stared down at her lap. She'd avoided thinking of the future as much as she could, preferring to focus on school.

252

Although the big questions loomed, she wasn't ready to face them. She'd known this was coming, knew that, technically speaking, her very existence in her current state was illegal.

She thought about her father, about what he would have wanted for her. It was true that he'd always spoken so highly of Thessaloniki, insisted that she know where she came from, but she didn't feel like she was from anywhere anymore. And a life with the newly-weds just might work. The more she thought about it, the more she liked the sound of it. If the last year had taught Lena anything, it was that life was too short to spend time wavering.

'Yes,' Lena said.

'There's honestly no rush to decide,' Clara said cautiously.

But Lena held firm in her decision. 'I don't need to think about it. My answer is yes.'

CHAPTER THIRTY-ONE

October 1943 – Thereseinstadt, Czechoslovakia

On an early morning, Alexandre opened his eyes. He'd slept fitfully, tossing and turning with the same kind of anticipation he used to feel when it was the night before his birthday. But today was going to be better than his birthday. Today was the day he and Theo were getting their freedom back.

He waited impatiently as Vasily and Attila dressed and left for work, pacing the tiny room like a caged animal.

'Hurry,' he urged Theo, glancing out into the hallway to make sure no one was there.

'It's better if I speak with him alone,' Theo said, lacing up a pair of boots littered with scuff marks and tiny holes.

Alexandre shook his head as he followed Theo down the stairs. 'I waited too long for this day. I'm coming with you.'

As he hurried to keep pace with Theo, Alexandre thought about Leike and felt his stomach dip. He'd discussed with the older illusionist the possibility of asking for her release as well. Even though he had every intention of returning to Lena, he couldn't leave Leike behind to perish, he thought, as they crossed the courtyard.

A guard standing outside the administration office surveyed the two illusionists before letting them in. Files of neatly stacked papers lined the shelves across the back and side walls. In the centre was a desk and behind it sat Anton Burger, hunched over a pile of paperwork, taking no notice of the two illusionists.

'Excuse me, sir?' Theo approached the commandant.

'Yes?'

'We're here about our contract,' Theo cleared his throat. At the word 'contract', Burger lifted his head. Theo took out the folded piece of paper and smoothed it out on the desk. 'We had an agreement to do one year of hard labour and performances.' He pointed to the date at the top of the sheet. 'We've now fulfilled our requirements.'

Burger fingered the paper, his expression unreadable. After what felt like an eternity, he put it on one side and went back to what he was reading. 'No.'

Alexandre felt the hairs on his arms prickle. Beside him, Theo frowned as he placed his hands on Burger's desk. 'We've a deal, sir. You can't renege on a legal agreement.'

Burger lifted his eyes to meet Theo's. Then he calmly picked up the contract and slowly tore it into tiny little pieces, which he then scattered on the ground. From the corner of his eye, Alexandre could tell Theo was starting to panic.

'Sir, we can't stay here. I have a daughter back—'

'You're aware of the Danes that recently arrived?' Burger asked. Theo nodded, anguish settling into the lines on his face. 'Apparently word has circulated about our town's "conditions". We're to put on a show for their king next year. A ridiculous use of time to squash these rumours, but it must be done. Such a lavish production will be too hard to pull off without performers of your calibre.'

A pit of despair gnawed at Alexandre's insides. Hadn't he warned Theo? Hadn't he told him to have a contingency plan? *Any true thief will always have an alternate way out!*

Beside him, Theo was still attempting a feeble negotiation, but it was clear where the power lay. Alexandre felt months of pent-up frustration rise within him, like a venomous snake uncoiling, readying itself to strike.

Crash. In one fell swoop, Alexandre had grabbed a vase off a nearby shelf and thrown it in Burger's direction, narrowly missing his head. He watched it strike the bookcase behind, sending a row of files tumbling before shattering into sharp, splintered pieces.

'You're a liar! And a murderer!' He tried to grab a paperweight but the guard behind him restrained him. At once Theo was at his side.

'Stop it!'

Burger, who'd recovered from the momentary shock of the vase breaking, stared at Alexandre with a renewed sense of interest. Slowly, he stood up and removed his gun, digging the smooth, gleaming tip of the barrel into the side of Alexandre's head.

Alexandre lurched forward to grab him, but the guard keeping watch had come forward upon hearing the crash. He pulled back on Alexandre's arm so hard that his shoulder wrenched out of its socket. He heard a sickening crunch and then yelled, the shock of the pain surprising him.

'You're the devil!' Alexandre screamed. *Thwack.* The cold, metallic bluntness of the gun dented the side of his head and he fell to the ground. He could feel a thick liquid slowly trickling over his head and a searing ache burrowing into the core of his brain. At last. It was over. No more fighting. No more running. No more guilt. It would be just him and his mother, reunited finally.

'Alexandre!'

Alexandre opened his eyes. A very blurry Theo was crouched over him, distraught. If he hadn't been so dazed he might have noticed the tears. *Please. Let me go. I don't want to be here anymore.*

Then he remembered Lena. What it felt like to kiss her, how much he'd wanted to change for her sake, and how the idea of being together again kept him going all these months.

'Get him on his feet.' Theo immediately jumped to Alexandre's

257

assistance, propping him up with his arms. Alexandre's head felt like it had exploded. His gaze dropped to the floor and he caught sight of his blood staining the ground. He twisted his neck slightly, toward a breeze blowing through an open window. The coolness felt soothing, and he staggered sideways, relaxing into Theo's arms. Burger leaned his ugly face into Alexandre's.

'Why don't you shoot?' Alexandre taunted. Burger laughed and his breath, stale with beer and last night's meal, cloaked Alexandre's face.

And lose a perfectly good worker? Not a chance. You two will stay here as long as you're needed. I will decide when . . . indeed *if*, your time is up.' Burger smiled and sat back down at his desk.

'One more thing,' he said. 'I'd think twice before trying anything like that again. I've seen that pretty little violinist following you around. Unless you're willing to risk her life, you'll do as I say.' He nodded to the guard, who shoved Alexandre forward, striking the back of his head with the blunt end of his gun again. The last thing Alexandre remembered was the sound of Burger's voice cackling, a sea of dark falling over his eyes.

CHAPTER THIRTY-TWO

November 1943 – Theresienstadt, Czechoslovakia

'Alexandre?'

Theo was here again, Alexandre thought, keeping his eyes closed, trying to lay perfectly still. It was a game he'd been playing for the last few weeks in one of the makeshift hospitals set up by the Jewish nurses and doctors. He'd lost count of exactly how many days he'd been inside after the guard had left him with a bad concussion, dislocated shoulder, broken ankle and an assortment of bruises and cuts, but he knew it had been longer than a month.

He waited until he heard a chair scrape, followed by the low murmurs of Theo and the nurse, and finally, the soft creaking of the hospital doors, opening and closing. Satisfied that Theo had left, Alexandre chanced a peek, letting out a sigh of relief when he saw that he was alone again.

He gingerly rolled onto his good arm and propped himself up to take a sip of water. He wasn't proud of how he was acting. Theo had saved his life twice, but he couldn't help feeling that he was also responsible for them being stuck in the town for as long as they had been. Hadn't Alexandre warned him? Hadn't he told him they should try to escape, many times? And now, after the display they'd put on in front of Burger, security around the two illusionists was even higher. If their chances of escaping before had been slim, now they were practically non-existent.

Alexandre glanced around. The hospital was peaceful sometimes and horrific other times. He'd seen men, women and children die, their bodies wheeled out on beds like they were nothing but worn-out household objects to be tossed out. And while he was grateful to have healthcare services at all, he couldn't decide if it was better to be in here, where he was free from his back-breaking work duties, or worse. In here, he was alone with his thoughts, with an abundance of time to think. And he'd learned over the last few weeks that that wasn't always a good thing.

I told you to run when you had the chance! But you never listen! That's the problem with you. You've always been too weak, too sentimental!

Alexandre groaned, trying to block the ghost of Jacques Robichaud from his mind and thought of Leike. Since the beating, she, like Theo, had visited any chance they got, despite the danger in put them in. And it was this act of devotion, coupled with the new and terrifying certainty that they'd likely all die in Theresienstadt, that had opened the floodgates for something more between them. Time was compressed in a place like this and it wasn't hard to succumb to her nurturing nature. He listened attentively as she told him stories and didn't complain when she tried to feed him. When his cuts had healed and he was feeling strong enough, one of the first things he did was pull her towards him and kiss her properly on her lips. He missed Lena terribly and would always love her, but what was the point anymore? Besides, it felt wonderful to make a choice for himself, to have a modicum of agency over how he wanted to live out the remainder of his short life.

He pulled the thin sheet up over his neck, shivering. He'd been lucky to avoid the diseases circulating and didn't want to take any chances. He yawned and rubbed his eyes. He wanted to stay awake in case Leike came, but he was feeling tired. Perhaps he would close his eyes for a minute, he thought, his fatigue getting the better of him as he drifted off into a dream.

Anja get out of the way!

No! He is a good boy! He's not like you!

Alexandre felt the heat of a burning rafter above him, making his eyes water. But he couldn't move. He was trapped.

He's my son, of course he's like me! He was cut from the same cloth, bred from the same bone. Now move!

No! Alexandre! Run!

A crash. A scream. The scent of burning wood, the heat of a hungry flame.

'No!' Alexandre yelled, reaching for his mother, tears falling from his eyes. She looked peaceful, even in death, he thought as he hunched over her. And then, a knife, a blow, and it was all over.

You want to be a coward? Then go. But remember this. You cannot outrun who you truly are.

Alexandre? Alexandre?

Alexandre moved again, shaking his head. This couldn't be happening. He needed to wake up. She was gone.

But her scent was almost real, her voice so close. He could see her, smiling, above him, touching his forehead the way she always did when he was sick.

Alexandre, you must never forget how much I love you. No matter where I am, you can always find me. Look up. I am in the stars, watching over you, always. You mustn't give up.

'I'm so tired! I can't do it anymore,' he sobbed.

Hold on just a bit longer. Don't listen to your father. You are bred from my bone, fed by my milk. I am you. You are me. I knew it the minute you were born. No matter what anyone tells you. You can always be who you were meant to be.

'Alexandre!'

Alexandre opened his eyes with a start to find the nurse on duty shaking him, a concerned look on her face. He looked down at his sheets and noticed they were soaked in sweat.

'Where is she? Where's my mother? She was here!' He looked around, desperate to see her again.

'Are you sure he has to go? He's feverish. It will impact his ability to work and perform,' the nurse said to a guard who was standing at the foot of Alexandre's bed.

'My orders were for everyone who could walk to be discharged.'

Alexandre squinted, the harsh German accent jolting his senses. He frowned and looked around. There were a number of guards crowding the hospital, ordering around the nurses.

'Fine,' the nurse beside Alexandre said, exasperated. She began pulling back the sheets on his bed. 'You'll be alright with another week of rest. Don't put too much pressure on your foot,' she said, leaning over to help him stand.

'What's going on?' Alexandre asked.

'We need the beds for the residents.'

Alexandre rushed to follow the guard out of the hospital, gingerly putting weight on his ankle at first and then beginning to lean on it more firmly. He gasped as the guard opened the doors to the outside world, inhaling the fresh, cold air like it was water. It wasn't until they'd crossed the main square that he realised how eerily quiet it was.

'Where is everyone?'

'Census. Burger's orders.' Alexandre was about to ask why they needed a census when the guard stopped abruptly in front of the Hannover barracks. 'Stay out of trouble,' he said, pushing Alexandre forward so hard that he fell to the ground.

Rubbing his knees and scowling as the guard stalked away, Alexandre dragged himself up and limped up the stairs, collapsing in a dusty corner of his old room. He never thought he'd be so happy to see the filthy, tiny space again. Alexandre leaned his head against the wall, listening out for voices, but heard none. He told himself he had to stay awake, that he had to see Theo to make sure he was safe.

But his exhaustion overcame him. His eyelids grew heavy and he eventually slipped into a deep sleep.

'Alexandre?'

Alexandre blinked sleepily and opened one eye. Theo's anxious face hovered above him. Next to him, Vasily clapped his hands excitedly.

'He's back,' Vasily said. 'He's back, he's ok!' the dancer continued, racing out in the hallway to tell the others.

Alexandre pushed himself up slowly and shook his head. Theo put his arm around him.

'Oh, bless you, Alexandre. I was so worried!'

'What time is it?'

'Morning. We came back last night and you were fast asleep.'

'Where were you?'

Theo shuddered. 'There was a headcount. Burger ordered everyone outside to line up and wait until we'd all been accounted for. People were collapsing every minute from standing out in the cold.' He shook his head. 'Word is that many have already died from hypothermia.'

Something clicked in Alexandre's brain. That was why they needed the beds.

'Is Leike—'

'She's fine,' Theo reassured him. 'She was asking after you.' He stood up and poked his head into the hallway. When he was sure the coast was clear, Theo crouched back down next to Alexandre. 'Alexandre, I was wrong. I should have listened to you when you tried to tell me we couldn't trust them.'

'It's ok. Not like we would have been able to do anything about it.'

'The reason they had the headcount was because a group of men tried to escape.'

'And?' Alexandre asked, but didn't push it any further when he saw the expression on Theo's face.

'I ... I don't know if I was too worried about Lena and what they would do to her, or if I was blind to my own faith in the Germans. I've lost us a whole year.'

'It's fine,' Alexandre said, resigning himself to the fact that they would be stuck forever. The two illusionists sat in silence for a moment and then Theo cleared his throat.

'No. It's not.'

Alexandre searched his face and, even in the dim light of the room, he could see the familiar resolve and fearlessness he'd missed in the old Theo coming back.

'What are you talking about?'

'We're going to do what we do best. Escape.'

Alexandre stared at the illusionist, wondering if Theresienstadt had finally turned him crazy. 'There's no way out. Even if we were going to try, do you know how hard it would be with the extra guards they've added?'

'The number of guards doesn't matter,' Theo continued, smiling. 'Think about it. When's the least likely time they'd be expecting us to make a run for it?'

'During a performance?' Alexandre, said, sitting up a bit straighter.

'Exactly. All we need is some kind of distraction to make them think we're not trying to escape.'

People can't see what they're not looking for. Jacques Robichaud's words came back to Alexandre, only this time, he didn't try to drown them out. 'A show,' he said, his excitement building.

Theo grinned. 'To end all shows! A jaw-dropping spectacular. Something that will have the guards so preoccupied they won't have a minute to notice we're gone.'

Alexandre nodded eagerly. He tried to think of what Horace would do if he were in their situation. 'Do you have any ideas?'

Theo's eyes sparkled. 'I've got just the thing.'

CHAPTER THIRTY-THREE

Taking a page from Horace's book, Theo decided to put on a performance inspired by the Moulin Rouge. His vision was admittedly much smaller, the costumes less sumptuous, but the intent was the same. Whereas their shows in Theresienstadt had, up to now, been a series of individual acts, this special presentation would bring everyone together, and drive the audience wild with their sybaritic delights.

The timing couldn't have been more serendipitous. Theo used the upcoming Danish visit to pitch his idea, telling Burger that they needed to start now if they were to convincingly masquerade as a model town in a few months' time. Burger was so pleased that he insisted on bankrolling the entire operation. Apart from starting on the aesthetic improvements for the town, Theo suggested they conduct a dress rehearsal just before Christmas.

'In order to iron any hiccups out. We want to ensure everything is perfect for the actual visit,' Theo explained to Burger, who readily agreed. Where there was never any money before, it magically appeared in the form of silk and taffeta bolts, spools of golden thread and sparkling red sequins.

Alexandre was tasked with inspiring the other performers to stretch their imaginations, but when he explained the concept, the inspiration flowed. Buoyed by the freedom to experiment, the residents banded together, eager to produce a show of the highest order. Natalia took charge of choreographing a Can-Can number, complete with high kicks and jewelled black garter belts. She was given the roots of a Rubia plant and spent an evening hunched over a steel washing basin, dying what was left of her and her fellow dancers' pointe shoes a deep red. Vasily teamed up with another man to perform a comedic act inspired by Foottit and Chocolat. One woman took on the challenge of singing an Adelaide Hall song and the courtyard was suddenly filled with a different kind of music – sultry, jazzy, sensuous. Leike would be part of an orchestral group that played an Ellington piece, but it was in the costuming department where she truly shone. After rehearsals, she sat for hours, her nimble fingers working by candlelight, stitching white and silver feathers onto corsets, adding gold trim to the hems of long, ruffled skirts, and creating a glorious red velvet tailcoat for Burger himself.

Alexandre once heard Horace say that with constraint came beauty and the statement could not have been truer now. There was a real joy pulsating in the air.

The grand finale act featured Theo and Alexandre being handcuffed together and then escaping from a tank full of water. What the others didn't know was that they were planning to swap with the guards, Erik and Friedrich, then leave whilst the impostors were trying to escape.

To divert suspicion, they scheduled a trial run with Burger, working round the clock to finish building their equipment. Because everyone in the workshop knew about the illusion, they didn't have to hide that part. They built a solid wooden framework and slotted extra thick glass panels into place on all four sides of the tank. Then, they created a simple pulley and harness system. During the trick, a guard would use it to hoist them above the tank before dropping them into the water. With some of the Rubia plant leftover from Natalia's show project, they'd tint the water red on the night of the show, and project lanterns from behind it, giving it a majestic, rich glow.

During their trial run, Burger placed two potato sacks over their heads, handcuffed them together back-to-back and secured the harness around their waists tightly. Once this was done, the guard attached a metal hook to one of the harness loops and pulled the two illusionists up over the tank. On Burger's command, the curtains opened, revealing the magicians dangling dangerously in mid-air. Then the guard released the rope, plunging them into the water. A metallic covering was then slid over the top of the tank, locking them in.

Most people could survive underwater for no more than two minutes. But Alexandre and Theo, skilled at holding their breath, could easily survive four. As they kicked and flailed, making it look like they were struggling to get out, Alexandre felt the sharp tip of the key to the handcuffs Theo had hidden up his sleeve. This was Alexandre's cue to take the additional key he'd hidden up his own sleeve, which was the one that would get them out of the tank. They'd built in a hidden lock on the inside cover, one that wasn't visible to the guards. With the murky red no one would be able to see Alexandre unlock it. They waited a few more seconds for dramatic effect, then swam up and burst through the top, catching their breath as they leaned over the side of the tank. Alexandre climbed out and tried to shake the water from his hair and clothes. It was only then that he heard the applause.

'Magnificent! It's magnificent!' Burger stood in the front row, clapping his hands exuberantly. Alexandre looked around. Everyone was on their feet. Guards had abandoned their posts to see them play with their lives. Their fellow performers were watching with a mixture of admiration and envy on their faces, jealous that their own acts would never be as thrilling. No one could take their eyes off them. It was going to work.

With the mechanics of the illusion worked out and preparations well underway, it was time to tell Leike the truth. Theo and

Alexandre both firmly agreed they had to take her with them. So they took her aside after a rehearsal one day and explained their plan.

'What if something goes wrong?' she asked, distraught.

'Something could go wrong,' Theo replied. 'But truthfully, I don't think any of us is going to get out of here alive if we leave it to chance.'

Leike looked uncertain and let out a weak cough. Alexandre frowned. Didn't she want to be free? She studied her hands, avoiding their gaze. 'If I leave, what will I have?'

It struck Alexandre then that he and Theo were in very different positions to Leike. Theo had a daughter to raise. Alexandre didn't know what the future held, but at the very least, he had a trade he could practise. Leike had no home or family. Though she was a formidable musician and seamstress, Alexandre knew that by sheer virtue of her being female, she would struggle to get work. He shuddered when he thought about her ending up in an orphanage, or worse, a brothel.

Have you learned nothing from the last month? Don't waste your time looking out for anyone but yourself!

As he stared at her sad face, Alexandre did something that he didn't have the courage to do until now.

'You have me.'

Leike's eyes flickered with doubt.

Alexandre took her hands in his. He didn't know how things were going to play out with Lena, but he had to take care of Leike, no matter what. 'Wherever we go, I'll be there. I promise.'

For a moment, Alexandre thought she was going to refuse again, so concerned was the look on her face. And then she collapsed into his arms, sobs of relief flowing out of her.

'It's ok.' He stroked her hair. 'Don't worry. Everything's going to be ok.'

*

With Leike on board, they divided up the remaining tasks. Theo's next job was to procure a few bottles of brandy from Burger and he played his part perfectly. During one of the rehearsals that he knew Burger would be attending, he threw his cards and fell to his knees, grabbing his wrists.

'Forgive me, sir,' Theo grimaced. 'It's the arthritis.' He cast his eyes in Burger's direction. 'It would be such a shame to not be able to perform for the Danes—' Burger straightened up in his chair.

'That's not an option. The town must be ready.'

Theo nodded, continuing to massage his wrists. 'Could I trouble you for two bottles of brandy? That usually cures it. Nothing too expensive, of course—'

Burger did the rest. 'See to it that this man gets what he needs, before day's end,' he shouted to one of the guards, who nodded. Alexandre smiled from his corner as Theo thanked Burger repeatedly for his generosity.

Leike proved to be a worthy partner in their plan. Between her skills as a seamstress and trustworthy relationships she'd built with the town staff, she quickly became the most valuable member of their team. Within a week, she'd created costumes for Theo and Alexandre and an identical set that they would use for Erik and Friedrich. She also got barbital, a potent sleeping pill, from the hospital. She'd spent so many days there with Alexandre that she knew the nurses' schedules like clockwork, and was able to procure a handful of pills in no time. She handed them to Alexandre surreptitiously during a break in rehearsals and he quickly wrapped them in a handkerchief, stowing them in his boot.

Leike's final task was to obtain the official train timetable. The administration office held folders with information on all the local transportation schedules. Because Leike had excellent penmanship, she was often called upon to transcribe records. When Frau Lauder stepped out to use the toilet one afternoon, Leike pounced on the correct file and quickly copied down the departure time of a supply train scheduled to leave Bohusovic for Prague on December nineteenth.

'I've got it!' she whispered at rehearsal that evening, pointing to her pocket. 'There's one at 21:27 on the nineteenth. It's perfect.' Overjoyed that everything was coming together, Alexandre swept her up in his arms.

'This is it, Leike,' he whispered, twirling her around. 'This is our freedom train.'

CHAPTER THIRTY-FOUR

Snow fell like a fine dusting of white sugar on the ground as they drew closer to the show date. The day before the big performance, Alexandre whistled as he walked to the canteen. Though the familiar chill of winter had settled in the air, nothing could harden his mood.

At the canteen, Alexandre spotted Leike hunched over in a corner. He grinned and carried his tray over to the table.

'Good morning!'

Startled, Leike twisted around. Alexandre's smile faded as his eyes moved from her frightened face to the handkerchief dotted with faint red spots. She shoved it in her pocket and stood up, coughing.

'I didn't see you,' she smiled, a little too eagerly, and reached for his hands. He pulled away.

'How long?'

Her smile flickered. She opened her mouth to answer but a violent cough escaped and she hunched herself back over the table. Alexandre ran his hand over her back, flinching when he felt her ribs pushing against the skin of her body. He'd been so busy planning their escape that he'd stopped paying attention to what was happening inside these walls. A drop of blood fell on her handkerchief. When she'd recovered, she reached out to him, but he stepped back.

'I asked you how long.'

Leike winced, refusing to meet his eyes, and instead looked at a group of children scampering by. When she spoke, her voice was soft and free of bitterness.

'Six or seven weeks?'

Alexandre swore under his breath. He hated himself. He'd let his guard down by letting her in and now he was on the cusp of losing her, too. Well, he wasn't going to let that happen so easily.

Grabbing her arm, Alexandre jerked her out of the canteen. She whimpered as he pulled her down the hallway, towards the hospital.

'Stop, Alexandre. Stop it!' Her feeble pleas escalated to a high squeal and he let go, watching her arm fall limply next to him.

'Did you see a nurse?'

She massaged her wrist and shook her head. He yelled and punched the wall in front of him. Leike began crying, which only made him angrier.

'Why are you crying! You knew and you didn't say anything!'

'I didn't want to worry you,' she whispered.

'Didn't you think I should know? Did you not care, coming and sitting next to me every day, what would happen? And what was your plan for when we got out? What was I supposed—' Alexandre stopped himself from saying the thing they were both afraid of, the thing that she'd probably accepted, but didn't want to discuss. 'Did you ever stop to think about that?'

'I only wanted to help,' Leike whispered. She slid to the ground and pulled her legs close to her chest, her calloused hands clutching at her kneecaps.

Alexandre noticed the cracks around her knuckles where her skin had become chapped from the cold. She shook with sobs, mumbling her apologies over and over again, while he stood over her, lost.

To his right, the archway to the courtyard framed the gravel-lined ground, shades of beige, grey and stark white. Exhausted, Alexandre sank to the ground, pulling Leike towards him. Her body, stiff at first, eventually relaxed and she cried into his shirt. He thought about Vienna and the medical facilities there. He wanted to ask her so many questions. Did she know any doctors who could help with tuberculosis? Why hadn't she told him? Didn't she trust him? *I could have helped you*, he wanted to say.

But nothing would come out of his mouth. Instead, they sat in the morning silence, two orphans who'd dared to dream, only to have fate deal them another wicked blow.

Alexandre's mood the rest of the day was complex. One minute, he was relieved Leike was alive. The next, he worried about how he was going to look after her. Then he started fretting about his own health, wondering if he'd got sick.

He skipped dinner and instead went to lie down in his room. Closing his eyes, he began going over the events for tomorrow in his head: the mechanics of pulling off the illusion, how much time they'd have to get to the station. He thought of Erik and Friedrich, and how thrilled he'd been just a few hours earlier at the prospect of never having to see their faces again.

He sat up and rubbed his head. Theo had stashed the brandy bottles in a box in the corner. He took one out and uncorked it. Tipping it back, he took a long sip. It burned as it trickled down his throat. After he'd had enough to satiate himself but not so much that it would look suspicious, he wiped his mouth and stowed the bottle away. Feeling sluggish, he slumped back to bed, allowing the sweet, comforting cloak of the alcohol to lull him into a deep sleep.

'Alexandre?'

Alexandre opened his eyes to find Theo shaking him. A dull pain stabbed at the front of his head.

'What time is it?'

'Late,' Theo answered. Alexandre pushed himself up and massaged his head. 'I came in earlier but you were fast asleep. Thought I'd give you a chance to get some rest before tomorrow.'

Alexandre stretched his neck. The earlier events of the day – Leike, his reaction, the alcohol, flooded back to him.

'Anything left to do?'

Theo glanced around the empty room. 'They're still in rehearsals.'

Alexandre nodded and pressed his forehead with the palm of his left hand.

'We don't have much time,' Theo continued.

'Time for what?'

Theo hesitated. 'There's something I have to tell you.'

'You can't back out!'

'I'm not leaving you,' Theo reassured him. 'But, in case something happens, and I don't make—'

'Of course you're going to make it,' Alexandre interrupted. His stomach sank when he saw Theo's expression. Was he sick too? His eyes darted over the illusionist's body, hunting for signs of disease.

'I'm not sick,' Theo said, reading Alexandre's mind. 'But we have to be realistic. One of us might die. And if it's me, there's something I need you to tell Lena, something I never told her.'

Alexandre felt what little enthusiasm he had left drain out of him sharply, like air being released from a punctured balloon. They were almost at the end.

'Please. It's important. You had the courage to be honest about your past. I owe it to you and Lena to do the same.'

Alexandre cleared his throat. 'What is it?'

'On the day Lena was born, I made a decision that would change our lives,' Theo began. In the dim light, Theo told his story. When Theo was finished, he wiped a single tear from his eye. Alexandre couldn't speak. He sat, dazed, wondering if he could still trust the person sitting across from him.

'Why didn't you just tell her about Isabella from the start?'

Theo looked like a little boy who'd just been found out by a teacher or parent. 'I didn't think she'd ever find out. But then Horace gave her that letter and . . .'

Alexandre thought back to when Lena had told him about her father's affair. But he couldn't have imagined this.

'Alexandre?'

Alexandre glanced up and saw the pain in Theo's eyes. He softened and squeezed his hand.

'It's not your fault. Gia didn't die because of you,' he said. Outside in the hall, the chatter of men coming back from the day's chores echoed. There was something he still didn't understand. 'But why tell her now? The damage has already been done.'

'Because everyone deserves to know the truth.' Theo said. 'I hate that I have this hanging over my head. Lena deserves an explanation.' He closed his eyes. 'Do I have your word?'

Alexandre leaned over and hugged Theo. He knew what Theo meant, about being honest, especially with those you loved. As hard as it had been to tell Lena about his past, when he'd finally done so, it was a huge weight lifted. 'I promise. But on one condition. If I don't survive, you must pass on a message from me to her.'

'Anything,' Theo said, nodding.

'Tell Lena that I love her.' Alexandre didn't hesitate when he said it.

CHAPTER THIRTY-FIVE

After a restless sleep, Alexandre climbed out of bed. He tiptoed into the hallway and down the staircase, shivering as the early dawn chill curled its icy fingers around him. He watched the sun slowly illuminate the courtyard. What Theo had told him last night didn't change anything. As he knew all too well himself, everyone made mistakes. And everyone deserved a second chance.

At breakfast, Leike confronted him, her face ashen.

'It's gone,' she said, anguish in her voice.

'What's gone?'

'The schedule I'd written out. It's gone.'

'Where did you last see it?'

'At rehearsal yesterday. I'd put it down on the pile of costumes and thought it was in the stack of fabrics I was carrying back to my room. But when I checked it was gone. I looked everywhere, I promise.' She looked like she was going to cry.

Alexandre cast a glance across the canteen. No one was looking at them suspiciously and he hadn't detected any strange behaviour. 'Was anything else written on it?'

Leike wrung her hands. 'Only the measurements for your costumes and the train timings.'

'Ok,' Alexandre said, glancing around again. 'I'm sure people will think it was something from the administration office.

There's nothing we can do now, but hope that no one suspects anything.'

Back at the barracks, Theo and Alexandre nodded at each other, silently acknowledging the events that transpired the previous evening. After Attila and Vasily left, they ran through the plan for the day. Satisfied they'd plotted things out as best they could, Theo headed off to *Badhausgasse*, leaving Alexandre to complete his final task.

Double checking that no one was around, he uncorked the bottles of brandy. With a stone, he ground up the barbital to a powder, then tipped it into the two bottles. Then, he resealed the bottles carefully and headed to *Badhausgasse*.

Alexandre couldn't concentrate all day. His hands fiddled with the stem of the table leg he was sanding. He was so nervous that he couldn't look at anyone else in the workshop. When five o'clock arrived, he hurried out, unable to cast a backward glance to the friends he was leaving behind. With the sun fading behind the clouds and residents filling the seats for the big dress rehearsal, he slipped quietly away to hide near Erik and Friedrich.

As the faint strains of the children's choir warming up filled the air, Alexandre heard Friedrich and Erik joking with one another. He peered around the corner, took a deep breath and strode straight towards them. They noticed him instantly, drawing themselves up. Grasping the handle of his bag containing the brandy firmly, Alexandre flashed a big smile.

'Gentlemen, what are you still doing here?' Alexandre gestured to the stage area. 'Seats are filling up.'

'Who gave you permission to address us?' Friedrich sneered.

Alexandre dropped his bag and held up his hands, making sure his bag was left wide open in full view on the ground.

'Forgive me. I simply wanted you to have a chance to experience the wonder of our magic.' He watched gleefully as Erik's greedy eyes shot to the bag.

'What are you doing with this?' he barked, yanking out one of the bottles. He shoved the bag towards Friedrich, who took out the other bottle.

'Burger's orders, sir. Theo required alcohol for his arthritis.' He reached for the bottles, but they both pulled away.

'Why don't you run along to your little practice play,' Friedrich said, clutching the bag. 'We'll keep this safe.'

Alexandre bit his lip to keep from laughing. It was almost too easy, he thought, as he watched Erik stroking the body of the bottle.

'You're not going to watch?'

A cold smile appeared on Friedrich's face, and he gripped Alexandre's shoulder with his large hand.

'Some of us have to work.' Friedrich pushed Alexandre with such force that he fell, sliding backward on the gravel. Dazed, Alexandre shook his head. It took him a moment to recover. But when he did, he couldn't help letting out a tiny smile. The scene of Erik and Friedrich leering at him as they sipped brandy laced with sleeping pills was too perfect.

Finished with the two guards, Alexandre joined Theo backstage. The performances were set to begin at 6 p.m. and last about two hours. Theo and Alexandre were the finale act.

'Is it done?' Theo asked anxiously.

Alexandre nodded as he peeked behind the curtain. It was a packed house, the entire town of residents and the administration crammed into the courtyard. Despite it being a run-through, there wasn't a single person who wanted to miss it. They waited backstage, watching performers warm-up and don their costumes.

'Where's Attila?' A resident in charge of stage production rushed up to them. 'I need him in makeup!'

Alexandre scowled, as he checked the clock. They needed to get back to Erik and Friedrich. 'We've not seen him. Try Vasily,' he shouted over his shoulder as he and Theo raced back to the place where Alexandre had left the two guards, finding them motionless on the cold ground. Alexandre knelt to check their pulses.

'Well?' Theo asked, his breath making misty clouds in the chilly night air.

Alexandre jumped up. 'Let's move.' Hauling the sleeping guards into the work wheelbarrows they'd been using to cart show props all over the town, they covered them with tarps then took a circuitous route back to the dress rehearsal area, stopping in a darkened alcove nearby, where Leike had left the duplicate costume set. As people clapped and whistled, the two illusionists worked to switch the guards out of their uniforms and into the show clothing. They grabbed the guards' guns, hid them under the uniforms, and tucked everything in one of the wheelbarrows under the tarp. When they were finally done, they knelt back, taking a moment to catch their breath.

'Ready?' Theo asked, panting.

Alexandre nodded, and they took off, steering the guards backstage, parking the tarp-covered wheelbarrows in a corner. No one would suspect they were full of anything but surplus fabric.

Nervous with anticipation, they waited anxiously as the performances went on, the vibrant costumes and live orchestra transporting the audience to the *boulevard de Clichy*.

By 8 p.m., everyone but Alexandre and Theo had performed and the backstage area was empty save for the guard waiting to raise the illusionists above the tank.

'Give me a minute,' Theo whispered to Alexandre before slipping out into the audience. A second later, he was back, smiling.

'I told Burger to stay out there, that we need to create a spectacle, get people cheering first. The curtains will open to reveal us suspended, ready to fall into the tank,' he said.

Alexandre nodded, casting a sideways glance at the guard. He turned to Theo, giving him a wry look.

Theo grinned. 'Would you do the honours?'

'Gladly,' Alexandre said. He approached the guard, holding out the handcuffs. 'We're ready,' he said. As soon as the guard reached out, Alexandre ducked, grabbing his legs. Caught off balance, the guard fell backwards, smacking his head on the ground. Theo crouched beside him, checking to make sure he was out cold.

In front of the curtain, Burger's commanding voice was booming out across the audience, who couldn't keep quiet.

'This next act is a masterful display of illusion by Theo the Magnificent and Alexandre, his apprentice!' A surge of applause filled the air. 'They will attempt to escape from a locked water tank while handcuffed and blindfolded.'

'Hurry!' Alexandre yelled. He'd handcuffed Friedrich to Erik and Theo was pulling the potato sacks over their heads. He fastened the harness around them and looped the hook through it. Then the two illusionists moved out of view and began pulling the rope, hauling Erik and Friedrich above the tank.

In front of the audience, Burger droned on. 'Behold! The greatest trick you will see tonight!'

Alexandre imagined him, waving his arms around, loving the attention. The curtains began to move and they heard the audience gasp, as they stayed out of sight, keeping the rope taught, waiting to release it.

'On my count,' Theo whispered. 'Three, two—.'

Splash.

The guards sank into the tank and Alexandre could tell from the way they'd moved that the chill of the water had woken them up. They watched as Burger pushed the cover over the top of the tank and secured it shut.

'Come!' Theo whispered loudly, clambering away from the stage area.

Alexandre wanted to wait. He wanted to see Erik and Friedrich squirm, to witness them experience just an ounce of the pain they'd inflicted on everyone else.

'Alexandre! Now!'

Alexandre said a silent prayer for everyone they were about to leave and ran.

Leike was huddled in the nearby alcove, waiting. Alexandre pulled her into a hug. Their biggest hurdle was clear. The two men quickly changed, pocketing Erik's and Friedrich's guns. They looked like they were part of the staff, accompanying a nurse out on the town. Once changed, they rushed to the post where they'd picked up the guards earlier and grabbed the bikes lying on the ground.

'Remember to walk slowly, like we have nowhere to be,' Theo muttered. They strode confidently across the courtyard, tossing out snatches of German here and there, saluting the guard at the inner gate.

'Where are you headed at this hour?' he asked, coming out from his booth.

'The lady wants a drink,' Theo said, gesturing to Leike.

'Haven't seen you here. I take pride in knowing all the nurses.' The guard smiled seedily at Leike, revealing a set of tobacco-stained teeth. He leaned towards her, running a finger down her cheek. 'Ah, to be so young again.'

Alexandre curled his hands into fists and readied himself to strike when suddenly Leike raised her arm in salute.

'*Heil* Hitler!' Her face was stony, her once-scared eyes now blazing with anger. Caught unawares, the guard stumbled back.

'*Heil* Hitler,' the guard said, saluting her. 'Please. Enjoy your evening.'

It took everything in Alexandre's power not to break into a run but he knew he had to keep up the charade. They walked out of the unmanned gates, past the ominous arch that had welcomed them a little over a year ago, and jumped on the bikes.

'That was too close!' Alexandre said, giving Leike, who was perched on the handlebars of his bike, a quick peck on her cheek. But there was no time for discussion.

'Go!' Theo yelled.

Alexandre pedalled faster down the road that led to the train station. As they rode further away from Theresienstadt, he didn't look back. There was nothing about that place he wanted to remember.

The station was two kilometres away, but they had to cut through a wooded area to reach it. Staying on the open path where SS officers and Czech gendarmerie regularly patrolled wasn't safe, so they jumped off their bikes at the edge of the forest about fifty metres out from the platform. Leaving the bikes on the ground, they walked briskly through the woods, not daring to look over their shoulders. So far it didn't seem like anyone had tried to follow them and even if they did, it didn't matter. They looked like staff members.

The forest was dark but fragments of light from the moon shone through, illuminating the station ahead. They stomped through the uncut brush, dark green fir and snow-covered roots, their breath forming pale, white clouds in the air.

As they approached the clearing, Alexandre felt something stir inside him when the train came into view, and he clutched Leike's hand tightly. It was waiting silently, curls of wispy smoke rising from underneath it. Alexandre didn't think he'd seen anything more beautiful. For a brief second, they halted at the edge of the wood. Theo and Alexandre exchanged a tentative glance. But, they couldn't help it and broke into nervous laughter, big grins plastered across their faces. They hugged and punched the air as they started across the clearing. Their weeks of planning had paid off. They'd done it.

Theo walked on ahead. The train would depart soon and they

were planning to jump into one of the last cars. The platform felt like a ghost town, not a person in sight. Still, it wasn't like they needed tickets with their uniforms and if anyone asked, they'd say they'd had orders from Burger to travel to Prague. Alexandre squeezed Leike's hand and smiled, watching her cheeks turn a rosy pink.

He was still smiling when the first gunshot sliced through the air, disrupting the eerie calm that hung around them.

And then everything happened in slow motion. Alexandre saw Theo's face, tight with fear, as he lunged towards him and Leike, pushing them out of the way. As his body made contact with the hard ground, he saw Theo pull out Friedrich's gun and aim.

But before he could pull the trigger, there was another gunshot, followed by a shrill scream. Leike flopped into the snow a few feet away. Dropping to his knees, Alexandre scrambled to reach her. She lay on the ground, breathing heavily, her face frozen in shock as she tried to orient herself. Blood seeped slowly from her shoulder into the white snow, turning it bright red. Without thinking, he heaved her up into the back of the freight carriage in front of him.

Theo.

There were too many things happening at once. It was hard to keep track. Alexandre spun around just in time to see Theo hurl himself at a Czech gendarme a few feet away, as Friedrich's gun slid out of his hand.

From the carriage, Leike groaned and Alexandre turned back, holding his breath as he hastily tried to check her wound. Unsure what to do, he tore off his jacket and threw it over her.

I can't leave Theo.

Alexandre realised that if he could sneak up and shoot, he'd be able to get Theo to safety. His hands closed around the cold barrel of Erik's gun and he drew it out of his pocket trying to figure out where to position himself. His eyes darted around him and fell on a nearby lamppost, just a few feet away, casting a hazy glow on a body. He ran over to it.

It was Attila. His eyes stared up at Alexandre, glassy and vacant. A chunk of his ear had been blown off, a bullet wound puncturing his chest. Blood pooled around his head, forming a dark halo. Next to him was the piece of paper Leike had lost. Attila, who couldn't let his suspicions go. Attila, who so badly wanted to be free and rid of the Germans, so much so, that he thought he could trust a gendarme, outing the plan Alexandre and Theo had made in exchange for his own freedom.

Looking back to Theo, Alexandre focused on where to aim his gun. But it was proving to be an impossible task, the two men moving so rapidly back and forth. He could hit Theo by mistake. Still, what choice did he have? Alexandre moved his finger over the trigger, his hands shaking. Just then the loud whistle of the train assaulted his ears. His shot went wide, and he watched, his heart plummeting, as the bullet hit the snow a few feet away from his target.

'Go!' Theo yelled, not taking his eyes off the gendarme.

Alexandre looked back to the carriage where Leike lay, her head raised slightly. He could tell she was searching for him, but the effort proved to be too much and she fell back down on the floor of the carriage. Alexandre hesitated and then made a decision.

'No!' he yelled at Theo, rushing towards him. He raised his gun, aimed squarely at the gendarme and shot.

Bang. The gendarme keeled over, grasping at his right foot, yelping, as his pistol fell to the side. Alexandre pushed Theo toward the train, keeping one eye on the gendarme. 'You have to go now!' he yelled, his voice raw.

Theo opened his mouth to protest but Alexandre shook his head. If only one of them could survive, it was not going to be him. He would not let Theo, who had sacrificed so much for him, die on his watch.

The train let out a loud whistle again and then started to come to life, moving slowly like a giant carnivorous animal stretching its limbs, readying itself for a sprint.

'Theo! Go!' Alexandre yelled more urgently. As the train lurched forward, Theo turned and raced to the back carriage, hoisting himself up next to Leike.

Alexandre swivelled to face the gendarme, who was using his arms to drag himself closer to his pistol. He snarled at Alexandre, who raised his gun and aimed. He could hear Theo yelling at him to shoot. Holding his breath, he cocked the gun one more time and pulled the trigger. Nothing. The gun was jammed.

'Damn it,' he swore, tossing the gun onto the snow. The gendarme, though not dead, couldn't get up and run. Behind him, Alexandre heard the steady motion of the wheels turning.

'Alexandre, run!' Theo screeched, the desperation in his voice cutting into Alexandre's thoughts.

Alexandre turned and sprinted toward the back of the train as it picked up speed.

'Come on!' Theo yelled. He was lying on his stomach, his hand outstretched. 'Run!'

Alexandre dug his feet into the snow, pumping his arms as fast as he could. The cold air made it feel like his lungs were on fire, but he didn't stop. He didn't know when he had started to cry, but tears had wrestled their way into his eyes and were now streaming down his face. He realised now that all he wanted to do was live.

'You're almost there!' Theo shouted. Alexandre strained his arms forward, his fingertips grazing Theo's touch.

'No!' Theo gasped.

Alexandre turned his head instinctively. The injured gendarme had retrieved his pistol and was aiming it squarely at them.

'Jump!' Theo screamed.

Alexandre took a deep breath and leapt, just as a gunshot shattered the still night air.

CHAPTER THIRTY-SIX

December 1943 – London, England

'Lena?' Clara called.

'In a minute,' Lena called back. She twisted to face the mirror and inspected her outfit one more time. Clara had braided her hair and looped it over her head, securing it with barrettes studded with pearls, so that it looked like she was wearing a crown. Lena had worn her smartest red dress for the occasion and she tugged at the waistband of her woolly tights, smoothing the skirt part down. Slicking on a bit of pink lipstick, she thought about the schedule for the day. After their appointment was over, Clara and Fitz were taking her for lunch to the public house on Fulham Broadway to celebrate welcoming her to the family.

'*Officially*,' as Clara had put it the night before. 'You were always part of the family, but after tomorrow we'll have the papers to prove it.'

Satisfied with her appearance, Lena glanced at the two necklaces lying on her dresser. She'd thought about wearing them many times but today seemed as appropriate an occasion as ever. She took turns fastening each one around her neck, then adjusted the strand of pearls and star pendant so that they were just above her collarbone.

'Lena!'

'Coming!' Lena grabbed her purse and walked out into the hallway.

'You look lovely,' Fitz said admiringly, handing Lena her coat as Clara draped a scarf around her neck. The trio walked out into the damp December air and poured into Clara's father's bright orange Peugeot. They were staying with Clara's family over the holiday break. Fitz was due up north in ten days' time and they didn't think it reasonable to rent a home that neither Clara nor Fitz would be able to live in. Clara had apologised for the transitory nature of the living arrangements, but Lena didn't mind. After so long without a family, it felt nice to have one to come home to, wherever they were living.

As they sped towards the town hall, Lena leaned her head against the backseat window. As terrifying as it was for her to admit, she was looking forward to making things official. She liked having tea and toast with Olivia every Saturday morning in the mess hall. She liked sitting in the warmth of Clara's tiny cottage, exchanging stories about the daily activities of the school, while the wind howled outside. Clara was less stern parent and more big sister. And though she didn't know Fitz nearly as well, anyone who could see the value in Clara was alright in Lena's eyes. Plus, she didn't think too many men would so willingly welcome a teenaged orphan into their home. The fact that Fitz did so without hesitation said a lot about his character.

At night Lena sometimes lay awake, feeling guilty about how quickly she was settling into her new life. It seemed too soon for her to be moving on. She wasn't sure if she should even be allowed to feel happy, thinking about the lives that her father and Alexandre would never get to complete. But then she'd remember her father's words about her mother.

She would have wanted us to move on and be happy, Lena.

In one of their biology units that term, they'd learned about adaptation. Lena liked the analogy of comparing her own life to that of the plants and animals they studied, that changed in response to their environmental conditions. In a way, this adoption was the same thing. She was simply adapting herself in order to fit in and survive.

Fitz pulled up outside a nondescript government building and turned the car off. The trio walked down the halls until they found the adoption and foster wing. Inside the office, the adults busied themselves with paperwork while Lena waited patiently. At length, the lawyer helping them through the process turned to her.

'Would you like to change your name?' He held out a form, pointing to the top section. On the first line, 'Helena' was typed out in block capitals. Next to it, the name 'Calista' followed and next to that was a blank space. She realised what the official was asking her.

'Papadopoulos' was the last thing linking Lena back to her father, to the Beddington and Sterling World of Wonders, to Alexandre and to the sunset-filled muggy nights in Thessaloniki. Did she really want to lose the name she'd been given, the name that tied her to her old life and her parents, now that they were both gone?

Then she thought about how it had all ended, and how she would carry the guilt of the way she'd treated her father in their final moments as long as she lived. The past year had taught her that true grief and heartache would never permanently disappear. She knew, deep down, that she would continue to feel the loss of Theo and Alexandre forever.

But time waited for no one. She had a chance now to step into a new life. She made a silent promise to never forget where she'd come from and to honour her father and Alexandre always, something she liked to think she was already doing by excelling in school. As she fingered the star of the necklace she was wearing, she hoped that in time the good memories of her childhood would overshadow the bad, but for now, she thought the best thing to do was to start afresh.

'If you like, it can be the middle name,' the official continued, writing it out for her. He turned it around. *Helena Calista Papadopoulos Thomson*, it read. 'Perhaps this is a good compromise?'

Lena glanced at Fitz and Clara, then looked at the lawyer and nodded.

'Welcome to the family,' Clara said, wrapping an arm around Lena and squeezing her shoulder. The official placed the paper in his typewriter and began clacking away. Lena sat clutching Clara's hand, listening to the sound of her identity being overwritten.

CHAPTER THIRTY-SEVEN

April 1944 – London, England

The journey to London had been a long one, spanning four months, multiple cities, and countless dead ends. And still, the man soldiered on. He had lost too many people at this point to give up on finding her.

As he walked south from the Fulham Broadway tube station, he consulted his map, noting that Parsons Green would have been a better choice. But no matter, he told himself, as he trudged past pedestrians, doing his best to blend in. Even now, months removed from Theresienstadt, it felt odd to be able to walk freely.

He looked around, taking in the crumbling buildings, rubble, and the film of dust that seemed to have taken up permanent residence in the air. With each passing step that brought him closer to the Smith family home on Chiddingstone Street, he felt his hopes falling. Judging by the scene unfolding around him, he would be smart to temper his expectations.

When he finally found the number he was looking for, he was relieved to see that it was still standing. Taking a deep breath, he walked up to the door and knocked firmly.

'There's no point in knocking.'

The man turned around to see a young boy standing on the pavement, a football tucked under his arm, eyeing him curiously.

'Oh, hello,' the man said. He gestured to the house. 'By any chance do you know if this is the Smith residence?'

The boy shrugged and began passing the ball back and forth between his hands. 'Might have been.' He jerked his head to the right. 'We used to live three streets over, but left on account of the raid.'

'There was a raid?'

The boy nodded. 'The Luftwaffe attacked, few months back. Operation Steinbock I think it was called. We moved to Brighton, where Mum's family is.' He frowned. 'Only back for a day because Gran's in hospital.'

'I'm so sorry,' the man said.

The boy steeled himself. 'Don't like hospitals. Funny smells and all. Dad said I could go for a walk, if I was careful,' he continued, dropping the ball to the pavement and dribbling it with his feet.

'So, this attack. They hit this street?'

The boy was concentrating on weaving the ball in between his feet, but nodded. 'Loads of people died.'

The man shook his head, trying to collect his thoughts. He looked at the house again. Though it showed signs of surface wear and tear, it was still intact.

'You said you used to live nearby. Do you know who lived here? Was it the Smith family?'

The boy shrugged again. 'I seen a family here a few months ago but I dunno their names. A young woman and her parents. No, wait – there was a teenage girl too, I think.'

The man perked up. 'Was the teenager using leg braces?'

The boy's eyes widened and he stopped kicking his ball. 'Braces?' He shook his head. 'No.'

The man sighed, rereading the address he'd written down on the slip of paper in his pocket. 'It's just . . . it said this was the Smith residence,' he mumbled.

The boy cocked his head. 'You can come back to the hospital

and ask my dad if you like?' Then the boy frowned, noticing something on his ball for the first time. 'Bloody hell, only been a week,' he complained, running his finger over a nick in the leather. He shook his head. 'How does that sound, sir? Sir?'

But when he looked up, the man was gone.

PART III

Our revels now are ended. These our actors,
As I foretold you, were all spirits, and
Are melted into air, into thin air.

—PROSPERO, *THE TEMPEST*

CHAPTER THIRTY-EIGHT

February 1952 – London, England

Horace took a measured sip of his pint, enjoying the warmth of the amber liquid streaming down his throat. He set the mug down and tugged at a stray blue thread that dangled from the cuff of his jacket. Gone were the expensive suits and custom-made suede shoes. Following a less-than-stellar run in Asia, Horace was now back in London with the only thing he owned: his home. The circus was no more. He had no wife, no children, and no friends to share his life with. Even Chadwick had up and left him.

He toyed with the idea of starting over in America. But at nearly fifty years of age, he was too exhausted from years of butting heads with creatives, producers and investors to do it anymore. The World of Wonders was now a thing of the past, like folklore. From time to time he overheard adults excitedly telling their children about the show as they stood in line at the Piccadilly or the Alhambra. But he never revealed himself and no one ever asked who he was, his creative genius hidden in the body of an anonymous man, unremarkable without his colourful attire.

In the years since the circus unravelled, Horace had tried to pinpoint the start of the demise, when the sparkle began to fade, when the glitter turned to dust. Still, he kept up the illusion long enough. No one could deny that he'd had a good run, he thought, chugging back the last of his pint. A thin layer of white foam settled on his moustache and he wiped his mouth with the back of his hand.

At times like this, he remembered the girl and her odd hobbies. He remembered her desire to become something, to not simply accept her condition, but to push past it. And he remembered the day the light went out in her eyes, when her father and that boy were taken.

He reached into his pocket, carefully counting out a few silver coins, before ordering another drink. As he sipped his ale, Horace's mind wandered back to a similar night, eight years ago, when he'd been back in London for a month that spring. He'd been minding his own business, seated at the bar, when he felt a hand on his shoulder. He remembered the horror he'd felt, what it was like seeing him reappear, like a ghost. He'd taken a seat next to him without asking and ordered a pint of lager. Horace had glanced around quickly, hopefully.

'Don't bother. He's not here,' his drinking partner had said gruffly.

There was no time for niceties. He'd grabbed Horace by his collar and insisted he hear what he had to say. And so Horace sat, listening to him tell tales of the horrors he'd witnessed, the pain he'd endured. And asking after Lena. Always asking after Lena. 'Where is she?' 'Didn't she tell anyone where she was going?' Finally, he'd left an address. 'If you hear anything. Now, tomorrow or in ten years. You must tell me.' And then he was gone.

And now here Horace was, with all the power to change things. He removed a folded up slip of newspaper he'd torn out of the *Daily Express* earlier that day, smoothing it out on the counter, a drop of ale turning one of its edges damp. He'd been happy to read it, glad that the girl was safe. He lamented the blame everyone had placed on him in the first place and thought briefly about doing nothing. What did he owe to anyone? Besides, judging from the information in the newspaper, it seemed like the girl's life had turned out fine. Far better than that of most cripples.

As he stumbled out of The Flask, taking a roundabout road to his home on Fitzroy Park, he remembered how the only person who'd been at the port to see him off was his grandmother, and how he'd cried, ashamed, years later when she died and he wasn't able to get back for her funeral. To lose a loved one was a terrible thing, he told himself, fumbling with the lock on his front door before careering through, nearly knocking over his coat rack in the process.

In the safety of his study, Horace took out a sheet of notepaper and a pen. In block capitals, he wrote:

I found what you've been searching for.

He paused before inserting the newspaper clipping inside. Then he sealed it and took out the worn piece of paper he'd carried in his breast pocket for the past eight years. He began copying the numbers and letters onto the envelope and told himself that he'd take it to the post office first thing in the morning.

Once it reached its destination, the recipient would be able to do the rest.

CHAPTER THIRTY-NINE

March 1952 – London, England

'After the lecture on molecular biology, they had a special one on epigenetics that wasn't even in the programme. I simply had to stay,' Lena said, trying to catch Olivia's eye as her friend roamed around. They were on the second floor of Selfridges, for what Lena hoped would be her final wedding dress fitting. 'Really sorry I was late again,' she said, looking forlornly at Marjory, the senior seamstress.

Marjory raised an eyebrow and pulled two pins out from between her teeth, sticking them in her pin cushion. 'Can't even be cross— I've no idea what you're talking about.'

Olivia laughed from across the bridal boutique in the flagship department store, fingering a pair of white pumps. 'You think you're having a hard time? Imagine growing up with her!'

Lena grinned. She was glad to have Olivia here, grateful that her closest friend from boarding school was still in her life. After the risk of an air raid forced Briarwood to close, they'd completed their A-levels at a school in Brighton, where Clara had accepted another role. After school, Olivia had done a short-hand course and gone straight to working as part of a typing pool at a publishing company in Soho, where she wowed the men and women alike with her razor-sharp wit. Lena had tried to convince her to attend UCL, but Olivia was having none of it. The promise of a steady income, a life away from her mother and the buzz of being young in post-war London was too enticing.

Despite their divergent career paths, the two girls remained close. They tried to meet up every week, Lena trekking down to Dean Street after classes on Mondays and Olivia coming up to Gower Street to sip martinis and ogle the university men on Fridays. Olivia had got married just five months earlier to a man she'd met at work named David and she, alongside Clara, had been instrumental in helping Lena prepare for her own upcoming nuptials.

'If you insist on twisting and turning like this, you'll have a dress that's half backward!' Marjory said, as Lena squirmed.

'Sorry,' Lena said. 'Oh and Liv, you won't believe what else,' she continued. 'I heard two students discussing Rosalind Franklin. She's a chemist at King's doing amazing work on X-ray diffraction images of DNA.' Forgetting her promise, Lena twisted her head around and knocked over the pincushion Marjory had placed on a footstool. 'Oh! Goodness, let me help you,' she said, bending down.

'You will do no such thing!' Marjory pretended to be upset but the truth was the elderly seamstress loved Lena's spark. 'Now keep still!'

Lena grinned sheepishly as Olivia came into view and perched herself on the armchair usually occupied by a husband waiting for his wife. She winked at Lena's reflection in the mirror as she removed a slim, gold compact from her purse and began powdering her nose.

'So,' Lena continued. 'Rosalind does all this research and gets no credit for it. But the men do, because they're men. Someone said she might leave King's, that's how bad it is.'

'That's good. More room for you.'

Lena shook her head modestly. 'She's got a PhD. I haven't even got a medical degree.'

'But you *will*,' Olivia said sanguinely, plopping her compact back into her purse.

Lena smiled, grateful for the faith her friend had in her and her abilities. But stories like Rosalind made her doubt her chosen career path. Lena had been trying for years to get accepted to one of the medical schools in London with no success. Despite a biology degree from UCL and work experience as a science teacher at the school Clara now owned in Islington, it still hadn't been enough. 'If a woman with a PhD can't get a break, what hope do I have?'

Olivia had migrated towards the accessories section and was eyeing a rack of bowties. 'You're different,' she insisted. 'Remind me again what colour Harry's shirt is?'

'The groom's clothing choices shall be dictated by the bride's attire, not the other way around!' Marjory clucked her tongue.

'Fair,' Olivia said. 'Oooh, this would be perfect for India!' She exclaimed, removing a colourful silk scarf from one of the racks. She draped it across her shoulders.

'Are you off to the subcontinent?' Marjory asked.

Lena felt her cheeks redden. Harry, her fiancé, had accepted a work assignment that would take him to Delhi for six months starting in August. He was a photojournalist with the *Daily Express*, assigned to the Asia beat. Because Lena would be off from teaching over the summer, she'd decided to go with him. It had worked out perfectly. They were to leave a week after their wedding, spend three and a half weeks together and then, if everything went her way, she'd be able to start medical school in September.

'We are,' she smiled, thinking about how excited Harry had been when she'd agreed to go.

'Mind your stomachs, the both of you. Right,' Marjory said, taking a step back. 'Take a look.'

Lena turned around and glanced in the mirror. She'd never been the type of girl to imagine what the perfect wedding dress would look like, but if such a thing existed, this had to be pretty close. The bateau neckline showed off her décolletage perfectly. Below it sat a hand-stitched lace bodice, followed by a full skirt that stopped just short of her ankles, giving the dress a modern spin on the traditional tea-length gowns she'd seen splashed on the covers of the fashion magazines Olivia and Clara had helped her look through.

'You look like a real princess!' Olivia said, admiringly.

'Doesn't she?' Marjory nodded her approval and held out a matching fitted bolero jacket.

'You're both too kind.' Lena said.

'And you're too modest.' Olivia said, grabbing hold of her friend's shoulders and forcing her to look in the mirror again. 'Look at you. I hope Harry realises how lucky he is.'

Lena blushed. She'd always prided herself on being rational but the truth was, she thought there had to have been some magic in the air the night she and Harry met. It had happened one evening at the Islington Assembly Hall. She and Olivia had got dressed up as they always did on Saturdays, heading for their favourite place on Upper Street. Though Lena could walk now with no aids of any kind, activities like running and dancing were still difficult for her. But she enjoyed the music they played at this particular hall and relished the chance to be in the company of people her age. She usually sat by herself, content with her role as observer.

On the night she'd met Harry, she'd been feeling an unusual pang of loneliness, watching Olivia glide across the floor with David. So she'd taken her cup of orange squash and wandered outside, thinking the fresh air would make her feel better.

'Got two left feet like I do?'

Lena had spilled a bit of her drink, startled to see a young man seated on the wall that ran around the perimeter of the entrance. He was hitting his legs against the brickwork, a lit cigarette dangling from his fingers. She noticed he was clutching a camera in one hand, a thick strap around his neck.

'I didn't think anyone was here.'

The man jumped down, stubbed out his cigarette and held out his hand. 'Didn't mean to frighten you. Harry. Harry Evans. Pleased to meet you . . .?'

'Lena Thomson,' she replied, taking his hand.

'Got a Mediterranean glow to you, Mrs. Thomson.'

Lena felt her face turn pink as she gently corrected him. 'It's Miss.'

Harry paused, shifting his camera from one hand to the other. 'My apologies, Miss Thomson. Are you not from here?'

'Well,' Lena started, wondering how to explain her childhood. 'I was born in Greece, but I suppose I'm from all over.'

Harry grinned. 'Well, hello, Lena from-all-over. How'd you manage that?'

'My father was part of a travelling circus.'

'This evening just got a lot more interesting,' he said, inching closer to her. 'What's a pretty girl like you doing out here alone?'

Lena felt her skin turn from pink to scarlet and wished Olivia would come outside. It wasn't as though she didn't like men, it was more that she wasn't accustomed to them noticing her. 'I just needed some fresh air,' she explained. Then, before he could ask her anymore questions, she pointed to his camera. 'That's a heavy thing to be lugging around on a night out.'

Harry patted the camera with one hand. 'She's the only girl who'll go out with me,' he said, and Lena giggled. She liked this man, liked how she immediately felt at ease in his company. 'I'm a photojournalist with the *Daily Express* – you ever read it?'

'No,' Lena said carefully. 'But I'll pick it up.'

Harry rolled his eyes. 'Save your money. I'm kidding, I'm kidding,' he clarified, watching Lena's confused facial expression. 'It's a good gig. I've been at it . . . six years now? Mostly in India, covering the move to independence.'

'Wow,' Lena breathed, a feeling of wanderlust washing over her. It had been ages since she'd travelled outside of the city.

Harry nodded. 'It's pretty amazing. But I was getting tired living out of a suitcase, so I asked to come home for a bit, pick up some local work.' He held the camera up to his eye and before Lena could stop him, he'd snapped a few photos of her.

'Don't do that,' she said, suddenly feeling very exposed. She looked away, tilting her head down.

Harry let the camera hang around his neck as he grinned. 'They told me to take pictures of every pretty girl I saw. So,' he continued, not missing a beat. 'You feel like going back in there?'

Lena bit her lower lip and frowned. 'I'm afraid I'm not much of a dancer.'

Harry removed his trilby hat and held out his hand. 'Me neither. How 'bout we go make fools of ourselves?'

They'd danced until Lena's feet ached. Much to Olivia's delight, Harry had insisted on escorting Lena home, but not before stopping for food at one of the Turkish restaurants nearby. They'd sat next to each other, Lena recounting tales of Hungary, Estonia and France as she nibbled on olives and creamy hummus. Harry explained that the *Daily Express* was one of the largest broadsheets on Fleet Street. As their main photojournalist in the Asian bureau, he'd spent the last five years snapping roll after roll, documenting the conflict in West Bengal, the war in Kashmir and the assassination of Gandhi.

Lena thought his life sounded both dangerous and thrilling and she sat, spellbound by his stories, hanging onto his every word. He explained that he liked photography because to him, it was one of the only universal languages.

'A journalist can only write in so many languages. But a photo – you don't need to be able speak a certain language to understand a photo.'

Almost overnight, their chance meeting blossomed into a fully fledged relationship. Lena no longer felt like the one tagging along on Olivia's coat-tails, or cringed when she went to dinner parties alone, feeling like the pity invite. She and Harry spent nights at a cosy gin bar in Stoke Newington, watched films at the Roxy and, when the weather was fine, drove out to Brighton in Harry's old car, the hot stones of the beach warming the soles of Lena's feet as Harry splashed her with cold sea water.

Lena loved that he was well-travelled, a rarity among people she met. She loved that he knew some of the places she'd been and that he spoke two languages. But what she loved most about him was that he asked her what she thought of things. Often he'd develop a series of photos for a work assignment and then ask for her opinion on it. While she'd never placed a premium on dating, most of the men Lena met were far more interested in her looks than her thoughts.

So when Harry had proposed to her with his grandmother's ring outside the hall they'd met at just seven months earlier, Lena didn't hesitate to say yes.

'Is the jacket comfortable?'

Lena blinked twice, realizing that Marjory and Olivia were waiting for her response.

'Yes,' she said, looking at herself in the mirror. 'Everything's perfect.'

CHAPTER FORTY

'I'm home,' Lena announced, entering the house she shared with Clara, Fitz and their two children in North London.

'Aunty Lena!' Harriet, Clara and Fitz's five-year-old daughter, came zooming into view and wrapped her arms around Lena's legs.

Lena laughed and stroked Harriet's reddish brown hair. 'Someone's happy to see me!'

'Have you got my dress?' Harriet was going to be a flower girl at the wedding. When Lena had told her the news, she'd been asking every day if her dress was ready.

'Not yet, but soon.' Lena removed Harriet's hands from her legs and led her into the parlour.

'You're just in time!' Clara appeared, carrying a tray of tea and biscuits, which she set down on the coffee table. 'How does it look?'

'It's beautiful. Marjory's done a fine job,' Lena replied. 'Is there enough for me?'

'Help yourself,' Clara said. She watched as Lena removed her coat and poured herself a steaming cup of tea. 'How were the lectures?'

'Really interesting, which is bad news! I've yet another speciality I'm considering,' Lena explained. 'Speaking of which, has the post come?'

Clara's smile faltered. 'It has,' she said, trying to keep her voice even. She picked up the pile of mail and handed it to Lena.

'Thanks.'

Clara waited, her heart sinking as she watched Lena thumb through the letters. She'd know when she chanced upon the one she was looking for. And sure enough, Lena's reaction was obvious before she'd even opened it. It was a thin envelope, stamped with the return address of one of the universities she'd applied to.

Lena thought back to the other letters she'd received, all in the same font, and of the same size and felt the familiar feeling of her dream slipping away from her. Bracing herself, she slit it open, and saw those all too familiar words – the ones she'd been reading for the last two years. *We regret to inform you.*

'I'm so sorry.' Clara said. She'd known Lena long enough to know that she needed time to process it and that she was far more resilient than people gave her credit for.

'It's alright,' Lena said quietly, feeling her stomach sink. She knew how lucky she was to have all that she did – Harry, a teaching job, and an upcoming wedding. But what she really wanted – what she'd always wanted – was to be a doctor. Acceptance to medical school was meant to be the icing on the cake, a reward for all her hard work. Still, it didn't seem right to complain, not after everything she and Clara and everyone else she'd loved growing up endured. She pocketed the letter and stood up, plastering a smile on her face.

'Shall I book a table for Joe's? Might make you feel better?' Clara asked.

'We're going to *The Gargoyle Club* with Olivia and David. But thanks,' Lena said, as she retreated to her room to get ready. She paused as she turned the doorknob. There was one option she hadn't mentioned to anyone. Perhaps it wouldn't be so bad to share it with Clara now. But then Lena thought about how hard it had been to tell people she'd been rejected from all these other schools.

She remembered the pitying looks on peoples' faces, mixed with the smug glances they couldn't help but cast her way. No, she thought as she pushed her door open. It was best to keep quiet.

The doorbell rang just as Lena was lining her lips with a deep burgundy lipstick.

'I'll get it!' Lena heard Harriet's high-pitched voice, followed by the pitter-patter of her tiny feet scurrying down the hall. She grabbed her purse and stepped into the hallway just in time to see Harriet tug open the front door and fall silent as Harry walked in.

'Good evening, Miss Harriet,' he greeted her, removing his hat and smiling down at her. With his charming personality, easy-going presence and sharp sense of style, Harry was immediately liked by everyone he met.

'Say hello to uncle Harry.' Lena leaned over Harriet to hug her fiancé. He was dressed in a charcoal grey suit, a grey wool coat, signature wingtip shoes, and had slicked his hair back.

'Hullo, uncle Harry,' Harriet whispered, as Clara came out from the living room.

'Harry, lovely to see you.'

'And you, Mrs. Thomson – are things well with the school? How's Mr. Thomson?'

'He's fine, thank you. As for the school, well it's never dull! Lena tells me you're off to *The Gargoyle*?'

Harry grinned. 'My publisher got us in.'

'What I would give to be young again,' Clara said, smiling. 'Can I get you a glass of scotch?'

Harry checked his watch. 'I think we'd better head out.'

'Bye, you,' Lena pecked Harriet on the cheek. 'Don't wait up, I've got my key,' she said to Clara.

Clara moved to close the door as the couple stepped out-side. 'Do have a good time,' she said to Lena. 'Everything will be alright.'

'What was that all about?' Harry asked as they walked to the taxi idling outside. He opened the door for Lena and she slid in.

Lena hesitated as the driver pulled the car away from the house. She didn't want to get into a discussion about it, not right before she was going out. But this was Harry. She was supposed to tell him everything. That's what couples did.

'A letter came from Guy's. I wasn't accepted.'

Harry's face fell. 'Lena. I'm so sorry.' He put his arm around her and Lena leaned in, resting her head against his shoulder. 'Did they give a reason?'

'They never do.'

'Was that the last one?'

Lena hesitated before nodding. She buried her face into the soft wool lapel of his coat and inhaled his scent.

'It's entirely their loss.' Harry said, stroking her hair. As the car sped towards Soho, they sat in silence, Lena feeling grateful that they were comfortable enough to not have to fill every minute they spent together with words.

As they turned off Theobold's Road and flew down the A40, Harry cleared his throat. 'Lena. Don't take this the wrong way, but if you don't want to go anymore, it's alright.'

Lena sat up. 'Of course I want to go. Besides, they'll have left Kensington, we can't very well leave them standing there.'

'I meant school,' Harry said, a concerned look in his eyes. 'No one would fault you if you didn't want to try again, least of all me. But I've been thinking ... maybe you could stay on in India? They're always looking for good English teachers at the missionary—'

Lena bristled. 'I'm not an English teacher! Why would you say that?'

Harry held his hands up. 'I didn't mean anything bad by it! It's just hard seeing you get down about these letters, that's all.'

'You're not the one having to deal with all the rejections,' Lena retorted. She crossed her arms, peering out the window. They were close to their destination, but Soho was always so busy at night, throngs of young party-goers crowding the streets, that they were crawling along at a snail's pace.

Harry took a deep breath. 'You know I'll support whatever you do, but you don't have to prove anything to anyone.'

'That's not what this is about!' she snapped. Harry didn't say anything and Lena glanced in the rearview mirror. She caught the driver's eye and wondered how many arguments he'd been privy to in his line of work. Sighing, she dropped her head in her hands as they rolled onto Dean Street. 'Look, why don't you go and have a drink with them. I'll head home.'

'Lena,' Harry said, taking her hands in his. 'All I'm saying is maybe there's an easier alternative—'

'I don't want "easy".' she said, stonily. 'I want to be a physician.'

Harry smiled his warm smile, the one that never failed to put her at ease. 'I know. And you'll get there.' He tossed his head towards the entrance to the club, where a long line of people had formed. 'Forget I suggested anything. Let's just have fun.'

Three hours later, a beleaguered Lena kicked off her shoes inside Clara's house, watching them fall with a thud onto the ground. She knew she should try to be quieter since the children were sleeping, but she was too tired to care. Despite her best efforts to stay positive, Harry's words had grated on her all night and drinks in the company of good friends had just worn her out as she pretended to be fine.

As she stumbled into the foyer, she couldn't stop repeating the words 'one whole year', 'one whole year' over and over again in her mind. True, she had one last option, but given her track record, it was a long shot at best. She'd likely find herself in the same position she'd been in last September, writing essays, asking for references and licking stamps as she crossed her fingers, hoping one of the applications would yield the result she desired.

She didn't want to stop trying, but as time marched on, her resolve weakened. Years of hearing the word 'No', of being looked at awkwardly at dinner parties when people asked about her life, of having to work three times as hard as every man – it was all beginning to weigh on her. She'd known it wouldn't be easy, but she'd also believed that hard work would triumph in the end. And though she put on a brave face, inside she was struggling. Every single rejection she received was like a tiny paper cut, wedging itself deeply within her skin.

'Lena?' Clara called out from the top of the staircase.

'Sorry,' Lena whispered loudly. 'Didn't mean to wake you.'

'You're home early.'

'I got a bit cross with Harry,' she rubbed at the mascara on her eyes.

'Sounds like you could use some tea,' Clara said. She wrapped her dressing gown around her and walked down the stairs. 'Go on, into your nightgown. I'll put the kettle on.'

Ten minutes later, wrapped in a cosy blanket, a mug of tea in hand, Lena explained what had happened.

'Then he said instead of medical school, why not stay in India with him and teach? He made out like it was so easy for me to just give up my life.' Lena's voice wobbled as the last word slipped out. 'Do you know what the worst part is? He's right.'

'Come now. There's no right or wrong in this case.'

'No, he's right. It's not as though I have a place at a university. Would it be so bad to have a change of scene, spend some time with my new husband?' Lena looked down into her mug. 'I told myself I'd try for two years. And now it's been two years, and it hasn't happened. Any sane person would stop. But I can't. There's something,' her voice wavered. 'I must be crazy to love something this much, something that isn't even real. It's not a person, or anything worthwhile.'

'The pursuit of academic excellence is entirely worthwhile,' Clara said. 'Besides, being a doctor is a noble profession.'

Lena sniffed. 'I can't believe he suggested I stop.'

Clara raised her eyebrows. 'In his defence, he never told you to stop. He merely suggested an alternative for the time-being. But the decision is yours. Do you want to keep trying?' She watched Lena nod. 'Then forget everyone else. They'll comment no matter what you do, so you may as well make the choice you want.'

'How did you keep going?' Lena asked. 'How did you not let it undo you?'

'Becoming a teacher is a bit more acceptable for a woman than completing medical school,' Clara pointed out. 'But it's the same as with anything. If you have a setback, you rest. Then one day, probably sooner than you think, you wake up, ready to try again.' She reached out and rubbed Lena's leg. 'Get some rest. There are few things that can't be fixed by a good night's sleep.'

CHAPTER FORTY-ONE

The next morning, Lena was up early. She'd slept soundly and, as Clara had predicted, was already feeling better. By 9 a.m, she'd made breakfast for everyone, washed and was getting ready to head to the Italian market in Clerkenwell with Olivia when the doorbell rang.

'I've got it,' she called, opening the front door, where a postman stood holding a box.

'Package for a Mr. Fitz Thomson?'

'Yes, that's us. I'll sign,' Lena said, taking the pen and scribbling her name on the form.

'Your post and the newspaper are underneath.'

'Thanks,' Lena said, letting him put everything in her outstretched arms. She edged back into the house, kicking the door shut with the back of her foot and set down the package on the parlour table. She checked the return address, wondering what it could be.

'For you?' Clara asked. She'd entered the parlour from the kitchen and was drying her hands on a tea towel.

'Fitz,' Lena said. 'D'you know of a company in Worchester?'

'I've no idea what he's gone and ordered this time. Hold on, I'll get a knife.'

Lena was so busy wondering what might be inside that she'd nearly forgotten about the post and paper. She slid both out from

317

under the box, placing the newspaper on the sofa before rifling through the mail. Mail order catalogues, ads for a new vacuum cleaner, a letter for Clara. And one for her. In a big envelope.

Immediately Lena felt her stomach flutter. She glanced at the return address, not daring to get her hopes up. Université de Paris, it read.

'Here,' Clara said, returning and holding out a knife for Lena.

Lena took it from Clara, slowly slit open the envelope and removed the contents with trembling hands.

Dear Miss Thomson,

We are delighted to inform you that you have been accepted into the Université de Paris School of Medicine. Your acceptance is for the Autumn term beginning September 1952.

Below, you will find details of our policies and payment information. We invite you to join us for a meeting in the coming weeks, as all students …

Stunned, Lena re-read the letter. She closed her eyes and opened them, not believing what she'd just seen.

Having seen the return address on the envelope, Clara's insides began swirling with anticipation. 'I thought you received all your responses?'

'Don't be angry,' Lena said, gesturing for her to sit. As Clara perched herself on the sofa, Lena launched into an explanation. 'After I didn't get into any schools in England last year, I thought I should have a contingency plan,' she said. 'Except, I didn't tell anyone. It's been so hard admitting defeat, telling people I still haven't been accepted. You know, sometimes it feels like people take a perverse pleasure in me not succeeding.'

'Ah, yes,' Clara said. 'I believe the Germans refer to it as *schadenfreude.*'

'Right. So, I applied to a school in Paris and … well … it looks like the French love me, she said, unable to hold back her news any longer.

Clara blinked trying to register Lena's words. 'Is that,' she pointed to the envelope. 'Did you?'

Lena nodded, handing the letter over to Clara. 'I did it. I got in.'

And then Clara threw herself around Lena with such vigour that she almost knocked her over. They were crying and laughing all at once, letting out shrieks that echoed up to the top floor, not caring if they woke Fitz Jr. They caused such a commotion that Harriet came running into the parlour, demanding she be included in whatever was happening. When they finally calmed down to catch their breath, Lena couldn't stop beaming.

'I'm sorry I didn't tell you!'

'Forget sorry! This is thrilling, just thrilling!'

Just then the doorbell rang again. Lena looked at Clara. 'Olivia,' she said, before racing to tug it open. Before Olivia could speak, Lena waved the letter around. 'I did it,' she said, unable to restrain herself. 'I got into medical school.'

'You're joking!' Olivia yelled, her jaw dropping. 'I knew you'd do it, kid, I knew it!' She leaned down and squeezed her friend as tightly as she could. 'We have to celebrate. You, me, David, Harry—'

Suddenly Lena's face fell. 'Harry! He's away on assignment till Friday – but belated celebrations Saturday?' Lena frowned. 'Oh, I do hope he won't be cross about having to wait to hear this.'

'Have you seen the way that man looks at you?' Olivia said. 'He'll be overjoyed!'

Lena grinned and re-read the letter again. 'I'm to travel to Paris to meet with them.'

'We'll get you on the night train from Victoria,' Clara said. 'Fitz will make the arrangements.' She clasped Lena's hands and smiled at her. 'I can't tell you how happy I am. And you know your father and Alexandre would have been so, so proud.'

'Thanks,' Lena said, feeling her throat clam up. As if on cue Olivia swooped in.

'Right,' she said, taking her friend by the elbow. 'If we can't have

319

a full-on celebration until Harry's back, then I'm taking you out. Cream tea on me.'

The next week went by in a whirlwind, Lena suddenly on an upswing, having to think about settling into a whole new life. She moved through her days in an excited haze and in the evenings, she sat with Clara, discussing where she and Harry might live, what courses would be best when it came time to specialise, and more. At night, she struggled to sleep, but for a good reason. No longer riddled with anxiety about what she'd be doing next year, she instead stayed up dreaming about doing rounds at a hospital.

By the time Saturday rolled around, Lena was bursting to tell Harry her news. She'd decided she couldn't do it over the phone. She wanted to see his face, to witness his reaction.

Olivia had booked them all a table at *Scott's* in Mayfair and Lena had asked Harry to meet her a little earlier so that she could share her news. When she saw him standing by the entrance, she rushed into his arms.

'Well, hello!' he said, laughing as he leaned down to kiss her. 'You're excited!'

'I'm just—' she paused. She wanted to be seated, with champagne at the ready. 'I'm just so happy you're back.'

'I should go away more often,' he said, winking as her took her hand and led her inside.

As they waited for their coats to be taken, Lena took in the lush surroundings. Black draperies fashioned from thick, heavy material lined the walls. Rows of expensive spirit bottles were stacked neatly at the bar and waiters in crisp black uniforms traversed between the kitchen and tables smoothly. A large chandelier hung from the centre. All around them, the moneyed people of Mayfair and Kensington sat, smoking and laughing, not a care in the world.

As the waiter led them to their table, Lena's mind flitted back to the circus. Horace would have loved this place, she thought somewhat wistfully. Although she had no desire to ever see him again, Lena had learned that the passage of time did something strange to memories. Ever so slowly it chipped away at the most painful parts, smudging the hurt and softening the aches, to the point that she could now almost reminisce about her childhood in a fond manner, without sticking again and again on the wounds.

'Lena!' Olivia exclaimed. She had a martini glass in one hand and was dressed in a silver silk sheath that hugged her slim frame.

'You're early!' Lena said, trying to mask her disappointment. As she hugged her friend, she felt her stomach dip. She'd wanted to tell Harry by herself. It would just have to wait, she thought, taking a seat. Olivia nodded and took a sip of her martini.

'David couldn't wait to come! He's been desperate to eat here for ages.'

'Can you blame a man?' David asked. 'It's one of the only places in the city with butter.'

The two couples ordered drinks and food and settled into a discussion.

'So, Harry,' David said, after they'd started on their main courses. 'Liv tells me you're off to the subcontinent?'

Harry plucked an olive out of his drink. 'We are. Continuing with the reporting on the ramifications of partition. Thought I'd drag this one along with me,' he said, rubbing Lena's leg affectionately. 'We'll be in Delhi most of the time, but I took a few weeks out for us to travel. We'll visit Agra and Jaipur. Then down to Kerala and Goa – they've amazing beaches there.'

David laughed. 'Sounds idyllic. Excuse me, waiter?' He flagged one of the waiters down. 'A bottle of Bollinger, please.' He looked back at Harry beaming. 'Let me be the first to say we're so happy for you both.'

Harry frowned slightly. 'That's very kind of you. There's really no need for champagne though!'

'News like this should be celebrated! Though I must admit, Lena, I was of the camp that thought it was impossible.'

'Thought what was impossible?' Harry turned to Lena.

Lena felt the colour draining from her face. Terrified, she glanced at Olivia, who seemed to be realising the exact same thing simultaneously.

'Darling,' Olivia turned to David, 'I told you not to embarrass them! Why don't you tell Harry about your latest investment deal?'

'Nonsense, it deserves a toast!' David drawled, picking up a flute of champagne, the yellow gold liquid sloshing around precariously inside. 'To Paris!'

'Paris?' Harry asked.

As David drank, Lena tried desperately to think of a way to explain his comment. She looked hopelessly at Olivia, who was mouthing 'I'm so sorry' to her over and over. But Lena knew she had nothing to apologise for. She was the one who hadn't been completely honest.

'What's happening in Paris?'

'Oh you are good, Harry!' David guffawed, draining his flute and gesturing to the waiter to refill it. 'If you ever want to give up photography for acting ... Liv, will you look at him, he looks positively perplexed.'

'Will someone please tell me what's going on?' Harry asked, the frustration mounting in his voice.

'David, I need to go to the bar!' Olivia shouted suddenly, standing up and dragging her husband out of his chair.

Harry put down his glass and massaged his forehead. 'Is it just me or is he really drunk? Paris! I mean ...'

Lena bit her lip, wondering if she should let it slide and tell him the truth tomorrow. But she knew in her heart Harry would know. Bracing herself, she took a sip of the champagne. 'Actually, he was talking about me. I ... I got into medical school there. In Paris.'

'What?'

Lena smiled a small smile but when she noticed that Harry wasn't smiling back, she quickly adopted a more neutral expression. She turned to face him, taking his hands in hers. 'I didn't tell anyone

I applied because I thought I wouldn't get in. It had been so hard with all the other schools, and then having to tell everyone I'd failed, again. I thought, why not try outside of London? And last week, well, they accepted me.'

'You got in?'

Lena nodded.

'And you weren't going to tell me about it?'

'I didn't tell anyone, not even Clara—'

'They knew!' Harry said, pointing to Olivia and David at the bar.

'Only because Liv came round the morning it happened. Harry, please don't be cross. I was going to tell you tonight! I wanted to do it in person, to surprise you!'

'Consider me surprised,' he replied, quietly.

They both sat quietly at their table. Lena kept her gaze on the slice of half-eaten bread in front of her, wondering when it would be appropriate to speak again. Harry was alternating between pushing around the cold bits of an oyster shell and poking at a lemon wedge. This wasn't how she wanted it to go, she thought, berating herself for having kept it hidden at all.

'You could have told me you were applying,' he whispered. 'I'm me. I'm your Harry. You can tell me anything.'

'I know,' Lena nodded, guilt coursing through her. 'I ... I just couldn't handle the disappointment again. Honestly, I'm as shocked as anyone.'

A sprig of parsley fell off the edge of Harry's plate and onto the glossy black table. Lena watched as he raked one hand absentmindedly through his brown hair. When they'd first started dating, Lena would sometimes sneak into the local chemist's shop, remove the cap from a Brylcreem bottle and inhale deeply, before quickly putting it away. She liked the way it smelled, liked that it reminded her of him when she couldn't be around him.

'And what about India?'

'We can still go and ... I guess you can join me afterwards,' she said, resting a hand on his arm. 'Harry, believe me, I wanted to tell you, I did.'

He pulled away from her again. 'God, Lena ... it's ... you made a fool of me in front of our friends! And we're to be married. Married people tell each other things!'

'I know,' she said softly.

Harry put his hands down on the table, trying to compose himself. Lena couldn't blame him. She watched a waiter carefully swerve away from their table, half-wishing he would come over and ask them both to leave.

Harry rubbed his eyes and looked at Lena, an expression of guilt clouding her otherwise beautiful face. He sighed and took her hands in his. 'I know the last few years have been hard. And this is, I mean it's ... I just wish you'd involved me in it. If you can't tell me this, what else are you hiding?'

'Nothing! You have to believe me when I say I didn't think I would get accepted. And then the way you spoke to me, about how I didn't have to prove anything to anyone.'

'I never said you couldn't do it,' he said firmly. 'I wouldn't put it past you to become prime minister if you wanted. But even the prime minister needs someone to walk beside them.' He sighed, shaking his head. 'I've lost my appetite,' he continued, taking out a few bills to pay for their meal and setting it on the table. 'Do you mind if we go?'

'Not at all,' Lena said, standing up and signalling to Olivia from across the room that they were leaving. A queasiness settled into her stomach as she followed Harry towards the exit. In all the conversation, he hadn't actually said anything about Paris or her getting in. 'It's good news, about school – isn't it?'

Harry dragged his hand across his face, forcing a smile. 'Yeah. It's great.'

CHAPTER FORTY-TWO

'Are you sure you'll be alright on your own?' Clara gripped the handles of her purse.

'I'll be fine,' Lena said warmly. It was a few days after the scene at *Scott's* and she, Clara and Fitz were all onboard the Night Ferry at Victoria station. After the scene at dinner, Lena had felt terrible and said as much to Clara. She'd called Harry four times the next day but he hadn't answered. Fearing the worst, Lena sunk into a stupor, worrying about what would happen, regretting her decision to keep it a secret.

Then Clara suggested she go to Paris. 'They've already invited you to tour the school. It would be a good idea, to get your mind off things. You can tell Harry all about it when you get back.'

So Lena had decided to go. She'd paid for a first class cabin, the sleeper kind, which meant her luggage was checked all the way through and she had her own bed, meals and an attendant who had promised to update the Thomsons on Lena's journey and not let her leave *Gare du Nord* alone.

'I promise to ring you when I get there,' Lena said, tucking her purse onto the opposite side of the bench. 'Give a kiss to Harriet and Fitz Jr. for me?'

'We will. Be safe. And Lena? He just needs time.' Clara said.

'Thanks,' Lena said, squeezing Clara's hands.

As the train gathered speed, Lena looked out the window, waving to Fitz and Clara. 'Goodbye!' she called. 'Goodbye!'

'Final stop, *Gare du Nord!*'

Lena stood up easing out the crick in her neck. She'd been awake for a few hours, the anticipation of her meeting with the admissions director making it hard for her to sleep. She peered out the window, taking in the scene unfolding as the train came to a halt. Well-dressed travellers rushed back and forth on the platform outside and the scent of petrol and coffee filled the air. A giant clock at the centre of the terminal read 10 a.m.

With the help of the attendant, Lena gathered her things and then managed to find a taxi. As they wove further into the heart of the city, Lena ventured a few tentative phrases of French with the driver. By the time they reached her hotel in the second arrondissement, she felt comfortable enough to hold a conversation.

The hotel was a smaller boutique one that Fitz had recommended. The first thing Lena did once she'd got to her room was yank open the curtains. Light streamed in, magnifying the dust mites and falling in a rectangular slant across the carpet. From the window, Lena could see the tip of the Eiffel Tower and she stood, her hands pressed against the chilled glass of the pane, gazing at the beauty of the city, imagining what it would be like to wake up here each morning.

A yawn escaped her mouth and she rubbed her eyes. Even though it was morning, she wanted to be fresh for her meeting with the admissions director the next day. Lena climbed into bed, rested her head on the pillow and drifted off to sleep.

The doorbell rang just as Fitz Jr. had fallen asleep for his afternoon nap.

'Mrs. Thomson?' Rose, the housekeeper, called out.

'I'm putting the baby down,' Clara replied.

'Mr. Evans has come calling. Says it's mighty important.'

'I'll be down in a minute. Would you mind seeing him to the parlour and offering him some tea?'

'Certainly.'

A few minutes later, Clara walked into the parlour, Harry's anxiety palpable even before she'd had a chance to greet him. He was standing stiffly by the mantel, a harried look on his face. Still, even under stress, he didn't forget his manners, removing his trilby hat when he saw her.

'Mrs. Thomson. I'm sorry for showing up like this, unannounced. I just need to see Lena.'

'You're always welcome, you know that. But Lena's in Paris visiting the school.'

Harry frowned. 'Paris? By herself?'

Clara sat down on the sofa. When Harry made no move to join her, she nudged him gently. 'Harry,' she said, pointing to the tea Rose had brought in. 'Sit. Have some tea.'

Harry opened his mouth as if to say something, but then shut it. His hair was uncombed and his clothing wrinkled. His eyes fell on a photograph of Fitz Jr.

'They grow like weeds when they're young,' Clara said, looking fondly at the picture. 'So. How's everything at the newspaper?'

Harry shook his head sadly, sinking into the chair opposite Clara. 'I'm afraid I've made a mess of things.'

'It's alright. Lena understands.'

'She didn't even say she was applying. Why wouldn't she tell me?'

'You know why,' Clara said, softly. 'Would you keep telling people you were applying for something if you kept getting turned away?'

Harry buried his face in his hands. 'We're supposed to tell each other things.'

Clara placed her teacup gently on the china saucer, taking in the William Morris flowered pattern adorning it. 'She didn't tell me she'd applied, either. As for going to Paris without telling you, well, she mentioned your argument.'

Harry laughed wistfully. 'I was trying to tell her I'd love her, no matter what. But it came out all wrong.'

'I'm not criticizing you. If anything, I admire how supportive you are. The truth is, Lena needs this. She's always found success in her studies, especially when she was a child and didn't have success in other areas. And now, she finds herself torn between two worlds. She doesn't want to choose.'

'Why didn't she say that?'

'I'm not sure she knows.' Clara replied quietly.

Harry stood up and walked to the mantelpiece, studying the photographs of the Thomson family. 'D'you know the reason I applied for that assignment in India was for her? We've got our separate travelling stories, but I wanted to make our own memories. I wanted to hold her hand on a worn leather seat bench on a train to Madras. I wanted to watch a snake charmer and eat spiced nuts out of a newspaper cone with her in Delhi.' He smiled as though he was reminiscing about a good time that had already passed. 'I wanted to watch a Keralan sunrise, sipping hot spiced tea with her at my side. I wanted to photograph her framed by a *haveli* and hang the photos in the hallway of our new flat.'

'You can still do all those things,' Clara urged. 'You might just need to rethink the timing.'

Harry ran a hand through his hair and glanced at the clock. 'You say she's in Paris?' Clara nodded. 'Should I go? It can't be safe.'

Clara walked over to Harry and gently laid a comforting hand on his shoulder. 'Let her concentrate on why she's there. She'll be back in a few days and you can talk then. If you like, I'll leave a message with the hotel saying that we talked. Actually, hold on,' Clara said, walking over to the desk in the corner. She scribbled down a phone number on a piece of paper and handed it to Harry. 'Here. This is the number of the place she's staying. Why don't you ring her yourself?'

'Thanks,' Harry's eyes glittered as he took the piece of paper and put it in his breast pocket. 'I'm not going to lose her. I love her.'

Twenty minutes later Clara was just sitting down to review the school financial records when the doorbell rang again. She heard Rose opening it and made a quick note to give her some extra pay. There'd been far too many interruptions today for her to concentrate on her work properly.

'Mrs. Thomson?' Rose called from outside. 'A gentleman caller's asking for you.'

Harry, Clara thought. He must have left his hat.

'It's not Mr. Evans, ma'am,' Rose said, as if reading her mind. 'Someone else. Says it's about Lena.'

Clara glanced anxiously at the clock. Lena had already called to say she'd arrived safely. If anything had happened to her, there would have been a phone call, not a personal visit. She walked out from her office to find Rose standing dutifully by the door.

'Is it the rag and bone man?' Clara asked, following her down the stairs.

'I don't recall seeing any products, ma'am, but perhaps I was mistaken. I believe he introduced himself as Alexandre. Alexandre Robichaud.'

Clara stopped dead in her tracks, gripping the edge of the bannister. 'What did you say?'

'Alexandre. Says he was an old friend. Did I not say it right? He sounded French.'

Clara couldn't move. It had to be a coincidence.

'Mrs. Thomson, are you alright?' Rose asked, wrinkling her forehead. 'You're lookin' flu-ish.'

'Are you sure that was his name?'

'Quite sure.'

'It's just, it's not possible,' Clara explained, as they reached the front door. 'Alexandre Robichaud is dead.'

Rose shrugged apologetically as she pulled open the door, leaving Clara to stare back at the man standing before her.

'Oh my goodness.'

CHAPTER FORTY-THREE

Alexandre stood shyly in front of Clara. He looked the same, albeit far removed from the awkwardness of adolescence. He raked a hand through his hair, which, Clara noticed, still had the same habit of falling into his eyes.

'Hello, Clara. I . . . it's me,' he said, his voice still carrying that unmistakable French lilt.

Clara rested her head against the doorframe, closing her eyes. Maybe Rose was right. Perhaps she was running a fever. She opened her eyes again slowly. He was still there.

'Is it really you?' she whispered, knowing how stupid she sounded, but unable to believe the incredible turn of events.

Alexandre nodded and a familiar shy smile tugged at his lips. 'Didn't mean to frighten you,' he said, nervously. 'But I assure you it's me.' His eyes caught the ring on Clara's left hand and he smiled. 'Belated congratulations are in order.'

Clara shook her head. 'Forget congratulations! An explanation is what's needed. Come in, come in. Rose,' she called out. 'Would you mind making a fresh pot of tea?'

Alexandre stepped up over the threshold. 'It's not necessary.'

'Nonsense. You've practically returned from the dead, I should think a bit of tea is the least I can do,' she said, ushering him into the parlour.

Once they'd settled down, tea in hand, Clara studied Alexandre whilst simultaneously trying to collect the stream of thoughts racing through her mind. 'You'll forgive me for my stunned reaction. You were the last person I expected to find on my doorstep this afternoon.'

'It seems there was a misunderstanding about what happened all those years ago.' Alexandre stirred a bit of milk into his tea.

'I'm not sure "misunderstanding" is the right word. Colossal mistake is more like it.' Suddenly, Clara sat up straighter. 'Hang on. If you're here, is Theo ...'

Alexandre stared into his cup. 'It's ...' he paused, struggling to find the right words. 'All due respect, Clara, but I owe it to Lena to tell her first. Theo was her father.'

Was her father. Crestfallen, Clara let his words sink in. 'Of course. It's just, for a moment I thought Lena would have everything back.' She sighed 'Now. Tell me. How on earth did you manage to find us?'

Alexandre explained how he'd returned to London after escaping from the garrison town he and Theo had been imprisoned in, only to discover that the World of Wonders was no more.

'Eventually I heard rumours that Horace returned to London during the spring and summer. I confronted him one night in The Flask. We exchanged words, but I wasn't interested in revenge. All I wanted was to find Lena.'

Horace had told him she'd gone off to school, Alexandre explained, so he decamped for St. Ives. But when he got there, they'd shut down on account of the air raids, and were instead operating a satellite location miles away. The interim head mistress at that place, he told Clara, had never heard of a Helena Papadopoulos.

'After that, I came looking for you. I had your old address from Horace. But when I got to the house in Fulham, it was damaged. A child walking by told me there'd been an air strike – Steinbock, I think – and that there were a number of casualties.'

Clara nodded. 'Our house was hit. Mother and father decamped to the North, like so many of our neighbours. We couldn't risk staying. And Lena and I were away at school, though even that changed. The war was just . . .' Clara shuddered, remembering the horrors of what they'd all lived through.

'The boy didn't know your names, but he thought he remembered a teenage girl living at the house. I got excited and asked if she had leg braces. And he said no. And then I knew it wasn't Lena.'

'Actually,' Clara began, clearing her throat and smiling. 'It probably was her.'

Alexandre's eyes widened. 'But . . . that would mean—'

'Took years of therapy, but yes, Lena can walk, unaided. She can't run or cycle or do anything too taxing, but considering where she began . . .' Clara shook her head. 'But I'll get to that. Tell me more.'

'At that point, I had to leave. I was on the run myself and I needed money.' He had supported himself by performing at one-man shows and opening for larger musical acts, slowly gathering experience and building up a consistent repertoire that wowed audiences over the years. But he never stopped looking for Lena. 'I couldn't accept that she'd disappear like that.' Alexandre paused to rub his eyes. 'Then last month, Horace saw Lena's wedding announcement in the *Daily Express*. He sent it to me and well, here I am.' He glanced around, a mixture of hope and nerves on his face. 'How is she?' His voice was husky but affectionate. 'Is she well?'

Clara set her cup down on her saucer. 'She is. I'm afraid you'll have to wait a few more days to see her. She's in Paris.' Clara's face spread into a wide grin upon seeing Alexandre's facial expression. 'I know, ironic. She's been accepted to medical school there.'

Alexandre's face broke into an astonished smile. 'What?'

Clara nodded happily. 'Mind you, it wasn't easy. She's certainly something. It's funny though, as proud as she was about the walking, I think she's come to realise it was never about being able to walk, was it? It was about putting her mind to something and achieving it. At some point she realised it wasn't her so-called physical flaws holding her back. Her mind was always sharp.' Clara looked pointedly at Alexandre. 'We have you to thank for that. You came in and turned her life upside down.'

'When does she return?'

'The weekend.' Clara hesitated before proceeding. 'Alexandre, you're aware she's engaged. That announcement wasn't a lie.' She watched Alexandre's face like a hawk. For a split second, she could have sworn she detected a hint of sadness, but the student had become the master and Alexandre continued as if nothing had changed.

'I would have never expected her to wait, but there's something important I must tell her.' He glanced at the grandfather clock in the corner. 'What time does the next train leave?'

'10 o'clock.'

'I must return to Paris immediately.'

Clara leapt up to stop him. 'Alexandre, don't. You simply can't walk into her life, unannounced, after years away. She's not prepared for it.' She nodded towards the sofa. 'Why not stay here? I'll have Rose—'

But Alexandre was already fastening his coat. 'I've waited ten years. I'm not wasting another minute. Now – could I trouble you for the address of her hotel?'

'Fascinating,' the admissions director said, ushering Lena out into the hallway the next afternoon. 'Miss Thomson, your achievements are most remarkable. I do hope to see you in the autumn, and I wish you a safe journey back to London.'

'Thank you,' Lena said, waiting until he'd returned to his office to take her leave. She took the lift down to the ground floor, then paused to watch the students entering and exiting the building, books clutched to their chests. She felt a ripple of joy when she imagined joining them in a few months' time.

As the cab driver drove back to the hotel, Lena thought about how she was going to spend the remainder of her time in Paris. She'd allowed herself a few extra days to reacquaint herself with the city after Clara urged her to take a holiday. Lena already knew her first stop would be *Stohrer*, a café she used to frequent with her father. It had been a childhood favourite. And then off to admire the glittering glass of Sainte-Chapelle or the colourful carousel in Montmartre, followed by a baguette from *Au Grand Richelieu*. But before all that, she needed to ring Clara from the hotel – she'd be dying to know how the meeting went.

After she'd paid the cab driver, Lena pushed through the hotel doors and walked to the concierge desk.

'Bonjour. I'd like to make a call to London. Can I do so from my room?'

'Madame, I will give you the instructions, but first – a gentleman has arrived for you,' the concierge said.

Lena's heart fluttered as she scanned the lobby hopefully, thinking Harry must have jumped on a train. But she couldn't spot him anywhere. Confused, she began a sweep of the lobby again, wondering if the concierge had mistaken her for someone else.

'Here are the dialling instructions,' the concierge said, holding out a slip of paper.

But Lena wasn't listening anymore because she'd seen him. Except it couldn't be him because he was gone. The lack of sleep must be getting to her, she thought. It wasn't possible. He was dead. And yet, there he was, not two steps away. And that was enough for her legs to give out. The last thing she remembered was hearing her name on his breath.

CHAPTER FORTY-FOUR

A few hours later, Lena's eyelids fluttered open. It took a minute for the scene before her to register but when it did, she rolled over and pulled the covers over her head, afraid of how real his presence felt. *He was gone*, she told herself. She'd held his mother's necklace in her hands. But something inside her was telling her otherwise, and so she sat up and slowly turned around.

Alexandre – her sweet, mischievous Alexandre – was dozing in the armchair that flanked the opposite side of the bed. Lena pinched herself to make sure she wasn't dreaming, then crawled quietly over the bedspread towards him, too curious to resist. When she was just a few inches away, she reached out and touched his hair.

'Alexandre?'

He stirred and Lena quickly withdrew her fingers. His eyes opened and, upon seeing her, his face stretched into a sleepy smile. Lena's hands flew to her mouth and she leapt back.

'Lena,' Alexandre said, leaning forward. 'It's really you?'

She nodded in disbelief, ten years' worth of sorrow and guilt rising within her. 'But . . . you were gone! The fire—'

'There was a misunderstanding.'

Slowly, Lena unfolded her legs from underneath her and stood up, trying to take all of him in. His skin was paler than she remembered and his jawline was sprinkled with stubble. His hair was still cut on the longer side and hadn't lost the habit of flopping into his brilliant blue eyes. Although his face now sported the hard lines that age and experience brought, his smile still had that childlike quality she had found so endearing as a young girl. She noticed he was pointing at her and she looked down at her body for signs for distress. 'What's wrong?'

'Clara said, but I never ...' He looked at her, momentarily overcome with emotion. 'You can walk.'

Lena smiled bashfully. 'Yes, I ...' Overwhelmed, she began to cry. 'I thought you were dead! All these years, I thought you and Papa—' she stopped. Her father. She searched Alexandre's eyes eagerly. 'Is he here?'

Alexandre's face hardened and he walked to the window to gaze out at the buildings. Lena followed him, noticing that the sun was now lower in the sky. She must have been asleep for hours.

'It's ok,' she said, trying to convince herself to believe her own words. 'At least you're safe.' She squeezed his shoulder.

Alexandre stiffened at her touch and he pulled away, avoiding her eyes, as he walked to the bed and sat down, burying his head in his hands. Lena's lower lip trembled as she joined him. She was almost too afraid to ask, unwilling to let him confirm the worst.

'You don't have to talk about it yet,' she whispered supportively.

Alexandre frowned, lifting his head. 'It's not that.'

'Then what?'

'Your father ...'

Lena waited with bated breath, anticipating his next words and when he said nothing, she braced herself for the terrible truth. 'Whatever it is, you can tell me. I can handle it.'

Alexandre took a deep breath before forcing himself to look at her. 'He's here. Theo is alive.'

CHAPTER FORTY-FIVE

Lena wasn't sure she'd heard correctly. 'I beg your pardon?'

'He's alive,' Alexandre continued, his voice low and gravelly. 'But he doesn't know I found you. After I got the clipping—'

'What clipping?'

Alexandre pulled the newspaper article announcing her engagement to Harry from his pocket and handed it to her. 'You had a different name. The photo, it looks like you, but I wanted to be sure before I told Theo. We've had a few near misses over the years, and each time it was heartbreaking, getting our hopes up, only to discover we were wrong.'

Lena didn't know how to react. After all these years, she was getting a second chance to make everything right. 'He's in Paris? Is he ok?' Alexandre nodded and she leapt up, trembling. She grabbed her purse and flung her coat across her shoulders. 'Please! You must take me to see him!'

'I will, but,' Alexandre hesitated.

'What is it? Is he injured?'

'He's not injured, it's,' Alexandre shook his head and gestured to her outfit. 'You have to change your clothes.'

Lena dropped her jaw in disbelief. 'I don't think he's going to care what I'm wearing!'

'He won't. But Count Beistegui surely will.'

According to Alexandre, Theo was due to perform that evening at a lavish masquerade ball being thrown by one of Europe's most eccentric millionaires.

'But I've nothing to wear.'

Alexandre pointed to two boxes in the corner of the room. 'It's all taken care of.'

Lena opened her mouth to say something but then closed it. Still feeling like she was lost in a dream, she grabbed the box and went into the washroom. Her brain was spinning a mile a minute and she really didn't have the focus to even think about changing, but if it was the only way to see her father again, she would have to do it. She opened the box, her eyes widening at its contents. On the top sat a navy-blue half face mask, with a spiral of golden feathers flanking the right side, arcing up in a half moon curve. Thin strands of golden thread created a subtle rose pattern across the bottom half. Tiny golden pearls dotted the rim and two thick, blue velvet ribbons were sewn on each side.

The dress came next. 'Oh,' she said softly, removing it from the box. It was midnight blue and trimmed with gold accents. She quickly removed her clothes and slipped into it, then spun herself around to look in the mirror. The iridescent material was sumptuous and as she moved, it shimmered in the dim washroom light. She fluffed the skirt, noticing tiny golden drop pearls scattered throughout. When she looked more closely, she realised they were the outlines of famous scientific constellations and she traced the path of Circinus up and down her torso.

The last thing inside the box was a pair of blue velvet slippers laced with braided gold trim. She felt a pang of love for Alexandre as she saw them, touched that he had thought to get her a pair of comfortable shoes she could walk in.

As she emerged from the washroom she heard a breath escape from Alexandre's mouth. He was holding a midnight blue *bauta* mask in one hand. His shirt and trousers were midnight blue and accented with bursts of white and there was a tiny golden threaded constellation on his right breast. She pointed to it, incredulous.

'Columba,' Alexandre said.

Lena gestured to their clothes. 'When did you have time to get all of this?'

Alexandre shrugged. 'Clara told me your dress size. Then I called my head costumier from London and asked for a rush job,' he said, smiling at the dress. 'They worked all night and sent it over while you slept.' He reached into his pocket and produced Lena's dove bracelet. 'Even though you were hard to find, I never stopped believing I'd see you again,' he explained, taking her hand and slipping it onto her wrist.

Lena twisted her wrist, admiring it and then suddenly remembered Alexandre's mother's necklace.

'Wait,' she said, rummaging through her purse until she found it. She picked it up and placed it delicately in his palm.

Alexandre gasped as his eyes fell on the necklace. 'How did—'

'Horace. They found it in the fire. I couldn't bear to part with it.'

'Thank you,' he said, his voice wavering. 'Now come. We've no time to waste.'

As they settled into a taxi and headed west, Lena clasped Alexandre's hands. 'Tell me everything. Leave nothing out.'

And so he began. He told her about the contract and Thereseinstadt, about the performances, and the absurd talent wasted within the town walls. He explained that the Nazis had built it as a model town, but that he was certain that the residents who left on the trains were later killed.

'It was horrible.' Alexandre's face clouded over. 'I wanted to leave the minute we arrived. I didn't trust anyone. But Theo insisted we stay, for the sake of your safety. He was so worried they'd find and hurt you if we dared break the rules.' He then explained what had happened when they tried to leave after their contract expired.

'Once Theo realised they had no intention of releasing us, we made a plan. We couldn't leave when they were expecting us to, so we did it when they least expected – right in the middle of an illusion.' He described the water tank, the train timetable, the rehearsal with Burger and the brandy. Lena noticed that when he spoke of a girl named Leike, his hand floated to a wooden rose pendant hanging around his neck.

'We were almost in the clear. Then we got to the train.' Alexandre's face darkened. 'Attila had figured out our plan and tipped off a Czech gendarme in exchange for his freedom.' Alexandre shuddered, the image of Attila lying in the blindingly white snow, blood spilling out next to him forever etched in his mind. 'The bullet from the gendarme's gun hit Leike's shoulder, so I put her in a carriage to keep her safe. And then the train started to move and I told Theo to go. I managed to injure the gendarme, but just as I was jumping onto the carriage, he fired at us, injuring Theo. I told him and Leike to hold on, that Prague wasn't far away. But ...' Alexandre's eyes filled with tears as he struggled to continue. 'I promised to look after her, Lena. But she was already sick.' He gripped the pendant harder. 'I took them both to a hospital as soon as we reached Prague. Theo's wound was severe, but with enough care and rest, they said he'd be fine. Leike, on the other hand ... she'd lost so much blood and she'd been sick for weeks before. She died not long after they admitted her.' Lena reached out and hugged Theo and they sat in silence as the car crawled along the left bank. After a few minutes, she pulled back and asked him how he had found her. Alexandre repeated the explanation he'd given to Clara, detailing the trip to St. Ives, the visit to Clara's family's home in Fulham, the drive to Dorset.

'I knew you had to be somewhere, so I kept trying. We both did. Once Theo healed, he went to Horace, badgering him for information about your whereabouts. We never stopped searching.

Three years ago, Theo and I contacted all the universities we thought you might be at: Cambridge, UCL, Guy's. But they wouldn't give out personal information. We never would have guessed you'd be teaching in London. And then Horace contacted me. I suppose he did one thing right after all.' He paused, scratching at the fabric of the seat. 'We tried to find you, Lena. We tried so hard. But it was like you'd ceased to exist.'

Lena thought back to the day she sat in the adoption office, telling the official to change her name. 'I didn't know.'

'Once I saw the newspaper clipping, I knew I had to see you, so I came to London. Clara said you'd be back in a few days, but I couldn't wait. I didn't know if you'd want to see me, given the circumstances,' he said, glancing at her ring, 'but I had to try. If only for Theo.'

A few minutes later, the taxi pulled up outside a palatial rectangular building. Lena craned her neck, reading the sign that hung outside.

'Alexandre,' she protested. They were at the infamous *Piscine Molitor*, an outdoor lido where the World of Wonders had often hosted post-show parties. Sometimes, on their days off in Paris, her father would bring her here, holding her up by her waist in the water as she laughed, the sun shining down on her from above.

Alexandre turned to her, a serious expression on his face. 'Lena, promise me one thing.'

'Anything,' Lena said.

'Give your father a chance to explain. He's not a bad person.'

Lena nodded understandingly. 'If it's about the affair with Isabella, it's alright. I knew, remember? But it's fine. I'm just relieved he's alive.'

Alexandre looked at her, a troubled expression on his face. 'Just promise you'll give him a chance.'

'Alright,' Lena said, looking at him funnily. He exhaled a sigh of relief and then nodded towards the building.

'Shall we?'

Lena stepped out, taking care not to trip on the cobblestones and followed Alexandre through the doors. As she entered the lobby, her eyes widened. Austerity, it seemed, was not among Count Beistegui's best traits. Hordes of partygoers clad in costumes and masks so extravagant they reminded her of the circus swarmed the lobby. Flashbulbs went off every few seconds, as society mavens posed and preened for the cameras.

'Is it always like this?' she asked, lifting her mask to her face.

'Trust me,' he said from behind his mask, leading her up a staircase that she now remembered led to the main deck. 'You haven't seen anything yet.' When they reached the main deck level, Alexandre pushed back a black curtain to reveal the pool area and Lena gasped.

All around her a nautical themed party and performance was in full swing. The deck had been transformed into a dynamic, outdoor interactive theatrical playground for what seemed to be the wealthiest of Parisian society. In the centre of it all sat the world-famous pool. It was filled to the brim with clear blue water that flickered brightly each time the white lights pulsated beneath its surface. In the middle of the pool, synchronised swimmers wearing navy-and-white striped swimsuits and matching swim caps created pinwheels and stars as partygoers whistled. To the left, a live band played as people danced. To the right, a giant glass aquarium filled with miniature tiger sharks swimming about had attendees ooh-ing and aah-ing.

'Do you like it?'

'Alexandre,' Lena began. She'd spent years avoiding anything to do with the circus. The excess, the wonderment, this world of pretend – she'd avoided it on purpose lest it bring back too many painful memories. And yet standing now as she was in front of the scene filled her with an energy she hadn't known she was missing. 'Did you do all this?'

'No. This is all the count. Much of this,' he swept his arms across the scene, 'is modelled off of *Le Bal Oriental*, the most incredible party ever thrown, according to many.'

'Does this happen often?'

'There are smaller salons every month. But the Count throws a few grand parties like this one every year.'

'And during the war?'

'No change. He identifies as Spanish and is the heir to a Mexican mining company. He was basically neutral during the war.'

A couple dressed as Antony and Cleopatra walked past them and then Lena felt a push against her back.

'Oh!' she said, as a masked gentleman dressed as a joker in shades of rust and mustard yellow tried to pull her into an embrace.

Alexandre stepped forward. 'She's with me.' Shrugging, the joker skipped off to find another lady to claim. '*Arlecchino*. A main character in the Italian theatre tradition known as *commedia dell'arte*,' Alexandre explained, taking her hand. They wandered to the far end of the pool where two bar-keeps dressed in navy uniforms with shiny gold buttons and jaunty white caps poured champagne into twinkling slim flutes studded with Swarovski crystals.

'Two glasses,' Alexandre said, handing one to Lena. He noticed she was scanning the deck area 'He's in the green room they set up by the changing area. He's due to go on any minute, but if you want me to take you to—'

Lena shook her head. 'No. We'll wait,' she replied, secretly relieved she'd have a chance to observe Theo before speaking with him. After so many years, it didn't make sense that she'd want to wait any longer, and yet suddenly, she didn't know what to say.

The synchronised swimmers finished their routine and were now wrapping themselves in silky white bathrobes, their teeth gleaming against the apple red lacquer on their lips. Below the pristine sheen of the water, a platform appeared to be rising. Lena glanced at Alexandre as they found seats on one of the *chaise longues* set around the pool's perimeter.

'Is he?'

Alexandre nodded.

Lena sucked in her breath as the platform emerged out of the water. It was covered in slate grey glitter and resembled a tiny rock island shining under the moonlit sky. Lena felt her skin prickle and she gripped Alexandre's hand in anticipation, as the lights dimmed all around them. A moment passed and then, they came back up, revealing a figure standing at the centre of the rock, alone. It was Theo. Her father was dressed in a lavish white and golden sun king costume, his face obscured by a *volto* mask. But it was him. She could see it in the way he moved, the deft touch of his hand, the charisma with which he commandeered the audience.

The melodic strains of a group of string instruments pierced the night sky and Lena looked up. A cello quartet were performing on the balcony directly above Theo. She watched as he seemed to become one with the music, moving his body slightly. And then, without warning, a shot of water rose, perfectly timed with a crescendo in the piece and Lena gasped. Theo was using water and music to create a completely immersive illusion. He shifted and moved, making droplets rise and fall around him, lost in his own world.

For the finale, Theo created what Lena could only describe as a symphony of water. First, he waved his arms, as though coaxing a living, breathing organism out of the pool. Then he made the water form a semi-circle that arched over the platform. He repeated this until there were eight small arcs and one big one right in front of him. Lena could tell that the music was coming to an end and on the top note of one of the last bars, Theo waved his arm, forcing the big arc to corkscrew out of the bottom of the pool and rise to the very top of the veranda above. The crowd gasped and leaned back, an immediate reaction to not wanting their couture to get wet. And yet the water didn't leave its place. With a flourish, Theo waved his arm dramatically and a frigid stream of air plunged across the desk, freezing the water in its tracks.

The audience erupted in cheers and looked up, pointing at what Theo had just done. The majestic corkscrew was still frozen, spiralling up like the top of a glass skyscraper. The eight arcs had stopped mid-air and beams of blue and yellow protruding from the lights around the pool were now dancing through them.

For his final move, Theo rose one last time and snapped his fingers. Immediately, the frozen water melted but remained perfectly in motion, nary a drop out of place.

The crowd erupted into electrifying applause, startling Lena. She watched her father take a gallant bow and then the lights went dark as he moved from the platform back to the deck. Lena felt Alexandre gently tug at her elbow, urging her to get up.

'What if he doesn't want to see me?' she asked, suddenly frozen.

Alexandre shook his head. 'That's not ever going to be the case. He's thought about you every single day since you were split apart. Come,' he said, extending his hand. Lena took it and they walked through the crowd, overhearing the guests praise the magical scene they'd just witnessed. When they were but a few feet away from Theo, Alexandre stopped and turned to Lena. 'I'm not saying what you're about to hear will be easy, but you shouldn't for a moment ever doubt his love for you.' He brushed a wisp of her hair off her mask, then stepped forward to greet Theo as he came striding towards them. 'A fine performance, sir,' he said jovially.

'Alexandre!' Theo embraced him. 'You should have told me you'd be here! We could have performed together!'

Lena swallowed. His voice. He spoke with the same gentle, reassuring tone he'd always used.

'I'm not here on business matters, I'm afraid,' Alexandre said, gesturing to Lena.

Lena bristled, waiting for Theo to react as he looked at her. But his face was blank, save for a kind smile. Her mask, she thought. He wouldn't have recognised her yet.

'I was wondering what was keeping you so busy these days.' Theo moved forward and reached for Lena's hand but she drew back, panicking. Theo shook his head. 'Of course. How silly of me.' He untied his mask, revealing a face that was so familiar yet changed. He still had the same kind brown eyes that sparkled, the same slim nose and broad smile with dimples in his cheeks, but she noted tiny flecks of grey in his once dark brown hair and faint lines set into his forehead. His strong jawline was no longer as defined as it used to be, but he was still handsome, still the man she looked up to.

Alexandre cleared his throat. 'Why don't we all sit down,' he suggested, leading them into Theo's dressing room.

Theo looked perplexed. 'What's going on?' he asked, as they all walked into the space and Alexandre shut the door.

Alexandre opened his mouth, preparing to launch into an explanation, but Lena stepped forward. It was now or never. Reaching behind her head, she untied her mask and faced her father.

'Papa,' she said softly.

'Lena?' Theo's voice was barely audible. He shook his head, stunned. 'But how—'

'I found her, sir' Alexandre said.

'Lena!' Theo took two big strides forward and pulled Lena into an embrace, his body shaking with emotion. She broke down in tears as she felt his strong arms around her. She'd missed that feeling for so long. Theo pulled back and stroked her cheek as if discovering her for the first time. They laughed through their tears. 'Is it you?' He shook his head in disbelief. 'My dear girl— you can walk?'

'Yes, Papa. It's me. And yes – I can walk,' she said, gripping his wrist, not wanting to take her eyes off him.

'How I've longed for this day,' he whispered. Lena noticed his dark eyes widening as she raised a hand to tuck a lock of hair behind her ear. 'You're engaged?' She nodded. 'Congratulations! What a joyous occasion! He is a lucky man.'

'I'll leave you two alone,' Alexandre exchanged a glance with Theo.

Theo and Lena looked at each other again, each unsure what to say. Finally, Theo gestured to one of the chairs in the room. 'Please. Sit,' he said, admiring her. 'We have much to discuss!'

Lena gathered the skirt of her dress as she sat down. 'Papa, Alexandre said—'

'Don't be angry with him. He's done nothing but protect me.' Theo sighed and Lena could tell he was about to begin an explanation she didn't want to hear.

'I know what happened. But it was a mistake and I forgive you. All I want is for us to be a family again.'

'Lena.'

'Please. It was Isabella, right? The lady from the letters? I don't care what you did. You've suffered enough,' Lena said, her eyes shining. She had only just got him back and didn't want to lose him because of a past transgression.

Theo shook his head firmly. 'Lena, you don't understand. I never did anything to hurt your mother.'

Lena frowned. 'But the letters. I read them.'

Theo took her hands in his and looked her directly in the eye. 'That's not what I lied about.' He paused and took one last deep breath. 'The truth, Lena, is this. I am not your father.'

349

CHAPTER FORTY-SIX

There were a few incidents in Lena's life that stood out above the rest – significant, life-altering moments that, if needed, could be brought to the forefront of her memory and relived like they had only happened yesterday. One was the day she'd met Alexandre. Another was the day her father and Alexandre were captured. Another was the time she'd received her acceptance letter to medical school. Today, the day she found out that her father, whom she'd presumed dead for the last ten years, wasn't really her father, would be added to the list.

Lena felt herself shrink away from Theo and then blinked, shaking her head. She couldn't have heard him correctly. 'Excuse me?'

'I'm not your real father,' Theo said softly. 'I never was. Gia was my sister.'

'You're my ... uncle?'

Theo nodded. 'Gia's older brother.'

Lena stood up abruptly, feeling like her entire world was collapsing inwardly. Of all the things she'd expected Theo to say, this was last on her list. 'This makes no sense!' she said, pacing up and down the small space. 'Have you been lying to me my whole life?'

Theo nodded ruefully and stood up. 'Please Lena, I'm so sorry, but I had my reasons for doing what I did. Will you at least listen to my explanation?'

Lena stared at him, dazed. She didn't know what to think. Now she understood what Alexandre had meant when he'd told her to give him a chance. She shook her head and finally took a seat.

'Ok,' she managed to say, still stunned.

'Thank you,' Theo said. He poured two glasses of water from a glass carafe and handed one to her. Then he shrugged himself out of the stiff white and gold matador jacket he was wearing, draped it across the back of his chair and sat down.

'I think it's best if I start from the beginning. Your mother and I were raised in a fairly liberal – at least at the time – household in Athens. Our father was a diplomat and valued education above everything. He was always giving me a hard time because I never had the head for traditional schooling. But Gia was different. She could read by the time she was three and was writing complete sentences before her fifth birthday. Though two years behind me, she was much smarter. She excelled in school and this brought pride and joy to our father. Despite my best efforts, I didn't have a talent for academics and I don't think my father ever forgave me for it.' Theo paused to collect his thoughts. 'Gia filled the void in his life that I'd created – that is, until she reached the age of eighteen. That was when most Greek girls were married off, and despite his forward-thinking mindset, our father eventually succumbed to societal pressures and began looking for a suitable husband for her.

'I had left school a few years earlier, convinced I was better off without it. I loved magic and performing and practised for hours each day. Eventually, I started picking up gigs on the weekends, performing at birthday and anniversary parties while working as a carpenter to pay my bills. When I was eighteen, I joined a tour and travelled all over Greece and parts of Europe. It rattled my parents, to have to tell their friends that their son had effectively joined a circus, but it was what I wanted. Still, it meant leaving Gia behind. We were always close, and I missed her terribly.'

Theo reached for a handkerchief on his dressing room table

and mopped at the sweat that had gathered on his forehead. Lena had forgotten how hot the spotlights could get, especially under all the stage makeup.

'Still, life went on. Two years into the tour and I had built up a good amount of money and a solid reputation. I'd also fallen in love,' he said, his face brightening. 'I'd met a young woman at a show in Madrid one night. Her name was Isabella. Though she wasn't part of the circus, we wrote to each other every week and very quickly fell in love.' Theo ran his hands over his thighs, as though bracing himself for something painful. 'Unfortunately, she came from an aristocratic family in Spain and, like our father had with Gia, her father had begun searching for a suitable match. She wrote to me regularly, saying she wanted to run away. I told her to stay put, that I would come for her once the tour ended, after which we'd elope. But I never made it.'

Lena interrupted him. 'Wait. This is the Isabella from the letter?' Theo nodded. 'But what happened? Why did you have to pretend to be my mother's husband?'

'Gia called me one evening, distraught. She'd been admitted to university a few months back and together we'd both managed to convince our father to let her keep attending her classes until they'd found a boy from a good family. But during this time, one of her university tutors had taken a shine to her. It wasn't hard to fall for Gia – she was stunning and brilliant. And this particular man said he would marry her and let her continue studying for as long as she liked.' Theo's face darkened. 'My sister was smart, but she was also naive. They began a relationship, but she soon discovered he was already married with two children. That was the night she phoned me, bereft. She was pregnant with you. She said the man she'd been seeing refused to acknowledge your existence once she'd told him and never wanted to see her again. She was terrified of what our parents would say – I couldn't blame her – but I knew we had to tell them. She couldn't hide her pregnancy

353

forever. So I took a leave of absence and returned to Athens.' Theo shuddered. 'I'll never forget the look in my father's eyes when we told him. He'd always considered me a disappointment, but to find out that his little girl had failed him, too? It was too much. He forbade us from ever returning, saying that if we were going to defy his expectations, we had to live with the consequences.'

'I'm so sorry,' Lena said, thinking how awful it would have been.

'The next day, Gia and I left. I quit the tour, wrote a letter to Isabella explaining what had happened, promising to return to Madrid when I could. Then Gia and I travelled north to Thessaloniki.'

'Where you told everyone you were a married couple,' Lena said, filling in the gaps.

Theo nodded. 'We stopped in Larissa on the way to get a fake marriage certificate. Your mother chose Thessaloniki because it was far away enough from Athens so that no one would recognise us. They'd also just opened a university. She hoped to return to her studies once she was able, even if she had to do it alongside raising you. She wanted to be a lawyer,' Theo said, smiling at Lena.

'What happened next?'

'We settled into a routine. I continued performing locally and Gia acclimatised to life in Thessaloniki beautifully.' Theo's gaze flickered. 'But things with Isabella hit a bump. She wrote to me saying she'd been promised to a man from a wealthy family, living in Seville. This was against her will, of course. I was devastated, but he was abroad for business and her wedding wouldn't take place for at least a year. I still had time. I didn't know how, but I promised Isabella we'd be together and I was determined to find a way before she was lost forever.

'About three months before you were due, Horace visited the city and saw me perform. He offered to take us onboard his new circus. Gia and I discussed it and decided it would be a good idea for everyone. I could keep an eye on both of you – remember, your mother was only eighteen – and Horace would provide the best of everything, plus a hefty salary that would let me set Gia up properly in Thessaloniki. I wrote to Isabella, explaining the situation and asked if she would also join me on board at some point.'

'What did she say?'

'She was so overjoyed, she came to see me!' Theo said. 'Now that she was betrothed, her father had relaxed his rules a little. She convinced her older sister to cover for her and came to Thessaloniki. We had but two days together and it was the most magical time of my life. Released from the prying eyes of those who knew her, we roamed freely all over the city.'

'Adelpha,' Lena said, thinking back to that day in Aristotelous Square, when she and Alexandre had run into Adelpha and heard her prophetic words. *Do not fall for his act. He is a good showman, that Theodoros.* 'She saw you with Isabella.'

Theo nodded. 'We spent the day and night together and even though we knew it was wrong, it felt right. We were meant to be. As I dropped her at the train station, I told her it wouldn't be long until I saw her again.'

Theo's face darkened. 'About six weeks before she was due to give birth, Gia fell violently ill with typhoid. It was the worst time of my life. To see my beautiful, bright sister, fighting so hard? And not only for her life, but yours, too? It nearly undid me.' Theo looked like he might cry.

'I took her to the best hospitals in Thessaloniki. The doctors tried everything. But it was no use. She had been fighting her whole life for acceptance and was done. You were her final gift to the world.'

Lena felt a lump in her throat.

'But things weren't over yet. You were five weeks away from being full-term, so it was risky to deliver you, but Gia insisted. You made it through, alive, but very weak. Things got worse from there. Your immune system and body were underdeveloped, and after only two days at home, we had to move you to a hospital with an incubator. It was a month before I was allowed to touch you again. I hated having to leave you in there. It was so unsanitary and ill-equipped for a child as sick as yourself. I'm sure that's where you caught polio, but, what could I do? I didn't have any of that equipment at home and you were too unstable for us to transport you to a hospital in Athens or somewhere like Paris or London. After three months, the doctors finally deemed it safe enough for you to travel, so we left.'

'What about Isabella?' Lena asked. 'You never contacted her again?'

Theo smiled softly. 'After you were born, I had a choice to make. But seeing you in your mother's arms, it wasn't really a choice. From the moment I met you, it didn't feel like a sacrifice. I had to do it. I wrote to Isabella a few hours after you arrived, and told her I had to think of you and to not contact me.' His eyes grew misty as he reminisced about his love. 'I thought it best to break it off quickly. But she was selfless and refused to give up on our love. She wrote back, saying she understood and that she'd wait for me, as long as it took.

'But her fiancé returned early and she had no choice but to marry him. I wrote to her sister, telling her how sorry I was and promised I would still come for her, one day.' He paused and looked at Lena.

'But you never did,' Lena said sadly.

'No. I did. But I was too late,' Theo said, his eyes heavy. 'After Alexandre and I escaped, I ended up in a hospital in Prague. I promised myself that if I healed, I would stop living my life in fear. I knew Alexandre was already searching for you, so on my way back to London to help, I stopped in Seville.'

Lena held her breath. 'And?'

Theo shook his head sadly. 'She was gone. Most of the people I spoke with said she'd died during childbirth, many years ago.

But that evening, as I sat drinking at one of the local tavernas, her maid came to see me. She said it wasn't childbirth that had killed Isabella, but rather, a broken heart.'

Lena fiddled guiltily with the pearls on her dress. Theo noticed her expression. 'It's not your fault. I made my choice, only it was too late.'

Lena sat silently for a minute, letting the news settle. 'Why didn't you just tell me the truth when I was old enough? Then you could have gone to Isabella and got married and brought her along with us.'

Theo looked down at his hands. 'Your mother made me promise two things before she died. The first was to ensure you got an education. The second was to never tell you the truth about who I was. She'd kept my affair with Isabella a secret, so to keep her secret was only fair. It was the least I could do. She knew that if people thought you were my daughter, they'd treat you in a more favourable light than if they thought you were a child born to an adulterer. She didn't want you growing up with the shadow of what she'd done following you around. As for why I went along with it,' Theo winced, like the pain of an old wound was flaring up again. 'My father abandoned us. He let his pride get in the way of loving his own flesh and blood and I promised myself if I ever had a child, I would never do that.' He shuddered. 'He could be difficult at the best of times, but he was still my father. Your mother was gone and there was nothing I could do to change that. But at the very least, I could be a good father.'

Lena didn't know what to think. Her life as she knew it had been a lie, but Theo had been untruthful out of love. All those years, he'd never said a bad word about Gia. He'd never wanted Lena to think ill of her mother.

'There's one more thing,' Theo said apprehensively. 'The reason I was so hesitant to let you pursue an education – even though Gia insisted upon it – was because I'd seen how girls were treated by men in positions of power. I couldn't bear the thought of what had happened to Gia happening to you. I think on some level . . .' He trailed off and paused to take a deep breath. 'I blame myself for having lost her. If I hadn't encouraged my father to let her study, she might still be here. After she died, I decided that too many risks, no matter the potential reward, weren't worth it. Now I can see how wrong I was.'

'That's why you were so upset about boarding school,' Lena said, finally realising her father's true motivations.

Theo nodded miserably. 'I thought it would be enough for you to learn from within the circus walls. But of course, you had your mother's spirit. It was a mistake to hold you back. I'm so sorry.'

Lena sniffed and searched the room for something to wipe her nose with. Theo pulled out a handkerchief and handed it to her. She blew into it once, twice, before handing it back to him.

'I know . . .' he paused, trying to find the right words. 'I know this is a lot to take in. But please know that I've never once thought of you as anything but my own daughter. And even now that you know, nothing has to change.'

Lena reached out and hugged Theo tightly, relishing the feeling of his arms safely around her. 'I'll let you get dressed,' she said. 'But will you meet me at my hotel tomorrow? It would give us a chance to speak more.'

Theo smiled. 'I'll be there first thing in the morning.'

'Papa,' she said, gazing up at the man who'd raised her. 'Thank you for being honest.' She hugged him one last time, then wandered back into the middle of the party, where she found Alexandre chatting with one of the barkeeps.

'Everything alright?' he asked, leading her to sit on one of the lounge chairs.

Lena placed her chin in the palms of her hands and leaned forward. 'It's a lot to take in.'

Alexandre rubbed her back affectionately. Around them, the

party was winding down. Lena yawned and checked the clock. It was past midnight.

'I should get back to the hotel.'

'The night is young,' Alexandre said, with a twinkle in his eye.

'Theo's meeting me in the morning.'

'I spent all this time searching for you and you won't let me have one night?' Alexandre asked playfully.

Lena stared at him, willing herself to make the right decision. It didn't seem fair that she had a chance to be with him now. She twirled the ends of her mask in her hands.

'I'm engaged.'

Alexandre rolled his eyes. 'Engaged. Not dead.' When Lena didn't reply, he pressed on. 'Come on. Where's that girl who ran through the streets of Barcelona, stole a bottle of Bollinger and wouldn't let me go?'

And suddenly Lena plummeted back in time to a place she'd tried so hard to forget. Flashes of that hot night in Barcelona, the turquoise, silver and yellow mosaic tiles in the Parc Güell. The bitterness of the iced coffee she drank at the Almirall Café, made sweeter by the taste of Alexandre's juvenile kisses. The blanket of stars overhead as they stumbled back to the circus, hand in hand, drunk on young romance. The headiness of the golden champagne, the sweet smell of alcohol and sweat mingling on their clothes. The blue fabric covering her, and falling asleep next to him, feeling safe. She wanted all of that. She wanted all of that and more.

'Where are we headed?'

They tore through the night, tiny golden halos of light from the lampposts that lined the city streets flooding the sky. As familiar buildings flew by and old memories resurfaced, Lena rested her head on Alexandre's shoulder.

When the cab reached the city's core, Alexandre insisted they get out and walk along the bank of the Seine. He'd grabbed two cashmere blankets from the swimming pool attendants, promising to return them the next day, and they each wrapped themselves in them and began strolling along the edge of the famous waterway as they caught each other up on their lives.

Alexandre told her he'd been living in Paris for the last five years. He had a weekly residency at the *Musée Grévin* for part of the year and toured Europe the rest of the time. He didn't belong to a circus, preferring to do things on his own.

'You have more control this way.' He talked about wanting to visit America and told her how an invitation had been extended many times from a wealthy oil Sheikh, urging him to relocate to the Middle East. 'It was a lot of money to turn down,' he said, as they approached *Pont Marie*, but for now he was content with having Paris as his base. He led, from what Lena could glean, a peripatetic existence and she wondered if it was solely because of his work, or if a piece of the young, scared boy she knew still lived within him, forever running from his past.

After he'd finished filling her in on his life, he asked her what she'd been up to and Lena launched into her own explanation, wondering how she could possibly summarise ten years' worth of living into a few hours. She told him about boarding school and Olivia and what it was like living with Clara and Fitz and their kids. She told him about the market she visited every Saturday morning in Clerkenwell and how, because it was run mainly by Italian immigrants, it reminded her of Mario and Anna Maria. She talked about teaching at Clara's school.

'I enjoy it – the children are lovely – but . . .' she paused, watching the street lamps illuminate *Jardin des Tuileres*, 'well, you know better than I do what I've always wanted.' Alexandre was quiet for a moment.

'And this chap you're with – Harry, is it?'

Lena blushed. 'Yes.'

'He's ok with you going to school?'

'He's a photojournalist, so he's used to travel.'

Alexandre let out a low whistle. 'Sounds smart. But not as smart as you. No one's as smart as you.'

Lena looked away, her eyes falling on a group of rowdy young men sharing a bottle of wine a few feet away from them. Despite the early morning hour, there were still many people out, enjoying the magic the Parisian capital had to offer. Every so often, someone would stop to stare at Lena, resplendent in her dress, but she didn't care.

'He is smart,' she answered eventually, meeting Alexandre's gaze. 'I'm very lucky.'

Alexandre smiled and then wandered down to the tip of the river bank, stopping just short the water's edge. 'Do you remember how we'd always skim stones down by Ladadika?' he asked, taking off his blanket and kneeling on the grass.

Lena nodded, watching him pick through the stones, finally procuring a few flat ones. He stood up and began skimming them across the body of water, leaning forward to reach the perfect angle. He was getting dangerously close to the edge and Lena, worried about his safety, hiked up her dress and rushed down to him.

'Move back.'

Alexandre laughed. 'That was what you always used to tell me! *Move back! You're too close! It's too dangerous!*' He skimmed a few more stones, not paying any attention to her warning.

'Move!' Lena said, more urgently, arriving by his side. She took off her blanket so she could move her arms more freely and tried to tug him closer to the grass.

Alexandre turned to her, a glint in his eye. 'Or what?'

'Or you'll fall in!' Lena couldn't help laughing, their faux argument bringing out a side of her she'd kept hidden for so long.

'You mean like this?' And suddenly she was in his arms and

then there was a splash and they were underwater, her dress billowing out around her, her shoes floating off her feet. Alexandre clasped his hands around her waist and pulled her up for air.

She burst through the surface of the river. Taking a huge breath, she raised her hands to push him back.

'Alexandre Robichaud!' Lena sputtered. She grabbed for his neck, fearful that she might sink but Alexandre had a firm grasp on her and was keeping her afloat. She glanced around self-consciously, noticing the passersby coming to the edge of the bank.

'It's ok. We're ok,' Alexandre sang out merrily, as he trod water, one arm wrapped tightly around Lena's waist.

Wet tendrils of hair clung to Lena's face and she shivered as a light breeze wafted over her exposed shoulders. She tried to scowl. Alexandre might still be caught in a world of magic, but this wasn't who she was now. She was a grown woman.

'Alexandre,' she began sternly.

But he was laughing at her, laughing with an abandonment she hadn't seen in him before. This Alexandre was free and unburdened, moving through life as though he had nothing to lose. Try as she might, Lena couldn't escape the feeling flowing through her. A surge of elation swirled in her ribs, threatening to burst through her chest. She loved Harry, but being with Alexandre felt so right, like a missing puzzle piece finding its home.

'Come, you'll catch a chill,' he said and he swam with her in his arms to the banks. He helped her out and she tried to wring as much water out of her dress, which was completely damaged, as she could. Her shoes were nowhere to be found but oddly enough, she didn't care. She let Alexandre drape one of the cashmere blankets around her shoulders. 'Well,' he said, looking out at the river. 'At least you've found your spot for your morning dip when you're at school.'

Lena hesitated, her mind flitting back to Harry, to the wedding, and to the life that was waiting for her in London. She pulled the blanket around her shoulders tightly.

'I'm not sure I'm going.'

Alexandre smirked. 'Nonsense. You have to go.'

'I don't *have* to do anything,' she said, suddenly irritated. 'People change.'

Alexandre balked at her. 'You've spent the past two hours going on and on about how exciting the curriculum sounds. You're going.'

'It's not that simple—' Lena began.

'It is. You're the one making it hard.' Alexandre scuffed the concrete part of the bank, frowning.

'What did you think was going to happen?' Lena asked, her anger flaring. 'That you'd show up to my hotel room and I'd leave behind my entire life for you? I love Harry! I know it hurts to hear that, but it's . . . it is the way it is.'

Alexandre's mouth fell open. 'That's why you think I tried so hard to find you? Because I wanted to ruin your engagement?' He shook his head. 'Lena, I came to London because I know what it's like to be an orphan! Theo isn't even your real father and yet he loves you more than my father ever loved me!' His eyes glimmered fiercely. 'If there was even the slimmest chance that my mother was alive, I would walk to the ends of the earth to find her. I tracked you down because I wanted you to have a second chance with Theo, not because I expected you to wait for me.'

Lena inhaled sharply, unsure how to respond. She stared at the ground and caught sight of a field mouse right before it scurried into one of the crevices lining the bank.

'As for Harry, at what point tonight have I asked you to leave him?' Alexandre challenged. He waited, watching Lena's face flame red. 'Exactly,' he finished off. He raked his hands through his hair, then let it fall across his face as it was wont to do. 'Look, marry him or don't marry him. But whatever you decide, at least have the courage to finish what your mother couldn't.' He sighed and held out his hand. 'Come on. I don't want you getting sick.'

On the train ride back to London, Lena thought about her breakfast with Theo earlier. He'd come to her hotel as promised and they'd spent the morning trying to catch up on the last eight years. Then he'd dropped her at the station, promising to visit her in London.

As she glanced at the green fields passing by her window, Lena twisted her ring. In the best of circumstances, she imagined she might have a different choice to make: Cambridge or Oxford, King's or Guy's. Never in her life did she imagine she'd be trying to choose between two men.

On the one hand she had Harry. Her Harry, a man she loved dearly and with whom she'd carved out the beginning stages of an adult life with. She thought of all the things they'd planned to do, all the trips they wanted to take. That past September when they'd driven out to Brighton, she'd swung her legs giddily as they sat on the Pier overlooking the water, listening to Harry talk about how he hoped to bring their children there one day.

'Nothing better for kids than a good dose of sea air and some handmade fudge,' he'd said, wrapping his arms around her. How could she give up the promise of a good life with a decent man? Not to mention her life in London – Clara and Olivia and the routine she'd created for herself. There was a kind of solace in certainty, and after a lifetime of tumult, she wasn't sure she could risk not knowing what would happen in her future again.

Her memories with Alexandre were just that – memories. They were both adults now, hardened by the passage of time and the hardships they'd both endured. Who knew if they could ever rekindle what they had had as children. They were so young when they'd fallen in love, she reminded herself. And she couldn't overlook the fact that Alexandre had lied to her, for years. Harry had never lied to her. If anything, she thought, frowning as she felt her stomach drop, she'd lied to him.

But how could she forget the night she'd spent with Alexandre? It scared her how strongly the feeling came flooding back to her, how easy it was to slip back into what they'd had. And she couldn't ignore the fact that even being able to go to medical school was in part due to what he'd glimpsed in her as a child. When everyone else was busy telling her what she'd couldn't do, Alexandre had always seen what she *could*.

As the grey streets of London came into view and the train lurched into Victoria station, Lena was reminded of something Olivia had said to her. She'd phoned her from the hotel the morning she got back from her night out with Alexandre and explained everything.

'I don't know what to do,' she'd whispered softly, wrapping the phone cord around her fingers.

'But it's not about Harry or Alexandre, is it?'

Lena frowned. 'It's not?'

Olivia had laughed. 'Course not! You already know what choice you need to make and it doesn't involve a man.'

She'd been right, Lena thought now, as she stood up to get her suitcase from the rack. She smoothed her coat lapels down and adjusted her hat as she waited for the passengers in front of her to disembark. Though she was tired, she was eager to see Clara, desperate to tell her everything that had transpired over a cup of hot tea. There was much to sort out. Theo had already phoned Clara and they'd made amends and now he was planning to come to London and stay a few weeks, getting reacquainted with all of them.

As she stepped off the train, she inhaled deeply, relishing the smell of petrol mixed with soot, newsprint and Cornish pasties. To anyone else it was an off-putting aroma – but trains had a special place in her heart. All the best things, she thought, happened on trains. Picking up her suitcase, she began pushing through the crowd towards the exit when she heard someone calling her name.

'Lena!'

She turned around and saw Harry. Her Harry. He was standing on the platform, holding a bouquet of daisies in one hand. With the other, he removed his hat and looked straight at her, his eyes holding the apology he hadn't been able to verbalise. And in that moment, Lena knew exactly what she had to do.

CHAPTER FORTY-SEVEN

August 1952 – Delhi, India.

Harry gripped the metal rung on the side of the rickshaw as the driver steered precariously through the streets of the Indian capital. *Bump, bump, bump* they went, Harry's stomach churning as though he were on an amusement park ride slated for a fatal outcome. A thick smog hung in the air and he blinked rapidly, trying to rid his eyes of the dust particles that had nestled their way in.

'Sir is wanting any woven rugs? Shawls?' the driver shouted over the din of the traffic. Taking one hand off the wheel, he slowed to a crawl and swept his hand towards a cluster of store fronts they just so happened to be passing.

Harry stroked the camera in his lap. The idea of haggling in the mid-afternoon heat was unappealing, but he decided it would be worth it in case he chanced upon another photographic opportunity.

'For you? Best price,' the driver continued, the unmistakable whiff of hope in his voice.

'Ok,' Harry said. 'But I may not buy anything.'

'Yes, yes, just looking,' the driver said, eagerly turning off the ignition.

Harry slung his camera strap around his neck, jumped down

from the rickshaw and paused to inhale. It was an interesting scent, the one in India. It hit you as soon as you arrived – a mix of petrol, spices, sweat and ambition. Once a relatively tepid government city, Delhi had boomed post-partition. No longer wedged under the heavy fist of colonialism, the place was abuzz with a burgeoning entrepreneurial spirit. Harry saw it everywhere he went, from the fruit stall owner offering a 'two for one' deal on misshapen mangoes, to the children who surfaced each time the vehicle he was in came to a stop in busy traffic, palms outstretched.

Harry followed the driver as he muscled his way into the first shop, a tiny sliver of a place. He stopped at the threshold, lifting his camera to snap a few photographs. It was amazing the way they managed to pack so much into such a tight space, he thought, capturing rows upon rows of coloured fabric bolts stacked to the ceiling.

'Something for memsahib?' the shop owner asked, as Harry lowered his camera and approached the counter. 'This Kashmiri wool,' he continued, holding out a cerulean shawl. 'Very warm. Very thin.'

Harry reached out and ran his hand over the fabric, picturing Lena wrapping it around her shoulders, her dark hair tumbling down, as she smiled gratefully.

Then he frowned, remembering the look on her face the day she returned from Paris. He'd known something was different the minute he set eyes on her on the platform.

Later that evening, as she'd intertwined her fingers with his while relaying tales of her long-lost father and a boy named Alexandre to a gob-smacked Clara, Harry watched, an uneasiness taking root in his gut, like a slow-growing cancer – barely detectable at first, but unstoppable in the end. It was as though a previously dormant fire within her had caught a passing flame and was now fighting its way back to full strength.

That first night back, she'd told him passionately, but firmly, that she had to go to medical school and asked him to join her after he'd finished his assignment in India.

'What's six months apart? I'll be too busy studying to be any fun,' her eyes sparkling as she brushed her hair, and Harry's heart had melted, reassured that despite the unreal turn of events, she still wanted him.

So he'd agreed and started to make the necessary arrangements, going so far as to interview with the Associated Press. He kept telling himself the change of plans was a good thing, that Lena was getting what she always wanted – and that included him.

But five weeks before their wedding, Harry could no longer ignore the sinking feeling in his gut. Lena's energy and attention was increasingly consumed with planning for medical school and rebuilding her relationship with Theo. She'd nod politely as he read passages from travel guides and smile briefly whenever he added a thumbtack to the map of India that hung in his office, marking yet another place he wanted to show her. But something inside her had shifted, like a piece of ice that had finally broken free from a large berg and was slowly drifting away. As he watched her one night, talking animatedly about all the patisseries she was going to take Olivia to when she visited, he knew that she no longer belonged with him.

He'd broken it off with as much dignity as he could, refusing to engage in a game of finger-pointing. He'd come to her one morning and said he was having trouble finding a suitable job and that as much as he wanted to go with her, he couldn't give up his career. She'd cried, devastated at the thought of losing the life they'd planned together. Her sadness quickly turned to anger and she beat her fists against his chest, telling him he simply needed to try harder. In a final act of defiance, she wrote to the university, requesting they defer her acceptance by a year. When, three weeks later, she received confirmation that she could, she'd thrust the letter in his face, as though it were the physical proof

Harry needed of her undying commitment to him, that there was still time to change his mind.

Harry felt terrible, but he knew her attempts to keep them together were in vain. No matter what he said or did, it always felt like he was holding her back. And even if she didn't understand it, he knew that the only way Lena could go to Paris and succeed was to do so unburdened by anything and anyone. And so, in his final act of love for her, he did what he had to and set her free.

'Sir?' The shopkeeper pointed to a row of shawls, shaded bright pink, sage green and mustard yellow. 'Perhaps you like embroidery?' He jerked his head at an assistant, who scurried into the back.

'No, no, nothing. Thank you,' Harry said, walking out of the shop. He could hear the driver scurrying behind him, trying to keep pace.

'Sir is wanting to see anything else? Some carpets?'

Harry stopped and bit his lip. He knew this was par for the course, that any driver he hired would have done the same thing, but he was tired of feigning interest in the merchandise that he was forced to look at each time they ventured out.

'I'm going to look around. Be back in twenty minutes.'

Without waiting for the driver to protest, Harry set off, picking his way around the shops and stalls, searching for a captivating subject to photograph. Since arriving in India four weeks ago, he'd focused solely on work, grateful to have something to keep his mind occupied. But his workload at the *Daily Express* didn't take up all his time, so he began pitching freelance pieces to other news outlets and magazines. So far, he'd had a photo essay on the Delhi Gymkhana's changing culture accepted in Italy's *Corriere della Sera* and just last week, an American magazine had contacted him about a series documenting the influx of Sikh refugees, and what it meant for the city's infrastructure.

Harry quickly found that photographing the mundane, daily

activities of ordinary people was preferable to snapping yet another dignitary or corrupt official at a state dinner. He couldn't pinpoint when the shift happened, but lately he'd been finding people of importance tedious. They were always full of stock clichés, too bothered about their own reputations to say anything of significance, or to really let their guard down.

So Harry began venturing out on his days off, shooting everything he saw. He captured photos of men who'd had their legs amputated, of Muslim families forced out of their homes by Hindu extremists, of the farmers' children, who travelled for days to the nation's capital in hopes of securing a better life, only to discover the reality was bitter and disappointing, and of mothers delivering babies on dirt floors, anguish seared into their foreheads. Pain, elation, boredom and happiness – whatever the emotion, he challenged himself to catch it all, a split second forever frozen in time. Words couldn't always describe a moment, but a carefully taken photograph could.

He smiled as he passed a stall owner peddling miniature limestone statues of Ganesh, but the man averted his eyes, twisting his body away from Harry. Despite having gained independence five years earlier, much of India still felt like it was trying to free itself from the shackles of imperialism and it was this that Harry saw in the untrusting glances that sometimes came his way. He didn't blame them. He was sure he'd have done the same.

The row of shops eventually tapered off, giving way to a run-down residential area. Harry stopped in front of one of the homes that looked like a hut with the entire front removed, so that anyone passing by could look in, observing the lives of the residents. In front of the space where a door should have been, three boys kicked a deflated football back and forth, bursting into laughter one minute and arguing the next. A woman who looked like their mother stood nearby, beating the dust out of a jute mat. A bit further back, an elderly woman whom Harry assumed to be the

371

grandmother, squatted over a hearth, slapping pieces of fat dough onto a steel tray, rolling them out into circular rounds with a thin wooden stick.

But it was the little girl who caught his eye. She was standing calmly at the edge of the house, watching Harry. Her eyes were a deep brown, full of wonder and curiosity. He took a step closer, expecting her to dart to the safety of the folds of her mother's sari, but she didn't move. She couldn't have been more than three, but seemed to possess the maturity and street smarts of someone far older.

'Sir, there are no shops here.'

Harry groaned softly as the driver materialised by his side. He pointed to his camera.

'Could you please ask their mother if I can take some photos?'

The driver nodded and went to speak to the mother while Harry dug around in his pocket for some coins.

The mother dropped the mat she was beating, wiping a sheen of sweat from her forehead as she approached Harry.

'Five *annas*,' she said.

Harry counted out the change. She smiled a gap-toothed grin and pushed her boys forward, speaking to them in an authoritative voice, which Harry understood to mean 'Stand up straight. Smile properly.'

Harry's camera whirred to life as the boys stood before him, chests puffed out, teeth gleaming against tan skin, not unlike the soldiers that had fought for their freedom.

'She say these boys are future,' the driver said. 'She want them to go abroad. Have degree from English college.'

Harry smiled. 'Tell her I hope they get the chance.' He clicked a few more photographs of the boys and then pointed to the girl. 'What about her?'

The mother shrugged and said something to the driver.

'She say if you want to, you can take photo.'

Harry thanked the mother and approached the girl, who hadn't let her gaze slip. He held out his camera and she reached up a hand, touching it. Then Harry lifted it to his eye and began shooting. He snapped photo after photo, praying that at least one of them would capture her steely determination.

The mother had given a stick of *beedi* to the driver, and he called out to Harry now, spitting tobacco juice on the ground.

'She saying, everybody have hope. Before, none. Now, new India is here.'

Harry nodded as he continued clicking away, until he'd finished the roll of film. He glanced behind him. The mother and boys were engaged in a discussion with the driver and the grandmother had moved on to chopping vegetables. No one was paying attention to the girl.

Taking a deep breath, Harry quickly bent down and pressed a few coins into the youngster's palm. He watched, his heart breaking slightly, as she swiftly tucked them into the pocket of her simple dress, away from prying eyes. It was a gesture that both pained him and made him proud. Already accustomed to being treated like a lower class citizen because of her caste and gender, Harry hoped she would use this to her advantage and fight for what was rightfully hers.

He stood up and scuffed the ground with the back of his shoe, kicking a cloud of red dust up around his ankles.

'Right,' he said, wandering back to the mother and boys, thanking them for their time. 'Could you drop me at the office?' he asked the driver.

'Sir is not wanting to go to the hotel?'

'I want to develop these.'

The driver shrugged and started walking towards the rickshaw. Harry followed him but stopped when he was halfway there. He turned back to get one last look at the girl. As expected, she was still watching him, her gaze steady. If he looked closely, he thought he could see a small smile on her face, like she was now the keeper of a secret that neither of them would ever share.

Harry stayed up all night developing the photos, the chemical smell of the dark room providing an odd source of comfort. As the liquid dripped off the edges of the pictures, he smiled. As he'd correctly anticipated, the pictures of the girl really stood out. He knew as he stood in the dim light that he'd captured something truly special. It was more than a picture. It was an attitude, a statement, as if she was challenging anyone who dared look at her and doubt her. It was as if she was saying 'I know my lot in life, but I'm not going to accept it'.

A week later, Harry would tuck one of the photographs of the girl into a letter he wrote to Lena, hoping she would open it and immediately feel what he felt.

He couldn't have known it at the time, but fourteen years later, Indira Gandhi would succeed Lal Bahadur Shastri as leader of the Congress Party, becoming the first female prime minister of India. As Harry watched Nehru's daughter from the comfort of the home he shared with his wife and two children, he would be reminded of the photographs he'd taken of the little girl with the arresting gaze. She would be grown up now, he thought. He'd lean forward in his armchair, wondering what had become of the family. Had the boys made it to England? Would their mother be proud? But mostly, he wondered about the girl. He hoped that wherever she was, she was watching Indira with the same intensity he'd captured with his camera. And he hoped that she would go on to defy the odds, just like another remarkable woman he'd once known had done.

CHAPTER FORTY-EIGHT

October 1952 – Paris, France

Lena tugged her chair closer to her desk, the feet scraping on the wooden floor, and unfolded the letter once again. It had arrived a few weeks ago in a pale blue envelope so thin it was nearly translucent. Her name was scrawled in Indian ink on the front, the last four letters hidden by the edge of a stamp depicting an intricately carved temple. She'd slit the edges of it open with a sharp kitchen knife, afraid that if she tried to use her fingers, she'd tear the words inside.

Dear Lena, it began.

She curled her right ankle around one of the chair legs, resting her cheek on her left hand as she read it for what must have been the hundredth time.

It's an exciting time and change is rampant, Harry wrote. *It's a privilege, observing a country going through a re-birth . . .*

I'm staying in a hotel in the centre of Delhi, not far from Haifa Road, where the PM resides. Every morning, a maid brings me a steaming cup of chai, which I sip outside on the veranda, watching the city emerge from its slumber.

Most of my days are spent as a silent chronicler of a monumental historic shift, but it is the portraiture work I've begun doing on my days off that I find most thrilling. I've included a photo that

I hope you like. I spotted this little girl on a rundown residential street. There was something about her gaze, so determined and focused, that reminded me of you. I also clipped a few petals from the tuberose plant (they call it 'rajnigandhi' here) on the hotel veranda and put them in – I'm hoping you can still make out their heavenly scent.

I truly hope you and your father are keeping well and that school is everything you dreamed it would be.

Take care,

Harry.

Lena looked at the photograph, trying to flatten its curled edges with the pad of her thumb. Each time she saw the girl's big, serious eyes, something stirred inside her and she'd smile, feeling achingly content that if they had to be apart, at least Harry was doing something he loved.

She scooped a few of the dried petals into her palm and brought her hand close to her nose. Closing her eyes, she inhaled, not just the scent of the flowers, but a life that could have been: navigating the swelling streets of Delhi as she walked to her job as a teacher at a local missionary, buying freshly ground spices from a local market, watching from the safety of a covered awning as the monsoon ripped through the city and sipping hot ginger tea, the liquid warming her throat, as a reward for a hard day's work – all with a man who loved her. It wouldn't have been a bad life, she thought, opening her eyes and letting the petals fall back into the body of the letter before laying the photograph on top. But as she was only beginning to acknowledge, it wouldn't have made her happy.

She folded up the envelope, and wedged it neatly between the pages of a dictionary, then glanced around her bedroom. She'd arrived in the French capital in August, with little more than the clothes in her trunk. At first, she'd said she would take up residence in a woman's rooming house, but Theo had insisted she stay with him, at least until she was settled. There were two bedrooms in his flat, he'd pointed out, and with his touring schedule, she'd have the place to herself for a few months of the school year.

'You'd be doing me a favour,' he explained. 'I wouldn't need to find someone to look after it.'

Lena had gratefully accepted and not only because she was excited at the prospect of having more time to spend with Theo. Up until a few months ago, she'd truly thought it would be Harry by her side as she stepped into her new life. With him gone, she needed every bit of support she could get.

Lena sighed as she surveyed her desk. It was littered with anatomical sketches and course notes sporting neat reminders she'd scribbled to herself in the margins. She stacked a few sheets of looseleaf into a pile, then paused, her mind elsewhere. She opened the top drawer of her desk and pulled out a packet of letters she'd exchanged with Alexandre. They'd kept in touch for a few weeks following their reunion in Paris. He'd come to visit her in London once, taking great joy in being able to see not only her, but Clara and her family. It had felt like old times, easy and carefree.

After he returned to Paris, they continued writing letters. But after a few weeks, the letters slowed and eventually, Lena stopped writing. She told herself he'd likely got too busy touring and that his silence had nothing to do with her relationship with Harry. The last time they'd had any contact was in May. By June, her engagement was off and she'd been too upset to try to tell him.

Lena thought about the irony of the situation as she flicked through the letters, reading snippets of their exchange. How could she spend a decade missing someone, only to let him slip out of her life again so easily? She kept telling herself she'd reach out when she felt ready, but as the sleepy Paris summer turned to autumn, she wondered if she was being entirely honest. She assumed her father had told Alexandre about the wedding being called off. The fact that he hadn't been in touch despite this only confirmed what he'd said that night at the Seine: being with Lena was never his end game – he'd merely wanted to reunite her with Theo, and for her to know the truth about who Theo was.

So Lena focused on the opportunity to do what she'd always wanted: she threw herself into school, arriving to lectures early and staying long after they'd ended. She spent any extra time she had in the labs or library, filling her head with facts about the respiratory and cardiovascular systems. It was better this way, she reasoned. With her workload ballooning and exams looming, there was nothing to distract her from doing her best.

She stood up, shoving her school books in a leather satchel from Ackery's, a gift from Clara and Fitz for starting medical school. As she slipped her feet into a pair of pale pink ballet flats and made her way to the kitchen, she reminded herself it wasn't a bad thing he'd not been in touch. Her heart had been through enough.

'Good morning,' she greeted Theo, who was taking brief sips of coffee in between chopping ingredients for breakfast over the stove.

'Lena!' He turned to her, beaming as he held up a fistful of fresh herbs. 'You have time to eat?'

'I'm late,' Lena replied apologetically. The one pleasure Lena allowed herself was time with her father. Often the two would be up till the early hours of the mornings, trying to make up for lost time. They'd play gin rummy and drink *retsina* and Theo would tell Lena stories about her mother and their childhood in Athens.

'You're sure?' Theo gestured to the eggs, tossing in another handful of chopped basil.

'Yes,' Lena said, bustling about the kitchen in search of something she could eat on the run. She was starving and wouldn't get a break until lunch.

'At least let me make you a panini!' Theo said. He plucked a fresh baguette off the table and sliced it in half, white crumbs falling across the wooden chopping board.

'Papa,' Lena warned, watching as her father stuck a spoon in a jar of fresh pesto, spreading big dollops of it on the bread.

'Now for some cheese,' he murmured, opening the fridge.

Lena pursed her lips and crossed her arms, but the truth was, she valued every minute they had together and wasn't going to waste any energy being frustrated with him. She plopped her bag on a kitchen chair and leaned out onto the Juliet balcony. The flat was in the Montmartre district, not far from the *Sacre Coeur*. The neighbourhood had a bohemian, artistic vibe and suited her father perfectly. They often strolled on the streets at night or visited one of the many cafés in the mornings, sipping lattes while they read the day's issue of *Le Monde*.

As Theo sliced up chunks of brie, he glanced at his daughter. He'd been overjoyed when she'd confirmed she'd be moving to Paris and had immediately insisted she stay with him. He didn't think he'd ever tire of looking at her, admiring how much she'd overcome to get to where she was. He'd be lying if he said he didn't have pangs of regret – how much more could she have achieved if he hadn't been so protective when she was younger? But as they both knew all too well, life was short and there was no merit to be found in dwelling on the past.

He'd been wanting to ask her more about what happened with Harry, the ring noticeably absent from her finger, ever since she'd arrived. But he respected her privacy and hadn't pushed. For the most part, she was in good spirits, thrilled that something she'd dreamt about for years had finally come true. Yet some days, Theo sensed a melancholic sadness weighing her down, like she was yearning for something – or someone – else.

'There,' Theo announced, rolling up the panini in wax paper. 'Remember, I'm performing tonight – you'll be ok on your own?'

Lena nodded, biting into an apple she'd pinched from the fruit bowl. Theo hesitated as he watched his daughter, his mind flitting back to Alexandre. He thought about the letter he'd received from him. If it had been any other two people, he would have stayed out of it. But he knew these two like the back of his hand. And life had taught him that one had to take risks, no matter how terrifying.

'He leaves tonight.'

Lena stopped chewing, feeling a trickle of tart apple juice race down her chin. She wiped her jaw with the back of her sleeve and swallowed.

Theo dumped the chopping board in the sink and turned on the taps. 'On the train to London. He'll do a few shows, then fly to America for six months. New York. Chicago. Philadelphia.' He paused. 'I thought you should know.'

'Thank you,' Lena said quietly. She picked up her panini, and tucked it into her satchel. 'See you later,' she rose on her tiptoes to kiss her father gently on his cheek.

'You didn't do anything wrong.'

'What?' Lena spoke so quietly her voice was barely audible.

'With Harry,' Theo said softly. 'You don't have to punish yourself.'

Lena sighed. She'd appreciated that her father hadn't asked about her personal life, that he'd allowed her to grieve and move on as she saw fit. But she knew that at some point she couldn't ignore everything she'd been feeling and that it might help to talk about it, even a bit.

'I hurt a good man,' she whispered, feeling her voice break.

Theo turned off the taps and wiped his hands on a towel, before putting an arm around Lena's shoulder comfortingly.

'You made a choice and offered him one, too. You couldn't control what he did.' He gently tipped Lena's chin upwards. 'Alexandre . . . he'd want to see you.'

'I'm too busy with school,' she said abruptly. 'Besides,' she continued, swallowing her grief. 'If he'd wanted to hear from me, he'd have said something. Replied to my letters.'

Theo frowned 'Lena. He doesn't know about Harry.'

'You didn't tell him?'

'I didn't think it my place.'

Lena frowned, letting this realisation fall over her, then shook her head. 'It doesn't change anything. He's leaving.'

'I only needed two days with Isabella to know she was the one. You two have had far more time than that.' Theo smiled, his dark eyes crinkling. 'Life is fickle, Lena. If you have a chance to be happy, take it.'

Lena stared out at the blue sky. It looked perfect, almost unreal. It was the kind of day where everything was supposed to go right. She took another bite of her apple and grabbed her satchel.

'Good luck tonight,' she called, as she walked down the stairs of the building.

Eight hours later, Lena sat in a classroom, twisting her neck from side to side. She was 15 minutes into her final lecture of the day, discussing a case in which an operation to correct a cardiac shunt had been performed using induced hypothermia.

'Cooling the body's temperature was the key factor in its success,' the professor explained. 'By keeping the body in a hypothermic state, less oxygen was required for it to function. Dr. Bigelow's pioneering technique has wide-ranging implications for the entire cardiology field.'

A young man two seats over from Lena raised his hand. 'How do we know it's safe to use in other surgical procedures?'

'You can't know. All you can do is make the best possible educated guess,' the professor answered. 'But understand this – if utilised to its full potential, cooling of the heart could change the face of surgery as we know it.'

'What about the risks?' Lena heard herself say.

'What's the risk if you don't do anything?' the professor countered. 'In the case of the shunt, the patient – a five-year-old girl – likely wouldn't have survived.'

381

'Surely we need more evidence before pushing something like this into the mainstream,' Lena said.

'And at what point will we ever have enough proof? Where do we draw the line?' the professor asked. When Lena didn't answer, he continued. 'Each decision we make, no matter how mundane, involves an element of chance. Everything from the food we eat, to the relationships we enter into, to the jobs we pursue – we all calculate the pros and cons, and then make the best choice we can, with what we have. It's the same with medicine. You can weigh the benefits and risks all you want, but at some point, you have to dive in and hope that the consequences are in your favour.'

The room was awash with murmurs as the moral and ethical issues weighed on the minds of the budding physicians.

'Isn't it a bit reckless?' Lena offered.

'Isn't inaction a bit reckless? Not giving this young girl a chance to live doesn't seem fair, given what we know from past experiments,' the professor said, not unkindly. He waited for the class to quiet down. 'What I'm about to say will go against much of the training you're about to embark on. No matter how much you learn from these,' he said, picking up a textbook, 'you'll inevitably be faced with real life situations you can't prepare for. After thirty years of practising medicine, the only thing I know for certain is that in the absence of evidence, we have to have blind faith. That's difficult for many of you to fathom – we're used to process, procedure, moving from point A to B and knowing what the end result is. But the truth is, progress in medicine – progress in anything – cannot exist without ambiguity and risk.'

Lena sat in her seat, the chorus of voices around her fading away as Clara's fateful words took hold in her mind.

Try or don't try. The time will pass anyway.

'Sir,' she called out, leaping up and grabbing her satchel. 'I've just remembered there's somewhere I have to be. I am so sorry!' she called, rushing towards the exit. A few seconds later, she

382

pushed open the doors of the university building and flew down the steps, en route to *Gare du Nord*. She didn't know what she was doing but she knew if she stopped to try and think about it rationally, she'd talk herself out of it. She strode north, past the *Pont Marie* and up through the Marais district. With each step, she felt her confidence bloom. *It'll be ok*, she told herself, over and over, till it became like a steady mantra. She kept walking, not stopping to think about the blister forming on her heel, or the sweat that had accumulated around the waistband of her skirt.

By the time she reached the station entrance, her feet were aching. Scolding herself for her poor choice of footwear as she ran into the terminal, she promised to reward herself with a glass of red wine afterwards to soothe her throbbing toes. Right now, she had no time to lose. Rushing up to the ticket office, she tapped on the window.

'Excuse me, where can I find the train leaving for London?'

'Platform seven,' the assistant answered.

Lena thanked him and began hurriedly scanning the platform signs. As soon as she spotted the number seven, she broke into a run, ignoring the pain in her legs, not stopping until she'd reached the train's first-class cabin. As she stopped outside, her satchel, which had been flying behind her, smacked her hip and she let out a howl of pain. Breathless, she hunched over, inhaling big gulps of air. When she'd caught her breath, she rushed to the conductor.

'Please, sir. I have to get on.'

'Your ticket, Madame.'

'I haven't got one. There's someone I need to see.'

'With no ticket, I can't let you on.'

'I'll come back off, I promise! I need to speak with someone on there,' Lena pleaded, pointing to the train.

'No,' the conductor said firmly, beckoning to the couple behind her to come forward.

Lena stepped back, trying to figure out her next move.

Tucking a few strands of loose hair behind her ears, she craned her neck, trying to gauge the carriage's length. It would take her too long to run up and down each side, and even if she did, Alexandre wouldn't know she was looking for him. She glanced at the conductor again and then did something entirely out of character.

'Stop!' she yelled, pointing to something behind him further up the platform. 'Thief! Stop him!' The conductor turned around and Lena used the split second distraction to leap onto the train. Not wasting a minute, she pushed open the door to the first class carriage and began walking as quickly as she could down the aisle, squeezing herself in between passengers stowing their luggage as they prepared for the journey ahead.

'Alexandre?' she called, looking left and right, only to be met with one confused face after another. As she moved further down the aisle, her stomach began to dip uneasily. What if he'd changed his plans and wasn't on this train at all? After all this time, she'd finally mustered up the courage to tell him how she felt and now he wasn't around to hear it. 'Alexandre!' she called, a little more desperately.

'Stop! Madame!'

Lena stole a glance over her shoulder and, much to her dismay, saw the conductor advancing towards her. Not willing to give up, she quickened her pace, apologising as she manoeuvred her way around a young girl and her mother.

'Madame!' Just then, a rough hand clamped down on Lena's shoulder. She stopped walking, squeezed her eyes shut and cursed softly under her breath. Feeling guilty, she turned around, trying to prepare some kind of explanation that would get her out of trouble.

'Lena?'

Lena whipped her head back to see Alexandre, just a few seats in front of where she now stood.

'Oh, thank goodness,' she said, relieved.

He walked into the aisle and rushed towards her, dumbfounded. 'What are you doing here?'

'I needed to speak with you. Please,' she said, trying to wriggle out of the conductor's grip. 'Tell him I'm with you.'

Alexandre stepped forward, exchanging a few words with the conductor, who reluctantly let go of Lena's arm.

'Come,' Alexandre said, steering Lena out of the carriage.

'You'll miss your train,' she protested, as they approached the exit. A hot blast of steam hissed from underneath the tracks as Lena stepped down and she coughed, the water and smoke curling up inside her nostrils.

'I'm right next to it,' Alexandre answered, a slight smirk on his face, joining her on the platform. He glanced up and down the station, then looked back at her in disbelief, raking a hand through his hair. 'Are you visiting Theo?'

Lena frowned, a wave of guilt crashing over her. She fiddled with the strap of her satchel, massaging a sore spot from where it was digging into her collarbone. 'I'm ... well, the thing is ...' she trailed off, meeting Alexandre's eyes and shrugging, like she'd been defeated.

Alexandre's eyes widened. 'Wait – you're in school?'

'Yes – I only found out today my father hadn't told you,' she said bashfully, her cheeks going red. As difficult as the break-up had been, Lena didn't think she'd ever tire of telling those who'd known her struggles that she was finally on the right path.

Alexandre looked at her, confused. 'I've not seen him for months. Only got home from my summer tour three days ago. I did write to Theo, telling him I'd be in town around now, but assumed he was visiting you. I meant to call him, but it's been ridiculous, trying to prepare for another six months away.' He shook his head. 'But enough about that! You did it! You accepted the place!' Alexandre swept Lena off the platform into a hug. 'I'm so pleased,' he continued huskily, his eyes glittering with admiration as he put her down. 'Let me guess. You're the top student and all the others hate you for it,' he teased.

'Hardly,' she swatted at him playfully.

Alexandre laughed. 'And Harry?' He scanned the crowd for Lena's fiancé. 'He's settled in?'

'He's ... in India. We didn't get married,' Lena said, in a resigned voice. As she waited for him to reply, she wondered if she'd ever utter those words as a simple fact and not feel a rush of sadness each time they came out of her mouth.

'Alexandre!'

Lena jerked her head towards the train. A young woman was hanging outside a carriage window, one arm nestled on the frame, the other beckoning to Alexandre elegantly. Her dark brown hair was pulled into a low bun, a few delicate wisps framing her face, her lips painted a deep red. 'Hurry up!'

'Two minutes!' Alexandre shouted back.

The woman frowned at Lena and disappeared back inside the carriage. Suddenly Lena knew why Alexandre had stopped writing and why he hadn't enquired after her. He'd moved on, she thought, the realisation washing over her like a bucket of ice water.

'Sorry,' Alexandre said, distracted. 'About Harry—'

'It's fine,' Lena whispered, her throat feeling like it was closing up. *What was she doing*, she thought. She'd walked out of a medical school lecture to tell a boy she had a childhood crush on that she still loved him. What was wrong with her?

'What did you need to tell me?'

'It's nothing, actually. I should go,' she said. Her heart felt like a balloon that had just been popped and was slowly deflating, the air hissing out of it sadly. Worried she might cry, she turned to make a swift exit, but Alexandre grabbed her wrist.

'Don't leave like that!'

'You're obviously busy,' she shot back, glancing at the train.

'She's a performer on the tour,' Alexandre raised his eyebrows.

Lena felt her cheeks redden and sheepishly let her arm go slack in his grip. 'Oh.'

'Lena,' Alexandre said, watching her carefully. 'Why are you here?'

Lena wished he would stop asking her questions and put two and two together. Wasn't it obvious? Why else would she come? She glanced at the clock: 17:56. Four minutes left to tell him, or he'd be off and gone for months.

Alexandre let out an exasperated sigh and pointed to the carriage. 'Her husband is sitting next—'

'I'll be twenty-eight,' Lena blurted out.

'What?'

'I'll be twenty-eight when I finish school,' she continued, standing up straighter. 'Maybe thirty. Practically an old maid by society standards. What do you make of it?'

Alexandre glanced at the clock, then back to Lena. 'Look, let me ring you from London—'

'I've no time for that and neither do you,' she said, lifting her chin, knowing that the words she was about to speak would define what happened next. 'I'll be twenty-eight. Or twenty-nine. Or thirty. And I'm asking you if you'll wait for me?'

Alexandre's hair flopped into his eyes. Lena watched as he instinctively shook it off to one side, just like he'd always done when they were kids.

'Is this . . . am I really what you want?'

Lena twisted the dove bracelet around her wrist. She realised she'd been holding her breath, a tightness gripping her chest, since she'd arrived. If she was being honest, it had been there for months, since the day she realised he was still alive. Because the truth was, no matter how much she tried to explain it away, she loved him.

'You are.' As she spoke the words she'd been so afraid of

releasing, freeing them out into the open air, she felt as though an invisible weight was lifted. She waited for him to say something, never losing his gaze.

Without warning, a loud whistle erupted from the train and Lena jumped, clamping her hands over her ears, her heartbeat sky-rocketing. To add insult to injury, the conductor blew his whistle, aiming in their direction, scowling at Lena. And still Alexandre did nothing. He just stood on the platform, staring at her, as though he were in some kind of trance.

Eventually, the silence became too much. Lena reached out to give Alexandre a light hug.

'Have a safe trip,' she said, smiling bravely. Sometimes, she thought, as she started to turn around and walk away, not getting an answer was an answer in and of itself. At least now she knew. At least now she could focus entirely on school and not be left wondering what could have been.

'It's a long time,' she heard him say.

Lena stopped. Slowly, she looked back. 'Very,' she said, taking a tentative step towards him.

'Longer than the distance from here to Mercury,' Alexandre said, a familiar hint of mischief beginning to swirl in his brilliant blue eyes.

'Yes.' She nodded, gripping the handle of her satchel tightly, her knuckles turning white. Two more steps. His face was still impartial, and Lena sucked in her breath, wondering how much longer he was going to wait before giving her some kind of sign about how he felt.

And then all of a sudden, she was spiralling back in time again, to a memory of her carriage on the World of Wonders, to the night of her thirteenth birthday when Alexandre had first admitted his true feelings for her and kissed her and she'd felt like she was walking on air. Except it wasn't a memory – it was all real. He was here, now, his lips pressed confidently against hers, one hand cupping the small of her back, the other holding her waist tightly, as though he would never let go.

The conductor blew his whistle aggressively and Lena and Alexandre pulled apart, laughing as he shouted a final warning. Lena grasped Alexandre's hands in hers, an unspoken agreement forging between them.

'So,' she said. 'Will you wait?'

Alexandre nodded and a smile burst across his face. 'I'll wait.' Then he kissed her again, winked at the conductor and darted onto the train. A moment later, Lena caught him sticking his head out the window, waving, as the train took a huge breath and began pulling away from the platform.

Seven years later, Lena would stand proudly at her convocation, becoming one of only two women in her class to graduate from medical school that year. She'd accept her degree graciously, as a cheering contingent that included Alexandre, Theo, Clara and Olivia, looked on proudly, marvelling at the woman she'd become.

Two months after Lena earned her degree, she and Alexandre would run down the steps of St. Stephen's Church on the *rue de Georges Bizet*, bells ringing loudly as well-wishers tossed rose petals in the air. At the reception that followed in *Tuileries*, Theo would raise a glass and tell a story of a love between two people so strong that they endured decades of heartbreak, loss and distance, ultimately defying all odds to find each other again.

A year after their wedding, Lena would give birth to a baby girl that she and Alexandre would name Aria. As they sat beaming at the bundle of light that had entered their lives, they promised to teach their daughter that one's past did not dictate future possibility, that she alone had the power to decide who she would become, and that if rationality and logic should ever fail her, she could always, always believe in magic.

But for now, all Lena could do was focus on the present. She watched Alexandre's train slink out of sight, waiting until the only thing left was a trail of white smoke and the memory of his kiss on her lips. Then she turned and walked towards the exit, elegantly dodging tourists who were oblivious to the happy ending and new beginning that had just transpired.

She passed under a magnificent archway and out onto the street, pausing to look up to the sky. No longer blue, it now resembled a watercolour painting, awash with swirls of mauve and dusty pink, the sun dipping slowly below the clouds. And as Lena walked down the *boulevard de la Chapelle* in search of a suitable café where she could rest her feet, she thought she could hear her father's voice swept up in the warm Parisian breeze.

'*Epiméno*, Lena. *Epiméno*.'

At the end of the day, that was all anyone could do.

Author's Note

Crafting any book is a daunting task, but writing historical fiction comes with its own unique set of privileges and challenges. On the one hand, it is a joy to travel back in time, delving into worlds that no longer exist. On the other hand, readers inevitably wonder how much of the story actually happened. Much like the World of Wonders toes the line between reality and fantasy, *The Circus Train*, while partly based on fact, does take artistic licence. I have tried as best I can to address here some of the choices I made.

Before I begin, I would like to acknowledge that despite my extensive research, I will never know what it is like to live a life like Lena's. Her character was never meant to be representative of an entire population – indeed, it is impossible to create a singular character who can speak for and accurately represent the lived experiences of a whole demographic.

I would also like to note that my publishers and I made the choice to use the word *disabled* throughout the novel even though *handicapped* would have been the more common term at the time.

Disability and Representation

At the core of the novel is Lena Papadopoulos. After contracting polio as a baby, she spends much of her youth in a wheelchair.

What's unique about the way I wrote Lena's experience is that it was both common and uncommon at the time.

Poliomyelitis (also known as polio or infantile paralysis) has been around for centuries, but large-scale epidemics didn't occur in the Western world until the twentieth century. In Europe, Greece and England experienced polio epidemics in the 1950s. At the time Lena caught it, it would have been endemic. It wasn't until the 1955 mass rollout of the polio vaccine developed by Dr. Jonas Salk that cases began to fall. Polio is an infectious disease that primarily affects young children. At the time the novel is set, it wasn't uncommon for children who contracted polio to be hospitalised, wear leg braces, and/or use wheelchairs. In some cases, children were not allowed to move at all, as treatments that favoured immobility were the norm.

However, with proper treatment and time, many children who lost mobility in their limbs due to polio were later able to regain full use and functionality. This is the case with Lena.

Sister Elizabeth Kenny, an Australian healthcare professional, revolutionised the field of polio rehabilitation. She developed a unique method that used heat and movement to relieve pain in patients with polio. She would wrap the affected areas in hot, damp cloths then gently introduce movement into the limbs. In the novel, Dr. Wilson uses this treatment on Lena.

Throughout her career, Kenny struggled to get backing for her ideas; many trained medical professionals criticised the absence of immobilisation and lack of traditional splints and braces to prevent muscular and skeletal deformity. But by 1942 her methods were being written about in *Time* magazine, which noted that Kenny's 'impressive 80 percent recovery rate forced doctors to recognise the unorthodox work she was doing.' The Kenny treatment, as it came to be known, went on to gain widespread acceptance.

I would also like to address how Lena is treated by others throughout the course of the novel.

Although much of the current Western world's attitude toward individuals with disabilities emphasises inclusion, equality, and autonomy, historically speaking this was not common. It certainly was not the case during the time period in which *The Circus Train* is set.

In a study titled 'Disability and Social Policy in Britain Since 1750: A History of Exclusion', the author and professor Anne Borsay details the experiences of people with both physical and mental impairments from the end of the eighteenth century onward. The study features testimonials from those who grew up in England during the 1940s and 1950s, often detailing the horrific treatment children with disabilities endured. It was not uncommon for disabled children to be sent to live at institutions, where they were often neglected, punished, and ridiculed by staff.

As well, for many disabled children, hospitals in England at the time of the novel's setting were not a place of care but rather of experimentation. Unnecessary surgeries were regularly performed in an attempt to 'correct' and 'fix' what was deemed wrong in children with physical and mental disabilities. For those interested in reading further on this subject, authors Steve Humphries and Pamela Gordon detail what it was like to be a child living with a disability during this time in *Out of Sight: The Experience of Disability, 1900–1950*.

In *Worth Saving: Disabled Children during the Second World War*, author Sue Wheatcroft crafts a moving account of the treatment of disabled children in England. She writes that although many children with disabilities were marginalised, during the war people ensured that disabled children were evacuated to live in safer areas.

But these efforts didn't come without problems: apart from logistical issues, there were reports of abuse and punishment inflicted upon children in their temporary homes. Wheatcroft does acknowledge that much of a disabled child's experience came down to other people and how they treated the individual. However, there still existed the general view that disabled children were a problematic group as a whole. Recipients of any type of care were expected to be grateful. Decision making was, more often than not, placed in the hands of people in power, removing what little independence a person with a disability may have had.

The rise of the eugenics movement served to further segregate physically and mentally disabled people from society. Eugenics is a movement that is aimed at improving the genetic composition of the human race. It gained widespread popularity in Britain, America, and Germany starting in the late 1800s. In 1907, the Eugenics Education Society was founded in Britain to campaign for sterilisation and marriage restrictions for disabled people in a bid to prevent those considered less fit from reproducing. In 1912, the first International Eugenics Conference was held in London. By the 1930s, membership in the British Eugenics Society had peaked and the movement continued to receive backing into the 1940s.

Things were no better in Germany. In 1933, the Nazi government implemented the Law for the Prevention of Progeny with Hereditary Diseases, a step toward its goal of creating a 'master race'. Supporters argued that people with hereditary diseases should be sterilised and thus prevented from passing on their so-called 'unfit' genes to future generations. Targeted groups included people with physical deformities and/or disabilities, individuals with mental health issues, and those who were blind or deaf. The passing of the law also increased the propaganda against people with disabilities, labelling them as unworthy of living and highlighting both the financial and emotional burdens they supposedly placed on society.

Just before the Second World War broke out in 1939, Adolf Hitler authorised a programme called *Aktion T4*. Developed by Dr. Viktor Brack (head of Hitler's Euthanasia Department), the programme involved the systematic murder of people who were mentally and physically handicapped. Under this secret programme, approximately 70,000 Austrian and German residents were killed. Following public outcry, operations were publicly halted in 1941, but the killings continued in secret. By the end of the war, the death toll of people with disabilities was estimated to be at least 275,000.

The following resources provide excellent accounts of the treatment of people with disabilities in Nazi Germany: Michael Burleigh's *Death and Deliverance: 'Euthanasia' in Germany 1900–1945*, Suzanne E. Evans's *Forgotten Crimes: The Holocaust and People with Disabilities*, and *Century of Genocide: Critical Essays and Eyewitness Accounts*, edited by Samuel Totten, William S. Parsons, and Israel W. Charny.

The above attitudes and treatments toward those with disabilities at the time of the novel's setting were part of the reason why I chose to make Theo the way he is. Although he may come across as overprotective of Lena, he had a valid reason for being this way. I hope that by providing a bit more of the historical context around attitudes to disability at the time I've shown how his desire to keep Lena close to him makes sense.

Circuses

I have always been fascinated by circuses, both past and present. Inspiration for the World of Wonders was drawn from many sources, including Cirque du Soleil and Les 7 Doigts, both of which have roots in my home country of Canada.

With respect to circuses during the Second World War, inspiration was drawn from German circus owner Adolf Althoff, who hid the true identities of a Jewish circus family throughout the war on board the Circus Althoff. Similar to Horace, when the Nazis came for their inspections, he would distract them with alcohol and food, giving the Jewish performers time to hide.

Please note that my novel was never meant to be a retelling of either Althoff's story or that of the families he helped save.

The rich history of the Cirque d'Hiver in Paris also proved to be inspirational, having continued operation during the German occupation of France. The years during which ownership lay with the Bouglione brothers were particularly useful.

Despite the above, the World of Wonders is a figment of my imagination. Having done research into circuses that operated at the time of the Second World War, it was obvious that it would have been difficult to travel across borders, especially as the war escalated. Some owners, like Althoff, managed to keep going, but it was not the norm. As such, my circus should be treated as fiction.

Magic and Illusion

Although my novel takes place mainly after the Golden Age of Magic in the Unites States, I drew upon this time period to help build my world. Late-nineteenth- and early-twentieth-century magicians and illusionists including Howard Thurston, Harry Kellar, and Harry Houdini influenced my creation of Horace. Jim Steinmeyer's excellent *Hiding the Elephant* provided both historical context and inspiration.

Magic and illusion also had a firm grip on European audiences. I focused mainly on France and England for my research. In France, early to mid-nineteenth-century watchmaker and illusion-ist Jean Eugène Robert-Houdin is widely recognised as the father of modern-day magic (Houdini drew his stage name from him). Robert-Houdin transformed magic from a lower-class hobby into a form of entertainment for the wealthy. Also in Paris, the small but delightful Musée de la Magie houses an assortment of magic and illusion-related memorabilia and a collection of automatons.

In England, members of the Maskelyne magic dynasty (John, Nevil, and Jasper) were influential, as was illusionist, shadow-graphist, and filmmaker David Devant. Venues like the historic Hippodrome, Egyptian Hall, and St. George's Hall, along with magic shops like Davenports, were also instrumental in allowing me to craft this story.

Theresienstadt

Please note that while I did undertake extensive research, I have also taken artistic licence with my interpretation of Theresienstadt. As such, it should be treated strictly as fiction, not fact. I encourage anyone wishing to learn more about Theresienstadt to consult third party, non-fiction sources and organisations, some of which you can find listed at the end of this author's note.

Perhaps the most horrific part of the novel occurs when Theo and Alexandre are sent to Theresienstadt. Located in the Protectorate of Bohemia and Moravia, Theresienstadt operated from 1941 to 1945, serving as a ghetto, transit camp, and concentration camp.

Theresienstadt was marketed to Jews as a 'spa town', and it was intended to house the elderly, privileged, and most famous Jews from Germany, Austria, the Czech lands, and Western Europe. What was unique about Theresienstadt was that it actually functioned like a proper town. It had its own governing Jewish council, its own currency, coffee shops, parks, a school, a library, and many more amenities. It even had its own football league, called Liga Terezin. Jews who entered the town were given jobs, which often involved back-breaking labour.

Theresienstadt was also unique for its cultural heritage. Some of the most prominent Jewish writers, artists, musicians, philosophers, and poets lived in the barracks, giving rise to a rich artistic culture. Although the show I write about is one I dreamed up, it was not uncommon for regular musical and theatrical performances to occur. If you were a Jewish performer, you were granted better living conditions.

Of course, all of this hid the truth. The living conditions, though better than the average concentration camp, were still abhorrent. Alongside the coffee shop, library, and school stood a prison and gallows. Many people died from illness and disease and many more were deported from the town to extermination camps. Anton "Toni" Burger was a real person, but I have taken liberties with his personal character, gleaning what I could from historical reports and my own research. Burger was the camp commander at Theresienstadt from July 1943 to February 1944. He had a reputation for cruelty. In one scene in the novel, the residents are forced to stand outside in the cold for a head count. This actually happened under Burger's rule. Approximately three hundred prisoners died from the resulting hypothermia.

After the war, Burger was arrested in 1947 and held in a camp in Salzburg. He was sentenced to death, but just before he was due to be executed, he escaped. He lived under a false name for a few years before being arrested again in 1951. However, he escaped a second time and spent the next few decades living under numerous aliases on the border of Germany and Austria. Burger spent his final days in Germany and died from natural causes in 1991. It wasn't until 1994 that his true identity was revealed.

Propaganda within Theresienstadt

Following the deportation of a group of Danish children to Auschwitz in the fall of 1943, Theresienstadt came under fire.

Prominent Danish officials, including the king, insisted on visiting the town to gain information about what was happening. The Germans reluctantly agreed and, toward the end of 1943, began preparing the town for the 'inspection'.

The Nazis stalled the visit for months, during which extreme measures were taken to hide what was truly happening within the ghetto. The Jewish residents were forced to 'beautify' the town, planting flowers, painting homes, and developing artistic performances for entertainment during the visit. The performance during which Theo, Alexandre, and Leike escape is a fictional early rehearsal of one of these shows. The Germans also increased deportations to other camps. In May 1944, just before the Danes were due to visit, more than seven thousand residents were sent to Auschwitz to alleviate the overcrowding.

The visit occurred in June 1944 and the Nazis successfully duped the Danes into believing that all was fine within the walls of the garrison town. Theresienstadt was eventually liberated by the Soviets in May 1945.

I would like to thank the following organisations, whose resources, documentation and archives were instrumental in my research of Theresienstadt: the European Holocaust Resource Infrastructure; archives from the United States Holocaust Memorial Museum; the National Archives in Richmond, UK; the Wiener Holocaust Library; the Jewish Museum in Prague, the Jewish Museum in Thessaloniki; and Yad Vashem – the World Holocaust Remembrance Center.

Acknowledgements

I joked at the start of this process that writing this section would be harder than penning the guest list for an Indian wedding. (Update: I wasn't wrong.)

To my brilliant agent, Thérèse Coen. Thank you for your hard work, persistence, empathy, kindness, and, most of all, your unwavering faith in me as a writer. I am so glad we get to go on this journey together. Thanks also to Nicole, Caroline, Jo, and Hannah at H&S.

To Iris Tupholme and Julia McDowell at HarperCollins Canada. I will be forever proud that a Canadian team placed the first bet. You took this novel and transformed it into something truly magical. I can't thank you enough for your vision, patience, and belief in my work. Thank you to my publicist, Rebecca Silver, and to the entire team at HarperCollins for working so hard on my behalf. Thanks also to Sage and Salt Books, especially Madison Parrotta, for the care shown in helping get this story just right.

Thanks to my UK editor, Rosanna Forte and to my US editors Tara Singh Carlson and Ashley Di Dio. Your insights helped ensure we had the greatest chance of success in different markets and I'm so grateful for the time and energy you gave to this story. Thanks also to the teams at Little, Brown UK, Putnam and to the myriad of international publishing houses who brought *The Circus Train* to life around the world. Lastly, I'd like to thank the booksellers and buyers who have championed Lena's story to readers everywhere.

In 2014, I walked into a boardroom on Haymarket and my life changed forever. Thanks to Erin Kelly, Anna Davis, Jennifer Kerslake, Rufus Purdy, and the rest of the CBC team. To my classmates: each of you inspired me with your words and pushed me to be a better writer. Special thanks to Laura Evans, Rachel Greene-Taylor and Rachael Revesz for reading endless drafts of my work. Without you, *The Circus Train* would not exist. A big thanks also to my Royal Court Theatre Writing Group and the Debuts 2022 UK Group for the comforting chats and laughter.

I'm eternally grateful to my friends for their encouragement over the years. Thanks to Natalie Bauer, Brendan Beesley, Ellena Bianchi-Barry, Akshara Chandhok, Adrienne Coucill, Rachel Cyr, Laura Delbridge, Pan Demetriou, Derek Deustch, Fran Harvey, Rakefet Hootnick, Shraddha Kothari-Walker, Elijah Lawal, Jessica Leung, Barbara Peric, Evan Placey, Corinn Pullen, Sarah Romeiro, Emily Schatzker (my head cheerleader!), and the many others who helped along the way.

Growing up as a shy child, books were where I found my home. Thank you to my teachers and librarians for creating a space where I could thrive. In particular, I would like to thank Mrs. Switzer from Cliffwood P.S., Ms. Ladoucer and Ms. Carli from Cummer Valley M.S., and Esther Yermus from Earl Haig S.S.

Thanks to Dr. Gelareh Zadeh, Dr. Rowena Ridout and everyone else at TWH for keeping me healthy. Thanks to Mike Carneiro, Eden Haugland, Matt Nichol and Martha Weizman for keeping me strong and inspired. Thank you to Carol Hasek for filling my life with song and a big thank you to all my former sports coaches, dance teachers, and music instructors. Being involved in organised athletics and community arts programmes as a child taught me to be disciplined, patient, and tenacious – things that proved to be invaluable when it came to writing this book.

To the Choraria, Jani and Parikh families: thank you for the constant support and interest in my work. Special thanks to my cousins for their never-ending enthusiasm: Smita Rossetti, Jaya Choraria, Priya Choudhari, Bhavna Choraria, Adesh Choraria, Anika Choraria, Neha Choraria, Rohan Jani, Nisha Wright, Nayana Parikh and Sanjay Parikh.

Finally, a huge thank you to my parents, Asit and Sushila Parikh, who are the most hardworking and selfless people I know. I don't have enough words to properly articulate how I feel, so I will simply say thank you for instilling in me a love of reading and a desire to excel at whatever I put my mind to from a young age. And to Rishi and Sahil Parikh, the best brothers a sister could ask for – I hope I've made you all proud.